... shortlisted ...

... que currently lives and writes ...
... ou can visit her website at www.m...

PRAISE FOR *SUN DOG*

'... l of sensuality . . . a delightfully unusual debut'
T... Times

'... hanting. Roffey handles this modern-day metamorphosis b... tifully'
I... Mail

'... to read a novel with such a big heart'
(...

'Be... ly written – an extraordinary first novel. Buy it, then tell ... our friends to do the same'
Hea...

'A high... original and imaginative literary love story. Bewitching'
Daily Express

'A brilliant idea, brilliantly executed'
Daily Mirror

'Striking, original and razor sharp'
Dazed & Confused

'A feast to the senses . . . Monique Roffey's rich imagination makes the ordinary feel exotic and the extraordinary seem as natural a... te for life'
Lindsay (...

Monique Roffey was born in Port of Spain, Trinidad, and educated in the UK. She has worked as a Centre Director for the Arvon Foundation and has held the post of Royal Literary Fund Fellow at Sussex and Chichester universities. Her highly acclaimed debut novel, *Sun Dog*, was first published in 2002 and her most recent novel, *The White Woman on the Green Bicycle*, was shortlisted for the Orange Prize for Fiction 2010.

Monique [illegible] in Kensal Rise, north London. [illegible] moniqueroffey.co.uk

[illegible] ordinary [illegible] and the extraordinary [illegible]
[illegible] the seasons. Her book sharpens the appeti[illegible]
[illegible] Clarke, author of *The Chymical Wedding*

SUN DOG

Monique Roffey

SIMON & SCHUSTER

London . New York . Sydney . Tokyo . Singapore . Toronto . Dublin

First published in Great Britain by Scribner, 2002
This edition published by Simon & Schuster UK Ltd, 2011
A CBS COMPANY

1 3 5 7 9 10 8 6 4 2

Simon & Schuster UK Ltd
1st Floor
222 Gray's Inn Road
London WC1X 8HB

Simon & Schuster Australia
Sydney

A CIP catalogue record for this book is available from the British Library

ISBN: 978-1-84983-303-5

Typeset by Palimpsest Book Production Limited,
Falkirk, Stirlingshire

Printed in the UK by CPI Cox & Wyman,
Reading RG1 8EX

In memory of my father,
Alan George Roffey

9 June 1927–13 July 1993

11 December

There'd always been a problem with the light. Ever since August had first opened his eyes, he'd found it hard to look out through them.

It was a problem with pigment mainly, or lack of it. He'd been born with the palest of blue eyes. Eyes filled with a kaleidoscope of the most delicate shades of ice. They were the eyes of a veal calf. The eyes of a worm; of a hermit crab, with pinheads all nervous on stalks. Eyes that smarted constantly, or seeped water. Eyes that blinked or peered. Squinted. Eyes that were always about to collapse on him, or so it felt, his eyebrows sagging like paunchy roofs.

His eyes provided little protection from the sun.

The problem was one he harboured and often took out of a black velvet pocket in his mind to brood over when alone; one he assumed, in a sorrowful and private way, was a trick of nature, one which made him feel naturally confined. It was almost always in his thoughts, that he cringed at the sight of so many things. The light, mainly. But other things too. Women. Children sometimes. Fish, clothes, car fenders. Knives. He was constantly blinking back these sights, searing the balls of his eyes.

Winter was the easiest time. Winter was kind. August could look at the world without too much difficulty, at the gun greys and milky skies of purples and lavenders and muted pearl blues. In winter the skies were also struggling; not to see, but to be seen. The floes of stars were fatter, more bloated with dust, moving heavily and sluggishly, as if drawing a screen of smoke between the sun and earth. In winter it was as if the sun itself was blind.

Often, sleep deceived him, soothed him, appearing to rearrange reality overnight. August frequently dreamed he was someone else and would wake up with this possibility faintly traced, as though with the juice of an onion, on his cool, white eggshell skin.

In the bathroom he'd avoid the mirror at first, absurdly half-playing a game with himself, half-believing a swap really might have taken place. He'd urinate. Blow his nose, stare at the wall – then turn round.

He didn't see Adam Ant or GQ Man or a young Peter Frampton, all of whom he thought of as ideal replacements. He saw himself: six foot four in his skin, elbows sharp as corncobs, collarbones protruding like the jaws of a great fish. He saw his lumpy, set-to-one-side nose, his large, spaced-apart teeth. His upright blood-orange hair which limbo danced crazily from his head, as though a madman lived there, leaping from a burning attic. His eyebrows and lashes were the same colour and he knew it made his face look as if it was crawling with fire-ants or some other kind of insect. It was a face which had lain dormant in youth, unformed – even plump. As he'd grown older it had thinned and then elongated and found itself, as faces often do, long after adolescence. It had climbed out of a bag of tricks, punching its way into its present curves and lumps, its monstrous dimensions, presenting itself in his late twenties with the innocence and confidence of truth.

That morning was different.

August woke from a dream with a start. In the dream someone was bending over his bed, peering at him, breathing into his face. He'd felt a light and tickling breath on his cheeks, his eyelids, across his throat. When he opened his eyes there was only his bedroom. Empty, yet still holding the essence and presence of a body. Something was etched in the air around him, the feel of someone – the heat, or perhaps just an imprint left from his imaginings. He lay under his covers, perturbed, focusing on a crack in the ceiling until the feeling disintegrated and the dream completely disappeared.

He looked at his bedside clock, saw it was 6 a.m. and groaned, annoyed he'd been jolted so prematurely from sleep.

He pulled back the covers and got out of bed.

In the bathroom August went straight to the mirror. He splashed hot water on his cheeks, picked up his shaving foam from the shelf above the sink and sprayed a ball of foam into one hand.

For five, maybe six years now, what he saw most mornings wasn't just a face he didn't like. It was a face which didn't fit.

August glanced at the mirror's edge.

An old photograph was wedged behind it. The photo, about three inches long and two inches wide, had curled with age and its colours had become a mixture of liverish browns and lurid over-processed inks: purples, greens. Framed in the middle, in a tank top and jeans stood

Luke, a smallish, wiry man with long blond hair and fine, even features. Cheekbones. Thin lips. Dark eyes. Tanned skin. Luke was handsome and impish; a vibrancy in his smile which spoke of an innate ease with the world. In the picture Luke had his arms folded across his chest and a large tattoo bulged high up on his right arm – Lucky Luke, the cartoon cowboy with the lounge crooner's eyes. Luke smiled out from the photograph with the sureness of that day's sunshine. With the abundance of the harvest at the time. With the ripeness of an afternoon. With the ease of evening.

The photo was taken the day before he died.

Luke, August's father, had died when he was two weeks old.

Small, sunny Luke.

Handsome.

Brown-eyed.

Lucky Luke.

August rubbed foam slowly, deliberately, across his cheeks making large smooth circles, his eyes picking over the photograph, Luke's hair, his mouth, his nose.

As the years passed, as his face had gradually formed, August had grown more and more suspicious of the man in the photograph. The more he examined Luke's face for clues: a curve of the brow, or even of the ear, moles, freckles, anything, the more he'd come to see their connection was plainly incongruous – he looked nothing like Luke. In fact, they were impossibly different. And this disturbing idea, now living with him for years, was made worse by the fact that Luke's picture triggered no emotion. No filial response. When he looked at Luke he felt nothing.

Carefully, he rubbed foam along his top lip.

His mother, he'd come to realize, also behaved oddly. As he'd grown older he'd come to see her thinness. She was internally thin. Collapsed in on herself; thin-voiced, thin-nerved. As a child he hadn't understood, hadn't pieced together her mannerisms: her permanently clenched jaw, her habit of looking away when she spoke, of keeping conversations short, of being afraid of scrutiny of any sort. Her stories about Luke had always been kept to the minimum, the same few details repeated. She was on bad terms with Luke's parents and had lost contact, never encouraged him to trace them. He'd added all this up.

Now he felt mocked.

His eyes like pools of fat, his golem's skin. His teeth, his height. His colouring.

All taunted him.

Most mornings.

That morning, as he smoothed foam along his jaw line, August felt a tingling in the backs of his forearms, a sheer blush of warmth. Peculiar, as though a battery had been switched on inside him; he could feel his blood cells multiplying in a dim frenzy.

He caught sight of one of his forearms in the mirror. It looked unusual. Something white, a pattern, was smattered along his arm, a rash of some sort. Perhaps he'd eaten something. Odd. He rarely got rashes, had no allergies that he knew of. The sensation spread up to his elbow, then his armpit, becoming warmer and more fluid. August peered closely at his arm. The pattern seemed to have risen up from under his skin, was part of it. In it, even. He rubbed it, pinching up the skin between his thumb and forefinger. It appeared to be made of fine particles which sparkled a little, like salt or sugar. Crystals.

The morning sky was low over London. Outside the darkness was just lifting and the air had the qualities of a lung; dense, absorbent. Muffling sound. August noticed tiny lilac globes, hailstones, scattered on the ground as he walked to work – the result of a clash between currents thirty miles up. The walk was short, all of three minutes, left out of his flat, up Lena Gardens and right on to Shepherd's Bush Road. At Finlay's Deli, he stopped and fumbled for keys in his trouser pockets. When he found them he let himself in, flicking on the lights as he walked through to the café at the back.

In the kitchen alcove he switched on the coffee machine, letting it warm up before he made himself the first cup of many he drank throughout the day. He went back through to the deli, slipping behind the long display fridge. On the counter a coffee grinder stood upright, battered, shoulders back, its funnel bent somehow at a noble slant; rows of brown-dusty drawers of unground beans ran under it, jars of ground coffee crowded around it. Behind the grinder was a small, portable radio-cassette player and some tapes. He selected some Colombian ground coffee as well as some cumbia, slipping the tape into the machine and pressing play.

August closed his eyes – his way of making himself vanish. The cumbia was slow and rustic, snaking around his waist, settling on the soft, butterfly-shaped area around his kidneys. Trumpets and horns. An accordion. Sticks. And possibly an old washboard for percussion. It was a simple melody and he imagined it came from the mouths of five ancient men, sitting on chairs in a dance hall, singing to a wedding party. He envisaged couples gliding across a vast polished floor, mutely pressed together. He began to sway carefully, from side to side, feeling the music in his mind, a lazy, friendly tune.

His hips began to swing in time to the languid song, moving effortlessly, as though his body and the music were one. He began to shift his feet. One step, then two. He shimmied forward, braver, the trumpets pushing him from behind. His hands floated upwards and began to knead the air in gentle, fluid movements.

August salsa-ed past the salami slicer, past the row of upright fridges which kept fine cakes and champagne, the quail's eggs and the Ben & Jerry's, past the entrance to the café. He danced blindly into the middle of the deli, danced around the wrought iron tables pulled in from the pavement. Danced, suspended in time, his face relaxed, different, a small smile pressed into his cheeks, danced graciously, loose-limbed, on his own. In Spanish, the old men were crooning, something about tobacco. August hopped a little, overcome with the rise in emotion in their voices, the increase in tempo.

He opened his eyes by accident.

Sweet Banana Wax Peppers.

The jar pulsed on the shelf in front of him; the peppers were gnarled and an eerie yellow, pickles from another world. He cocked his head at them, trying to realize them, absorb their freakish nature. Something about their twisted form was strangely soothing.

The music was stronger than him now, picking him up and coursing through him. Near the peppers were rows of condiments. August ran his eyes along the jars: Jamaican Pepper Jelly, Spicy Sri Lankan Balti Paste, Green Olive Pâté. Their thick textures were somehow reassuring, he felt stirred at the thought of their locked secrets. He danced on, past the wall of pasta sauces, marvelling at their flavours, silently mouthing their long, onomatopoeic names: arrabiata, basilico, puttanesca, vodka, campagnola. He stared closely at a jar of tightly packed anchovies. Silver-white fillets. Tiny fish darting through the water. Now naked and standing on their heads. He could taste them: gluey, vinegary. He danced past bags of lumaconi pasta. Like giant snails. He hadn't ever tried them. He must, he told himself. With cream and porcini mushrooms.

He danced on. His body had warmed. His blood was loose and roamed freely over his back and shoulders. He twirled his hands and rotated his hips in graceful circles. It felt natural and he smiled. People did things like this all the time, he thought, without having to close their eyes. August snatched up two tubes of pretzels from a small table and shook them like maracas. He had rhythm and movement. Momentum. He salamandered backwards, towards the door, hands and hips in sync, feet like crabs darting from side to side. He was suddenly excited, thrilled he could move so fast. A flurry of strong feelings rushed around in him.

A sharp banging rang out above the music.

August became instantly rigid.

The sound rang out again, unmistakable: knuckles rapping on the glass.

August remained frozen, cat-like, as though about to pounce, pretzel tins still in his hands.

Slowly, he turned to look outside.

A young woman was standing on the pavement, about three feet from him. She was pretty, her hair running down her shoulders in two silver rivers. Her face was lightly tanned and her neat, black eyes were narrowed. Her arms were folded across her chest. August dropped the pretzel tins and they clattered to the floor. He moved quickly across the deli towards the display fridge, slipping behind it to the small portable radio-cassette player and switched the music off. He could feel all the heat in him rushing up his neck, into his face. He glanced out the window again.

The young woman was still waiting, her eyes more like slits.

At the door his fingers trembled at the lock. Panic flooded him as he felt his hair, his nose, his teeth, his entire body re-emerge from wherever it had gone.

He opened the door.

'I'm s-sorry,' he stammered.

August's eyes tried to meet hers but instead found her chest. He smiled apologetically.

The young woman pulled her head backwards. Her face hardened as she scanned his features. She gazed openly for a moment, as though she didn't have to be polite.

'Your cheese,' she said curtly.

August was puzzled. 'My . . .'

But the woman turned, cutting him off before he could

finish his response and stalked back towards a van parked nearby.

* * *

The storeroom sprawled like a catacomb beneath the deli. Its walls were pistachio green and lined with shelves crammed with tins and jars of overstocked goods. In one corner there was a kitchen with a large oven used for baking, fridges for the cakes and salads, also two cold rooms, one for cheese, the other for meat. In another corner there was a door which led to a small office.

August let the box of cheese fall to the floor with a thud. He shuddered as he thought of the woman who brought the delivery, remembering the way she wouldn't look at him as he wrestled the box from the back of the van. With a Stanley knife he sliced the top flaps open. Shiny new hay protected the cheeses inside. He grasped a handful, put it to his nose and inhaled. It smelt of cows. Open pastures. Mountain streams. That morning, the cheeses had been flown in from Normandy.

As he scrabbled through the hay he imagined the affineur they'd come from, a middle-aged man with a grey tonsure and cheeks like ripe apples, his skin the colour of tea. His fingers were callused and he had haemorrhoids from eating too much cheese. His 'caves d'affinage' were large dark rooms with fat dimes of cheese stacked high to the ceiling. Though August had never been to France, he'd seen pictures of French dairy cows with distended udders like hot pink torpedoes. Milked twice a day – they needed to be. An Emmental, he knew, was made with 900 litres. He imagined the affineur as a man of great natural balance, a virtuoso of alchemy who could make cheese from the milk of trees.

He found a large envelope resting on the first waxy package, a large wheel of Brie. In it there was a list in turquoise spidery writing.

2 Chaumes
3 St Maures de Touraine
2 Camemberts de Normandie
3 Bries de Meaux
Pont' L'Evêque – 1 kilo
1 Roquefort
Comte – 3 kilos
12 Crottins de Chavignol
6 Pouligny Saint Pierre
1 Boule de Lille

Boule de Lille. This was a new order, one he'd avoided having in the deli but couldn't any longer. Customers kept asking for it. Recipes often recommended it. It was a bold, rich cheese, fine for cooking and eating, good in salads and in canapés. Excellent for crudités. Now, he found himself impatient to see it. Hastily, he began to unpack the box, gathering the three large Bries to his chest and stacking them on a shelf in the cold room, then the Camemberts and the Roquefort and the smaller goat's cheeses. He left them wrapped, not interested in any of these. He wanted to hold the Boule de Lille.

When the other cheeses were stacked he looked down into the box. The way the Boule de Lille was nestling in one corner was deceptively timid. He picked it up and weighed it in his hands; it was heavy, he mused, almost three kilos.

'Mi-mou,' August said the words out loud as if to a small

face he was holding in his hands. *Half-soft*. Mimolette was its more common name. He carried it to the window, his pale eyes watering as he held it up to the light. The cheese was perfectly spherical, a compact, heavy ball. Its surface was peach coloured and pockmarked, lunar even. The cheese could be a small planet, he imagined, Mars or the moon. He saw the large vats of milk, the kind used in dairies, the curds rising, the whey falling away leaving the concentrate. *This is what the cheese looks like*, he decided, *the earth's concentrate*. A planet's core.

He knew he'd find it hard to look at the cheese once cut open, hard to look at its colour.

Blood-orange.

Unlike him, the cheese wore the colour easily, projecting it and flaunting it openly. He'd often seen the cheese in other delis, sitting composed in the fridge with its brilliant orange on display, rude as open legs, and as brazen. Attracting people. Charming strangers. Mimolette was always popular, it was vivacious and robust – a jester amongst cheeses.

Now he looked at the cheese half-wanting it to speak, to release the secret of its confidence, of dealing with its extreme colour, also half-fighting an urge to hurl it out the window.

Upstairs, the front door banged open and there was the sound of clumping feet and singing. Henry.

'Où est mon beau haricot?' she shouted.

The French had been going on for weeks, since she'd met her new boyfriend Yves. She'd decided the language was spoken loudly and in the tones of the BBC.

'I'm here!' August replied from the catacomb.

He gripped the Mimolette in the crook of his arm and climbed the stairs to the café. Henry was in the front of the shop, dragging one of the wrought iron tables out on to the pavement. He was glad to see her, as usual, to take note secretly of her hair. Before working at the deli she used to be a hairdresser's assistant and her hair was always different. Today she'd woven her long, black tresses into two side-plaits which had been carefully wound to make deck quoits above her ears.

'Fous le camp!' Henry snorted, her back to him.

August grinned.

'That's fuck off, not fuck me,' he corrected, joining her.

'I don't care, help me out, chéri.'

He picked up the other side of the table and together they carried it out on to the pavement.

'Merci,' she smiled when the table was on the ground.

Outside, the cold air was like fire, burning the end of his nose, stinging his cheeks.

'Is your boyfriend learning English?' he inquired, shivering.

'No.'

'Why not?'

'Because French is the language of *love*!' Henry winked.

Henry's hairdo was both unflattering and endearing, both matronly and sleek, giving her an air of a young Eastern-bloc Olympian starlet. The dark down on the edges of her face, along her jaw line, had collected moisture. Her pear coloured eyes prickled from the cold. August found her utterly captivating, as usual.

He tried to smile at her but his lips wilted.

'And the language of cheese!' she laughed and began to unbutton her long quilted jacket. Underneath, her brown cardigan was silky, as though knitted from the ears of an exotic goat. He saw that it clung to her body, rising with the swell of her breasts which seemed large and firm and delicate all at once, then fell into a wide waist which somehow seemed small. Her body was a gentle place, August thought. Gentle, like sleep.

There were morning rituals. Together, they went about them with a practised ease. The white tureens of olives needed to be brought up from the fridges downstairs and laid out on the large, black, wooden table opposite the till. There were half a dozen different types. Mauve Italian olives the size of quail's eggs. To August they were sinister, a gutter full of decomposing bodies. French olives, black and swollen, the size of prunes. Bald, yellow, Spanish ones which tasted like old socks. Green olives, tiny rugby balls, marinated in basil and lemon. Oily, Boscailo olives with garlic and red peppers. The small, black Niçoises fermenting in a claret coloured water could be cherries. There were also pestos and pickles, capers, woodland mushrooms, sun-dried tomatoes. Fresh bread and pastries were delivered to the back door every morning and needed arranging in baskets. Quiches and pies and tartlets on little silver platters were placed in the window.

'Je vais faire le awning,' Henry informed him, carrying the long hooked pole like a lance as she walked outside. August watched as Henry lunged upwards and missed.

'Merde!' she laughed through gritted teeth.

She wasn't tall enough to do this job, but she always tried. She smiled through the window at August to signal she was fine. He grinned and shook his head, walking out on to the pavement. Henry jumped again. August said nothing. Instead he grabbed the top half of the pole, his arms reaching up, way over her head. Henry held the bottom. Together they pulled as if on the rope of a church bell, their bodies close, facing each other. August felt a flutter inside his chest being so close to her, her smell. Pears soap. As Henry looked up through his arms, her eyes landed on the scoop at the base of his neck, the pale skin there, smooth as the skin of a seal. August blushed and grinned, showing his teeth. Henry's eyes flickered and then glanced away again. They pulled and the awning slowly unfolded like the hood of an old jalopy, clicking into place.

Their arms dropped and they stood for a moment on the pavement. Next to them, on Shepherd's Bush Road, the morning's traffic was grim and stationary. Like baby elephants each car stood patiently still, holding on to the tail of the car in front. Metres from them, the road was lined with hulking, flaking, long-faced, Victorian terraced houses. Around, above and beyond, the sky was resentfully nurturing a pastel yellow bruise.

'In December everything becomes ugly,' Henry grumbled.

August disagreed.

He looked up, admiring the plane tree above them. Its slim belly had turned a silver khaki and it rose from the pavement, a great cobra with combat fatigue skin, leaning into the road, above the traffic with its ten arms stretched out above it as if to dance a salsa. One arm was shorter and stumpy. August decided this was its head, a mossy Afro, thrown back in a laugh. The laugh rustled high above them, rattling him, making him feel suddenly, unaccountably watched.

He shivered.
'Il fait froid,' Henry said, thinly.
'Oui,' August replied. 'Il fait très froid.'

The first customers were usually mothers with toddlers dropping their older children to school. Or builders, or people coming off a night shift. People stopped for a takeout coffee on the way to either Hammersmith or Shepherd's Bush tube.

Finlay's Deli was owned by Rose Finlay. Painted tomato red, and sheltering two nests of tables and chairs under its awning, it was a homely and welcoming landmark on the long and mostly featureless Shepherd's Bush Road, part of a small stretch of shops a little east of Brook Green. On one side of the deli was a Chinese takeaway, on the other a newsagent run by a Muslim family. Across the road and along, next to Pollen, the flower shop, there was a tapas bar. Further towards Shepherd's Bush Green the terraced houses were mostly dingy hostels, most full of asylum seekers, who, when bored, hung around on doorsteps, or patrolled up and down in groups. To August these surroundings were fascinating, glamorous even; a mix of customs and cultures from countries he'd only ever read about or seen on TV. Most days it was possible to overhear a dozen languages spoken in the street.

First thing in the morning the shop and the café were full, but easy to deal with. People weren't themselves in the morning. It was like attending to a swarm of smoked bees. People were stingless. Quiet, vague. Happy to wait in line. People were still dreaming. It wasn't until later, when the day had slapped them in the face, that customers could get demanding. By lunch time things were different. Rose came at midday to help.

As August served the sleepy, he fantasized about having sex with Henry.

The fantasy was always more or less the same.

There wasn't much space behind the display fridge and often their bodies grazed each other during the course of the day. In his fantasy the deli was empty. It was late afternoon. They bumped into each other. A coffee cup dropped. It shattered and they both knelt to retrieve the pieces. On the way down their noses clashed, foreheads bumped. Lips met. They kissed deeply. Passion had been brewing between them for almost a year. Henry's voice was thick as she began to tell him what she would like to do to him, how long she'd thought about doing these things. She bit his ear. They rose, joined at the hips. He slipped his hands under her shirt, felt her smooth, warm skin. He pushed her back gently, her buttocks sliding effortlessly across the marble counter in front of the fridge full of cheese. He saw her thighs open towards him, felt her mouth on his throat. His fingers found her underwear, fine black lace. They twisted in them. As he pressed her neck with kisses he slid his fingers inside her. It was wet and warm at her centre and he felt happy and relieved. They laughed and stayed like this for a brief moment.

Then she fell into the cheese.

Sometimes, when they were on the olive table, she fell, heavily, off the table. Or if they were on the sink in the café, she fell into the sink. When they were on the stairs which led to the storeroom, she fell down the stairs. Other times they were attacked by a swarm of locusts. Once they fell into a hole, a deep black hole. It just appeared. They were having sex on a ladder and they fell in. Another time they were attacked by a whale.

Henry had just fallen into the cheese when a man walked into the shop. August was mildly aroused; under his apron he was semi-erect. He was staring at his shoes. When he looked up, he saw the battered cowboy hat and the long square face. Instantly recognizable, but also a blur in his memory. The same face but different. August was suddenly faint, crowded in. The man smiled and pointed at a blueberry muffin.

'One of those and a double espresso.'

The voice.

He remembered the voice, the garbled monologues; he used to talk fast and nervously, sucking air up, catching wind in him. August walked from the deli to the coffee machine in the café. The hat. Could it be the same hat? On the same head? Would a man wear the same hat for over twenty years? He scooped coffee into the espresso filter, slotted the filter into the groove in the machine, pressed the switch. It lit up. *Blood-orange.* Two feet away, Henry was making peppermint tea. She smiled at him. He stared at the delicate black hair on her bare forearms; he could see under her trousers she was wearing a G-string.

'Ça va, ma pomme frite?'

August's face was grey.

No, he wanted to say. *No, I'm not all right. I want to lie down, go to the toilet.* A feeling of dread ran through him, liquid, as though ink was being poured into his head. Thick, strong coffee flowed in a stream into a demitasse. When it stopped August unlatched the scoop from the machine and placed the little cup on a little saucer. He slipped back behind the fridge, walked to the counter where the man was still standing, already eating the blueberry muffin.

'That's two pounds fifty, please,' August said stiffly.

The man dug in his jeans pocket. His flowery shirt was open to the chest, exposing grizzled hair underneath. Over it he wore a large, sheepskin jacket which was stained with what could have been fox blood or battery acid, or children's hand prints. The man smiled broadly, handsomely, as he'd always done. He handed him the coins.

'Thanks,' August mumbled.

The man picked up the muffin and coffee and walked out of the deli on to the street. He sat at one of the tables, looking around expectantly, as if he was waiting for someone, his breath like steam.

August watched the man as he looked up into the plane tree. *Drink your coffee*, he thought. *Drink your coffee and leave*.

When the man left, August ran downstairs and locked himself in the bathroom. He stared in the mirror for a full minute only seeing past himself – to a room with red walls, to something he'd seen a long time ago and a sound like panic. Years, a lifetime it'd been. An age had passed since he'd last seen Cosmo. A hotness rose in him, flooding his face. He caught a single tear with his finger and wiped it away. He turned his head, one way, then the next, scrutinizing his mug-shot.

When he was a child he'd feared asking his mother questions. Feared, superstitiously, in the way of children, the effect they might have. They could cause her to do unexpected, undesirable things. As a child, questions were potentially disastrous. And that fear still persisted. He was still unwilling to upset the carefully arranged order of things between them, what little they had, even though it was all on her terms. The prospect of questioning her was too enormous, the risk of losing her too big.

And so he'd never quizzed her about Luke, never held the photo up to his own face and drawn attention to his fears. But now Cosmo had appeared, from nowhere. A different cowboy. August's eyes filled with an opaque hatred, his mouth turned downwards.

Cosmo.

August stared at his face, inspecting its shape, his nose, turned his head from left to right, sniffed. He was deserted by ideas, by any reliable information and the result was a thickheadedness. A frustrating emptiness.

August spent the rest of the day bumping into things, feeling vulnerable behind the glass battlement of the display fridge. At three his shift ended and he walked home, noticing on his way that the winter sky was unsettlingly bleak and low and that he still felt watched.

* * *

In his kitchen, August gulped down guava juice, draining it straight from the carton. His arms were tingling again, pleasurable somehow, a sudden surge of health. He stopped drinking and rolled back his sleeves, holding his arms towards the window for a better look. Both forearms had the white rash now. It was curious, unlike anything he'd seen before. It was both crisp and slippery, velvety-rough, the kind of pattern he'd seen on frozen things.

When the door bell rang August stood still, planning not

to answer. Old ideas, like dried seeds, had scattered in him and he wanted to gather them back. He wanted time to think about Cosmo's appearance, what it might mean.

The door bell rang again.

This time the caller kept their finger on the buzzer, the noise like a very big and loud mosquito.

'Go away,' he muttered.

The ringing stopped.

August re-examined his arms, touching them gently, running his fingers along them. His thoughts drifted back to Stonegate Hall, a sadness welling behind his sockets, the skin on his cheeks. Cosmo had been the antithesis of a ghost – a real-life shock. But now, re-visualizing him, the man he'd just seen, he realized, disconcertingly, that this Cosmo was thinner than the one he remembered, and much older, less attractive, dirty. Slightly decrepit even. He was an old man now, like any other. If anything, in the cowboy hat, the open shirt, the sheepskin, Cosmo looked pathetic.

The ringing started again.

'Okay, okay, okay.'

He left the kitchen and walked down the hall, opening the inner door to the landing he shared with his neighbour. He turned the lock on the front door, pulling it open.

His mother was standing on the top step. In her arms she was holding her customary offering, a large, wrapped bundle of flowers.

'August!' she snapped, exasperated.

'H-hello, Olivia.'

August didn't open the door wider. He felt a swell of resistance and remained in the shadows of the landing. What with Cosmo, he'd forgotten Olivia was coming and now wanted to see her even less than usual. Since they'd left Stonegate Hall she'd behaved as though Cosmo had never existed. None of it had. Those long years had been sliced from her life with the precision of a surgeon's knife. As with a tumour, 'Cosmo' had become an unspeakable word between them.

Olivia was eyeing him with irritation.

'Are you letting me in or not?'

August continued to stare. Her brown eyes were still clear, and somehow innocent. Her lips were un-aged, ridiculously plump and firm. The rest of her was old, though. Despite good bone structure, her face had slipped and withered. Her red hair was browner, still long, but flecked with grey. Her neck was papery, her breasts had flattened, her waist had gathered rolls. Her ankles had thickened.

'August!'

August opened the door. Taking the bundle from her, he turned before she entered, walking back into the kitchen.

In the kitchen he rested the flowers on the counter top. He reached up and took a large crystal vase down from a shelf and began to fill it with water from the tap. His mother stood behind him, watching, saying nothing, and he could sense her impatience. She never liked the way other people did things.

'I need to talk to you about Christmas,' she said quickly, addressing his back.

August began to unwrap the bundle.

'What are you planning to do?'

He didn't answer, he knew he needn't.

'You can't come to me.'

The flowers were hollyhocks. He liked hollyhocks. Delicate purples and pinks. Probably imported. He began to single them from each other and stab them into the water, listlessly.

'I'm heading for the sun. Mustique. Fred and I are staying with Jean. You know Jean. She has such a lovely house out there. All those pillars flown in from Rajasthan. Sorry, baby. I couldn't say no. I'd have asked if you could come too, but you know your eyes couldn't take it.'

She sighed, as if truly thwarted.

August continued to stab the stems into the water. They were far too long for the vase, even though it was quite deep. The flowers had fallen to the sides and looked awkward, but he didn't care. He tinkered with them, ineffectually.

'Oh, *God*, August!'

The sharpness in her voice was familiar. He was always amazed at how near the surface her anger simmered, how it could spill over so easily.

Olivia pushed him out of the way and made a terse, strangling gesture around the neck of the vase. His inadequacy at anything to do with flowers or plants, even mowing the lawn, had always made her angry.

'Why are you always so *hopeless* at this! Look, there, see,' she began arranging the flowers more artistically. 'See? It's so easy. So eas-y. Simple. I've never known anyone to be so bad at such a simple thing.'

She huffed.

August watched her without emotion. He should've remembered to let her arrange the flowers, let her be the child. *Cosmo*, he would like to lean over and whisper in her ear. *He came into the deli today. Your old boyfriend. One of them.*

Remember him?

But he couldn't. Saying Cosmo's name aloud would make him real. For the moment he could pretend he hadn't seen him, and he might never see him again. It was probably a one-off coincidence. He knew he had every right to ask these questions. But he felt powerless and unsure, somehow fundamentally without rights. She had made him and his life.

'Mustique,' he said. 'How lovely. I already have plans for Christmas. Jim's asked me to spend it with them. Send a postcard.'

But his mother wasn't listening.

When she'd gone, August went into his bedroom and lay down. He hadn't discussed Christmas with Jim and he didn't plan to either. Jim was broke and had children to feed and his home in Harlesden was tiny. He decided Christmas on his own would be a treat. He'd stay in his dressing gown and slippers all day, drink a fine wine and listen to the Queen's speech, later watch a black and white epic on TV. He'd buy a carp. Stuff it with chestnuts and bake it. Eat it with noodles. He imagined them, a mound like a glistening castle, slippery, translucent. For dessert, he'd make something easy, perhaps some flaming peaches.

Mustique – his idea of purgatory. It wasn't a place, even. More of a floating golf course, by the sound of her other trips and the photos she'd shown him. He had a list in his head of a hundred places he'd like to visit. There were a hundred other places he could add to the list before even considering Mustique. This choice was typical of Olivia, a non-place. A visit to nowhere.

August rubbed his eyelids gently. Underneath them, his eyes burnt as they did at the end of most days. Cosmo, Christmas, he pushed these ideas away, closed down on them. He was tired and demoralized by his mother's visit as usual, inextricably bound to her. Her past was his and the cold fact of it always made him moody and irritated. He'd never be able to cut himself free. The past was as unshakeable as a friendly dog.

And now Cosmo had reappeared.

He felt black as he lay on his bed.

His eyes stung.

When August arrived at the deli the next morning he was anxious. Unusually, Rose had come down early and he found he wanted to confide in her immediately, throw himself on his knees. Wrap his arms around her waist. Tell her, *a man came into the deli yesterday, just thinking about him makes me feel sick*.

But this was impossible. She was standing on a ladder when he came into the shop, a box of jars from Tulip Farm at her feet. Cobwebs of sunlight were pressing against the large windows, paralysing him. Rose was humming to herself, making room on the shelves for the new delivery. Henry was on her own serving customers, a long queue.

It wasn't until the morning rush had died that he could approach Rose. Her small task had become a mammoth operation. Every pot and jar had been taken off the shelves: vinegars, mustards, pasta sauces, dressings and syrups, jams and pickles. She'd polished each jar lovingly and put it back on to newly dusted shelves. The box from Tulip Farm still lay untouched at her feet; it was a good excuse to join her.

'Can I help?'

'Thank you, August,' Rose purred, in her mild Scottish lilt.

The jars in the box were mostly jams and pickles. They glowed dark and unctuous. Deep purples, maroons, reds and oranges – individual cells from a vampire honeybee.

August reached down, picked one up and handed it to Rose; in it white bulbs bounced in amber amniotic fluid.

'Oh,' Rose squeaked with glee. 'These are superrrb.'

August smiled insincerely.

He wanted to say: *Who do you most dislike? Who would upset you most if he or she suddenly walked into your life?*

Rose was wearing a powder blue kilt and a matching twinset, a string of pearls at her throat. Her silver hair was combed, as usual, into a neat pixie cap. Her shoes were flat moccasins with toggles.

He doubted Rose had real secrets. She lived a humdrum life in the flat above the shop with her lethargic, half-dead pug Hilary. She had no private life to speak of, only other spinster friends with whom she took holidays several times a year. She went for walks on weekends, she liked fine food. She never talked about her family in Edinburgh. He supposed Rose had always been like this. Tidy, tubby, conservative. He was unable to put a different face on her, a younger one.

August handed her another jar, garlic pickle, the colour of crushed sun.

He didn't know how to start, but an urgency made him feel incautious, indifferent to beginnings, middles and endings. He and Rose often talked, they were confidants of sorts. They shared a love of food and cooking and often discussed recipes or swapped cook books. Sometimes they talked about music, or customers who came in, or they gossiped about other shops. It'd often occurred to him that Rose treated him like a son – and that he liked it.

He handed her another jar.

She took it without looking at him.

Who do you hate most?

She was dusting, her eyes on the shelves.

'Rose?'

The ladder creaked a little as she shifted her weight. The bulge of her stomach was very close to him and he watched as she tugged at her twinset, trying to conceal it.

'Who . . .'

Rose continued dusting, only half-listening.

How could he word it right?

He handed her a jar.

'Who have you . . . have . . .'

She took it from him. 'Have I what?'

He held a jar of red cabbage in his hand, trying to arrange his feelings into words.

Rose moved up a rung.

Cosmo's face materialized in front of him, indifferent, bleary.

'Who do you hate most?' he said.

Rose didn't answer. She continued to arrange the jars.

August's ears burnt. He wanted to snatch the words back.

'Sorry,' he mumbled. 'I don't know what I'm saying . . . I . . .'

'My father,' Rose said, in a steady voice, her eyes on the jars.

August reddened and handed her the jar of cabbage.

'He wasn't a very nice man,' Rose continued, looking

down at him calmly; her small grey eyes were pellucid and she seemed at ease.

'Another jar, please.'

He handed her one. Grapefruit marmalade, a ring of citrus rind gnashed against the glass, dentures suspended in a gummy green. She looked at it, turning it in her hands, then put it on the shelf. She huffed and began arranging the jars in alternating colours.

August bit his lip, feeling oddly upstaged. He continued to hand her more jars, but the atmosphere between them had changed. Rose had begun to dust and hum again, louder, this time, as if a drawbridge had been pulled up. He'd always instinctively liked Rose, found her smallness, her neatness, inspiring. Next to her he felt so big and heavy-boned, reminding himself of something too large, a great dog of some sort.

He passed up more jars. As he did he found himself wondering who Rose loved, and who had loved Rose. And what her underwear looked like.

Lunch time passed.

The afternoon sky rumbled, as though great tablets of stone were being pulled away from the mouth of a cave. The clouds turned mauve, then orchid purple, but no rain came. *Funeral weather*, August thought, shaking off a crawling feeling between his shoulders and peered out the large plate-glass windows, wishing for milkier skies. Rose had disappeared upstairs to give Hilary her daily ginseng, Henry to the storeroom to find herring fillets. In the premature dusk, the deli was cosy. Two metallic lamps on chains were slung low in the room, throwing a watery consommé of light on to the walls. On the radio Roberta

Flack was singing slowly, hauntingly. In the deli, August felt secure again.

He usually did.

Food he understood. Food was complex and didn't speak. The deli was an oasis in the real world, a crowded room full of strong personalities, a party he felt comfortable at, a gathering of fellow mutes. It was his private salon, a coterie of eccentrics he knew and enjoyed being with.

The deli's two rooms were spacious.

The first, looking on to the street, was the delicatessen. It smelt like a gastronomic locker room, August thought, one where the heavyweight odours of cheese, coffee and dried meat had gone to recuperate after a bout of fifteen rounds. It was the smell of a full-flavoured clash, of the aftermath of a tie-break. All August's clothes had the same smell, his skin too. But for all its force, its invisible chaos, the smell, he always noticed, was curiously subtle.

The deli's saffron coloured walls were lined with bulging shelves, its wooden floor was bordered with baskets of dried produce and boxes of vegetables. Pushed against the shelves were three tables: one large one for the olives; the other, smaller ones permanently heaped with a changing selection of imported delicacies – Bayonne chocolates and Dutch biscuits, bags of handmade pasta, Venetian polenta, Milanese panettone, Caspian caviar, all sourced by Rose, all chosen as much for their exquisite packaging as for their craftsmanship.

The room was dominated by the L-shaped glass display fridge which ran the length of the shop, ending at the till. Chest high, the fridge formed a natural barrier behind which Henry and August served customers. To August it was a trick wall, its contents, the cheeses, the charcuterie, the pâtés and salads, were land mines scattered in a two foot wide no-man's-land between himself and other people. It was a wall behind which he could both hide and be seen.

The long fridge also hid the tools of the trade: the meat slicer, the coffee grinder, some scales, a microwave, plastic tubs, clingfilm and fine tissue, the small portable radio-cassette player. The radio was almost always on, tuned in to Radio 2.

The second room, the café, was light and pretty, painted butter yellow, with mint green curtains and plastic table-cloths. In a corner, behind a barrier, was a kitchen alcove with the coffee-machine, where lunch-time meals were prepared. The café was often busy, mainly with customers who lived locally, most of them women.

August was refilling an empty salad bowl with his own leeks *à la grecque*, when he noticed a young woman bending over the olive table. He hadn't seen her come in. She was pressing her fingers to her chin and her brow was puckered with concentration, her eyes sharpened by the sight of the heaps of olives, trying to decide which to choose. He noticed she was wearing an apron too, white, like his, with green stains on the front. She had on a tweedy skirt and long, pink woolly socks under gumboots. Between the skirt and the boots her legs were bare and he could see the valleys in the backs of her knees. The skin there was smooth as a plum and pale as a white opal. Chalk blue veins, like subterranean rivers, crossed underneath.

Somewhere in him, August felt a pull. He straightened up behind the display fridge.

'Can I help?' he asked, blushing at the sound of his own

voice. But she didn't seem to hear. She scooped large, green olives into a small Styrofoam pot from a stack on the table. August's insides began to jangle with self-hatred, waiting until she turned around and flinched. He wished his skin would drop off like a suit revealing another man, a young Peter Frampton. She turned, and looked around.

'Hi,' she beamed.

August blinked. The soles of his feet started to melt like cheese toasties, melt and stick to the insides of his trainers. The woman had long auburn hair, wiry, tied back loosely, an aquiline nose, and pale but freckled skin.

August tried to smile but couldn't. His throat was a vacuum.

'Can I help?' he croaked the question this time.

'Oh, no, I'm fine.'

She glided over to the till and put the pot on the counter.

'I'm Leola,' she said breezily. 'I've just started working across the road.'

August couldn't speak. He nodded. His ears, he was sure, were melting, falling from his head.

'At Pollen, the flower shop.'

August nodded again and rang the amount up into the till.

'One pound twenty,' he said in a voice which had almost evaporated.

She smiled, reassuringly.

'I–I'm August,' he said. He couldn't look at her. He looked at her neck.

'Nice to meet you.'

'Yes,' he replied.

She looked at him uncertainly, a look he knew so well.

There were a hundred things he could say, a hundred platitudes, anything, but nothing came.

She handed him the money.

August leaned forward to take it and as he did so, his long T-shirt sleeve slipped up a little. She glanced at his forearm quickly, at the odd rash which had been exposed; then, puzzled, she stood still, regarding him, his face.

She smiled, faintly.

August opened his mouth, trying to smile, showing his large spaced-out teeth.

'See you around,' she said before walking out on to the street.

August leaned against the back counter, feeling hot and short of breath, fighting back a flood of fresh and ancient disappointment.

He hooked his fingers in the corners of his mouth and pulled upwards, then took his fingers away. The smile he was left with was inane. He tried again, without his fingers. This smile was open, toothy, cavernous. He smiled quickly and then stopped. He smiled again, quickly. Then stopped. He practised smiles until another customer walked into the shop.

Outside, Mrs Chen walked past. August nodded and she nodded back. She usually started work at the takeaway next door at around five o'clock.

August liked to practise different languages, even though he'd never left England. He often dreamed of travelling, only to places where the sun wasn't too strong: Latvia, Lithuania, St Petersburg, or even Ireland. But he couldn't travel very far. Motion sickness always struck, either that or mild nausea. There was something about being moved, about being taken or carried without his actual body doing the moving that panicked him. Something he didn't quite trust. He'd learned to drive, but never enjoyed it. He got car sick on a bus. He had fear of flying though he'd never flown. The one time he'd taken a train from York to London, he'd had a panic attack. He loved to swim, but had a fear of boats.

Travelling, he'd always thought, was where he'd meet his other self. Somewhere in a foreign place, he would bump into the bit of himself which was lost. Travelling would bring him upon himself, would force him upon the unknown, upon the fear of being totally alone. It would force him to think about who he was, give him courage to trace himself. This is what he fancied, anyhow, on gloomy mornings in Shepherd's Bush.

Out there he was.

But he never went.

Instead he read books about other places. Encyclopedias, atlases. Pored over maps. And he visited Shepherd's Bush market once a week to browse in the shops and stalls which sold falafels and dasheen, plantain and fufu flour, red snapper and bacalao, great tongues of dried beef. The market was a mini-world.

A toddler on a plastic trike cycled into the shop. August looked down and practised a smile. The little girl had long, white-blonde hair spread like floss over her back. Her mother followed. Her face was scrubbed and she had short, thin, brown hair; she was wearing tight trousers. She selected two batons and a soda bread from the basket in the window, handing August a ten pound note. Her smile was pinched and she stared at his hands as he handed back the coins.

'Thanks,' she said quietly.

Her daughter gazed up at him as she wheeled out of the shop, her mouth gaping.

'What a wonderful arse!'

The loud, rusty voice rang out from behind a bowl of Belgian truffles.

Cedric was standing in the middle of the shop, preening his long white druid's beard. His long, white hair was rustling up around his head a little, like in some kind of electrical experiment.

'Cedric, be quiet!' August couldn't help laughing.

'My kingdom for an arse like that. Oh God!' Cedric made a motion in the air with his hands as though he was weighing melons.

'Blondes in tight pants. Oh my ticker!'

'Calm down, Cedric.'

'Blondes, fronds, ponds, wands. I feel a poem coming on.'

'Good. Go outside. I'll bring you a cappuccino.'

'My pecker is tingling.'

'Cedric, go outside.'

Cedric's large, oystery eyes watered a little. He didn't move. Instead he weaved a little on the tepee of his legs, blowing his nose into a rumpled hanky. After a few moments he remembered he'd been told to go outside and looked annoyed at August, weaving a little more. Then he wandered out.

August watched him like a parent through the shop window, feeling what he always felt for the old man, exasperation mixed with fondness. Also, dimly, a recognition of his future self.

On the pavement Cedric was unsteady on his feet as he examined the traffic, staring as if he'd never seen cars. Then he looked up, into silver dancing arms.

'What a tree!' the old man shouted.

August smiled.

He could smell Pears soap: Henry was back from the storeroom, making herself a coffee at the machine. August joined her to make Cedric's cappuccino, admiring her hair. Today it was styled into a neat, compact doughnut on her head.

'Ça va, ma puce?' she grinned.

He wanted to kiss her and say: *Oui, mon petit lapin. Ma petite grenouille, my flower, my flea. Mon petit fromage.*

'Cedric's here,' he said.

'Slime ball.'

'He's not that bad.'

'He always stares at my tits.'

'He's old.'

'I don't care. Why doesn't he wear long trousers in the winter?'

'I don't know.'

'I do.'

'Why?'

'He's kinky, that's why. It gives him a thrill.'

'He's eccentric, not kinky.'

'He is. I bet he reads porn – kinky magazines. I bet he's into chambermaids, likes a little slap and tickle.'

'Henry!'

Henry danced her eyebrows up and down at him to stop him from continuing.

'My boyfriend's taking me to see a film tonight.'

'Yves?'

'Oui. He wants to see a French film.'

'I thought he was taking *you* out,' August smiled.

Henry looked puzzled.

'He is.'

When the cappuccino was ready August sprinkled it with chocolate. He carried it to where Cedric was sitting, back hunched, at one of the tables on the pavement. He was writing something on the back of a napkin, a poem or a billet-doux. He sat for hours sometimes, scribbling and muttering, staring into space, drinking cups of coffee which August let him have for free. Cedric had always been part of the deli. Like the slicer and the coffee machine, he was a fixture, thrown in; Rose had inherited him when she bought the shop.

'There you go,' August placed the cup and saucer down on the small table.

Cedric pretended he was too absorbed to notice him.

'Your coffee, Cedric,' August said louder, smiling at this game.

'Oh,' Cedric replied, looking at him as if for the first time. 'Thank you, darling.'

August stared at Cedric's soft, girlish legs. He was wearing thin, khaki shorts and an old racing green school blazer. Under the blazer he had on a dirty, white shirt with its tails hanging out. He wore this outfit – an outsize schoolboy's uniform – throughout the year but August had never dared ask about it.

'Well?' Cedric sulked. 'Don't you want to read it?'

'Oh, of course,' August said politely, as if he'd forgotten. 'Another one, so quickly?'

Cedric blushed.

August picked up the napkin and read:

Blondes in Tight Pants

O Queen of wands, let me play your knave:
Blondes in tight pants! Let me be your slave.
Let me be your wood pecker
Let me drill a hole in your bole
Let my hypodermic beak
Pierce your bark!

O Queen, such larks!
And yet, too late I speak:
For time, relentless ticker
Leaves me my soul, but moves the goal.

Ever closer now the grave, and Lethe's languorous ponds;
I sit and watch the fireflies, like strength,
Fading midst the limpid fronds.

August stifled the urge to laugh aloud.

'I like it,' he said to the old man. 'It has swagger.'

Cedric became serious and nodded.

Again, August felt someone was watching him. He looked around. People hurrying past were walking as though to a wake, head down, eyes vacant. Across the road a street cleaner leaned on the railings with a roll-up cigarette. He looked ill. *The weather is corrosive*, August thought. Like acid, it could eat through clothes, into skin and bone marrow.

The trees along the Shepherd's Bush Road had shrugged off all their leaves and the upper branches, the finer twigs, resembled some form of netting on a ship. From it dangled clusters of large pods. In each, small seeds were fast asleep. As August contemplated them, their peace, he sensed a presence behind him, an instinct to look up the street.

Walking quickly, stumbling past, legs collapsing inwards, head back, nostrils flaring into the slight wind and hands holding on to the lapels of his jacket for support, came Cosmo.

He stopped abruptly, in front of them.

'Hello, there.'

August's insides plummeted. Heat swilled in the bowels of his ears.

Cosmo smiled, politely. ''Fraid I'm a bit lost. Looking for Sulgrave Road.'

Cedric cleared his throat.

'Continue up, first left and then first right,' he gestured.

A wild, anarchic joy rose in August. *Cosmo didn't recognize him.* They were inches apart, and it was clear Cosmo didn't know who he was.

'S-sulgrave Road,' August stuttered and smiled as if only casually interested. 'Why're you going there?'

'Moving in,' Cosmo replied proudly. 'Next week, number ten. I'm off to sign the lease.'

August nodded but his sight filmed over, his pale eyes swam in their sockets. He pushed his bottom lip out and shook his head as if he had no further interest.

'Thanks, anyway,' Cosmo smiled again and winked at them, then pushed on past the deli heading east.

August was taken by surprise at his awkward gait, a puzzle of legs, about to trip, but just saving himself. He'd forgotten the walk, or perhaps this had developed with age.

'Sulgrave Road?' Cedric repeated, scratching his beard and squinting. 'Isn't that where *you* live?'

August smiled at the old man and nodded. He wanted to cry.

'I live at number two.'

'Lovely new neighbour,' Cedric teased. 'Three doors away?'

'Four,' August replied.

* * *

August stared at the fluorescent digital figures of his radio clock, 4.17 a.m. In his sleep, an ocean had been rolling him in his bed, an ocean of alkaline and acid. Refusing to neutralize. Instead, curdling his body's systems, causing them to thin and separate and then riot in his bloodstream. Cosmo, his walk, stumbling through his dreams, hurrying up the Shepherd's Bush Road, hurrying away from him or towards him. He couldn't make out which. For hours he'd been watching him on a silent movie screen, projecting the image again and again.

He felt confused and weak, barely aware of the previous day's events, their order. A silk-like agony lived somewhere, dimly, in his muscles, smothered over by exhaustion. He lay in the darkness for some time, floating in and out of consciousness.

Eventually he closed his eyes again.

He dreamed of a woman.

She had long, auburn hair.

In her hands she held an onion.

'Its skin is hard,' she said, pressing it to her lips. She smiled kindly at August who was sitting outside the deli on a milk box, legs crossed.

'That means a bad winter,' she continued.

She began to ease off this tough layer with her thumbs. It crumbled. Under it there was a layer of yellowish crystals – olivine. She peeled this layer too. Under this garnets sparkled. She peeled more layers: orange, green, blue. The layers melted. A hot liquid dripped in her hands, ran down her forearms.

At the heart of the onion was a diamond. She put it in her mouth and sucked it clean.

'Keep hold of this,' she said.

The diamond was the size of a peach stone. She handed it to him.

'Don't let it go,' she cautioned, before she disappeared.

*

August's eyes flicked to the curtains. Through the open V he could see the morning sky was mottled and worn thin, the colour of old denim. A javelin of light fell into the room, across his bed and his forearms which were now both completely covered in the strange sparkly rash. The pattern it made was fine, intricate, a faded stencilling of talc: old somehow, and pretty. He let his fingertips brush one arm ever so slightly, distractedly.

His thoughts were still infested.

He remembered Cosmo – shaving one morning, stripped to the waist, the day's first whisky beside him on a chair. Thin lines of sweat ran down Cosmo's ribcage. They smelt acidy, as though his insides were leaking. That smell had been the hardest to get away from, following August around for years. He remembered the hawkish look in Cosmo's eyes when he'd caught him watching, like he was inspecting a worm which wasn't worth eating.

'That you, shy-boy?' Cosmo had jeered.

But he'd flitted away quickly.

For hours afterwards he'd pondered on that word – *shy*. What did it mean? Did it mean him? It sounded right and oddly, it rang with meaning. He wondered about it all day, and for days afterwards. Then almost every day ever since.

Shy. It was the first time the word had ever been used about him.

August thought again of Stonegate Hall, the old house in Yorkshire. The commune. He pictured himself standing alone in the open field in front of the house, looking at it face on. As he did, the familiar feel of the place descended on him, one of wearying unhappiness and uncertainty.

It was a plain house to look at, remarkably so; a large

rectangle on its side, like the houses children draw, with smaller rectangles for windows and a flat, upturned boat for a roof. Built in the early nineteenth century, it'd once been a modest home for local gentry. But August had always imagined whoever had lived there in bygone eras had also been troubled. The house possessed an inherent air of discord. At times, in the corridors, on the stairs, he'd heard the faded whispers of other orphans. Other children had lived there unhappily before him, he'd known that, sensed it all those years.

Around it the gravel driveway was studded with weeds. A small, unkept, once formal garden fronted the house like an apron. Beyond it lay a wide, open field at the bottom of which there was a small copse. A stream ran past this at the end of the property. There was a paddock behind the copse which bordered the road.

Made of stone, the house was always cold. August grimaced, remembering the dark halls, the murky windows, the smell of sour milk. No heating at all. And bodies. Bodies everywhere, mainly in the common room. Large, hazy forms lolling into beanbags, asleep or smoking. Vast clouds of smoke and bodies, like packs of dogs, slumped in corners. The air in the summer was thick with moths, the curtains always drawn. The carpets were threadbare, torn. An atmosphere of latent menace born from boredom. Pink Floyd's *Dark Side of the Moon* was always on, somewhere in the background.

Under the duvet August curled himself up into a ball. His blood still went cold at the thought of the commune.

On the ground floor there was a large dormitory for the children, a different bed every night, the same dirty sheets. The faint ammonia of dried urine. The floor above them was where the adults slept, in their own dormitory. The third floor was semi-derelict and even colder than the rest of the house. Up there, broken windows let in the elements and the odd nesting bird. Leaks in the roof had rotted the wooden beams and the floorboards. No one went up there. It was used for storage mainly, though one room was sporadically used as a school room.

He was on the third floor when his mother left the first time. It was the only quiet place in the house and he often escaped there for hours as a small boy, unlooked for and unmissed. He liked to gaze at the emptiness of the rooms, or look out of the high windows at the ruggedness of the surrounding moors. It was May and the bluebells were out in the copse at the bottom of the field, thousands of them. He was always drawn to looking at the copse; it was an island of some sort, in his thoughts; it changed colour with the seasons, each hue raging full and rich before dimming and melting into the surrounding scenery. The trees in it were oddly grouped, their backs to him, making them appear enviably self-sufficient. The copse was its own tiny world, a microcosm of earthly intimacy.

That day one window was open, spears of light thrown through it, on to the bare wooden floor. He was standing, gazing out at the copse, mesmerized by the indigo sea.

Outside a horn honked and he looked down. His mother was below, on the drive, sitting in an open-topped jeep. She was with a man; he recognized his cowboy hat. Cosmo. They were waving to the others in the house. Her long red hair was loose, the sun shining on it, turning it into a piercing copper mass. The jeep moved off, away from the house. As it swung around the first bend in the long drive, the wheels disappeared behind tall green grasses. When it picked up speed the jeep appeared to be hovering, slicing through the greenery. Tails of red hair, green grass, bluebells.

Looking back, it made him shudder. At Stonegate parenting was shared, theoretically, just like the housework and everything else. So she hadn't worried about leaving, hadn't told him she was going.

He'd waited three days and nights for her to come back. After that, her face disappeared from his memory.

When she returned three months later he'd run away from her, screaming.

August felt the first sharp feelings of hunger in his stomach and thought of breakfast. He swung his long, lithe legs from the bed to the floor, his big feet curling to grip the carpet. He could hear the man downstairs pull the bathroom light on, the flow of his bath tap. He padded to the kitchen, flicked on the kettle and peered through the kitchen window. He could feel a hot ball up there, somewhere, only today it was distant, the sun's rays straining to warm this half of the planet as it leaned back on its axis. He was glad for this little warmth, though, for this faint but persistent smile from the sun, knowing something inside him was perpetually cold.

He blew breath out and it steamed the glass of the window. On the sill outside he could see a thin hoarfrost; the crystals were startling, prickling like lemons. The kettle clicked off. He spooned Lavazza coffee into a cafetiere and poured in the boiled water. He put the plunger in only halfway, leaving the coffee to brew. He opened the fridge. In it there was a jar of coconut marmalade and a giant squab on a plate, looking a little blue. He'd been meaning to cook it for days, a recipe he'd clipped from an old Larousse. He closed the fridge and took a mug and the cafetiere back to his room.

In bed he sat upright, drinking his coffee slowly, staring at the wall.

Cosmo.

August tried to do his sums. He'd left the commune with his mother when he was twelve, so it must be over twenty years since he last saw him. Time in which he'd trained himself to think of something else whenever his thoughts strayed to Cosmo, whenever he popped up in his daydreams.

Besides his acidy sweat, Cosmo reeked of whisky. When he was a boy, he used to think that was why Cosmo's eyes were the colour they were, clouded whisky. Because he'd drunk so much and the drink had filled up inside him. He remembered he talked too much: Buddhism, time travel, unicorns. He talked on and on as though trying to stop something from happening; as though if he stopped, the earth would stop spinning. Sometimes he'd start swaying to the words he was saying, making winding movements with his hands. Remarkably, people listened to him, especially women. He always wore the same clothes. Brown flared corduroys and a green cheesecloth shirt with wide lapels. A soft packet of Camels was always in his top pocket. The cowboy hat was always on his head.

That was when he wore clothes.

August rested one hand on his stomach. He could feel an old sadness and an old hatred sway around in his gut. Cosmo's stench, his nakedness, it'd all been too much. Too much to look at.

The day flew. August hardly noticed what he was doing for most of it. When Jim rang in the afternoon, suggesting August meet him and his brother Gabriel for an early drink, August immediately agreed. Seeing Jim and Gabriel was always a relief, a welcome break from his usual surroundings. Separately and together, they had something about them that parted the curtains of the conventional world and let him step into the unusual space they occupied.

On the way to his flat August instinctively looked up. A procession of heavy, pewter clouds were trailing him in single file, making him quicken his pace a little.

In The Green Man on Askew Road, Jim and Gabriel were sitting in a corner, Gabriel vigorously finger signing, Jim nodding as he listened.

'Hi there,' August said loudly, making sure to look straight at Gabriel so he could read his lips. Gabriel waved and Jim nodded and said hello.

'Another drink?' he pointed to their full glasses of bitter.

They shook their heads. August went to the bar to

buy himself the same and returned, pulling a stool up to their table.

'Gabriel's met a new woman,' Jim said teasingly, signing along.

Gabriel smiled and crossed his chest, the sign for love, and flamboyantly pressed his fingers together to make part of the letter B, gracefully opening the other fingers on the same hand like a flower, the sign for beautiful.

August was unable to muster a spontaneous look of goodwill.

Gabriel continued to sign, telling August she was posh, drove a truck, was an interior designer and had gold, flowing hair.

After knowing Gabriel for so many years, August knew enough sign language to communicate more than adequately; knew it was best to keep sentences short, as if sending a telegram.

'M-e-e-t?' he spelt out on his fingers.

'Friend's house one night,' came the reply. They'd got talking, she'd asked him to help with some building work. He'd agreed. They'd spent most of their after work hours together ever since.

Gabriel pointed forwards, then opened two flat palms in front of his face.

'Er-ry daes,' he said, with a conspiratorial wink.

August smiled, insipidly.

Gabriel loved people, loved being in large groups, liked being included in social occasions in which he was often the centre of attention. He'd never had any problems with women, or children, had no barrier between himself and living.

August had met Jim when he was twelve, when he'd

left Stonegate and had finally gone to school. Even as a child, Jim'd had a quiet confidence, something adult and self-assured the other boys couldn't penetrate. He was good at football which also made him popular. Jim had adopted him, August had always suspected, out of his natural protective instincts; because his younger brother was stone deaf and he'd grown up around his learning difficulties; he had a heightened sympathy, a sensitivity which was predisposed towards the weak. When August arrived at secondary school he could barely read.

As an adult, Jim had the air of a novice priest. He was slight of build and gentle, with wide glamorous eyes and a baby's head of mousy hair, thin and silky and receding back over a smooth, delicate skull. He dressed in dark, second-hand suits and dark shirts buttoned to the neck. When he sat down he crossed his legs like a scholar, one thigh slung casually over the other, toe upright, the bottoms of his trousers revealing mismatched socks. He always wore battered Eton boots and fiddled constantly with his wedding ring. He had a benign, glowing smile and a way of nodding when he listened – and smiling with his big, raw eyes. He was August's closest friend, his only real friend, apart from Gabriel.

Gabriel was younger than Jim by two years. Like his brother he was slightly built. But, whereas Jim was gentle and calm, Gabriel was wild to look at. Whereas Jim was a listener, Gabriel liked to talk. While Jim had the presence and manners of a man filled with the stillest of waters, Gabriel was on fire. His veins ran with lit tequila; his long, feather-soft hair was often damp with perspiration. His eyes were soft and bovine, his lips were fixed in a permanent, inward smile and his hands were small sharks snapping through the air around him as he signed.

August put two fingers to his forehead.

'Name?' he asked.

'I-a-bel,' Gabriel said and signed proudly and stared happily at August.

August always had the impression that somewhere, living maliciously inside Gabriel, was a sprite with an acid which dissolved the words he tried to say. His speech dropped out of his mouth as though from a wind turbine, the words twisted and half formed and sludge-like. But this didn't deter him from speaking as he signed.

August smiled at him. 'Isabel, that's nice.'

Gabriel grinned.

Love, August thought. He looked at Gabriel, trying to see if there was something different about him, if you could tell if someone was in love or if they were loved from their aura or their body language, or the way they were sitting, anything, something. If there was a sign. But Gabriel looked the same as he always did. He thought of the woman who'd come into the deli the day before, Leola. He remembered the way she stood, her shoulders back, the way it lifted her breasts up. The way she'd moved across the deli's floor, her natural poise. Thinking of her made him feel queasy. Unlike Henry, there was something about her he'd recognized: her face had been a front behind which he'd sensed a waiting, a kind of patience. He frowned. It'd been years since he'd had anything serious with a woman, years. Not since Stella and that felt like another world away.

'Love. What feel like?' August slowly finger signed.

Gabriel gazed up at the ceiling for a moment as he

thought, then he pointed to his heart and his kidneys and other organs and gestured that before they were outside him and now they were in.

'Whole,' he signed.

August nodded and sipped his pint. Silently, he wrangled with envy as he looked at Gabriel the handsome, natural extrovert. Gabriel with no boundaries. Gabriel who felt whole and was loved.

Gabriel was staring with interest at August's hands. He touched a blue vein on his wrist, the sign for blue, then tapped his finger to his left shoulder, the sign for why?

August spread his hands on the table, fingers wide.

Jim leaned forward, over them. 'They *are* a bit blue,' he agreed.

August leaned over too and studied his hands. They were bluish at the very tips of his fingers, and oddly, where there was this colouring, his fingers felt warm. His hands were blue with warmth.

All three men stared at his hands for several moments. 'They look like beautiful, blue starfish,' Jim said.

Gabriel looked flummoxed. He turned his lips down and shook his head, almost amused.

Disconcerted, August nodded slowly. 'Yes, I suppose they do.'

Gabriel gathered his fists to his chest and pretended to shiver and said, 'Old.'

The walls of August's living room were a pale, egg brown. Book shelves were pushed against them. Maps were pinned to them. A patch of damp made a sepia coloured shape of Africa on the ceiling. Piles of newspapers rose like high-rise buildings from the floor. A leather sofa, soft and worn, had teeth made of battered pillows. There was a wide bay window looking on to the train depot opposite, old grey velvet curtains framing it, a long wooden table in its alcove. The room smelt of wood smoke and oranges. There was a big mirror above an old stone fireplace in the far wall. The vase full of hollyhocks stood on the mantelpiece, shrivelled. August had a habit of never removing the flowers Olivia brought, until she brought new ones. He always kept the dead ones there until her next visit. If he left them she'd come back. He always left them and she always did.

When August returned to his flat it was still early, only nine o'clock. His white forearms, his blue hands, Cosmo moving in a few doors down. He told himself there was no connection. Nothing so overwrought, so completely improbable. There was a virus going round, or something he was wearing had run, a dye of some sort.

Once inside, he put on some Curtis Mayfield to help banish his anxiety.

In the bathroom he unzipped his flies and peed, relief pouring from him. Dark yellow liquid.

The colour of whisky.

He frowned.

As a child he could never get away from Cosmo, or so it felt. He was in the garden, in the house, behind every wall. His hatred felt old and unfathomable, something which had rubbed itself into him, into his mix. It wasn't possible to isolate it, separate it from himself. Cosmo was part of him, part of his substance. Cosmo was like a relative.

In the kitchen August took the baby pigeon from the fridge and dug in a brown paper bag on the counter for some sour apples he'd bought the day before at the market. If the music hadn't driven Cosmo from his thoughts, following the recipe he'd remembered would.

As he began to stuff pieces of apple into the squab he started to feel strange. A queer feeling began to heat up in him, in the small of his back. He ignored it at first. He knew the squab's cavity also needed to be seasoned with salt and pepper and after he'd stuffed it with the apples, the neck had to be sewn up with string. It would then be basted with butter and browned in a casserole dish for about twenty minutes. Shallots and thyme and cloves and half a bottle of cider were to be added to the pot. The squab would then need to stew for another twenty minutes.

But something was happening to his back, at the base of it. August closed his eyes. It felt as though someone was blowing into it, into him, gently. The feeling was comforting, as though a faint and tranquil breeze was running through him. He opened his eyes and stared out the window on to the wet, black road in front of the kitchen. Headlights skated across his line of vision. A person was walking away from him, half-lit under the streetlamps. And something else. Trees. A man walking towards them. A big man. The feeling was spreading gradually, a creeping euphoria. It was light, like smoke, except inside him, not out, rolling up through his back and into his shoulders.

August stopped what he was doing, propping the squab up on the chopping board.

In the bathroom he turned around so he could see his back and lifted up his T-shirt.

His back was blue.

Blue as a blue whale or a blue dolphin. Nature's blue. Like sea or sky. Blue like feathers or fins, or scales. Blue like a parrot or a parrotfish. He looked at his hands. They'd faded, but there was still a bluish tinge to them. His forearms sparkled.

Tears welled in his eyes. A surge of panic rose in him. He ran back to the kitchen. On the counter top the squab was sitting up on its neck, naked and grotesque, its little wings like thalidomide fingers. It was sweating a little.

Sweat.

He stared at the bird. Before, it'd also been a bit blue. Perhaps it'd warmed up. Perhaps that was it. He was cold. He needed to warm up. He needed to sweat. He rummaged in the drawer under the sink and pulled out a thin box of cling film. With panic-stiff fingers he began to wrap the film round his naked torso, round and round. Over his shoulders. Round his arms. Pulling off his trousers, he began to wrap his legs in plastic film. Wrap it round his groin, his arse. His hips, his stomach. When he was finished, only his head wasn't covered.

His face was white.

His hair was a torch.

He stood for a while in the kitchen wondering what to do next, staring dumbly at the naked squab. His brain pulsed and he felt dizzy, thickly terrified.

He picked up a handful of apples and continued to stuff.

* * *

The next day the blue had faded a little.

Late morning August stood in the queue in the Midland Bank on King Street. His head was still thick with sleep, anxiety still stumbled in him. Sleep laced the rims of his eyes. Earlier he'd rung his GP's surgery and made an appointment. It had to be an allergy of some kind, he knew it was, he'd ask for one of those tests, with pinpricks and little vials of allergens inside, wheat, eggs, that kind of thing, it was something in the deli.

He recognized one or two other shop people needing change, a girl from Ryman's, the man from the fruit stall on the pavement. They gave each other an early morning smile, polite and mutually standoffish. He and Henry took it in turns to get change from the bank. While one of them was gone, Rose covered.

In front of him a small boy standing next to his mother was staring into a thin book with comic pictures. In a second August recognized the comic strip and wished he hadn't.

Lucky Luke.

The story of Luke's tattoo was one of the few his mother had told him more than once.

She'd met Luke in the late sixties, travelling in the southern states of America. They'd stopped for the night in a small town in Louisiana, a hellhole, malaria ridden and humid with rain coming down in beaded curtains. The people all looked depressed and had tattoos because that was all there was to do. They'd got drunk on the local hooch and visited a tattoo parlour.

'I'm a lucky person,' he'd told the tattooist, a man with anaconda arms and stubble like molasses smeared across his face. 'I'm Lucky Luke.'

The man had grunted as he pressed the needle into Luke's arm, but Luke was so drunk he felt no pain.

August practised a smile at the boy who was staring at him. The queue had shortened and his mother was nearly at the front. The child's eyes were like spotlights, full and on, staring at his hair the way only children were allowed, with open mistrust. From time to time he thought about dying it, or shaving it all off. But then he'd have to dye his eyebrows and lashes too – difficult. There would be a problem with root regrowth, or growth in general. There was no escaping it. Mostly, he wished himself totally bald, hairless, wished an illness would make all his hair drop out.

August walked back towards the deli, up Shepherd's Bush Road, past Brook Green, past the entrance to Tesco, past the big old pub on the corner which was always empty. As he walked he became conscious of the closed-off feeling of London. Cars zipping past were closed, shops were closed, so were residential buildings. People walked past with their faces closed, as though obeying an unofficial code of conduct, an oath of self-abasement. Though London was busy, it felt the opposite, somehow derelict, a place that was moving slowly. It was more of a ghost town in winter: eerie, cold, quiet.

August shivered into his denim jacket as he walked, digging his fists into his pockets alongside the bags of one pound coins and pennies. The pavements were wet and the air was laden with moisture. On his right, outside Pollen, the flower shop, the pavement was crowded with plants, large palms, firs, small holly trees in terracotta urns, clipped into the shape of a lollipop. Ivy was bound in great clusters to the railings. Part of the pavement had been transformed into a small forest.

August stopped and stared at the shop. He envisioned Leola inside. Her long pale legs, the faint rivers of blue chalk, bending over buckets of flowers. *Actually, we'd be completely ill-matched*, he knew. Plants rejected his tending. He'd tried once or twice to hand rear his own herbs, simple hardy plants like bay or thyme, plants which needed virtually no attention. But these had all died. He'd tried house plants too, a yucca, a rubber plant, a frizzy fern; they'd died too. Even a cactus once.

Plants are lungs, he thought, complex and delicate. They need a special touch. Not his. He imagined a single buttercup in a flower pot, its yellow head was an open mouth, breathing in. Its two green leaves opened and shut. He imagined hundreds of buttercups standing on the earth's crust, breathing, their little leaves like gourds filling and then puffing out pure air.

He walked on, pulling at the long sleeves of his sweatshirt from the insides, tugging them downwards under his jacket. He was ashamed of his earlier panic. The rash was most likely an allergy to something unpasteurized, a cheese, a blue one, or a new order he'd sampled. It could be a kind of fungus, he reasoned, in the hay he'd touched, or in the box.

He stopped walking.

The Mimolette! In the last delivery from France. The truth jumped out at him, as if from behind a bush. He laughed out loud. It was the great round, blood-orange cheese, of course. It had to be. He remembered how he'd held the Mimolette up to the light, the light which so often hurt his skin, his eyes. No wonder his hands were blue. The bacteria in the cheese must be photosensitive. It'd brushed against his hands and reacted with his skin. Spread to his back. He'd been poisoned!

August quickened his pace, feeling easier than he had in days. When handling the cheese from now on, he'd have to use gloves.

* * *

In bed that night August was more relaxed, reading a novel. He had a strange relationship with books. He had the notion that people who wrote novels were also lonely. He believed this more and more, reading between the lines of the novels he'd loved. Most books were about one kind of loneliness or another, about people who couldn't get what they wanted, people who found things hard, who were slow, or sad or difficult. So he read most evenings, finding a comfort in following words written by someone like him.

When he thought of a writer he conjured an image of a small vampiric creature. His skin was as hard as wood and his head was the shape of a peanut and bald, with two loose strands of hair which flew in the wind. He wrote in a cupboard for eight hours at a time without stopping. He wrote with pen and ink, by the light of a candle stub, his forehead shining with concentration. At night he came out of his cupboard to drink absinthe and eat very little, perhaps a few Brussels sprouts. He wore black always – black trousers and a jacket – both too short. He was bow-legged and thin. A writer was part-man, part-beetle.

Some books sucked him in, took him into another world. Some didn't. But he liked to read these just as much. These books did another trick, they lifted him half off the ground. They got him *read-dreaming*. They triggered his own stories, real and imagined, present and past, made him relive his own forgotten narratives. Invent new ones. Bad books got him thinking.

He was read-dreaming when he heard a sigh he recognized immediately, a woman in the throes of orgasm.

His bedroom was directly above his neighbour's and the floor between them was thin. The man downstairs was short. He had a loud voice and ears which protruded like funnels. Whenever they passed each other on the street he smiled at August, a tidy, restrained smile. But he never ventured a word, just his small smile, a little gate.

August listened.

The woman sighed again. *A wonderful noise*, he thought, the most honest sound in the world; the sound of woman loosened from her body, a sound she couldn't keep in. Like a laugh.

Another gasp rose from the room below. It floated like a note of a song. August felt sad. He imagined his neighbour's new girlfriend downstairs on white sheets;

she had thick hips and red lips and a warm smile. For some reason, his neighbour wasn't around. Instead, she beckoned him to her and he took a step towards her from the shadows. Frustratingly, he couldn't get closer; every step he took forward moved him backwards.

He remembered the first time he heard a woman make this sound. He was eighteen, with Stella, his first love. They were lying on her old iron bed, kissing. The room had sky blue painted floors and a high white ceiling. A broken white globe, a paper shade, hung from the bulb, a fallen moon. The window was open and outside he could see the clouds had been shredded. He was aroused, wanting to push himself inside her. But something was wrong, somehow he'd slipped from his body. Every time he tried to pin his thoughts down, fasten them to himself, they moved a little, squirmed away from him. He wanted desperately to feel a connection, a oneness with her, but his mind kept filling up with random thoughts: his bike which needed fixing, his dentist appointment the next morning.

The harder he tried to concentrate, the further away he slipped. He could smell apple cigarettes in her hair, on the sheets, feel pips of sweat breaking out on his forehead. He wanted to freeze time, to look at her body, the half-moon of where her ribs met her breasts, wind sculpted, like a sand dune, her mahogany coloured nipples.

But he felt nothing.

Intimacy had made him numb. The moments stretched, paralysing him. There were questions he wanted to ask. *What do I feel like inside you? How can I make you come?* He never knew if or when she had an orgasm, couldn't see or feel her have one. Sexual pleasure, he was beginning to suspect, was an isolated experience. It was something one felt alone, even when physically joined together.

He was slipping away again when he heard her sharp intake of breath. Felt her hand on his.

'Wait,' she said.

Gently she pushed him off.

'Let me show you,' she whispered, almost to herself.

She rearranged her body so she was lying in his arms. Her eyes were closed, her long blonde curls twisting down her body. And then she dipped her fingers into the slit between her legs and began to move them quickly, he was amazed at how quickly. As quick as a man. Quick and hard on herself until she began to writhe and gasp and arch her back and make *that noise*, those sighs, like a song. He held her in his arms and watched as she came in front of him, several times, and all the while making that noise, a loose, thin note of music. The sound made him feel peaceful.

Like being asleep.

He spent weeks afterwards discovering how to make her make that noise. He learned to use his lips and his teeth. His tongue. His fingers. His nose, even.

August wriggled to get comfortable under the duvet, bicycling his legs for warmth.

If only things were so easy, he thought. He found out later that few women made this noise. Mostly it was a different sound, moans which sounded too of-this-world, too loud, like talking, too flat. Even when he used all the techniques he'd learned to use on Stella, there was no gasp of shock. No release. *Moving a woman is like trying to move a mountain*, he thought, dismally. It was random, hidden. It had nothing to do with technique.

August lifted the duvet.

He peered down the length of his pale, smooth body. The blueness had more or less gone. He was wearing jockey shorts, and for a moment, in the quilted coffin of his sheets his body looked lifeless and bloodless, fished from a cold river. A dead man's body. Not his. *My body is unfair*, he thought. Or more accurately, its colours. Carrot. Pumpkin. Marmalade. These were his colours.

Carrot eyelashes.

Pumpkin eyebrows.

Marmalade hair.

A halo of coppery hair glowed around his nipples. His armpits looked as though they were home to a nest of angry fire-ants. His pubic area was just as difficult. An army of red ants lived there too, one which was forever scaling the walls of his hips, looking for more territory to conquer.

He was ashamed of his erections. His penis, when hard, was purple. Purple against copper. Women had had varying reactions. Fright, instant mood change, a sudden greyness around the lower face.

He was ashamed of himself.

Ashamed of his hair and eyebrows, his colouring.

His orangeness.

The next afternoon snow fell from the sky, the flakes mad and stray, like ash from a fire. August walked to the window to watch the flurry, rubbing his arms, tucking his hands under his armpits. Dramatic weather always gave him a kind of solace, made him feel alone in a way he liked.

The shop was quiet.

From the kitchen downstairs, the smell of Rose's spicy haggis stuffing had levitated up through the floorboards and roamed like a low-lying cloud through the shop, overpowering all others. Rose had left him to keep an eye on it and gone to Borough market. Henry was on a late lunch hour trip to Hammersmith library. To keep himself occupied, August decided to stock-check the salamis. Two thirds of what they sold was Italian. Napoli, Milano, Felino, Varzi – names people could usually identify. The dried meats were stacked like a pile of logs in a corner of the display fridge. He began to count through them, one by one, checking to see if anything needed to be reordered.

When he was done he eyed the Mortadella. Rumoured at one time to be made from donkeys, it was his favourite object in the deli. The one they had at the moment was enormous, vulgar. The orange plastic casing was like sunburnt skin. The open cross section was as wide and round as a dinner plate, the meat inside was bandage pink. In it discs of fat resembled bumper cars chasing each other round in circles. August imagined it was what you'd find if you severed the thigh of a Miami tourist.

He bent into the fridge to wipe around the platter it sat on. A flake of bread fell from his shoulder on to the cool metal surface. He pressed down on it with his finger to pick it up but the flake melted at his touch. Another fell. He pressed that one too, with his finger. It melted also. Another fell and then another, gauzy white flakes the size of thumbnails – falling from his jumper. He flicked at his chest.

More flakes fell.

August glanced around him.

Through the window he saw that outside the initial flurry had stopped. Now, the snow was falling thicker, fatter, dropping past the window, falling to the ground, silently, easily, drifting past the glass. As August watched he glimpsed a similar movement, just above his eyeline, inside the shop. August felt terror like a wire, drawing a circle around him, pinning his arms to his body. He stood stiff as a soldier, fixing his eyes on a jar of comb honey on a shelf opposite.

Snowflakes were spiralling around his head.

They moved sluggishly, in a mass, an aurora of fuzzy crystal stars.

August's mind filled with shock. His body surged with warmth and a feeling like he had no inner stuff, only air inside him, pure and ethereal. Water fell from his eyes, unsalted tears. Fresh water ran down his face, down his chest in thin rivulets. He found himself releasing his breath in little hiccups.

Mechanically, he strode into the café.

In the kitchen alcove he clasped the two jutting stems of the coffee machine's filters as though they were electrodes, staring into the dullish silver chrome of the machine's façade. He saw himself: a blur of blood-orange, a galaxy around his head. He smiled. An intensity pulsed inside him, a sureness. As each flake fell away from him, he felt a tug, as if it'd been leached from some delicate muscle inside him, then sucked out into the whorl. They spun away slowly, dropping to the floor, leaving a sense of amazement and an uncomplicated happiness.

August gazed out the back window. The snow had stopped as silently as it'd started. At his feet a thin puddle of water had appeared. He ran his hands through his hair. It wasn't even damp. In the chrome the galaxy had vanished. Beyond the café he heard the deli's door open, the sound of feet on the floorboards.

'Excuse me?' inquired a female voice.

August floated back through to the deli.

Leola was standing in front of the high glass fridge.

She smiled.

'I'd like some of that cheese,' she said, pointing to the Mimolette. August blinked at the cheese. A third of it had been cut away and he could see into its core.

'Of course,' he whispered.

He slipped behind the long fridge. As he bent into it he felt a flaring under his skin, an outbreak of warmth on his chest. His head hurt, his stomach boiled.

'I love that cheese,' she said brightly. 'It's so rich, like some other food. Pawpaw or mango.'

August tried to smile as he picked it up. The cheese smiled back, flashing its brilliant shade of blood-orange. *Blood-orange, tangerine, brandy-on-fire*, its colour flared and converged in front of him. He wanted to stop what he was doing. Shock had begun to take hold, stalling his ability to coordinate his movements. His thoughts were also breaking up, floating away from him like pieces of ice on a floe. He fretted surreally – whether she would notice the cheese matched his hair, whether she'd ever seen an orange-haired man naked, whether he'd ever have children.

He managed to carry the cheese to the marble counter behind the high cooler cabinet, where a long steel wire was attached to the side.

'How much?' August asked her shoulder.

He'd positioned the Mimolette square on the marble. On it, the cheese looked like a small ginger head on a block. Leola came closer to the glass cabinet, intent on observing the execution.

'Just a small piece.'

August steadied the wire, but his palms had begun to sweat. It was a larger cheese than usual, hard and fully mature, and he found it difficult to grasp; his hands couldn't quite span its girth and so he held it awkwardly. He pulled the wire up with his other hand, aiming to cut a small segment. As he pulled down there was a loud crash and he slipped, the wire slicing his thumb and grazing the side of the cheese. Grazing it hard and at an angle, causing it to take flight and sail across the space behind the counter, across the room – suspended in mid-air – a heavy but agile football, travelling slowly, spanning three, four, five feet. As it pirouetted away from him August admired its grace, its ease. He lifted his injured thumb to his lips. He watched as the cheese clipped the pastry basket, sending pastries scattering across the floor, watched calmly as it smacked against the window, bounced backwards, and landed in a plate of pork pies.

Leola's eyes were wild.

'I'm so *sorry*!' she exclaimed. As she'd leaned closer to watch she'd knocked over a pyramid of sardine tins on the top of the fridge.

'Your thumb, I'm so clumsy, clumsy, clumsy!' she wailed, one hand clutching her throat.

August looked at his thumb and noticed the wire had drawn blood.

'Please. D-don't worry,' he tried to soothe her, desperate to draw attention away from himself. His face flashed. His ears had ignited. 'It's n-nothing. Nothing, really.'

'Are you sure?' she asked, appalled.

'Yes, just a tiny cut.' August held up his thumb. A hair of blood was slashed across the pad.

Her face flinched. 'Oh, God, oh no,' she said, inconsolable.

'Please don't worry,' August grinned, clutching his thumb. He noticed there was heat in her voice. And she was blushing like a beetroot.

When Leola eventually left with a small piece of Mimolette, August found a Band-Aid in the medicine box under the counter and wrapped it round his thumb. He locked the door of the shop, pulling down the roller blind, and went downstairs.

In the bathroom he shut himself in. For a minute he rested his back against the door, trying to regulate his breathing, trying to process the last hour's excitement. He tried to think, not panic, think carefully through the bizarre things that'd been happening to him. Since the rash and the blue flushes had emerged, he'd been careful to wear long sleeves. He hadn't mentioned them to anyone, hadn't been sure what to say. No one had seen his forearms. Only Jim and Gabriel had seen his blue hands. The snowstorm around his head had been his imagination in overdrive. *It was the cheese*, it had to be. He'd forgotten to use gloves. His thumb. He'd been grazed, the wire had drawn blood. But now he could feel something hot on his chest and under his arms. He stood in front of the mirror on the wall, afraid.

Carefully he held the hem of his T-shirt and peeled it upwards.

August stared at himself like a child.

His chest sparkled.

A fallstreak of crystals hung on his upper body, a bird suspended in mid-flight. They sparkled yellow, orange, violet, red, as though his skin had been grazed, exposing a quartz mine. He walked to the small window above the toilet, nudging it open with the steel lever. The ledge outside was covered in a fine layer of white. He looked at the ledge, then at his chest. It was the same. He picked at the white powdery layer on the ledge, rubbing it between his fingers. It was cold and crystalline. And it sparkled. He touched his chest and the crystals on it warmed. Frost.

When Henry came back from the library he told her he felt unusual. Not himself. Before leaving he went downstairs to get his jacket and noticed a saucepan on the stove, steam issuing in curtains from under the lid. He dashed to it and turned the flame off. When he peered inside he saw Rose's haggis stuffing was done to perfection.

* * *

In the GP's waiting room August held a copy of *Parent and Child* in front of his face to camouflage his red eyes. His hair was plastered to his forehead, his face seemed smaller somehow, shrunken. He hadn't slept for two nights and had taken two days off work. The frost-like rash had spread to his back and legs. It was velvety and white and sparkled and was very odd. Very rare. Symptoms of a syndrome, he was sure.

A buzzer sounded. The nurse took the next card wallet from a pile lined up on a grey filing cabinet.

'August Chalmin?'

She scanned the faces of the people waiting. August nodded and stood up.

In the consulting room the doctor behind the desk had a nicotine-yellowed face and thin, shiny black hair glued over his forehead. He didn't look up from writing the last patient's notes. He kept writing, saying nothing, as if August hadn't arrived. August sat down in the chair in front of the desk. As he waited he studied the framed certificates on the wall, the fake ferns in the hanging planter, the tiny sea horse frozen in a glass paperweight on the desk. Being ignored made him feel even more anxious, foolish. After a few minutes, the doctor pushed his notes away and looked up, straightening his tie. He had walnuts for eyes. He stared past August and smiled, a watery smile.

'How can I help?'

August had prepared a speech, something brave, stating his case, his reasons for needing tests, for there being a legitimate fear of his having a unique and potentially fatal allergy to cheese. He'd planned to sound knowledgeable, articulate, to push for his rights. He took a deep breath and said:

'I have frost.'

The doctor made a cathedral with his fingers, collapsing it slowly with a small sigh. He nodded his head slowly, with concern, and then began to write on his small prescription pad.

'In the mouth or genitals?' he asked.

The following morning August returned to work. The doctor had finally diagnosed eczema, a severe outbreak. Stress related and non-contagious. He'd prescribed some ointment which had already helped. August had decided to hide it as best he could, wear his shirts buttoned up to the neck, and to the wrists, wear a scarf if need be. He'd have to be vigilant, so as not to alarm the customers.

As he stood near the window, refilling the bread basket, he saw Cedric sitting at one of the tables on the pavement. On his head he was wearing a red woolly hat with a pompom on top and earflaps which tied under his chin. He would have waved but Cedric was gazing in the opposite direction, out across the traffic. August stooped to see what his target was.

A woman stood on the other side of the road, waiting at the crossing in front of the deli.

The green man flashed, the cars stopped and she crossed towards the shop, her face coming closer into focus. Immediately August noticed her eyes – like winkles –

small and wet and grey and curled up tight. Her skin was dappled and stone-like, a smoky shade of lilac. Her lips were thin and straight as a sardine fillet. And her hair was arranged in a perplexing style, battleship grey and hovering around her head, framing her face with a brain of curls. As she advanced August saw she was a big woman, probably around Cedric's age. Her shopping bags appeared heavy, her shoulders were dragged down by them and sadly, she seemed tired.

As she drew closer to the deli a loud noise went off in the line of traffic, a car backfiring. It sounded like a clap of thunder. He saw Cedric look up at the sky, incredulous. As the woman entered the shop Cedric took his small note pad from his pocket, a pen from behind his ear, and began to scribble.

Sensing the possibility of a skirmish, August left the window and retreated behind the display fridge.

The woman was queuing behind two other customers when Cedric entered. Hands clasped behind his back, he wandered slowly around the deli as though perusing a garden, peering at bags of red pasta with suspicion. August tried to make eye contact, but Cedric studiously ignored him. Instead, he casually picked up a pot of Dijon mustard and joined the queue, waiting patiently behind the woman, turning the pot in his hands, reading the label.

'A little bit of seafood salad,' the woman said to Henry, when it was her turn to be served.

Her tone was flat, August noticed, her accent east European. He tried to guess where she might be from, somewhere in the Former Yugoslavia perhaps, Albania? She looked tough, like the kind of woman who knew how to shoot a gun. He liked her on sight and found, disconcertingly, that he recognised her.

Next to him, Henry leaned forward into the glass cabinet and began to scoop up squid rings, tentacles, mussels. As she did, she saw Cedric behind the woman and frowned. The woman looked up. Hanging on blue ribbons from a large wagon wheel suspended from the ceiling were pavlova casings, wrapped in cellophane.

'What are those?' she asked.

'Meringues,' Henry replied, straightening up. 'For pavlovas.'

The woman nodded.

'As well. Just one, please,' she said, pointing upwards.

Henry put the pot of seafood on the counter and went into the café to find a chair to stand on. August felt curious and embarrassed for Cedric all at once. He thought of the flying cheese, his disaster earlier on. Leola probably thought he was some kind of weirdo. He found himself rooting for the old man, willing things to be different.

On the other side of the glass wall, Cedric and the woman stood alone in the shop. Her back was turned to him, broad and tall as a granite tor. They stood in silence.

Cedric edged closer.

The woman looked away.

August felt heat in his ears.

'Very good with clotted cream and raspberries,' Cedric informed her.

August cringed.

The woman turned around, startled. One corner of Cedric's mouth twitched involuntarily as he smiled. His eyes were friendly. The woman blazed him with hers, staring like a boulder, ignoring his comment. Then she moved herself a little further away from him.

Henry came back with the chair, positioning it under the wagon wheel, then stood on it.

'They're made from free range eggs,' she said, untying the ribbon. 'We make them on the premises.'

August saw Cedric wasn't put off and noted his courage: maybe it would develop as he got older.

Cedric stood pondering a line of white chocolate mice on the top shelf of the fridge. One had no eyes. He winked at it. Then, quietly, he stepped forward, a small step, towards the woman. Surreptitiously, he tried to slip something into her coat pocket.

'Cedric!' Henry shouted.

The woman jumped with fright, pulling her coat away from him. Cedric's hand was still inside her pocket.

'What are you doing?' she demanded. Her eyes were angry. She yanked the coat and a folded piece of paper fell to the floor.

'It's all right, Madam,' Henry said, quickly. 'He's not trying to steal from you.'

Henry glared at Cedric. 'He's just mad,' she glared at him even more. 'Un vieux fou.'

Cedric was unruffled. With an air of dignity he bent slowly to the floor and picked up the piece of paper.

The woman stared at it.

Cedric stood formal and composed, regarding her.

'You, Madam, look like a force of nature,' he said, his voice cracking a little. 'So I penned you this sonnet.'

He handed her the poem.

The woman was caught off guard, her cheeks coloured. She took it from him, her mouth plump with distrust.

Henry snorted.

'Et vous,' he said, turning to Henry. 'Vous n'êtes qu'une brise d'été.'

Henry looked blankly at him.

August felt pride. Pride brimmed up to his nose for the old man, pride and hope. He loved Cedric, he wanted to be him.

Cedric opened the door of the shop and flounced on to the pavement. The three of them watched as he walked up the street, the pompom on his hat waving like a big, red sea anemone.

All day August sensed the possibility of courage. He forgot his troubles. His rash. The snow. Cosmo. Luke. His orangeness. At lunch time Henry went downstairs and rearranged her hair into two knots on her head, Mickey Mouse ears, and this also cheered him up.

She babbled incessantly about Yves, about the library book she'd taken out on the French Revolution. About France, about her eagerness to know more about French culture. He'd listened politely, abstracted, wanting to kiss her on the back of the neck while she was grinding coffee. Wanting to be Zorro. Or Nureyev. Henry, he imagined, would then collapse into his arms, her body limp and yielding. He smiled to himself at this thought, knowing it was ridiculous, knowing it was something he'd never imagine doing to Leola.

All day Henry talked and August fantasized. She chattered and he daydreamed about her stomach, the curve of it. He liked to look at the parts of her he thought might fit into him, the grooves in her neck, her shoulder area – where he could rest his head. The places he could put his knees. She talked and he dreamed and it always struck him as incredible that she never noticed.

At five thirty he saw a man standing under the plane tree. He was medium height and lithe, his black hair longish and lank, his eyes like holes, his face sharp. He stood waiting, looking detached and bored, smoking a cigarette.

Henry's eyes lit up when she saw him through the window.

'Mon amour!' she gushed and skipped out to greet him.

August watched as she reached up to his mouth for a kiss. *So that's Yves*, he mused. French, swarthy, louche – all in real life.

Yves pulled his head back as Henry tried to kiss him, his eyes on her hair. Henry looked at him as if he was joking.

Yves shrugged.

August could see Henry was hurt, her cheeks flushed pink. She pulled sharply away from Yves.

Yves simply raised his eyebrows, like he was being patient.

Henry turned, hot-faced, and ran back into the deli, flashing past August in an attempt to hide her embarrassment. August heard her stomp and kick things downstairs in the storeroom. He stayed behind the fridge, feeling awkward and slightly blown about. For the second time that day he'd witnessed a small tornado, one which could hit at any time, when you were in love.

Henry came back upstairs clutching her satchel.

'Good night, Gus,' she smiled, her cheeks stained with tear trails. Her hair was down, her mouse ears ripped off.

August looked at her, questioningly.

'Yves has been working so hard,' she said, in a clipped voice. 'He's not himself.'

Henry's face was sprayed on, her smile twittery. She winked as if to make sure he was okay, then walked out the shop, banging the door behind her.

Yves, August noticed, had disappeared.

He watched as Henry searched the street for him, looking left then right up the road. She spotted him, setting off at a brisk walk.

Courage, he thought. *Courage, ma petite souris.*

* * *

Shepherd's Bush market was busy, as usual, and August felt glad to be out and about. The market was really a long corridor which ran underneath and alongside the strip of tube line between Goldhawk Road and Shepherd's Bush tube stations. The corridor was lined on both sides with individual stalls: halal butchers, fishmongers, fruit and veg. Carpets, hardware. Pots and pans. As he milled amongst the other shoppers, brushing past so many large shapes looming brown and indistinct, August couldn't help but think of cattle. Big and docile and warm. The market was always a safe place to come, to lose himself. It was one of the main reasons he'd never left Shepherd's Bush. It was always a small adventure of sorts, only walking distance away. It was both familiar and exotic, foreign and his own home turf. It both opened his world and was near it.

The rash on his chest and back seemed to be much better. *Frost*, how stupid. *Cheese*, how ridiculous. He'd panicked when he first saw his skin. The blueness had probably come from something in his flat, some kind of dust on the walls, or perhaps he'd been past a building site, had brushed against a wall which was being painted or demolished. The snowstorm; he was embarrassed, that day some snow had obviously blown in from the door. Or else he'd been hallucinating, wildly, about a dry scalp.

Stress.

That was what the doctor had said.

He found himself thinking of Leola, the backs of her knees. He saw himself kissing them gently, kissing the rest of her legs, her feet. He pondered her as though she were an art exhibit under glass. For so long he'd known only the same thing, day after day, the same reality. Loneliness. An inability to change. A loneliness he was used to, harvested even. He hated but also liked being apart, he needed quietness like a dirty man needed a bath. Quietude was his soap.

He made his way to his favourite part of the market, the indoor Caribbean fruit and vegetable stalls. They had a close smell, earthy and sugary with fruit. The wooden shelves were painted red, and illuminated by spotlights; tinny strands of calypso emanated from a small radio hanging from the ceiling. He wondered at the dark brown mountains of hairy root vegetables: yams, dasheen, cassava, eddoes. He marvelled at the plantains. There was something obscene about them, black and leaking at the tips, hot with clouds of tiny flies. *Cosmo's penis dripped the same fluid sometimes.* He closed his eyes and shook his head, trying to shake this image.

Quickly, he left and pushed on through the crowd outside.

He stopped at a stall selling bolts of colourful African material, and rifled through the offcuts box. The women sitting next to this stall always intrigued him; their skin was so supple and polished it was hard to guess their age. Their heads were magnificent, wrapped like warrior goldfish in the colourful cloth. They nodded and chatted and smoked cigarettes, a great mauve cloud of smoke dissolving into the air above them. If he narrowed his eyes, he could see them in Senegal.

He moved on.

At a small green stall in a short row in the centre of the thoroughfare, he stopped. A sign above it read *Mahmud's Oasis*. Inside, a man with a wide face and heavy cheeks was standing at a large frying vat. His hair was black and crispy. He looked up from his gentle job of tapping chickpea balls in bubbling oil, saw August and smiled.

'Marhaba,' August blushed. 'Keef hallaq?'

The man chuckled, pleased at this attempt at Arabic. 'Kwayyis, kwayyis,' he replied. 'The usual?'

August nodded. He'd been coming to Mahmud's Oasis for years. Mahmud's falafels were the best in London, a weekly fixture in his life. He watched as Mahmud lifted the balls from the oil in a giant wire spoon, then peeled open the soft warm pitta bread, spreading its insides with hummus and chilli sauce.

'Shukran,' August said as Mahmud passed him the small towel of food. Mahmud nodded and then stopped, something catching his attention. He stared at August for a moment, as though trying to place him. He shook his head.

'I'm leaving here,' Mahmud said cheerily.

August's cheeks bulged.

'When?'

'Soon.'

'Where're you going?'

'North, my wife's mother is sick.'

August chewed, gulping down this information. 'And the business?'

'The space here has already been taken. I'll sell falafels up north.'

'Where, up north?'

'Morecambe.'

August nodded.

Lancashire, not so far from where he'd grown up. It was a small, broken-down holiday resort where the sea was radioactive. Mahmud was Palestinian, married to an English nurse. He'd escaped Gaza. Morecambe, August imagined, wouldn't be too different.

'I'll miss you,' he complained.

Mahmud made lover's eyes at August, doe-ish.

'I'll miss you too, habibi.'

'Who's taking over the site?'

'A hippie,' Mahmud replied, pronouncing the word *heeppe*.

August laughed.

'Very old.'

'Oh, no!' August imagined the worst, a man with a thin grey ponytail and a flute.

'A cowboy hippie,' said Mahmud. 'Cosmo something. He talks too much.'

August choked. His eyes watered and he tried to catch Mahmud's eyes to signal he was fine.

'Here,' said Mahmud, handing him a paper cup of water. August took it, pouring the water down his throat. As he drank he closed his eyes, feeling his ears catch fire.

'Shukran kittir,' he said, handing back the cup.

'Afwan,' Mahmud replied, shaking his head. August looked at Mahmud's large, heart-shaped face upholstered with soft, doughy skin, his small, intelligent eyes. He saw a man who was content, loved by his wife.

August quickly crossed Goldhawk Road, turned right and then left at the bus depot. At the end of the depot there was a narrow dog-leg alley which led into Sulgrave Road. As he hurried, he pulled his jacket closer to his body. There was a wind. It picked up a crisp packet on the pavement in front of him, shooting it off like a startled squid. He nodded as he passed a bus driver he recognized, and the driver nodded back, a little distracted by something he saw.

An icicle was dangling from one of August's ears.

* * *

August didn't like the look of Gabriel's girlfriend at all. Isabel had all the hallmarks, he'd decided, after watching her for most of the evening, of a clever, neurotic upper class woman. There was a sullenness about her manner, an aloofness which a person from the upper classes expected to carry off as neutral. He'd seen it many times, amongst his mother's friends. And in his mother. An ease born from privilege, a subdued arrogance which came with affluence. But somehow, as with his mother, he saw a tension lurking beneath the still surface. Isabel's gaze was studied and her chin set as though trying to control a floodgate of something strong. In fact, there was something constrained about every feature, her lips, the inward slant of her eyebrows; something brittle, as though she could easily and often snap, releasing vodka or vinegar. She held her head away from whoever she was talking to, he noticed, her eyes peering downwards. Or else she leaned in far too close, and talked into a person's face. She both held back from and invaded other people's space. She was self-conscious, her eyes hard, her voice stern. And though she was classically beautiful her face was somehow bland, tamed of any unexpected quirks or emotion. When she smoked she tapped her ash vaguely towards an ashtray.

Next to her Gabriel seemed so wrong. Watching them from the other end of a long table in a pub near Ladbroke Grove, August wanted to intervene, take Gabriel aside and tell him he was being used as some kind of servant. A mute. She will have given Gabriel a demeaning nickname of some sort. August looked at him, more closely. He'd never considered Gabriel objectively, had only ever seen him as essential and alive, only ever envied his *joie de vivre*. Seeing him with Isabel, who was looking at him as he signed with a kind of amusement, a schoolgirl's malice barely concealed, made him realize there was something he couldn't see, or know about Gabriel. His sexuality was invisible.

August knew he, himself, was drunk.

When nervous he mixed his drinks. Being in a group of people he didn't know made him nervous and so he'd had lager and spirits and red wine and his head was swimming.

After hearing Cosmo was setting up shop in the market he'd rung Jim. Jim was off to meet Isabel for the first time, in a pub near Ladbroke Grove, and had invited him to join them. Isabel had brought two other girlfriends, Anna and Jane, and then other people she knew had turned up and he'd found himself separated from Jim and Gabriel, crammed in around the table between strangers. On one side a couple sat deep in conversation, the man's back to him. On the other sat Anna. When the man she was talking to left to get some drinks, she was momentarily alone. She glanced quickly at August, then away. Then she reached for her handbag under her seat, took out a lipstick and small mirror, and began to paint her lips.

Blood-orange.

Like Isabel, she was patrician. She didn't want to look at him, let alone talk to him, August knew. Everyone around them was in deep conversation and he watched them for clues. It was a mystery, social ease, a world behind a wall or a secret curtain he couldn't see through. He didn't have the secret code or a collection of conversation ammunition, a stockpile of ready-made things to say. In these situations he was deserted by his inner flow of dreams and observations. They dried on him, shrivelled.

He peered across at Gabriel, whose hands were a flurry of wings.

Anna made kissy lips into her mirror and continued to paint. August stared into his beer. It was no use pretending any more. His hands clasped around the glass were still faintly blue. Sorrow's blue. Dipped in the colour of shyness. The blue had never really gone away; the sparkly rash wasn't receding either. Under his clothes his body felt extraordinary, full of air and a sensation of lightness. And he hadn't noticed the cold since the blue came; his body had stopped sensing any change in temperature, as though his blood and the air were the same. And the lights in the pub, the strangest of all. Usually they'd make him squint, but tonight they didn't.

He was already some kind of freak: he found the changes both hard to believe and hardly surprising; he felt dull about them, morbidly indifferent.

He looked at Anna. She'd finished her lips and was twisting the stem of her empty wine glass, eyes glazed. He hadn't spoken to anyone all evening. He smiled nervously at her, exposing his teeth.

'Y-your lips look good,' he stammered.

She shot him a look of incredulity.

'They match your skin.'

He smiled and his pale eyes grew.

Her eyes turned to lead.

'I mean,' August back-pedalled. 'Your skin colour, it matches your lips, it isn't like mine. Your skin isn't as white,' he smiled again and his teeth poked out like chairs.

She grimaced as he spoke, pulling her head back a little.

'I . . . I mean, it's okay on you. It looks *great* on you, the colour. Not like me. I'm like a parrot.'

She was quivering at his blundering, his total lack of social grace.

'Yes,' she said coldly.

August felt as though he'd swallowed a rock. Anna had abruptly turned the other way and was trying to spot her companion at the bar. He wanted to disappear into the slit in the world, the place where things came from, grace, social ease. Wanted to vanish, pouf! Like a genie.

'I'm just going to the toilet,' he said too loudly.

Anna nodded, sickened.

August stood up, swaying a little.

Against one wall of the large, crowded room there was a

long black sofa. At one end he saw a space still left on it, big enough for his body. He made his way over, dropping heavily into the deep cushion when he reached it. At the other end a couple were eating each other's lips, the man with his hand up the woman's skirt.

August looked the other way.

The room was full of beautiful people. Women with wonderful hair which was long and sleek and brushed a hundred times, men with a great deal of self-assurance. They were staring and smiling into each other's eyes, laughing and flirting. Together they presented a wall of locked conversations, a chain of backs and elbows.

August groped in his back pocket for his wallet. In it he'd stuffed the photo of Luke. He pulled it out. He stared at it, wilting it with his gaze, trying to imagine having Luke's fine features. He didn't look like either of his parents. His mother had been beautiful, his father handsome. Neither was particularly tall. They both had dark eyes and skin which could absorb the sun's rays. His height, he'd imagined, might be his mother's great-grandmother who was half-Danish. His hair was all he'd inherited. His mother's.

He stroked the photograph. Luke was another story, somehow linked to him, but not in the way he'd been told. He'd existed, sure. Been his mother's lover. But there was something else. He knew it by nothing present or concrete, more by a series of absences. The information he had about him was sparse and poor; even tactical. He'd been fed just enough.

When he was ten, Olivia had told him how Luke died.

It was early September, she said, still warm. One morning Luke got on his motorbike.

'I'm going for a ride on the Downs,' he'd told her. 'I won't be gone long.'

She'd been restless, concerned they were overstaying their welcome with Luke's parents, worried about money.

'Soon we'll move out of here,' he'd whispered in her ear. 'I promise.'

Luke's parents had lived at The Elms, a low and rambling house near a village called Ditchling in Sussex. They weren't happy putting the couple up. First it was a month, then six, then a year; then Olivia fell pregnant. By then it was almost two years since they'd moved in. Luke's parents never liked Olivia. They thought she was above herself with her arrogant, aristocratic manner. They didn't like her *wild ways*, her clothes, her eating habits. Her incense. They thought she was spoilt, conceited.

Most of this she'd told him.

Some of it he'd put together over the years.

Perhaps Luke had accelerated a little too much as he rode along the country lanes. He'd always imagined Luke's blond hair had been bleached and his body was browned from the long summer months. He didn't see or hear the tractor, large and green, a giant insect crawling slowly and heavily towards him on the other side of the road. He'd been singing to himself, his mother told him. Luke liked singing loudly to himself as he rode his bike. The tractor rounded the corner, a tight bend, with no path on either side. Luke had no time to brake. The bike slammed straight into the huge fender.

He'd felt nothing as he flew through the air, felt nothing as he hit its windscreen with a loud rushing *thwack*.

His skull had smashed on impact.

A week later, Olivia had left The Elms.

A friend, Jude, lived in a large house called Stonegate Hall, a commune, up in Yorkshire. Jude had said it was fine for them to stay, her and her newborn baby, August.

* * *

On his way home August turned right down Lancaster Road, skirting his way through the quiet, fashionable streets until he came out on Holland Park Avenue. He crossed the roundabout at the end and then the Green, turning again at the top of Shepherd's Bush Road. At the car wash he stopped abruptly.

A group of men were talking outside it, their thin legs silhouetted against a wall on which was written *Car Wash and Go, £5.00 only* in faded purple letters. He noticed one pair of legs in particular, the shape of them, sharp-angled and spindly, as though callipers were attached underneath his tight jeans. The man talked with his hands and the other men laughed. He saw the hands make a spinning motion, as if trying to reel the listeners in. He'd seen the man standing a thousand times like this, in the centre of a group, making others laugh, holding their attention. He heard a sudden storm of laughter from the group, saw the legs move off. Cosmo waved and the other men waved too. Voices trailed off. Then the legs, feet turned inwards, stumbled off down Shepherd's Bush Road towards the deli.

August stood with his feet pasted to the pavement, unable to move, unable to lose sight of Cosmo, though he was already gaining some distance. He watched as Cosmo walked further away from him. There was weight in Cosmo's step, his destination was somehow important, even if he was only going home. August watched and felt a pull at his centre, as though Cosmo was holding a string attached to his navel.

August began walking quickly to catch up, then hung back. There was something about Cosmo's lower half, his legs, their gait, which he found hypnotizing. Cosmo's legs didn't quite fit under him. But his body anticipated this constant fall, and compensated. Cosmo didn't fall, only seemed to be constantly falling. He walked with his head up, looking out at the trees lining Shepherd's Bush Road, at the traffic. Cosmo walked like a man without a care in the world.

Cosmo turned right down Lena Gardens and August's stomach contracted. He followed, repulsed to be so close. At the end of the street Cosmo turned right again into Sulgrave Road. August stopped dead, unable to continue. His own house was the first in the street. As Cosmo continued on August stood on the bottom step of the stairs which led to his front door. He took a step upwards for every house Cosmo passed.

one

two

three

On the fourth he stopped as Cosmo did, watching as Cosmo patted himself for his keys. He watched him climb three more stairs and then stop suddenly, sensing he was being observed. Cosmo turned his head and squinted across the line of houses, directly at August. Under the streetlights both men were lit up. They stood on their respective stairs leading up to their respective houses, four houses apart. They stood for a second which felt like a minute, a drizzle blowing in a gentle hula behind them out on the road. Then

Cosmo waved, a small wave, as though he was waving a handkerchief.

August nodded, hardly moving his head.

Then he vaulted up the last remaining stairs, ramming his key in the door, disappearing inside.

August threw himself on to his bed. Again he tried to batten down his bile, his revulsion. He sat up again and began to pull off his clothes, first his jacket, then his fleece, then his sweatshirt. He sat on his bed in his T-shirt and jeans, slowly massaging the sockets of his eyes with the backs of his hands.

His eyes hurt.

And he was tired. Tired of himself. Tired of half-living, tired of his loneliness, of living off his own emotional fat. For years it'd been okay, he'd accepted his shyness, his awkwardness, as an invisible disability. He'd seen others with it, met others who lived alone, slept alone, woke up alone every day. He'd accepted all this as his lot in life. Blamed his looks. But now, he'd had enough. He pulled his T-shirt high up over his head, pulling it off, flinging it to the floor. He stood up, half-naked in the middle of the room and walked to the full-length mirror on the wall. He lifted one arm up, exposing an armpit.

A chill ran through him.

Suspended in clusters, attached to the wiry orange hair, were long, thin fingers of ice, stalactites, dangling from the caves in his arms. He moved his arm slowly up and down and the ice tinkled a little. He raised his other arm and saw the same, a spray of razor sharp crystals – each armpit held a small chandelier.

He snapped off one long filament, holding it flat in the palm of his hand.

Trapped in the ice was himself: his sweat, his own body fluid.

His body, the changes, they should worry him. But they didn't. They were frightening, but also, oddly, they were comforting. He looked at the icicle again. It was beautiful and extraordinary, a diamond in the making.

He snapped one, then a few.

Each time he pulled one from its roots he sighed, feeling a jab of ecstasy.

When there were no more icicles August studied himself carefully again. 'August,' he said his name out loud; he was named after the month in which he was born. But this name was also a cruel joke. He'd never felt august, ever. Quite the opposite.

In the mirror he saw the truth: a thin white man, aged thirty-three, a man who looked more like a large boy. A man-boy who had the wrong body and the wrong life, who didn't know who he was. Who'd give anything to start again, as someone else. He saw a person who'd never felt comfortable, who couldn't smile at a pretty woman. He saw a monster, a man with hair which frightened children.

He looked past the mirror and saw Cosmo standing in a room at Stonegate Hall.

The room had red walls.

He could see his mother too.

She was lying on a bed on the other side of the room, her hair falling over it. He could see her white calves, lolling open, could see up, into her thighs, into a deep slit between them. He heard Cosmo and his mother laughing, saw Cosmo unbuckle his belt and let his trousers fall to the floor. He saw a rope of some sort, though upright, like a stamen. He watched himself, a small boy, shut his eyes and begin to cry, holding on to the door handle. He saw Cosmo thrust the stamen into his mother, the muscles of his buttocks, the hair on the back of his thighs, his mother's small white fists clutch the edge of the bed.

The sound like shouting.

His mother caught sight of him, standing at the door.

'Get out,' she snapped.

Cosmo was grunting, moving up and down, his buttocks thrusting, his scrotum banging and flapping.

The little boy began to cry, his tears were an ocean falling from him. It fell from his penis too, as he cried and pissed himself.

'Out!' she screeched. Her eyes were hard.

The little boy still clung to the door handle. He stood and wailed as Cosmo fucked his mother, the noise they made like the sound of panic.

August looked at himself.

His breath was slow, his chest rising up and down in a careful, even rhythm. It was clear, clear as crystal, what was happening. The sparkly rash, the blueness, the snow – and now this. It was clear. The idea Cosmo might be his father had brought on something; it was making him physically sick.

Outside the rain poured. August stood in his bathroom looking up at the chrome shower fixture suspended over the cast iron tub. He reached forward and turned on the taps, the hot then cold, mediating them until he found the right warmth; thin jets of water sprang from the shower head, wetting his arms. He stuck his head under the warm lively spurts, letting them paste his hair into a kind of woodpecker's quiff over his face. He stayed there for several moments, bare-backed, enjoying the water as it became a faint and comforting sound joining and then becoming the sound of the rest of the world.

His bent-over back was long but perfectly proportioned, his backbone a line of small eggs pushed up under his pale, seal-smooth skin. His waist was slim, tapering into angular, narrow hips. He unbuttoned and unzipped his trousers, letting them fall, stepping out of them, stretching his long dancer's legs into the tub.

* * *

In the deli the next day the radio was playing Bob Hope songs. Downstairs, Rose had been cooking tournedos with anchovies, and again the deli was overcome.

August was standing on the ladder, his mouth full of thumbtacks, feeling distinctly nauseous. In an attempt to hide his hangover, he'd offered to help Rose with last-minute Christmas decorations. Rose stood at the bottom of the ladder this time, a box of Christmas decorations at her feet. The decorations were the same every Christmas, a delicate curtain of red balls across the window, strings of tiny white lights around the frames. He and Rose decorated the shop together every year, usually much earlier, before anyone else had ideas. Last year Henry had wanted fake snow and tinsel, and Cedric had offered to stand in the window as Father Christmas, for a small fee.

'What are you doing for Christmas?' August asked Rose through the tacks. He knew she'd booked a fortnight off and he was going to cover as manager for most of it, except the three days when the shop was shut. The last time he'd inquired she'd been evasive. He was always intrigued as to why she never talked about her family in Edinburgh, hoping one day she'd tell him about the dispute.

'I've just booked a cruise,' she said, proudly.

'Where to?'

She smiled. 'The Antarctic.'

August stopped what he was doing for a moment, impressed.

'It's summer down there, dazzling light all day long.'

August imagined himself on deck, crisp and burnt, his face wrapped in bandages.

'I get low in winter,' Rose explained. 'Not enough sun.'

August nodded politely, as if he understood. 'It's quite a way away; how do you get there?'

'By ship. I fly to Buenos Aires first and then on to

Santiago and then a port called Punta Arenas in Southern Chile. The boat leaves from there. It'll be a long trip, but worth it.'

August had read about the bleakness of the Antarctic Circle, the dry valleys where nothing lived, where the wind blew even the snow away. It was like being on the moon down there, on another planet. He envisioned grand craters of nothingness. Nothing could survive the climate at the South Pole, only a few emperor penguins, and they were both crazy and unique. It would make for a stark and lonely holiday, he thought.

'Why did you choose there, of all places?'

Rose looked sad for a moment, then serene.

'It seems like somewhere peaceful,' she said plainly, then began picking about in the box of decorations.

Enviably, Rose travelled a lot. But it seemed she'd lived in lots of places too. It was hard to put a chronology together of the places she'd been. She was always unforthcoming whenever he'd tried to pin her down to dates, changing the subject when it turned to anything she did before owning the deli.

'What about you, Gus?'

August reddened.

'Oh, I'll probably spend it with my mother.'

Rose nodded.

'How is she?'

'I haven't spoken to her in a while, but the last time she was fine. Still with Fred.'

'Such a glamorous woman,' said Rose.

'Mmmm . . .'

His mother appeared in the deli from time to time, unannounced for dramatic effect, usually whenever she came to

London to shop. She'd never moved from Yorkshire and lived in a small stone cottage outside Hawes with a man ten years younger.

'You look like her,' Rose said.

'No I don't!'

'Yes, you do, you've the same colouring.'

'Mine's worse,' August said, reaching far into the corner of the window with a string of lights.

'But more grace,' Rose added, quietly.

August heard this but continued pinning the lights, not knowing what to say.

'Who do you look like?' he asked, when the lights were finished.

Rose glanced out the window, then back at him.

'My Aunt Evelyn,' she replied, smiling at some inner joke.

August sat on the top rung of the ladder. The window was done.

'Did *you* like your father?' Rose asked quickly. 'Was he a nice man?'

August was taken by surprise. No one had ever asked him this, or anything about his father. He thought about it for a moment, caught. He looked at Rose.

'I'm . . . not sure.'

Rose frowned.

'I was told he . . . died when I was two weeks old.'

'Oh . . .' Rose was slightly startled. 'I'm sorry. You've never mentioned it.'

August tried to cover her embarrassment. He went red.

'No. I . . . mean, I've never really . . . known. My mother, she's told me about a man she was with when I was born, Luke. But . . .'

Rose's eyes were wide, her mouth a prune.

'I have my doubts.'

'Oh.'

August scratched his arm.

'And you've never asked your mother?'

'No.'

'I see,' Rose said slowly. 'Yes, I can see why that might be . . . difficult. She's very . . .' she smiled, searching for the right word, her eyes falling on his arm. She breathed in. 'Or your grandparents?'

August's eyes widened as he shook his head.

Luke's parents, the Chalmins, they were his only grandparents still alive. Once, years ago, his mother had mentioned they'd moved to northwest London, to Harrow-on-the-Hill. But this fact had always lurked dimly in his consciousness, he hadn't paid it any heed. Their lack of contact had been implicitly understood and he hadn't tried to see them either. Instead, he'd made excuses, vague, formless reasons for not knowing them, slipped the fact of it into a slit in the story of his life. But they were important now, his only real lead. Perhaps he could pay them a visit. It would mean travelling, he knew. A car trip or a tube.

'Gosh, what's that?'

August started a little, then rubbed his arms, realizing he'd been careless to expose them.

'A rash,' he replied, trying to be nonchalant. 'Don't worry. It's under control. The doctor's given me some cream.'

Rose came closer, peering at his arm with concern. 'That's funny.'

'What is?'

'Your rash.'

'Why?'

'It looks odd.'

'What do you mean?

Rose made a face.

'Like frost.'

August quickly pulled down his sleeves.

'No, let me see,' she said, pushing the sleeve back up.

They both inspected his arm, August dispassionate, if anything slightly annoyed, Rose a little startled. His skin was similar to a frozen leg of lamb's: the top layer was covered in a whitish fluorescent velvet, underneath it was stiff, slightly mauve. Rose crinkled her face and breathed out deeply, unhappy, rejecting what she saw. Her mouth pulled itself down into a small 'o' and her brow furrowed.

'If the cream doesn't work let me know, I've something which I use on Hilary.'

August screwed up his face.

'Don't worry, it's fine for humans too.'

August climbed down from the ladder as Rose left. He wanted to tell her he hadn't been feeling himself recently.

He'd been feeling good.

Good in his skin.

When Rose went upstairs for the evening he locked up and left the shop, his Walkman clapped to his head. The soca he was listening to was infectious and it was hard to keep his feet on the ground. The calypsonian's voice was full of laughter, the horn section was a traffic jam, melted and turned to honey, releasing a mild charge up the back of his legs.

He hopped a little, as he walked towards Sulgrave Road.

*

August stood in front of his stereo.

It was midnight, calm and quiet.

Dancing and sadness went together, he knew. Like lemon on fish, or butter on bread, dancing enhanced the flavour of sadness. He rifled through a pile of CDs heaped like rubble next to the stereo until he found what he wanted. He pressed a button and the stereo slid out its thin, rectangular tongue. Carefully, he placed the disc in the shallow groove and the tongue took the disc back into its mouth.

He pressed play.

The diva was West African, her voice rooted in a wet red soil. The melody she sang was as rich as palm oil, slipping between his flesh and skin, slowly embalming him. Cooling him. Children joined her, and a man with the voice of an oak. He could hear *harmony*. It sounded like a crowd talking. Goose bumps rose on his arms. His spine loosened. He was alone with a force. The sound of the world laughing, the wind blowing.

A sea.

A snake.

A horse running.

His hips gave.

He danced until his body was weightless, until his hair was damp and his skin was like warm milk. He danced for hours, slowly, loose-limbed; danced until he was somewhere else.

12 March

August sat in the margarita-coloured bath water, staring at his feet.

For a minute or so he'd been examining a bud nestling in the fork of his toes, wet and small and naked, tilted to one side, as though singing to him. It reminded him of the delicate skull of a newborn chick, its eyes gummed by grey petals, its beak a sheet of opaque tissue. He wriggled his toes, and the bud moved a little.

Spring had brought many buds.

They emerged in the bends and folds and sluggish estuaries of his skin, quiet places. Behind his ears. Between his buttocks. In the crooks of his toes, his fingers. Under his foreskin. They emerged silently, without pain, in ones and twos, overnight, or sometimes during the day. Occasionally, when he was at the deli, serving a customer, or making coffee at the machine, he sensed a burrowing just beneath his skin.

A bud emerging.

They weren't like barnacles, or molluscs or chickenpox or anything hard or itchy. More like soft-shelled snails cleaving to his body, the root a wet mouth gently sucking, lightly kissing unusual parts of him. Scavenger fish, cleaning him. He was loath to pick them off, but he did and they came off easily, with a gasp. He pulled them off every morning, sometimes as many as twenty.

By evening more had emerged.

August leaned forward and picked the bud from between his toes. He held it up close to his face, as though it was a rare gem he was inspecting.

Winter had been long, chilling the earth and spreading itself like an unwelcome visitor, aware yet uncaring of its size and strength, its overbearing manner. After the first outbreak of frost in December things developed quickly. He didn't have eczema, that was plain, and he'd thrown away the cream. He'd decided to go back to his GP, this time armed with notes. He'd made a graph, charted his symptoms, written them down in a small notebook. He'd dated and timed his body's changes, established patterns. After the icicles, a pattern emerged very quickly.

Whatever the weather did, his body copied. January had been the most difficult month. When it rained, which was often, water seeped from under his arms. Thin rivulets ran down his torso, his legs. His body rained. And he was lighter afterwards, as if he'd lost weight. He began wearing more layers of clothes to work, brought towels which he hid in his rucksack. He tried to spend as much time as he could in the storeroom, to be near the bathroom. One morning he'd woken up encased in ice. But instead of feeling cold, he was warm, cosy as a coal, as though he'd woken up in a secret place, a pocket or a hole – or a sarcophagus, lined with the fur of an arctic bunny.

Still, he'd kept careful notes.

He continued to hope there was a straightforward

answer, a scientific explanation. Whatever he had was rare, he knew, but somewhere, in some medical journal, in some old and forgotten periodical, other cases would be recorded.

He had to be patient.

His notes became meticulous. Next to columns of facts and dates about the various eruptions, he'd pencilled in suggestions for the trigger. He was convinced if he found the cause, he'd find the answer – and the cure. He knew it was madness to think it was all to do with Cosmo. Cosmo wasn't his father. The dates didn't add up. He was *already born* when he and his mother moved to Stonegate Hall. It was irrational. Cosmo wasn't the trigger.

Incredibly, Cosmo still hadn't recognized him, made the connection between child and man. Time must have transfigured him a great deal, making him unrecognizable. His voice had broken. So had his nose, moving furniture once. In his late teens he'd shot up, filled out. Now he looked like someone else and Cosmo hadn't made the link. Once or twice August had caught him narrowing his eyes, as if trying to place him. But so far he hadn't guessed – August's only respite, the only barrier between his present and the past. Besides, why should Cosmo remember him? There were so many children in that house, so many came and went. Why would he remember one with flame red hair? It was a long time ago, and Cosmo was always drunk. And so, gradually, he'd become less afraid of Cosmo, as loathing, as resentful, but less worried.

For some time he'd continued with his theories, knowing they were hopelessly far-fetched. The rain on his body: could it be due to over-heating in the deli, a kind of super-sweat? The bouts of icicles, a metal allergy, or very high salt deposits in his blood? The buds. Perhaps his skin had developed a hormonal imbalance, or even something predetermined with an internal clock which had gone off. Or perhaps the trigger had been inhaled; there were so many strange smells in the deli, so much was made from old rot. Or maybe it was an unusual type of acne. He simply had spots. He was sure it all had a rational explanation. For some time he tried to pacify himself; he procrastinated, delayed any conclusions. Many natural things, he knew, could appear supernatural. Clouds which rained fish or spoons or frogs – he'd read about these stories. Sometimes objects and animals whipped up in a storm in one country could get dropped back down to earth in another. Ghosts? They could easily be explained: walls were the same as cameras, using the light to absorb an image and projecting it, forever. He was no oddity, he kept telling himself. He wasn't growing fins or gills or complex eyes that swivelled. What was happening was unusual, maybe, even phenomenal. But not a miracle.

The colder it'd become, the worse the weather, the more his body had reacted. And the better he'd felt. The eruptions sent dull waves of pleasure through his body and he'd been constantly relaxed. Coital.

In early March the plane tree outside the deli began to bud. He'd watched the first shoots emerge, wishing he knew more about trees. Even though high up, the buds were visible, grasshopper green scarabs. He'd watched with anticipation, impatience even, wanting to see whether the changes in his body would continue or stop. Then, as his body responded, he shed his rational approach. He began to feel more alive, as though waking from a deep slumber. For days he could sense a breaking inside him, cells pulling themselves apart, his bones moving minutely; movements inside him which were small explosions, air rising inside him, or expanding. He could feel life inside him, starting. Something extraordinary *was* happening.

Obliquely, privately, he held on to a crazy idea, one lodged like a pea under a thousand feather mattresses, an idea too foolish to let on, an idea which was more of a superstition.

Something had come to help.

Soon afterwards, he'd found the first bud under his tongue: tiny, like a swamp mussel. He'd let it stay sucking at the bed of his mouth, a minute angel, a pearl, a pulse. It made him feel relaxed, the opposite of ill. It gave him a strange sense of solace. For the first time in his life, apart from when he danced, he sensed a calmness in his blood, an ease in himself. Balance. He stopped taking notes when the buds appeared in clusters. His body delighted and frightened him at once. Buds appeared all over his body, egg-greyish hives. He'd thrown away his notebook, torn up the charts. Instinct told him there was no reason to panic, there would be an answer. Whatever was happening had its own methods, its own logic. He would watch and wait, see it out. He never went back to the doctor.

In the bath August held the bud out in front of him, balancing it on the back of his hand. *It's so small*, he thought, *perfect, peacefully asleep*. He regarded it with something akin to love, feeling a kinship, an unspeakable alliance. The bud resembled a small, exposed heart.

The morning was fine.

The sky was baby blue and the air had a bite. Big, mother-of-pearl discs of sunlight, strung on threads, came travelling through the large windows, into the deli where Henry and August were working side by side. Roy Ayres was on the radio, singing about wanting to kiss a woman on her poo poo la la. The words were making August nervous around Henry and he hoped she wasn't listening too closely. Henry's hair was tonged into a sleek black bell which curled round her face and turned up and out at the ends. She'd tied a paisley scarf through it. Her eyes had grown bigger, greener since the spring, the hair along her jaw line lighter, softening its angles.

She talked to herself when she wasn't talking directly to anyone else. Not always words or sentences, sometimes little oohs and ahhs and tuts, exclamations at whatever she was doing. Or she whispered to herself in a clattery cod French, a stream of words taken from a school book. August noticed she ate things without realizing she was eating, then hummed as she chewed. She often licked the corners of her lips, or bit them. Sometimes she sang.

'Oohh,' she muttered to herself, taking the wrapping

from a bowl of foie gras. The pâté, which came in a deep stone bowl, was sealed with an inch of yellow duck fat. 'Le pauvre canard,' she muttered to herself. 'Je vais tuer le chasseur. C'est un chien, un cochon . . . Où est le chasseur? Dans les champs. En plein air. Il est mon frère. Bon, je vais tuer votre frère . . .'

August listened to this stream of words as he was taking a newly arrived South American lamb pie from its box. He tried to pin down exactly what he liked about Henry, tried to picture her in his mind's eye. When he did, one thing stood out. The way she bit into her smile, her teeth like a strong stitch on a fat man's jacket, straining to contain what was inside. The smile always made him blush, made his organs feel slippery. She had no idea how much he liked her, what she had inside. Whatever it was, vivaciousness, gaiety, an inherent cheer, it had taken a physical, exterior shape, expressing itself in curves. Her cheeks, chin, throat, eyes, breasts, shoulders, hips, legs were all one type of curve or another, as though pushed out from the inside.

August surveyed the pie. It was enormous, the size of a manhole cover and possibly the same weight. He held a large knife in one hand as he tried to envisage the best way to cut into it. It was another new order, his idea, an experiment from a different outlet, a change from the usual conservative ham or turkey from Pie in the Sky. Recently Rose had given him a freer hand with the order book, encouraging him to find new savouries for lunch time customers, try new salads. He'd already had his way with the cheeses and she'd seen the result – new customers, more regulars.

Spring brought a change in people's eating habits, a lighter palate, and he'd created a few salads, just for the shop: cucumbers with crab, crawfish cerviche, a gado-gado with almonds and sweet potatoes. The mini-quiches and tartlets sold better in the spring; people liked to buy small things they could take to Brook Green for a picnic. He had plans for other delicacies too, Lebanese kubbe, Cuban meat loaf, Vietnamese spring rolls, hoping to let customers travel a little.

As he was surveying the pie, he sensed someone enter the shop.

'Your aura today is beautiful!'

August looked up.

'Monsieur Cosmo!' Henry squealed.

August breathed out heavily through his nose, bridling, and stared intensely at the pie, noticing it'd been glazed with egg and the glaze had reddened and cracked, splitting the crust like the surface of a parched desert. He plunged the knife into it, pretending he hadn't noticed Cosmo.

'All right, Gus?' Cosmo muttered, walking past him with a brief, almost imperceptible nod. He sauntered over to the far end of the display fridge and leaned on it, all dusty and heavy and loose haunches. His ripe, rude smell walked in too, following him like a noxious vapour.

Cosmo smiled and stared deep into Henry's eyes. Henry stared back. She was holding a large carving fork and for a moment she looked like a circus tamer holding a whip.

'I've missed you, chéri!' she said, tapping the fork at the air. 'Where've you been?'

'In my wigwam, my little . . .' He eyed a vase of daffodils behind her and stopped for a moment. '. . . *flower*,' he said in a French accent.

Henry laughed.

August glanced at him, disapprovingly. 'Fleur,' he said quickly.

Cosmo looked over at him and smiled, patiently.

'The French word for flower is fleur,' August mumbled, his insides plummeting, his throat contracting.

'Yeah, right,' Cosmo agreed and laughed. He focused again on Henry.

August was relieved. He cut another side of a wedge. Fine seeds and black seaweed were sprinkled on the top. He thought briefly of Japanese fishermen, dolphins caught in their treacherous nets. He slid a spatula under the slice of pie, pulling it away. Inside there were strata of red and green peppers, lamb and spinach, tomato sauce. He lifted the pie segment on to a smaller silver platter to put in the window. A fly buzzed near it and landed on the counter. Before he knew what he was doing, August smashed it with the spatula, making a loud smack.

Cosmo and Henry stopped talking. Henry glanced across at him, astonished.

August turned to them, slack-faced, embarrassed, and shrugged.

'Err . . . come round to the kitchen,' she motioned to Cosmo, glancing sideways again. 'I'll make you your usual.'

Cosmo nodded, following her as she waved him into the café with her whip.

In the café August could hear their banter continue. He looked guiltily at the squashed fly. It was completely flat and slightly sticky, the only thing he'd ever murdered.

How could Cosmo possibly be attractive to women? he smouldered. He must be *over fifty*, for God's sake. Fifty. And severely pigeon-toed. And he didn't know the French word for flower. *He's ignorant*, August railed. Ignorant and base.

Malodorous.

Oleaginous.

Illiterate.

If only Henry knew the truth. That Cosmo was a liar and a thief. At the commune he used to boast about his illicit dealings, the drugs he'd dealt, the stolen cars, the forged cheques. Many of Jude's friends had trust funds, weren't poor by other people's standards. They had impossible things: private bank accounts, titles. Cosmo's cheating, he'd always suspected, was born from the need to keep up.

August cut more wedges of pie, placing several on the small platter, wrapping the remainder in clingfilm. He carried this through to the café.

'I'm going downstairs for a minute,' he addressed Henry. 'Can you watch the till?'

Henry nodded, but her eyes were filmy. They didn't notice him going.

In the storeroom August sat down on a large trunk freezer. His head ached, his eyes were sore and weeping, slightly. A tingling began on his left hand, between the knuckles. A gentle burrowing had started under the skin, as though a bubble was trying to rise up through his blood. He watched his hand as the feeling intensified. Rings of warmth pooled outwards from where the bubble was rising.

It emerged in a blink.

As if through sand, a small bud appeared between his knuckles: a dusty garnet, a seed from a pomegranate. And he was warmer suddenly, more relaxed.

Lucid.

Cosmo was trouble in more ways than one. The first time Cosmo had walked into the shop, he'd seen the most obvious link, the most likely way he might get entangled with him again. Henry. She was a magnet for him. He'd known Cosmo would charm her, and that she'd like him.

Since the night he'd followed Cosmo home his dreams had intensified. He'd seen himself as a tiny man, a centimetre high, standing in front of an enormous, slowly rotating mandala, at its centre the face of a bearded old man. The man's face was benign and the mandala had a pull, the magnetic tug of an enormous planet. These dreams soothed and frightened him. Often they appeared when he'd barely closed his eyes, looming immense and three-dimensional in front of his face, unlike other dreams. So encroaching were they, some nights he was afraid to close his eyes.

He'd been aloof with Cosmo and courteous, avoided him whenever he'd come into the shop. In return Cosmo had ignored him at first, then treated him with a wariness one might reserve for a weird child.

Cosmo had become a regular. Coffee most mornings, a tiny espresso, and sometimes afternoons too. Henry had taken to him immediately, going out of her way to serve him herself if he sat outside or in the café, teasing him in French with little pet names she'd previously reserved for August. August had said nothing, watching helplessly. Cosmo was cautious with her at first, slow with his body, quick with his eyes – while she was nervous. If he was honest, he could see Cosmo was still handsome, had something, a type of manliness unusual in English men. A weather-beaten face. Loss in his eyes. An easy flirtatious manner. Cosmo, if he remembered right, was half-Spanish.

He'd watched helplessly over the winter months as Cosmo slowly insinuated himself into his life. He sighed, smiling down at the bud between his knuckles, picking it off.

He rolled the bud between his fingers before putting it in his mouth.

After lunch August busied himself in the café, clearing tables, washing up. Rose and Henry were in the deli, serving stragglers. Despite their differences, they worked in comfort, a natural symbiosis. Henry's constant chatter was a little girl's, but one Rose responded to. Every now and then Rose interrupted one of Henry's self-addressed questions with an answer or a comment. Mostly, Rose smiled to herself as she listened, as if taking notes. They moved around each other without effort, one slow and careful, the other busy. One old, the other young; both very feminine.

This was the first occasion the two women had worked like that since Rose had returned from her Antarctic trip and he'd missed them together. Since her trip Rose had come down less, adopted a perceptible air of mystery. He'd expected stories, or mementos shown; she often brought back gifts from her travels, items of food or a trophy of some kind, but this time, nothing. The trip had made her more introverted, silent – a tiny deprivation. August wondered if something had gone wrong but felt unable to pry. He liked to eavesdrop on Rose and Henry's conversations. When they thought he was out of earshot they were less formal, said things they wouldn't with him around. He stood at the sink in the kitchen alcove, quietly washing up – listening.

'Can I show you something?' Rose asked Henry when the shop had gone quiet.

'Mais, oui.'

August heard the rustling of paper and guessed Rose was taking something from the shelf under the till. There was more rustling, paper being torn.

'Comme c'est joli,' Henry exclaimed. 'Where did you buy them?'

'I didn't.'

'Someone gave them to you?'

Rose laughed modestly. 'I *made* them.'

'Rose, you're so clever.'

'It's my hobby, I do it for pleasure.'

'Pleasure? We had cross-stitch lessons at school, they were torture. I remember having to sew crosses on pieces of gingham. I was terrible at it.'

'I wish I'd had lessons at school,' Rose said, her tone gloomy.

'When did you take it up?'

'Oh, not long, a couple of years ago maybe.'

'I don't have the patience for sewing. My fingers are too big.'

A customer came into the shop, there was more rustling of paper. August would've liked to know what was in the bag, but sensed it wasn't for him to see. He waited as Rose served the customer, and heard the sound of the door closing.

The shop went quiet again.

'Rose?' Henry's voice was off pitch.

'Yes?' Rose's was ladylike.

'What do you think of anal sex?'

August stopped washing the plate he had in his hands. There was no immediate reply, though he could picture Rose's flushed face, see her fidgeting with her glasses.

Henry pushed on.

'Yves wants it all the time.'

The shop was as quiet as a church. August was blank with surprise.

'And I hate it.'

He washed the plate slowly again.

'I mean I love him. But he doesn't know what it's like. I bet he couldn't even get a pencil up his bum.'

Finally Rose released a nervous giggle.

August grinned.

'He says it's more enjoyable than real sex. Enjoyable for him!'

August put the plate on the wooden drainer. Lines of water rolled down its face.

'For me it's agony.'

August stopped what he was doing. He couldn't help wanting to take responsibility for Yves, feeling a ludicrous, ancient chivalry. He wanted to rush into the deli to say *Stop seeing this moron . . .*

'Never,' said Rose, her voice was slow, measured, 'do anything you don't want to do.'

Henry remained quiet.

August stared down at his washing-up gloves. He imagined Henry bent over a table with a man holding her there. He saw tears in her eyes and she was biting her lips, this time to suppress pain. He picked a dirty cup from the Formica and plunged it into the suds.

'For men sex is easy,' he heard Rose say. 'It's not a complex procedure. There's no hidden place, no enigma. Most don't enjoy foreplay. They don't want their ankles kissed. Or to be caressed, they don't need lots of time.'

August was amazed.

He rubbed the cup with a J-cloth, then put it still soapy on the drainer. To him Rose had always been virginal. She hadn't had sex, or a past, past lovers, past relationships. Past anything. He knew this wasn't very generous, but this was how he saw Rose. Without sex. And anyway, she was wrong.

He wanted to run around again to say . . . *No! Sex for me is difficult* . . .

'I love him so much,' Henry said in a thin voice.

'Then he should respect you.'

'I know he loves me. But . . .'

'But what?'

There was a silence.

Henry snivelled.

'He likes . . .'

'What?'

'Pornography.'

August was frozen with interest. Yves, the rake, the wolf. It was hard to imagine any man wanting a substitute for Henry. He listened closely.

'I can't understand it,' Henry continued. 'Why he needs to stare at other women. Why?'

Rose didn't answer.

'The women he brings home, with their legs spread and their shaved pussy. Playing with themselves. Uggghh . . . It makes me feel . . . he makes me feel . . . prudish, unsophisticated. I hate them, I hate those pictures.'

She didn't stop.

'He brings home other stuff too, harder porn. Women with deformed bodies, breasts like balloons. Opening those magazines always feels like . . . a blast in my face.'

The door opened again.

Another customer came in.

'Can I have two slices of the tortilla in the window?' a man's voice asked.

There were footsteps to the fridge, a suck as it was opened, footsteps back to the till.

In the kitchen, August felt mildly depressed.

Dimly, privately, in a way he couldn't express, he knew what Henry meant. The sight of so much flesh. At the commune, he'd seen so much . . . It had a force, hard to explain, but potent. It was something he didn't talk about because he didn't know how.

When he finished the dishes he went downstairs to the office. He took a sheet of paper from a pad on the desk and on it wrote:

Dear Henry,
I think foie gras is terrible too. We'll stop ordering it.
Yours, August.

He folded the note in half and slipped it into an envelope. He slipped the envelope into her satchel.

* * *

Jim had married Louise, his art college sweetheart, when he was just nineteen. She was a great friend of Stella's and the four of them spent a lot of time together in and out of art college in York. August was the best man at the quiet wedding in a registry office, and Stella was maid of honour. Six months later Louise gave birth to a baby girl, Kathy. Three more children were born, Kathy was now fourteen.

In The Green Man Jim and Gabriel were sitting together, Jim laughing at something Gabriel was signing.

'What's so funny?' August asked, when he came closer.

Jim was unable to contain his amusement, his face was flushed at what Gabriel had just said.

'Gabriel saw Alex busking outside our local sweet shop yesterday.'

August smiled, also amused. Jim's oldest son, Alex, was eleven.

'He was with a couple of his friends from school.'

'What were they singing?'

'They weren't.'

August looked at Gabriel for more light on the subject.

Gabriel made a gesture like he was playing a saxophone.

'They were playing their recorders,' Jim added.

August laughed. 'Serves you right for taking him to Glastonbury last year. He's become a hippie.'

Gabriel laughed, agreeing.

'He wants to be a classical musician,' Jim continued. 'He's just decided. For his birthday he wants a lute.'

August smiled. 'Good. Lutes are unpopular and uncool. He won't have much competition.' He sat down and began to unbutton his jacket.

'Lutes cost a *fortune*.'

August was suddenly drawn up, mindful of Jim's expenses. He frowned.

'He doesn't get it from me,' Jim went on. 'I've never played an instrument in my life. Louise is tone deaf. He wants to join an orchestra, play at the Albert Hall.'

'He could get a scholarship,' August encouraged. 'There's all kinds of funding for young musicians these days.'

'Really?' Jim gazed into his pint and smiled, really quite proud. He huffed and picked it up and took a long swig then put it down.

'Funny how things turn out,' he said, wiping foam from his top lip.

'What do you mean?'

'How your children grow up.'

August nodded, uncertainly.

'The world forms them, really, not you. School, their friends.'

'Nurture,' August added, his eyes crinkling at saying something so corny. 'The people they're most exposed to.'

'Indeed,' Jim nodded. 'Our neighbours are musicians. Always rehearsing next door. Always playing music. That's where he gets it from, I think.'

Gabriel began to sign, saying Alex had inherited his desire to perform from him.

Jim and August smiled.

'How's Isabel,' August signed.

Gabriel smiled, dreamily. He gave August the thumbs up.

August nodded. 'I didn't speak to her that time we met, but she seemed nice.' He felt his ears go hot, lying.

'A real peach,' added Jim.

Gabriel signed to say they had been together for four months.

'And long may it last,' said Jim.

August made a small nod in agreement and left to get a drink.

As he walked home, along the Uxbridge Road, August looked upwards, using the blackness of London's night sky as a canvas for his thoughts. There was no moon up there, no stars or clouds, just a screen, a blindfold around the earth. He imagined the earth as his head, a world on his shoulders, a purple satin scarf tied around it. He saw himself walking blindly on the pavement which was also a plank of wood high above the ground. He closed his eyes and walked slowly, one foot in front of the other, spreading his arms like aeroplane wings for balance. He was surprised at how steady he was, not blind at all, but guided. He continued walking like this, eyes closed, for several moments. A bud popped from one of his nostrils, clinging and sucking him, a fat, velvet tick. Tendrils of pleasure tumbled from it into his bloodstream. He breathed in, taking longer steps, more confident, picking up his stride, walking as he would with his eyes open.

As he walked he sensed a pull in him, through him, from the pavement to the sky.

He doesn't get it from me . . .

Jim was right.

His inheritance hadn't come through a blood line.

He kept walking.

When he got home he took the phone book for west London from the shelf under the phone in the hall. He brought it to the table and sat down, flicking through to the pages of C's. He found there was only one Chalmin listed.

August had never registered himself, his home number was his landlord's. Until then, he'd never looked for his own name. Now he stared at it, speculatively. W. J. Chalmin. A beginning. Where he should start, at least. The address, The Elms, 85 Valance Rd, dispelled any doubt. Luke's parents had obviously taken the house name with them from Ditchling.

On the table he spread a tube map out and traced his route. Thirteen stops in all. One change, at Baker Street for the Metropolitan line which would go out overland for most the journey, to Metroland. Half an hour, possibly a little longer on the tube. So close, he marvelled, round the corner, almost. He rubbed his chin and thought about it, briefly massaged the back of his neck, looking down at the map. He could wear magnets on his wrists. Or take a book to distract him. Or maybe half a Valium – that would settle him down.

In ten years of living in London, he'd never taken a tube.

A woman examined the sandwich basket. She was sleek to the point of being gaunt and a chopstick was stabbed through her oriental hairdo. She whispered into her mobile phone as she selected two dusty white rolls stuffed with Mozzarella and salad. Another woman, older, parked her bike up against the railings outside the deli and ran inside. She stood in the centre of the shop for a minute, her face blank, clothes pegs were clipped to the ankles of expensive grey trousers, before realizing she was in the wrong shop, then ran back out. She cycled off.

August hadn't spoken much. He'd worked as if in a trance, as he often did in the late morning, between the breakfast and lunch-time rushes. He liked to watch people waltz in from Shepherd's Bush Road, talking in low tones, smiling weakly at him, as though only using their ear muscles. Londoners were still winter-drowsed. Still sluggish from the long chill, stalled and stricken uncharacteristically coy by the appearance of the sunshine.

An hour ago the sun had been flimsy as a hanky but the ground had remained cold. Now he could feel a palpable sulk in the sky and there were freckles on the pavement from a rain shower he didn't remember. April's showers had started in late March.

Henry had also been quiet. She hadn't talked French much – to herself or anyone else. Her hair was in a single ponytail. August wondered if she'd found his note about the foie gras, regretting it in case she was annoyed he'd gone into her satchel without asking. She'd worked in the café most of the morning while August had been behind the fridge in the deli. He'd noticed whenever he needed an extra pair of hands she'd appear at the right moment, and then silently help him. Despite this, she was distracted.

Her silence had been worrying his skin.

Behind his knees, in the crooks of his arms, buds were emerging in twos and threes. They were gorgeous and perverse, rosettes of tiny, bodiless nymphs lapping at him, sending waves of ecstasy up his legs. Making him feel loose.

He watched Henry refilling the pastry basket, remembering what she'd told Rose, realizing there was a lot he didn't know about her. He didn't know her family or friends, what her home looked like, didn't know what she cared about most. Having overheard the conversation he imagined a seamy life for her now. A bedsit at the top of a boarding house. It had small, double glazed windows and a futon on the floor, a lamp covered by a scarf. He saw once white walls with grey ghosts around the edges of the radiators and a toffee coloured carpet littered with used matches and shreds of tobacco. A *Playboy* magazine lay open on the carpet, its centrefold pulled open at Miss April. She lay back on a hay stack, her legs open, eating an apple. Her clitoris was just visible between her legs, a bashful mauve bud.

Since Henry had gone quiet, he didn't know what to say to her and felt at a loss, the only thing he could think of sounded inappropriate.

Would you like to dance?

During the lunch-time rush they worked together in the narrow space behind the till and the display fridge. Rose came down to run the café.

They sliced, weighed and wrapped food. They talked to customers, ones they knew, and ones they didn't. They closed the door when it was open, filled and refilled the salad bowls, swept the floor. There were noises: the chink of change, the song of the till as it opened, the whirring of the coffee grinder. They worked effortlessly together but didn't talk much. Once they reached for the same knife and their fingers touched. Another time they brushed hips as Henry handed over a parcel of chorizo to a customer.

The rush died, as it always did, at around two thirty. It was quiet again and August began to tidy the cheeses. A new Mimolette had been cut open and then into pieces which were so big and firm, the orange so rich, they could have been slices of pumpkin. Next to it, the vacherin was tired. Its innards were the colour of creamed banana and sagged from the suitcase of its rind. It was a winter cheese. French farmers stopped making it at the end of March and its disappearance from the deli was always a defining marker of spring. He reached into the fridge to clean it up, smoothing its melted stomach, stroking it with long, deft fingers. A bit had come away and was impossible to save and so he found a flat spatula knife and eased it off, balancing it expertly on the gleaming edge. Unconsciously, he threw his head back, lifting the knife with the dripping cheese an inch above his lips. He closed his eyes as he dropped the cheese into his mouth. The cheese was perfect, warm, soft and undercut with a taste which spoke of the mountains where it was made. As he savoured it, he imagined himself as a French herdsman, bringing his cows down the grassy slopes of the Massif du Mont d'Or, imagined himself tapping the haunches of a cow with long eyelashes and a rusty bell around its neck. These thoughts were interrupted by the sound of crockery hitting the floor.

'Merde!'

Henry had knocked over some coffee cups. She was standing next to the grinder, looking at him transfixed, clutching a bowl of ratatouille.

'I'll get them,' August offered, jerked from his day-dream.

'No, I will,' Henry snapped.

She placed the bowl on the counter and bent to pick up the pieces, August bent too. On the way down their noses bumped, their heads banged together.

'Owwww!' Henry cried, clutching her head. Her teeth were clenched.

'I'm sorry,' August cringed.

'Stop being so sorry all the time, Gus!' Henry snapped again.

'Sorry.'

'Gus!'

August was dumbstruck. He'd never seen her angry for no reason. A bud-nymph sprouted at the base of his spine and he had to concentrate to stop himself from moaning with pleasure. Quickly, he picked up the pieces of china on the floor, using one hand as a cradle, afraid to look at her. For a few moments they cleared up together in silence.

Then Henry stopped. He heard her inhale and snag her breath in her chest. Hesitantly, he looked up to smile at her, to say something, anything, to make her feel better. She squinted at him, struggling with what looked like pain in her eyes, resentment.

'I think you're wonderful,' she said, quietly.

August screwed his face up with surprise. Henry looked away and rose from the floor. She hovered above him for a moment, looking down, then uttered a small, strained 'uh' before rushing into the café and down the stairs. August remained crouched, shocked, staring at the broken china on the floor, wondering if he'd heard right, fighting a new feeling which had suddenly sprung in him for Henry, a terseness in his body, as though he was being instinctively held back.

Henry avoided him for the next hour, busying herself in the kitchen downstairs until he took a late lunch break and a sandwich to Brook Green.

August sat on a bench, chewing slowly, thinking about Henry. This would change things, throw their friendship out of balance. August thought of his fantasies as harmless, well-meaning, without outcome; he'd never really imagined taking them into action, into the possibility of really having Henry as a lover. He liked to imagine them together, carnally, the way they might make love, what Henry might look like naked, her curves. But it was just a dream, his own in-mind home-porn – and even then it often got stuck on pause. A real kiss? Or an actual connection of this kind? With Henry, big-boned and luscious – but. But in reality it was a slap in the face, a pinch on the arm. She was too young. Too unsure of herself. Too much. It meant a clash he hadn't intended, wasn't suited for. He felt annoyed with himself now, all mixed up.

He looked around him, chewing.

The sun had gathered its strength and was pouring on to the grass. Normally, he'd have also taken sunglasses to the park. He was used to having a pair glued to his head from the birth to the death of the summer months. Now he sat without protection. Above him the sky was as loud as an orchestra, as full of boldness, but painless. Rays of light weren't fingers poked into his eyes. The light was soft as honey as it spilt into him. Kind.

As with all the other changes, he'd decided to be cautious. Perhaps it was temporary, something which wasn't going to last. He surveyed the park, testing out his new sight. There were people about: a man in track pants practising acrobatic jumps, a group of homeless men and women drinking cans of strong lager further off, a girl playing with a small dog and a Frisbee hoop. Brook Green was only a postage stamp of grass with a steady flow of traffic zipping past, yet once the weather broke, once there was some sun, people treated it like a beach.

August continued to eat in silence.

Something about the men and women on the bench reminded him of Stonegate Hall.

Commune. A word which made him laugh. There'd been no shared community, no goodwill, no common goals. Only sloth and neglect, petty battles. The house was owned by his mother's friend Jude, a derelict heirloom she'd inherited and couldn't afford to keep up. So she'd filled it with friends, other upper class hippies, drifters, homeless families, hoping if she provided a roof, everyone would chip in.

That was the idea.

But it was the seventies. Ideas were big. The adults had lots of them, all with names. Egalitarian. Utopian. Radical. Cooperative.

August's eyes wandered to the girl with the little dog. He remembered the cold flagstones beneath the stairs to the adults' dormitories. There was a bathroom on that landing in which he'd often hidden late at night, talking for hours into a portable cassette player. He'd make tapes to send to an imaginary family, sisters and brothers he didn't have; even Luke, somehow still alive. In his tapes he'd recount an imaginary life, one where he lived in a small house with his own room and had his own little dog.

The stairs leading to the adults' dorm were green felt worn black. The landing at the top was a trapeze platform, way up in the billows of a circus tent; death-defyingly high up. He pictured himself walking up the stairs, a small boy, climbing each step one by one.

He swallowed the remainder of his sandwich in one gulp.

He'd never been back to Stonegate Hall, ever. He'd never go back. Even the idea made him uncomfortable.

After twelve years, his mother eventually chose to leave. He'd never cared what made her decide to move to York all of a sudden, one summer. It'd been his chance, his ticket.

'We're moving to the city,' she'd announced one evening. There was a red dust in the air in the kitchen, swirling around her head.

'Start packing.' Her eyes were serious.

A week later they were gone.

He remembered people waving goodbye, seeing the copse for the last time as they drove out the gate. Trees. Stiff, upright. Standing in a community too, ceremoniously sending them off. For some reason, Jude hadn't come down to say goodbye.

There'd been a hostel for a few months before York council found them a flat in the suburbs. He'd started school that September. Immediately his teachers had realized something was wrong.

At the commune there'd been a school room up on the third floor, a room with a blackboard and some chairs, one long table. An old man called Martin had lived at the house for the first six years and he'd taught the younger children the alphabet, how to make words and sentences. How to read the words. But Martin suffered from bouts of depression after which he wouldn't feel like teaching at all. He'd repeat what he'd already taught. There were no books to practise with between his depressions, only what they could write to each other. August would write long stories, or letters to himself and read those for practice. When Martin left, a young woman with long blonde plaits called Jill taught them for a year. She taught arithmetic. Poetry. Beekeeping. They had swimming classes at the local pool. After Jill there'd been Sabrina, and then Harry. Even his mother had taught them briefly. Flamenco lessons. This had been his education for years, broken, random, mostly useless. When he turned up at secondary school, he was more or less illiterate. He was lucky though, it was a small school, they had time to help. He attended remedial classes until he was sixteen.

Those years were busy.

Outside class he read everything he could: books on fish and fishing, cook books, books on heraldry, on canals, on how to shoe a horse. Books about England, about other countries. Books about churches, about the early Hebrews, the Christian fathers. Books about wars. About witchcraft, about making wine. He'd been starved for years, malnourished.

Once free, he ate.

He ate books.

And there was Jim. Jim's parents had moved up from London the year before which made him different also. Jim took care of him in the playground, liked his company, saw his hippie background as exotic. Jim thought Olivia was impossibly cool and liked to come over in the evenings to listen to her Dylan records.

No, he would never go back to Stonegate Hall; it had a kind of gel around it in his reckoning, an aspic of memory, of a time when he had no control, an age of desperation. It was somewhere he'd been lost. He thought again of his mother in the kitchen, of Luke, of Luke's parents not far away. Going back to Stonegate was impossible.

August rubbed the toe of his Adidas Sambas along the grass under the bench. He glanced at his watch and realized he'd been out longer than planned. He stood up and stretched, then examined his hands for buds and saw there were none. He walked across the grass, towards the pavement, stepping over the railings of the small park.

On the outside corner he stopped. Several yards away was the flower shop. The ivy and the firs had gone. Now there were daffodils and tulips and buckets of blossoming buds, tiny rose bushes and snowdrops. In a box full of what looked like swordfish swords there was a sign saying *Fresh Aloe Vera*. There were cramped and twisted bonsai trees and some white jasmine. Spring, August noticed, had brought a more capricious type of plant.

Leola came out of the shop with a pair of secateurs in one hand.

August immediately wished he could disappear, run.

As she bent to snip the ends off some blossom stalks, he saw the pale, smooth backs of her knees, the chalk blue rivers running under them. Again, he felt a tug. He saw the cheese flying across the deli, spinning away from him, crashing into the pork pies. His face flushed. He remembered how she'd apologized profusely. *Clumsy*, she'd said repeatedly, meaning herself, not him. Now she didn't look clumsy at all. When she straightened her back after bending to snip the stalks he saw she was tall, and had a graceful way of holding herself.

Consciously, he stopped himself. *It's got to end* he chided, his wild imaginings, his constant dreaming.

August didn't call out or say hello. He stood waiting on the pavement for a gap in the steady stream of cars.

Leola had become a regular too. As with Cosmo, for different reasons, he avoided serving her. He found he became even more awkward around her. Intensely so. He was unable to look at her without getting a seizure in his eyes, a driving desire not just to stare, but to gaze at her for minutes at a time. It was embarrassing. So he hid. In the café, or behind the slicer.

'Would you like some peach blossom?' Leola called into the shop.

August stepped off the pavement and walked across the road, his head turned slightly so he could see her. Leola disappeared back inside.

Cedric was sitting at a table on the pavement outside the deli when he returned. He seemed unusually quiet, caressing his beard, sipping his coffee. August sensed the old man was play-acting, as usual. That was how he usually went about, as if at any moment, he would be called on to claim his rightful role on the world's stage. He had his notebook with him, open, the pages rustling over each other. Then August saw Cedric's audience. Four feet away, at the other table, on the other side of the doorway, sat the woman with the winkles-for-eyes. She also sat sipping coffee.

'Good afternoon, Cedric,' August said cheerily, as he passed. But Cedric pretended he hadn't heard. He continued to sip and stroke his beard and looked away from both August and the woman.

She stared into a magazine.

In the deli August felt tense around Henry for the first time. He noticed there were chocolate crumbs on Henry's T-shirt and a brown smudge in the corner of her mouth. He wished she'd speak some French, try a new phrase out on him, wished a whale spout of hair was dancing from the centre of her head. It was disconcerting to find being finally noticed by Henry felt wrong.

Henry was wordlessly polishing the till. The rest of the counter had also been tidied. Her cheeks were plump with shyness.

'Ça va, mon raisin?' he tried.

'I'm fine,' she said, without meeting his eyes.

He pushed on. 'How long has Cedric been outside?'

'I don't know. But that woman needs saving.'

August looked out the window at the two tables.

'No, she doesn't.'

'What do you know?' Henry puffed. 'Cedric is going to corner her again, any moment.'

August reddened.

'What's wrong with Cedric?' Despite everything, he wanted Henry to tell him. Spell it out. What was wrong with him?

'I don't know . . .' she shuddered. 'He gives me the creeps, that's what.'

August nodded.

'I wish you wouldn't encourage him, Gus, he made quite a scene in here that time. I'm surprised she's come back.'

'He was being rather sweet, I thought.'

'He's screwy, not sweet. Why can't you see that?'

Henry, petulant, was vigorously dusting behind the coffee grinder without really looking at what she was doing.

August looked at the couple outside. Then he saw what was going on: they were ignoring each other, playing some kind of charade. He was suddenly conscious of them, *another pair at odds*, mocking himself and Henry.

'Has Cedric paid for his coffee?'

'You know he never does.'

Henry was right. He spoilt Cedric, let him have whatever he wanted, encouraged him to hang around. He read his poems. Listened to his ideas. August watched Cedric writing in his notebook, his back to the woman, one arm used as a shield.

He'd had enough.

Or perhaps the opposite. He *hadn't* had enough. He wanted courage. To buy flowers from Leola. Ask her out, take her to the pictures, or for a walk along the canal. He wanted Henry to lose her new mood, her odd behaviour, wanted the confidence to clear the air between them, discuss what had happened humourously. He wanted Yves to go back to France. He wanted Cedric to evaporate into a green cloud of smoke.

Tying his apron around his hips, August strode outside. The woman was still reading her magazine. Cedric was still writing.

'Cedric,' August's voice was unsteady, his legs were slightly unstable.

'Have you paid for that coffee?'

Cedric didn't look up.

August stooped to get nearer the old man.

'Cedric!'

Cedric's great hair-blinded head rose from his note-book.

'Have you paid for that coffee?'

'I'm not deaf!' Cedric shouted.

August reddened.

'Well . . . have you?'

'You know very well I haven't,' Cedric replied curtly.

'No I didn't.'

'Yes you did. Are you stupid?'

'No.'

August clenched his fists and breathed in quickly, then

let his hands go limp. He was ashamed at being riled by the old man but he also felt mad, reckless, as though at any moment he might throw himself into the traffic.

'*You* are stupid,' he said to Cedric.

Cedric's eyebrows rose in challenge.

For a moment they regarded each other, for the first time ever, in combat.

'And you are a heartless barbarian,' Cedric replied, speaking down his nose. 'A worm. A jellyfish. A roll-mop!'

August pursed his lips together in consternation and began to pace about the pavement.

Henry came to stand in the frame of the door to watch.

'I can't let you do as you please any more, Cedric.' August raked at his hair. 'If you can't pay I think you should leave.'

Cedric picked at his nails.

August glared at him.

'Poppycock.'

August gasped. 'No, it's not. You take me for granted. From now you'll have to pay.'

'You know I've no money.'

'Oh God!' August moaned, stuck, wishing he hadn't said anything.

'I'll pay,' said a female voice.

The woman at the other table stood up.

'No, Madam, please,' Cedric baritoned. 'Stay back.'

'No, you please, you're giving me a pain in the head,' she said in her heavy, east European voice.

'I'm so sorry,' August tried to sound professional. 'We didn't mean to disturb you.'

'You wanted the money for the coffee. Here, take it.'

The woman walked over to Cedric's table and slapped down two one-pound coins on it. She gave Cedric a slow wink, then turned to go back to her seat. On the way she stopped and stood in front of August. She really was big, August noticed, only an inch or two shorter than him and a foot wider. He had the same impression as he'd had before. He knew her, somehow.

Her eyes were grave, pensive. They flicked over August's face, studying his features, his upright red locks, his bumpy nose, his spaced-out teeth.

After a moment she said:

'You have a twig in your ear.'

In the bathroom August locked the door and switched on the light. He pulled his fist from his pocket, unfurling it under the bulb. *It isn't a twig*, he thought. Too young. The stalk lying across the palm of his hand was green, not brown. Perhaps the woman hadn't known the word for shoot. On it there were small green leaves, curled, like miniature lettuces. Inside each, he knew, was a tiny, crisp heart.

His rucksack was on the floor in the corner. From it he took out the small hand mirror he kept for these checkups. He held it in front of his nose, his ear flush to the bathroom mirror. He leaned closer to the mirror, but saw nothing. He turned his head and peered down the other earhole and saw nothing there either. He checked up his nose, then in his mouth. Under his tongue. Nothing. He could feel something, though, an itch.

In his crotch.

August put his fingers to his lips and for a moment

he tried to pray, remember words he'd learned from his childhood, school, anything, anywhere. No words came. He rubbed his cheek with one hand. With the other he began to unbutton the flies of his jeans. One button, then another, shutting his eyes the lower his hand went. The words 'poison ivy' flashed in his head and he shuddered. The jeans fell from his hips, then his thighs, around his ankles. He stood in his Y-fronts, his eyes now open, fixed on the bulge of his genitals. He pulled down the waistband of his underpants.

He saw his penis, shrivelling from the sudden cold and he saw the familiar nest of fire ants.

But nothing else.

As he climbed the stairs back to the café he could hear Henry talking.

'Oui, Madame, une tarte aux fraises, deux cafés au lait . . .'

He wasn't surprised to see Cosmo sitting at one of the tables in the café, smoking and smiling openly at the other customers, trying to make eye contact with any one of them. He was glad and annoyed he'd brought Henry back to life and hurried past Cosmo without as much as a nod.

I'm growing twigs from my ears, he thought. *I haven't time to make small talk*. Like a mosquito bite, the more he scratched the surface of his feelings for Cosmo, the less relief he got. He'd just have to block him out.

In the front of the shop, polishing the already polished till, he decided he'd make a poultice for his body, something with yogurt and eggs, something cold and hopefully neutralizing, something that would dampen things down.

He'd become too passive about the changes; because he was enjoying them he'd been careless, and now – the twig. He was sprouting and it was showing.

As he continued to polish he noticed Cedric and the woman were still outside, sitting together at Cedric's table. Cedric saw he was spying and raised his eyebrows over his spectacles, competitively. Then continued to talk intensely. The woman was listening, her eyes full of impatience, her mouth a small grin. August tried to think where he'd met her before, but it was hidden in a maze in his mind. As he leaned into the window to gather other empty platters he saw they were holding hands.

'A bientôt, Monsieur,' Henry said loudly, behind him.

'Namaste, my cherry.'

'*Chéri*, not cherry,' Henry laughed.

As Cosmo hovered near the till, August moved away from him, towards the window, bending his body into it, counting spinach rolls.

Henry cruised up against the counter. 'You've bought flowers, how lovely!' she gushed.

Cosmo was happy someone had noticed. 'Yeeahh. For my flat, aren't they cool?'

'What are they? Elles sont belles.'

Cosmo looked at the long furry branches wrapped in the brown paper in his arms, sniffing at the pink buds. 'They're peach blossom,' he said, proudly.

* * *

That evening August spooned yogurt into a bowl. His kitchen was a cramped, fusty place resembling an ancient apothecary's. Against faded pink walls leaned wooden shelves stuffed with jars and pots and little bags full of seeds and dried herbs and shrunken things: pods and unbelievable twisted fruits and curled-up waxy, suspiciously pungent strips of what could be either vegetable or meat. There were also pestles and mortars and grinders and small bowls of dust, which might be leftovers from a recent dish: cinnamon, ground allspice, harissa, lemon grass. There were bound bundles of sticks and leaves, jars of pulses and beans. Many of his finds were from the market and he hadn't got round to using them, they'd been impulsively acquired for their appearance. Others he understood and had mastered. There was something which had been sitting on one shelf for over a year – an enormous purple-black rotting parcel of banana leaves, its contents still a mystery. When he'd asked the African lady on the stall what was inside, she'd fixed him with a dismissive, uncompromising expression and shaken her head.

'It's not for you,' she'd replied.

August stirred the yogurt, mashing any lumps away. On the counter top there were a dozen eggs, also for the poultice, a carton of goat's milk, and a bag of lotus tea leaves.

As he cracked an egg he thought of Cedric and the woman outside the deli. Something about her matched with Cedric. It'd been annoying him all day, but now he had it.

Her eyes. They were the same colour as Cedric's. Their eyes were the same; they looked the same, were the same intangible shade – of sea. Or seaports, or shipwrecks. Or perhaps just that. Of wreckage. He cracked another egg into the bowl. *Our bodies know before we do*, he thought. Which was why the heart was a symbol of love. But somehow the heart was wrong. It was a muscle, over-used and overworked, with no time for such a delicate job as love. Choice, he was sure, came from tissue and fibre, bone marrow, somewhere deeper and darker – a blacker organ than the heart, more hidden. He remembered Gabriel's demonstration, his organs being put back in. Gabriel was right in a way. Our feelings lie dormant, asleep in our very darkest parts, in our organs, waiting to be germinated.

We choose with our liver, he decided. Choice comes from the dark. From nowhere with reason, nowhere with thought, or decision. *The liver is the organ of love*. At first, we only register a pull, towards this person or that. Sometimes people walked towards the pull. Others thought the pull was something else – low blood pressure or a headache.

August poured the goat's milk into the bowl, stirring it into the mix, then switched the kettle on. He was happy for Cedric. He knew Cedric lived alone in a small house nearby. The bailiffs had collected most of his furniture, BT had cut him off. Cedric lived off £18 a week, what the state provides if a person is jobless and unwilling to work. He doubted Cedric had ever worked. His family were wealthy. He'd been educated at Eton, then read Greats at Oxford – then had a breakdown. At some point, the wealth or his family's goodwill had dried up.

August was sad for himself, though, knowing he often wished happy people ill. He wanted their happiness to be untrue or flawed, wanted to believe his truth was the norm.

The kettle switched itself off and steam billowed from the spout. The poultice was for the outside of his body, the tea an inner cleanser. The lotus leaves would also make him sleepy and he looked forward to this retreat. He put the leaves into a small strainer and balanced it over the glass, pouring the boiling water through it. He took the bowl and the glass to his bedroom, placing them down on the small table next to his bed. He pulled off his shirt and trousers and lay down.

There were buds, as usual, under his arms, around his nipples, all over his torso. He thought of Leola, the backs of her knees. That was when he'd felt the pull. He'd felt it again today. Dull, like an ache. Like being tired. He sighed heavily. He didn't know any more, didn't trust his judgments. There was a gap in his means of processing, between fantasy and the real thing, a gap he'd lain dormant in for too long. And now his skin was crawling, growing, sprouting, as if something was under it.

August reached for the bowl, stirring the poultice with a spoon.

He scooped a spoonful of the cold, white mixture from the bowl and dropped it on to his chest, making it contract in little spasms.

He scooped up more mixture from the bowl and dropped more of it on to his body. He scooped and dropped, scooped and dropped, until each bud was covered with a soft white nub and his chest had a range of tiny snow-capped mountains running down the middle. August lay back, remembering the French farmers, their cows, and how soon the production of Vacherin would stop. From the window, a faint and amiable light fell on him, across his bed, across the small mountains on his stomach.

Jam tarts had arrived from Gertrude's – small, heavy volcanoes with red magma oozing from a hole in their lids. August stared at them with indifference, taking them from their box and slowly arranging them on a silver cake pedestal.

All day he'd been worried, about Cosmo and Leola. A kind of heaviness had set in; about Henry, and what he should say if and when they were alone again; about his poultice, which hadn't worked.

Cosmo. He'd charmed Henry. And it was plain he was after Leola too. Peach blossom. He'd bought it from her. The disappointment was terminal, all-pervading. Cosmo was like a fog. Everywhere, unstoppable. He couldn't turn for seeing him, having him around.

There was an image in his head which wouldn't dissolve. Cosmo and Leola, walking along a beach hand in hand, both grey-haired and wrinkled.

On her head, a crown of peach blossom.

Confidence should be deserved, he thought. Meted out, like aid to the needy. It was unfair some fools had nerve, or people who were irresponsible had good looks. While others live trapped within themselves, unable to smile, talk, look at the opposite sex without turning red. These inner abilities and disabilities were so unevenly shared out. The gift of body-confidence should be bestowed on a dwarf. The beautiful should also know what it was like to feel trapped. These thoughts had been stirring up in him all day.

As he placed the last tart on the pedestal he heard the sound of a throat being cleared behind him.

'A penny for your thoughts,' Rose murmured.

August made a bearish moan, then smiled, glad of her presence.

'Aren't those tarts wonderful?'

August turned to look at her and gasped.

'Oh, my . . . !'

Rose was different. Her hair was thicker, still short but sleek, a richer silver, a wave through it. Her eyebrows were thinner, more defined. Her lips were a soft pink. She was wearing a smart green and black tweed skirt suit.

Rose blushed, picking up an empty coffee cup from the counter, dotting crumbs with her finger from where it sat, dropping the crumbs in the cold coffee dregs.

'Where are you going?' August asked.

'Out for tea.'

August said nothing, not wanting to say the wrong thing, making connections. Her air of mystery, her being less around. Once he'd heard arias booming from her flat. Rose had been seeing someone.

'Somewhere smart?'

'The Waldorf. Tea in the Palm Court.'

August was stabbed by a tiny pang of resentment. Even Rose now had a suitor. He tried to picture him, an academic, or an antiques dealer, another shop owner perhaps.

Someone tidy and demure, like her, their courtship conducted amongst the bone china and scones.

Have you fallen in love? he wanted to ask.

'I just came down to let you know I'll be upstairs if anyone asks for me.' She smiled, then turned to leave.

'R-r-rose,' August blurted.

She looked warily at him as if he might again say or ask something too honest again. Her small, old face had been painstakingly scrubbed, then subtly and expensively painted over; it was clear she was self-conscious of how she appeared.

August smiled. 'You look pretty.' His ears caught fire.

Rose blushed. 'Why thank you August,' she smiled. 'Thank you very much.'

Henry'd had her nose in her library book all day. She'd kept it behind the alcove in the café, reading it during slow periods and during her lunch hour, times when she might ordinarily have chatted.

August had kept his distance.

He felt bad. He should acknowledge what she'd said to him the day before. *There are other problems in my life*, he told himself. Not least the tiny leaves unfurling all over his body. They had come on now, in a rush, in a profusion he was unable to keep up with. The plane tree had them too, small green pads, stretching for the sun, arching their spines like high divers. He could try another doctor, he supposed, or a hospital, and get laughed at or misdiagnosed again. But he didn't want to be treated like a crank, or a guinea pig. He didn't want to be tested or have tubes stuck in him, up his nose or down his throat; didn't want to stop or interfere with what was happening.

He stared out the window at the plane tree. It had shed its combat fatigues. Now its lithe belly was a pale lilac brown and the tree appeared to be leaping from the pavement – in a catsuit. The same arms were raised high above its head, the same Afro head laughed with arrogance. But the colour of the world had changed recently. The tree, the road, the passing cars. Even the houses were a different hue. The concrete, the wood were brighter. The air had changed too, from a grey wash to blue, as though the world's lighting had been amplified. For the first time August saw the nuances a new season brought, the change in tone of everything around him. He examined his hands. They were warm, glorious. He could feel the bones in them, the gelatine, like Turkish Delight, firm but light. Rose pink. He'd never been aware of his insides before. He looked at the tree again.

He knew how it felt.

August took a small paring knife from a magnetic strip behind him and chose a Cox apple from a basket displaying fruit near the till. Absent-mindedly, still staring out at the plane tree, he began to undress the fat juicy thing, neatly inserting the knife's tip just under the skin, pulling gently and carefully, parting it from the firm sponge underneath.

'Did they kill all their aristocrats?'

Henry was standing next to him, hesitantly, holding her library book, jolting him from his reverie.

August smiled at her, closed-lipped.

'All the main ones,' he replied. As he continued to cut, the skin was unravelling in one single ribbon of frosty pink. 'Some of the minor ones fled, to the French colonies, to other countries.'

'You're always staring at the tree,' Henry said, watching his hands.

'Am I?'

'All the time, especially recently. What are you looking at?'

'Nothing.'

'Then you're always looking at nothing.'

She watched the apple, brooding, pink lace falling as it lost its decency.

'I'll try to stop. How's Yves?' The ribbon was dangling over his hands and forearms, he bit it and crunched and smiled at her.

'He's in France,' Henry said, annoyed. 'For a few days.'

August nodded, still eating, trying to focus his full attention on her. Henry had become slimmer, he realized, not overnight but over weeks – and her hair, it'd been in a ponytail for days. He hadn't noticed these things until this minute. He stopped eating and swallowed.

'Your French is much better,' he said, wanting to draw her out.

'Merci,' she replied matter-of-factly.

How's his English? he wanted to ask. He stopped cutting and held the firm naked apple in the palm of his hand, smiling at it proudly. Henry looked at it too, appalled, heat in her cheeks. August began to cut it up into wedges.

'Has he gone to see his family?' he asked, slicing.

She nodded, watching the apple come apart. 'He's one of twelve brothers and sisters.'

August was instantly jealous. 'It must be wonderful,' he said, putting a wedge in his mouth.

'He says it's awful.'

'Why?' He held an apple wedge towards her, as an offering. His eyes were friendly, conciliatory, pale as two boiled sweets.

Henry shook her head.

'I dunno,' she huffed. 'It makes him feel like a number, he says. His mother never knew their names.'

Henry stood for a minute, not really interested in talking about Yves, restless. She bent and picked up a plum tomato from the box on the floor and rubbed its smooth skin slowly across her lips. As she did she smiled at August, oddly.

August didn't see this.

'I found your note,' she said.

August felt the muscles in his face go slack. He looked at her.

Henry stood still for a moment, holding the tomato against her lips. Then she turned, breathing in deeply, pushing out her chest – and took the tomato with her into the café. He heard her go downstairs.

August rubbed his forehead. He was mystified by Henry these days. She'd become unpredictable and weird. Flirtatious. Not in her usual harmless way. Friendly one minute, and then distant.

A man walked into the deli. He was tall and dark with a sun-blasted face and a great chilli pepper of a smile. He walked directly over to August.

'I am looking for Rose Finlay,' he said, as though delivering a secret message.

August couldn't hide his look of surprise. The man looked elegant, worldly, someone who owned polo ponies.

'Yes, of course,' he replied. He picked up the phone and

dialled her number, waiting as it rang. The man leaned closer to him, as if wanting to hear Rose's voice.

'Rose, there's someone here for you.'

Rose gasped on the other end of the line.

The man was pleased.

'She'll be down in a minute,' August said, embarrassed. The man made him feel silly. He also had a large, droopy moustache and moustaches were funny. August wanted to laugh.

The man blushed.

They waited in a polite silence. While Rose's friend inspected a bottle of Hershey's chocolate sauce August peeked at him from behind the display fridge, admiring his colours, strong reds in the skin on his face; his dark hair was a woman's, unruly with long curls he'd tried to tame with oil. He wore a navy overcoat and smelt of limes or some kind of citrus fruit. His shoes were enormous, like alligators.

'My Scottish Rose,' he declared when Rose appeared. He clicked his heels together. 'Good afternoon.'

August could feel It instantly. Between them there was a tension.

'August, this is Salvadore,' she said, smiling at the man. She pecked him on the cheek.

August blushed.

'I'll be one minute.' She disappeared into the café.

'What wonderful tarts!' Salvadore was eyeing the pedestal. August tried to place his accent, Spanish, South American?

'Would you like to try one?'

'No, no,' he tapped his stomach. 'We're about to have tea.' His voice was strong, each word perfectly enunciated.

Rose came back, a handbag dangling from one arm. 'See you tomorrow,' she said to August.

He nodded, briefly, noticing Salvadore was staring at his hair.

'Cheerio,' Salvadore said, precisely.

They left the shop arm in arm.

August watched, his spirits somehow lifted.

For the final hour of the afternoon, August worked in the front of the shop. Outside the sun was soft and molten-white, leaking its iridescence into a bleached blue sky. It still amazed him that the light wasn't affecting his eyes, rather the opposite – it was a balm. It cleansed rather than burnt, it soothed rather than stabbed. It made his eyes alive, alert.

Late afternoon was a time of quiet, the time the earth slept. Trees caught their breath. It was a time before a time, night. It was when August most thought about his mother.

He liked to remember her when she was younger. She was more tangible then, there was more colour in her face, her hair. She had a stronger presence, or so it felt – there was more of her. Over the years at Stonegate it was as if she'd been slowly rubbed out. She became more and more distracted over the years, often overwhelmed by whatever it was she could see in front of her. She would spend days staring out the window, at the copse.

She threw herself at men. As a child, this had been a great source of distress, an unstoppable compulsion on her part, something he'd watched again and again, sad and dismayed, hoping for a cure and not getting one. It was something he alternately hid from and studied.

Every man she slept with was an easy conquest, each she tossed aside. For some reason, Cosmo had hung around the longest, appointing himself her official guardian, a joke even Cosmo went along with. At Stonegate love was free. Sex was free-floating. That was the idea. But it only cultured an atmosphere of doubt and uncertainty, a dense cloud of sexual jealousies and unsaid fears. Cosmo didn't like or get these ideas at all and lingered around Olivia regardless of who else she was sleeping with.

Olivia had been the most attractive woman at Stonegate, by far. August had been aware of that. The community centred around her, or so it felt. It'd been a strange thing to witness, a tangible force, like a suck in the air, towards her. People were always looking at her or for her, or talking about her. It was there, always. But it wasn't.

Olivia, however, he knew was bored and often irritated by the attention. He'd sensed it made her feel trapped. He'd always had the impression she'd gone to Stonegate to hide rather than stand out.

The next day was the spring solstice and the clocks went forward, stretching the days. August had never really felt the change; until then it had simply meant more light, longer hours of discomfort.

He lay in bed breathing thinly while the planet shifted on its axis, keenly sensing the turn. As the earth tilted minutely, leaning forward a little closer to the sun, he felt a small movement in his spine, a gentle realignment of cartilage and bone. His neck felt looser, his shoulders too. His ribs floated wider, or seemed to expand. It was a moment, just a moment, of release, followed by a slower feeling – a pushing movement through him. Bones and the muscles around them unlocked as the feeling travelled down his torso, his legs and arms.

Outside the birds talked, the streets were quiet.

August got up and dressed quickly without fuss, ate a breakfast of brown toast and coffee. When he opened his front door the dawn greeted him, pale, steely, marking itself across his cheeks, his body. Higher up and behind, an immense expanse of sky hung yellow and creamy, a haze of warmth soon about to impose itself on the earth. At its centre he thought he could see a more defined blur, an orange swipe of pollen: the sun, struggling.

He could get to Harrow-on-the-Hill and back before the deli opened, if he hurried. There were so many things now pressing at him from behind, prodding him, phantom fingers in his back. They made his questions about his father seem a less difficult knot to unravel. He'd already decided not to ring first, not give the Chalmins the option of instant rejection, cutting him dead in the darkness of a phone call. What could he say in a second of introduction over the phone? No, he'd take his chances, turn up. It'd be early morning, eight-ish when he arrived. He saw no reason why it shouldn't be easy. They would know the answer to his question; was he or was he not their grandson? It was as simple as that. It would either be a denial or a confirmation. The onus was on him, not them, and he'd already guessed the worst. He took no props, no bands for his wrists, no book. No pills. He wanted to be awake not drugged, present for the journey and what he might find at the end of it.

On the tube he sat primly. Ankles together, back straight, hands on knees. Eyes closed. He sat and concentrated on breathing evenly: in and out, in and out, taking shallow, measured breaths. He could hear the train rattle, feel it jerk and roll as it sped along its way. He heard the doors open when it came to a station, sensed the rush and rustle of bodies entering and exiting. He could smell malt vinegar faintly, and Ribena and million-year-old dried skin. He heard a Walkman on loudly, near him, playing the new album by The Chemical Brothers. The journey was okay. Not too bad at all, as long as he kept his eyes closed.

*

The Chalmin house was set back from the road in a residential street in a smart part of Harrow-on-the-Hill. As he looked at it from the gate his skin crawled a little with a kind of guilt, as though the house was looking back at him with an aloof insouciance. A green Volvo Estate was parked in the drive. In front of the door there was a brass mud rail for shoes. Freshly planted crocuses in the window boxes. The house, detached, with a sloping roof, was outwardly correct. It wasn't too big or too small, or unusual in any way. Its neatness was self-assured. It was a home. Carefully tended, sharply restrained.

August loitered and thought about the gap between himself and the front door. It was a small distance, maybe twenty or thirty metres. The people inside hadn't seen him since he was two weeks old. Their worlds had never clashed by accident or design. They had never, for whatever reason, wanted to know him. He could keep it that way if he chose, he could leave quietly, content with seeing the house – not walking into their world. They'd moved away from Sussex, from the death of their son, turfed his mother out, years ago.

But he'd come all this way.

Thirteen stops.

It would be quick, over in minutes maybe, perhaps smoothing everything into place.

He opened the gate, feeling his legs weaken as he stepped towards the house. He had to push himself, drive his body as he walked, his resolve thinning, his nerves in revolt. When he got to the front door he saw a button bell neatly fastened to the side of the frame. He put his finger on it lightly, stroking it for a moment, his questions both crammed in on him and vanished, not knowing what his first words would be, his cheeks smarting, his eyes feeling loose in his head. He pushed the button and it buzzed coldly, abruptly, the sound of an electric shock. He closed his eyes and swayed and smiled to himself and breathed in. He waited for several moments, letting the time extend, loosening the fear in him.

No one came to the door.

He even buzzed again.

He went to the side of the door and peered over the white netting in the window, into a room of browns and coldness, lots of wood. He examined the petals of the crocuses in the window box on the ledge, their thinness: slivers of skin. Despite their random and vibrant, tigerish colouring, their Bohemian brilliance, there was something about the way they were planted that was fastidious; unsuitable for them. He bit his lip and his eyes filled a little. He turned and walked back to the gate and slowly, heavily, back to the station.

* * *

By the time he got back to the deli he'd recovered from his disappointment, harboured it and anchored it to himself, letting it bump along inside him in some quiet hidden bay. It was okay. He'd go again, another day. It'd been good for him to do and not imagine, to see and not wonder about the Chalmins, where they lived. He'd go again.

The deli stopped selling chocolate around the same time as the shift in seasons. The shop became too hot. So for most of the morning he and Henry filled in their spare time unpacking alternatives to chocolate from boxes: sesame snaps, natural fruit bars, cinnamon balls, amaretti biscuits, flapjacks, doughnuts, stem ginger, liquorice. They arranged these on the top of the display fridge, making it even more of a battlement, the treats like broken glass along the top. They worked in comfort, a passive rhythm, and August was pleased. He still couldn't understand Henry's recent mood swings. Had she made a pass at him the other day? Had he been ungracious? Maybe her pride was wounded? Or maybe there was nothing to it.

They worked together without mishap until the end of the day. There'd been a steady flow of customers and a large order delivered from a French patisserie, several trays of tiny exquisite cakes and petits fours: rich, three-finger-deep ovals of cassis or mint stamped with black cherry crucifixes, hearts of the densest, darkest chocolate mousse decorated with sugar violets, rafts of Madeira sponge piled with strawberries dripping in glycerine. All too much for Henry, who glowed visibly at their appearance and then instantly took control of arranging them in the fridges along the far wall. It kept her busy, her back to him, for most of the afternoon.

When business slowed and finally dwindled to an empty shop, August felt more relaxed. He wanted to get Henry back, as his friend, as quickly as possible. He looked over at her. She was opening the last cake box, laying its flaps open on the shelf in front of the cheeses. He breathed in deeply.

'Y-you know what you said.'

Henry looked up. She frowned, as though she didn't.

'The other day.'

She went red. Her lashes skittered.

He wanted her to know his genuine affection for her, that she often made him laugh or smile, that she'd always provided him, vicariously, with a sense of buoyance. That she made his world better.

'Well,' August smiled at her shoulder, a full, wide smile, his teeth like sticks of chalk. 'I . . .' his lips quivered. 'I think you're wonderful too.'

There was a long silence.

Then Henry laughed.

August's lips and teeth stuck together, air knocked against his throat. He saw himself on the deli's floor, his eyes closed.

'Uuh. Forget it, Gus. I . . .'

'Oh, of course . . . I was just wondering. I just thought . . .'

'No, I mean. It was nothing. I . . .' Henry's cheeks were crimson. For a second he thought she was going to cry.

'Heeeey!'

Cosmo was standing in the entrance to the shop.

'Mon champignon!' Henry shrieked.

'Cherry!' Cosmo shouted back.

August groaned, but also felt relief. For the first time he was glad Cosmo had interrupted.

'All right, Gus,' Cosmo said, flatly.

August didn't answer. It was minutes before the shop was due to close. He began to collect pies and tartlets from the window.

'What're you doing next, beautiful?' Cosmo asked Henry.

'Nothing. My boyfriend's out of town.'

'Stupid man,' Cosmo drawled. 'I'd never leave you alone for a moment.'

Henry giggled.

'Come and have a drink with me, round the corner.'

'Now?'

'Why not? My special lady's gone away too.'

August fought to stop himself from turning round.

Henry looked at him, surprised. 'Who?'

'The babe from the flower shop across the road. She's stood me up. She was supposed to have a drink with me tonight, but she's gone away for a while they said at the shop. To nurse her old aunt.'

'Oh.' Henry's eyebrows knitted, thrown.

'Oh, gooo on. Make an old man happy.' Cosmo smiled, showing a movie star's set of teeth; he danced his eyebrows up and down and then made a strange growling noise.

Henry found this amusing and smiled, but seemed unsure of herself. She glanced at Cosmo, then at August's bent-over body in the window.

'Can Gus come?'

August felt his ears go hot. 'I can't,' he said loudly, straightening up.

Cosmo looked annoyed, his eyes flared a little. 'Perhaps he's got something else to do.'

August turned to look at Henry, trying to shake his head minutely.

Henry lowered her eyelids.

An excuse didn't come fast enough. He knew he couldn't keep this up, keep Cosmo away from him. Contain fog.

'Okay,' he said. 'Just one.'

'Cool, man,' Cosmo replied, covering his displeasure. Trying to appear in control, he began moving his lips as he read the words *Patam Peperium* on a pot on top of the cheese cabinet.

While August and Henry shut up shop, Cosmo stood and watched.

The Fat Brown Horse on Uxbridge Road had brown walls and beige flock wallpaper inlaid with lyres. Smoke turned liquid hung in the air. The drinkers were mainly men, middle-aged with pink bald spots and yellowed hair. Behind the main bar there was a large room with tables and chairs and moss green banquettes. Cosmo sat on a banquette, bongo drumming on the table top to a tune in his head. Henry was in the Ladies.

August made his way back to the table from the bar with the second round he'd bought, Cosmo having forgotten his wallet.

'Gusss,' Cosmo hailed him when he sat down, still drumming. Behind him, on a large VH1 screen, played an old video of Prefab Sprout singing 'Appetite' and August wished Cosmo would shut up so he could listen to it. The drumming, the half-baked New Age jargon; Henry lapping it all up. August had sat through the first pint seething. Also taking the opportunity, now they were finally face to face, to study him closely, the long head and long chin with its permanent grin. Deep lines around his mouth, grin lines. Grin lines around the eyes too, making them seem youthful, cute even. Strong arched eyebrows. And thin, wispy brown hair, a little grizzled. Cosmo, he realized, looked nothing like him. Cosmo hadn't noticed him staring.

'Want one?' Cosmo asked, proffering a bag of Pork Scratchings August had also bought him.

'I'm fine.'

Henry appeared back from the Ladies.

'Uggggghhhhh!' she made a face at the packet.

'Oink, oink!' Cosmo laughed, waving a scratching near her face.

'You eat filth!' She screwed her face up in disapproval.

Cosmo oinked again, then laughed. 'I used to eat macrobiotic,' he said, through a mouthful of pork fat.

'What's that?' Henry grimaced.

'Eating like Yin and Yang.'

August cringed and rolled his eyes with impatience.

'You know.'

'No, I don't,' Henry retorted.

'With the seasons.'

August shook his head and almost laughed at the ridiculous prospect. He smiled kindly at Henry, unable to contain his silence any longer. 'It's a special diet,' he said shortly. 'Tailored to a person's *spiritual requirements*.'

Cosmo was pleased, nodding his head in agreement. 'Yeah, man. I used to grow my own vegetables too, once. Had a huge vegetable garden.' He chewed. 'When I lived in a commune.'

August's pale eyes bulged. All those days he didn't eat. In the kitchen, the rotting sacks of potatoes. The thin soups, like gutter water. *Stop talking*, he wanted to scream. There was no vegetable garden, only mud and refuse and a caravan on bricks outside in the ruined garden. A derelict chicken coop. No broccoli in season, no petits pois.

He picked up his pint glass, tilting it to his lips. *Incredible.* Cosmo was older, he was older, old enough to be unrecognizable. Decades had passed, the world had changed around them. But his feelings, they were still the same. Still as strong. Mischievous as a poltergeist. Cosmo had taken off his jacket and he could smell the acidy sweat, sharp in his nostrils. He saw the lines of sweat dripping down Cosmo's stomach as he paraded his cock about in the garden.

'Gus used to live in a commune,' Henry said, smiling proudly at him.

August's pint glass slipped, pouring beer over his throat, his shirt. His stomach dropped through him. He'd never told Henry about his life at Stonegate, never told anyone in fact. He put down the glass.

Cosmo, visibly surprised, stopped drumming.

'How do *you* know?' August asked, dabbing at his shirt.

'Your mother mentioned it once, when she came into the shop. Why, what's the matter?'

'Nothing.'

'Where was it, man?' Cosmo asked. He started to drum again.

Where was it, man ... August thought. *A long way away, years* ...

The drumming picked up speed, Cosmo's eyes were on him, a line of sweat rolling from his temple ...

Where was it, man? ...

In you, August thought. *That's where it was. In your hands.*

'Yorkshire,' he said quietly.

The drumming stopped again. Cosmo's face lit up.

'Whereabouts?'

'In the Pennines, the northwest. Near a small village.'

Cosmo's eyes filmed with water. 'No!'

Yes, August thought. He nodded, this time taking a measured swig of lager.

Henry was staring at him in disbelief.

'Lothersdale,' he said slowly. 'A house called Stonegate Hall.'

Cosmo clutched his head with both hands, squashing his cowboy hat. 'No way!' he shouted. 'I've had this feeling all along. I know you, man, but I . . . dunno. I wasn't sure. Wow.'

August had nurtured a dim hope if this bomb ever went off, it might be in a controlled explosion. This hadn't happened. August was sullen. His present, his future, his life, again in the hands of a moron.

Cosmo glowed at August. 'Yeah, you've always looked familiar. It's been bugging me for months. Where had I seen you before, where?'

August shrugged politely. He knew Cosmo hadn't given him a moment's thought.

'So you lived at the big house?'

He still doesn't remember me, August realized.

'Yup.'

'When?'

'When I was a child.'

Cosmo's face was serious.

'You're . . . No.'

August nodded. 'Olivia's son.'

Cosmo nodded his head also. He kept nodding, absorbing this information, quite obviously amazed.

August stared sadly at his pint glass, almost empty.

Then Cosmo rose, his eyes teary, his arms open. 'Brother!'

He hugged August across the table, crushing him to his chest, holding him for several moments.

August froze in the hug.

Cosmo released him after a while then sat back on the banquette, rubbing the skin around his eyes.

'Jesus, God,' he said shaking his head, incredulous. 'Little August. You grew big.'

August said nothing. He hadn't expected to feel what had welled up. From nowhere, a sentiment, betraying him, his past. Nostalgia. The same need to make friends, to be recognized by Cosmo.

'I *knew* all the time, man. Yeah.' Cosmo's eyes flickered over August's hair. 'But you know,' he tapped his head. 'I was boozing then. The old grey matter turned to mulch. It was a long time ago.'

'Mmmm,' August agreed.

Then Cosmo stopped, as if just struck with a clever idea.

'Did you recognize me?'

August shook his head slowly, innocently.

'No.'

Cosmo looked hurt, then dismissed this feeling.

'Yeeeaaah,' his face suddenly changed, becoming pinched. Then cold. He pursed his lips together in displeasure. 'Yeah, I knew Livvy quite well, hah!' he squinted, as though trying to recall her face. 'We were together for a while.'

'I think I remember,' August nodded.

'The tart she was, old Livvy,' he chuckled.

August felt himself grow, the nostalgia vanished; he wanted to pulverize Cosmo's face.

Henry's eyes were wide. 'That's not very nice,' she reprimanded him.

Cosmo snorted, uncaring, and laughed at her as though

she was possibly the same type; like it was all waiting for her too.

'Olivia? Noooo. She was cold-hearted. Had it coming to her, she did. She was kicked out in the end. God she was mean. Hope she's been hurt like all the hurting she did. She happy now, is she?'

Cosmo shook his head, his eyes widening, suddenly remembering something interesting. He stared at August, his eyes became even wider as the idea spread, his face slowly forming into a knowing grin. August was uncomfortable: this was the Cosmo he was afraid of. Cosmo's face had turned derisive. Wicked.

'And you, little August. You've changed a lot too. Grown so much like your father.' He smiled as he took a sip of his pint. 'Haven't you?'

Goosebumps rose on August's neck, a thin panic gripped him, flittered about inside. He knew this was why he'd agreed to come to the pub. He was numb, and now forced to say something ridiculous. Cosmo's eyes were on him, knowing his thoughts, watching him squirm, barely able to contain his secret knowledge.

August remained silent.

Cosmo snorted. 'Hah!' he laughed to emphasize the point. He laughed some more, shaking his head.

August felt himself liquefying in front of Cosmo. Henry was staring at each of them, shocked.

'You mean you still don't *know*?'

August's mouth was dry.

Every sad moment he'd ever had in his life, every self-hating day, all these days fell on him. He felt fragile and fierce at once. Impatient and slow. His body was failing him quietly, he wanted to know and then leave.

'About who?' he asked.

Cosmo sipped his pint, then put the glass down on the table. Carefully, he laid both his hands on his thighs and began to stroke them.

'You ask your mother,' Cosmo said, looking at him, slow and deliberate. Loving the power he had right then. 'About Edward.'

The words shot past August like missiles, words he'd always wanted to hear. They were out. Edward. A name. It was solid, like an ingot. A father he looked like. Edward, he'd been *right*.

August rocked backwards and forwards in himself, in a vacuum of sound, hating Cosmo and his reason, a cruel one, for telling him this. Getting his own back on his mother. Cosmo wanted to put him down, hurt him for being made a fool of. Hurt his mother. Instead he'd done him a favour.

August's legs trembled as he stood up from the table.

'You must have known,' Cosmo half-laughed, looking him up and down.

'Yes,' August said, thinly.

Henry talked excitedly all the way back to the deli, trying to be supportive and comforting, but she was more shaken up than he was, and managed to say all the wrong things, annoying August, making him close up. He'd wanted to go straight home to be alone to absorb Cosmo's information, to stare at a wall for hours. But Henry had forgotten her satchel at the deli and persuaded him to walk back with her to get it.

When they reached the deli August put the key in the front door, pausing for the familiar give as it turned, the clunk of metal. When he opened the door, he was caught off guard by the lifeless shop. The windows were empty, the olive table bare. The ceiling seemed higher, the walls thinner. The pavlova casings tied to the wagon wheel dangled like lynched bodies.

They walked through the deli into the café and August switched on a lamp. The butter coloured walls were instantly warm and soothing.

'I'll wait up here,' he said to Henry.

She nodded and went down the stairs to the office. August perched on one of the café tables and closed his eyes. There was so much to think about he couldn't think at all. Edward. He bounced the word off the walls.

Edward, Edward, Edward.

Ask your mother.

He could already hear the sound of her voice. There was something pathetic about it, reeking of insincerity, manners. Platitudinous charm. Except when she was really angry, only then was she sincere. Then her voice had a coldness which made him shiver. She bared her teeth when she was angry and her jaw became implacably set. It was only when she was angry he could see who she was.

He sensed heat from another body, could smell Pears soap. He opened his eyes.

Henry was standing in front of him, frowning.

'You're always so sad,' she said, shifting her weight from one leg to the other, moving a bit closer to him. August breathed out audibly, downcast, his eyes tracing her throat, her ears, the down on her jaw line. Henry reached out and put her hand on the side of his face. August held it, instinctively, pressing his lips and nose into her palm. Henry stepped closer, into the open V of his thighs. He looked up and smiled at her, carefully. She touched his lips, running her fingers along them and then along the sharp edges of his teeth.

'I like these,' she whispered.

She stepped closer and they embraced with the tightness of a clam closing, arms and legs slipping into one another, stomachs and chests flat.

They began to kiss.

August tried to kiss Henry with all the tenderness he had, to entwine his tongue gently, lovingly, with hers. Tried to give her all the warmth and love he had inside to give someone; everything which had lain wasted for so long.

But something was wrong.

Henry's tongue was thin and stiff, like a budgerigar's and deep inside her throat.

He tried to find it, but couldn't and his own tongue waved thickly, like an eel. He kept trying, but her mouth was slippery, empty. *Oh no*, he wailed inside. In his fantasies, their tongues *fitted*, locked easily.

She began to pull at his clothes and they struggled slowly, biting softly at each other's shoulders, throats, chins. Pulling each other's hair. All the while, August fought back his disappointment. *I can't even kiss properly*. Desperate, he began to unbutton her blouse. She was wearing a pale blue bra underneath and her breasts were soft and heavy, her skin white as flour. He reached out to touch them, but she stopped him, unzipping his jacket.

'Laisse moi,' she whispered.

August was horrified. All he wanted was love. Intimacy. Good kissing.

Henry bit the top button of his shirt, tugging hard at it. It came off in her mouth. She glowed at him with a wide and alluring grin. Then swallowed it. She unbuttoned the second with her fingers, still smiling into his eyes; then a third, a fourth, the fifth. As she opened his shirt gently August floated. He closed his eyes, arching his back a little, hearing a beat in his head, a pulse, *his* pulse in his temples, a rhythm. The melody was like lava, flowing richly in him. Inside him plates were shifting.

Edward. He wanted to know who his father was. See him, stare at him, marvel. Hold his hand, pinch him. Watch him laugh. He wanted to know his opinions and what he smelt of. Did he have any odd marks on his skin? He wanted to look at his father. Watch him sit, eat, sleep. Absorb the things he always did unconsciously, his everyday habits. Imprint them in a moment on his memory, the things he would've seen him do over the last thirty-three years. He wanted his outline traced on him, an intrinsic recognition. He felt well for the first time ever, since he could feel. He was floating in fluid – warm, saline, quiet.

'*Oh, my God!*' Henry screamed.

August looked down at his chest.

In his navel had sprouted a small whorl of leaves.

The next morning, August woke up with a dream still present in his memory.

He was standing in a field hospital, in a jungle. Outside the tent it was humid, the air full of rain flies. He stood in the middle, in a wide, central aisle. On either side of him were rows of women in green canvas makeshift beds. Each woman had just given birth and lay waiting to be attended. Their placentas were still attached to them, brown and viscous, draped over their legs and bedclothes. He was mesmerized by the sight, unable to move. Though he knew they needed it, he couldn't help them.

Something Cosmo said now stuck out from all the rest. *Kicked out in the end* . . . He struggled with this, half-knowing it was the truth, hauling it out from behind his dreams. An anxiety leaked inside him, a liquid fright; his mother, the past, it was all slipping out from behind an infinite blacked-out pane of glass.

He remembered the fight.

'Fuck you,' he'd heard Jude shout. He was watching them from the corner of the common room at Stonegate Hall. He was a boy, maybe twelve years old.

'This is the last straw, Olivia. You want it all, every man here. I've had enough, so have we all. Making a play for Michael. He's mine, keep away from him, can't you? It's as if you have no centre of your own. Nothing that's yours. So you run about trying to fill a hole, plug it with a man. You're so empty.'

Jude stopped, her fists clenched. She was a heavy woman, passionate and uncomfortable with her body. Her eyes were completely engorged, staring at his mother, but also into a void.

'I want you out, out of here,' she said, simply. 'I should *never* have let you stay in the first place, I should've known you'd be trouble. But I felt sorry for you, after Luke died. I should've been suspicious. Should have realized something was up. You think I don't know who that man was, the one who came looking for you,' her voice wavered. 'I *saw* him,' she spat. Luke was a friend of mine too, remember? I knew him long before he met you. You're so *transparent*, Olivia. I want you out, as soon as possible.'

Jude's face was contorted, the rims of her eyes were red.

His mother had kept quiet, stood looking out the window, into the copse, with her arms folded on her chest.

This memory spilt from August quietly, like a vapour, bringing with it a feeling of guilt. Jude's anger was out of his grasp and he struggled to process its cause. His mother had left the commune because Jude had kicked her out.

He thought about what Cosmo'd said.

Edward. Was it a name picked from a hat? Someone Cosmo had confused with someone else, fabricated through the mist of his hangovers? Was he a man he'd invented as an excuse for his own romantic failure with his mother? Could he possibly believe Cosmo?

He'd watched a lot at the commune, mouth closed. That was how he'd spent his childhood.

Now it appeared he'd missed something.

He pictured Luke thrown from his bike, through the air. *Thwack.* Felt a faint thud against his chest. Why had she persisted in telling him he was Luke's son? What was wrong with Edward? Why hide him? Was he the man Jude had mentioned? He looked across to the curtains and saw the morning was bright, the sun's strong, morning rays prodding against them, trying to get in. He groaned, not wanting to leave his bed.

He felt unwilling, like not playing the game, wanted to remove himself from the world he'd woken up in. The shift had finally come but it'd made his heart falter. He'd woken up with new possibilities, but didn't want them.

He got up.

He wandered aimlessly around his flat. After a while he put on Massive Attack's 'Light my Fire'.

* * *

Henry was late into the deli so August went to the bank instead to get change. On his way he crossed the road to walk past Pollen. As he did he peered quickly inside, but couldn't see Leola. *My special lady* . . . what had Cosmo meant?

And Henry. That had happened too. He winced, ashamed of his navel, his body, what she must have seen and now think. His orangeness, his glowing nipples. Had she kissed him out of pity after what Cosmo had said, had it been a female act of compassion? It had to be. He was hardly her type, not macho like Cosmo or Yves – whom she was in love with. The embarrassment of the encounter ached. How could they ever get over it? And on top of it now she knew about Edward. Henry was the wrong person to know his secrets; she was still trying to forge her own identity and could be unpredictable. Overnight his identity had changed. He vowed to talk to her later, put her off – tell her Cosmo had lied.

When he reached Brook Green, he stopped abruptly. Not far off Cedric was sitting on a bench, talking to the woman who saw the twig in his ear. Her dress, all lilac and cream, all skirt falling in creases on her knees, waist disappearing into large folds of bosom, was a rapid of water lilies. Her eyes were peering into Cedric's and she was smiling at what he was saying. She had a Tupperware box on her lap.

August watched as she fed him a pickle, then wiped her fingers on her skirt. He saw her great breasts move sideways as she laughed, Cedric's hand resting on her knee, the gaze they held when they looked at each other.

He remembered his bad kissing, all the disappointment he'd had for so many years. Bad sex, quick, snatched, impersonal, unloving. Sex on drugs once, on drink many times, all with strangers. Nights of mistake.

Five years alone, and then what had happened with Henry. How could he have forgotten about his body? He'd been taken off guard. Her breasts, the small blue bra, her arms around him.

August walked on.

He could feel seedlings tickling him behind his ears. Little sprouts. Their fine roots entwining themselves with his blood's capillaries. His scalp moved sometimes, of its own accord, as if there were earthworms moving through soil underneath. His stubble tingled every morning, as though his face was alive, breathing. But he didn't want to say anything, to anyone. This resolve became stronger every day. The changes were the only things he felt sure of. They were company.

When he returned to the deli, Rose was grinding coffee into a bag, staring into space. August had never seen her dreamy. He guessed she was thinking of Salvadore. He took the bags of coins out of his pockets and put them on the counter.

'Pennies for your thoughts,' he said loudly.

'Oh,' she jumped and turned round to look at him. 'Oh, you caught me. I was far away.'

August smiled and showed his great big teeth, winningly.

'Where?'

Rose blushed.

August blushed back.

'I thought Salvadore was very dashing,' he said, encouragingly.

Rose nodded.

'Did you meet him on your trip?'

'Yes.'

'He looked like a real gentleman.'

Her eyes became distant and she nodded again. She pursed her lips together as if she was about to say something reluctantly.

'That was how we met. He helped carry my suitcase when we boarded the ship.'

Despite her initial shyness, he could tell Rose wanted

to say more. The deli was empty. Henry, he guessed, still hadn't come in.

'Then what happened?'

Rose's eyes shone.

'We had dinner that night,' she said, imagining the ship's dining room in front of her. 'And then every night after. It was . . . yes, some time before I realized his interest in me was . . . romantic.'

August went pink.

'Oh, August. It's all so . . .' She looked at her feet then up again. She smiled, shyly. 'His presence in my life is still a bit of a shock. Like it's happening to someone else.'

August nodded. A lump had gathered in his throat.

'I know what you mean. My whole life is over there,' he made a motion towards the window. 'In the distance.'

Rose looked at him, the skin between her eyes pleating. She continued.

'At first I just thought it was the voyage, you know. The constant light. It was dazzling. I thought it might be tampering with my senses.' She smiled at herself. 'But, slowly, he made his . . . intentions known. He always wanted to hold my hand when we went for walks on deck. It was very icy, you know.'

August nodded as if he knew.

'Oh, he's a gentleman to the core.' Rose became more confident. Her eyes widened with more memories. 'We went on trips! To see the seals, in one of those wee outboard boats. And the penguins too. We walked on ice floes.'

She blushed crimson.

'We drank champagne from a *thermos flask*. Can you imagine!' She clutched her neck, catching her breath.

August was hopelessly swept up.

'And the landscapes. We gazed at them for *hours*. Like nothing on earth, nothing I'll ever see again. Ice as thick as the walls of Fort Knox. As solid as concrete. All *pushed* up from the planet's crust. It made sculptures. Rolled itself into flaps . . . like some enormous white carpet.'

August wanted to go there. Now his eyes were better, he could go anywhere.

'One morning, I saw an orange smudge in the sky. So delicate,' she blinked at him earnestly, trying to make him see it too. 'As though a flower had rubbed pollen against the sky, as though the sun had grazed itself against the world. At first I thought it was the sun, but it wasn't. The real one was much stronger, above it and behind.'

Unaccountably, August felt uneasy.

'I know it sounds silly. But I'd hoped it was a sign. You know. About Salvadore. That things would be fine between us. It was so unusual. Everything around me was.'

August suppressed the urge to walk away.

'Salvadore knew so much about the region, about its climate. He put me right.'

Rose imitated his voice. 'Ahhh, that is something unusual, something quite brilliant. A spectacle.'

August's throat constricted, his breath became audible.

'What was it?' he asked.

'A sun dog. A mock sun. Ice crystals in the air were being refracted in the light. It made an illusion. It only looked like the sun, behind a cloud. But it wasn't.' Rose smiled proudly at this knowledge. 'It's just one of nature's many tricks.'

August wanted to tell Rose about Edward, ask her stupid, ludicrous questions. Compare his life to hers. Ask her if she knew how it felt to spend a lifetime under a vague, looming cloud. To be constantly aware of an impinging greyness, a presence which was large and indistinct always in the background. Tell her about the falseness in his life, the father he'd never known; that he didn't know whose son he was.

He showed his teeth and smiled.

'I'm sure it was a sign,' he said to Rose.

When Henry breezed in she was flushed and bothered.

'My alarm didn't go off. I'm sorry.'

She didn't look at August.

'It wasn't too busy. Don't worry,' Rose reassured.

August shuffled his feet and cleared his throat. 'I'm just going downstairs,' he said to neither of them.

Rose smiled and Henry avoided his eyes.

He left the deli and went downstairs, much more bothered about their kiss. *Not again*, he railed inside.

After putting his jacket away he went into the café and began wiping down the coffee machine. He was annoyed with himself, preoccupied with Henry's aloofness. As he wiped, he strained his ears to overhear Rose and Henry talking.

'What's wrong, dear? You look lost.'

'Oh . . . no, nothing,' Henry muttered.

'Are you sure?'

'It's just . . .' Henry stopped.

'It's just what?'

'I don't think August is . . .'

'What?'

'Well.'

'*Well?*'

'Ill.'

'You think he's ill?'

'Haven't you noticed?'

'No.'

There was a silence.

'Well . . .' Rose ruminated. 'I suppose . . . yes. There was something. In the winter, his skin was quite bad, on his arms. It was eczema. Poor thing.'

'I don't know about eczema,' Henry replied.

'Oh?'

'I think he doesn't wash.'

'What do you mean?'

'Bad hygiene.'

'Oh, *no.*' Rose tutted. 'Oh, I don't think so. Not August.'

'I do.'

'Whatever makes you think that?'

'Oh, nothing special,' Henry said quickly.

August stood very still in the kitchen alcove, both relieved and alarmed by Henry's deduction.

* * *

That day spring unfolded its arms, relaxed and settled. The trees lining the streets danced with blossom. White and pale pink. Fuchsia. The blossoms were heavy, blowsy with adolescence. Above them, the sky was a bolt of china blue, the finest satin. The good weather had meant a steady stream of people into the deli. There'd been early lunchers, lunch-time lunchers, and in mid-afternoon, people were still wandering in to buy picnics to eat on the Green, or to eat in the café.

August had worked distractedly. While prepping up the lunch-time sandwiches, he'd been preparing his speech to Henry. While serving gnocchi au gratin to customers, he'd been deliberating on how best to approach his mother. A letter, a phone call? Should he just show up at her cottage? Edward; did the Chalmins know him? Could he ask them? He made a mental note to ask Rose for the morning off as soon as possible so he could go back to Harrow-on-the Hill.

He was garnishing two French onion soups in the kitchen alcove when he heard the familiar rusty voice from the deli.

'Where's August this fine day?'

August smiled, imagining Cedric – glaring at Henry.

There was no answer.

'Has he vanished? Has he?' Cedric demanded.

'No, he's next door,' Henry replied curtly.

August watched the large, tectonic crusts of bread float on the surface of the soup. Shifting. He saw Henry standing in front of him, right there at the table the soups were going to.

'There you are, my gorgeous cockatoo.'

Henry who wasn't talking to him or looking at him.

'One minute, Cedric.'

Cedric waited near the alcove while August carried the soups to two women by the window. He took bread and cutlery too. Cedric. He felt a stab of guilt. The last time he'd seen Cedric he'd been mean and unreasonable. On his way back, he stopped at the cappuccino machine.

'I'm sorry . . . I was so mean the other day.'

'Good, I'm glad you are.'

'Will you forgive me?'

'In a few weeks.'

'I saw you on a bench on the green earlier, with the lady who was there that day.'

'Ah, Flora.' Cedric's baggy grey eyes watered. 'Isn't she lovely?'

'Very. Her face is familiar.'

'Most classical beauties are. Anyway, I came to thank you.'

'For what?'

'For being mean to me.'

August shook his head.

'Oh, it was rotten. But if you hadn't been so beastly, Flora would never have rescued me.'

August sighed.

'She's Polish, you know.'

'Really?'

'Fled the Nazis, lives round here. Lots of Poles in Chiswick.'

August nodded.

'I'm in love.'

'Good.'

'You don't care.'

'Yes I do.'

'What's got into you these days?'

'Cedric, I'm busy.'

Cedric peered at him over his spectacles. He kept peering as August made a pot of tea, stuffing bags into the pot, putting cups down roughly.

He leaned a little closer.

'You have a twig in your ear,' he whispered.

August jumped, batting the side of his head. 'Jesus Christ, Cedric!'

'Only joking,' he giggled.

'Cedric, go away!'

'You're angry.'

August took a deep breath, counting in his head. He looked the old man in the eye.

'I'm not well at the moment.'

'Ahhhh.'

'Not well at all.'

'What is it?'

'I don't know.'

'Twig fever?'

August stopped what he was doing. He turned, hands on hips and breathed out. 'Yes. Something like that.'

'Then I have the cure.'

'What?'

'Tea tree oil.' Cedric guffawed into his beard.

'Cedric, I'm busy.'

'I'm leaving, I'm leaving.' He held up his hands as though at gunpoint.

'Cedric.'

'What?'

Does Edward look anything like you?

'I'm happy for you.'

Cedric peered at him over his spectacles.

'Thank you. For a moment I thought you were jealous.'

Cedric blew him a kiss and left.

In the office August hurried through some paperwork, aware the day was almost over and soon Henry would leave. He had plans. He'd apologize, ask her for a drink, tell her he'd developed a strange and unusual allergy. Explain he'd kept it hidden, had been worried it might make Rose unhappy to have him around the food. He'd tell her it was receding. He'd ask her to ignore what Cosmo had said, he'd been drinking. He needed to throw her off, make a quiet place for himself to find things out, at his own pace.

His head hurt. The floor of the office was cool. August decided to lie down on it, take five minutes to breathe, empty his head.

He lay flat on the floor and closed his eyes. Behind the dark soapstone colours of his lids he saw Luke, arms crossed, laughing down at him, his Lucky Luke tattoo bulging on his arm.

Are you lucky? he asked.

His mother was behind him, her hair flying behind her head; she was being driven down a long drive. Next to her sat a cowboy. He couldn't see the cowboy's face, only his hat. Luke was laughing again, looking down at him.

All the time, he jeered, *you thought it was one of us*.

'Gus?'

Henry was standing at the door of the office, her eyes trying to conceal her amusement. August sat up quickly.

'Are you off?'

Henry nodded.

He spoke from the floor. 'I need to talk to you.'

'No you don't, Gus, really.'

'No, I do. I want to explain.'

'It's okay.'

'No, it's not.'

'I can't talk, Yves is waiting for me outside.'

'I have an illness,' August blurted.

Henry nodded.

'I don't know what it is. An allergy, a fungus of some kind. I've had it for months. At first the doctor thought it was eczema. In the winter . . .' he broke off.

Henry's eyes were glassy. She didn't want to know.

She wanted to forget about last night, pretend it'd never happened. He could see it in her eyes.

'Gus . . .' she started.

The phone rang. He looked at her, pleadingly.

Her face was sad all of a sudden, her eyes turned wet. The phone kept ringing. On and on. He ignored it, willing her on. *Say something*.

The phone bleated.

Henry walked to the desk and picked it up.

'Finlay's,' she said into the receiver.

August stared at his feet, a big man's feet.

'I'll just get him.' She motioned with the handset and he got up.

'Don't go yet,' he whispered, holding his hand over the mouthpiece. Henry put her finger to her lips. 'Shhhh.'

'Hello?'

'Hi, it's Jim.'

'Bye, Gus,' Henry whispered. She turned to go then stopped. She returned and stood in front of him, her eyes on his. 'You worry too much,' she said. 'Don't.'

She turned again and this time slipped out the door.

August waved, a little wave to where she'd been standing.

'What's up?' Jim asked.

'What?'

'What's up? What's going on?'

August looked into the palm of his free hand.

'I don't know. Nothing.'

A small pink flower had blossomed at its centre, pale pink, with five petals opening from a cluster of tiny, velour anthers.

'Are you okay?' Jim sounded a little worried.

August marvelled at its flawlessness, a star fallen from a distant planet.

'No, I'm fine. Busy day, that's all.'

'Isabel's having a party. Can you come?'

'When?' He was barely listening. He was gazing at the flower. He'd known it was only a matter of time.

'Next Friday.'

'Fine.'

'So, you'll come? I know you don't like parties.'

'I'd love to.'

'I haven't seen you for a while.'

'I've been ill.'

'You sound ill. What's wrong?'

'Nothing. I'm better.'

'Good.'

'Goodbye.'

August put the phone down.

He inspected his other palm. A flower had emerged there too. His hands had pale pink petal stars in them. Stigmata like blooms of breath, each petal a tiny dog's tongue. He brushed one against his mouth, letting the petals tickle his lips. It smelt of cut grass, mildly spiced. Chlorophyllic. He held his hands out in front of him. Flowers on flesh. Pink on pink. He felt glad for them, proud of them. Exquisitely adorned.

They were some sort of blessing.

Carefully, he picked the flowers off and saw they left no mark.

On his lips were yellow dots of powder.

August left the deli late. There'd been invoices that hadn't been filed or sorted in weeks. Being the start of the month there'd been credits that would soon be chased, new orders to make. When he eventually locked up it was dark. An unusual breeze stroked him between the shoulder blades. He looked up at the plane tree. Its arms were very far up, its leaves were limp with moisture and hung like bats. August walked to the edge of Lena Gardens and turned left. At the end of the street, from the far side of the road, he could see his front door. He frowned. Someone had left a roll of carpet on his front steps. It looked dirty and heavy. Perhaps one of his neighbours was moving out, or had just had a new one installed. He quickened his pace.

When he reached the bottom of the steps he realized it wasn't a carpet. A man was slumped on his stairs, asleep. August recognized his jacket, the skinny legs, the smell of stale whisky.

'Wake up, Cosmo,' he said as he began to climb the stairs. A surge of impatience rose in him.

'Cosmo, you bastard,' August said louder, in his ear. 'Wake up.' Beneath him Cosmo reminded him of a dead spider, crushed and shrivelled. He fought the urge to step on him.

Cosmo began to stir.

'Huh? Is that you . . . August?'

August put his key in the door. He wanted to leave Cosmo outside like the refuse he was, or to turn and kick him hard for all the wrong ideas he'd absorbed. For being kept so long in the dark. He wanted to kick Cosmo until his ribs broke.

'Gus, Gus, I was waiting for you. I didn't want to come to the deli. I know I embarrassed you. I . . .'

August still had the key in the door.

'I know I'm pathetic. A pathetic old man.' Cosmo sat up

but didn't look at him. 'I just wanted to talk.' He stared out at the street. 'After the other night, you know. I'm sorry I said what I did about your mother, telling you about Edward. It was wrong. I loved Olivia. Years ago. We all lived in the same house. Me and you. And her. Those years were my life, man. Everything. I just want to shoot the breeze. I was remembering all the times I had with her. I had a drink. She never really cared for me . . . only for him, you know. Edward.'

The words were like eels, alive in August's belly. He pushed his front door open.

'Come in,' he said, quietly.

Cosmo sat on the old leather sofa with his hands between his knees. His head was bent, his shoulders rounded. His battered cowboy hat nodded forward. He shifted a little, awkwardly.

'I've some whisky,' August offered.

Cosmo looked up, grateful.

August returned from the kitchen with a single malt, a couple of inches left in it. He handed Cosmo the bottle and a glass. Cosmo poured it, timidly.

August watched.

He was so obviously harmless, he mused, so obviously defeated. Just part of the puzzle; as stupid and hapless as himself. He didn't know exactly what he wanted to get out of him, why he'd let him in. *Tell me everything*, he wanted to say. *The full story. Order it chronologically. Speak slowly.*

Cosmo drained the whisky and rubbed his knees, wincing as he rubbed.

'Arthritis,' he complained. 'In both knees. Painful.

Especially in the winter.' He continued to rub, seeming lost, or to have forgotten what he was going to say.

'My mother,' August said, quickly. 'You said she never cared for you.'

Cosmo continued to rub his knees, as if he hadn't heard.

'Livvy?' he said after a long time.

'Yes.'

Cosmo looked up with bloodshot, vacant eyes and smiled.

'She'd had a bad shock. Cried a lot when she first came to live at Stonegate. Been turfed out by her in-laws.'

August's eyes widened. 'What do you mean?'

Cosmo shook his head. 'They'd thrown her out. After Luke died. I don't know why, exactly . . . there was trouble.'

'They hated her,' August retorted. '*She left*. They didn't want to support her after my fath . . .' he stopped himself. 'After Luke died,' August continued, reddening, keeping to the story he'd heard all his life. 'Sh-she t-told me she wouldn't let them keep me. They wanted to raise me. Look after me themselves. But she left. To bring me up her own way.'

Cosmo wasn't interested, he continued to rub his legs.

August was angry. For the first time it hit him, the full and inherent rot of the lie he'd been told. How could Luke's parents *ever* have wanted to keep him? He wasn't their grandson.

Cosmo looked up and smiled faintly. 'All I know is Livvy was in a jam when she arrived.' Then his face became blank. 'She kept to herself, wouldn't speak to anyone for a long time. But eventually . . . after a couple of months, she thawed out. *I* joked her out of it. I did it.' He came to life again, shooting August a look of pride. 'But . . .' he let out a heavy breath, pulling his bottom lip over his top. 'I always knew. Yeah. Always did. She was using me. I think she used me for some kind of . . . warmth. That's what she said it was anyway, when she was drunk. But I,' again he sighed heavily as though annoyed he was talking about it all. He sipped his whisky. 'Never made her happy,' he shook his head regretfully. 'Never did. She never saw me. For years I tried . . . to joke about. Make her see I was a laugh. Damn it! I was a handsome son-of-a-bitch back then . . . I tried to make her see that other women noticed me. Make her jealous. Lord knows I tried with your mother . . .' he sniffed and looked innocently at August for support.

August frowned, repulsed.

'Then this man turned up. Years after she arrived. A giant he was. Big face. Big, shaggy beard. Older than your mother by ten years or so.'

August felt his eyes prickle. He didn't want to hear.

'Livvy wouldn't talk to him. So he sat outside on the stone step for a whole night and day and wouldn't go. He had something with him, wrapped in a bundle. Said his name was Edward, kept asking Jude to pass her notes. So she spoke to him eventually. God did she! Flew at him in a rage. Then she cried when he left. Never understood it. We never saw him again. Livvy never mentioned him either. But we all knew who he was. It was obvious.'

'Why?'

Cosmo's eyelids fluttered. His face took on the same derisive expression as in the pub. It made August feel right to hate him.

'His eyes.'

August's eyes began to water. He wiped them and tried to concentrate. He studied Cosmo, picking around Cosmo's form, trying to root inside him for a shred of integrity, gauging Cosmo's evidence. Hating him. Needing him to tell this story. Could he ever believe him, a drunk who'd loved his mother and whom his mother had rejected?

Cosmo looked up at him again and held his gaze.

'This man's eyes had no colour either. Nooossir,' he shook his head. 'Pale as ice.' He shuddered. 'A spook's eyes. That's what'd been bugging me about you all this time. It was your eyes. I'd only seen them once before.

'*I* was the one who told Edward to clear off, told him we'd get the police if he didn't leave. I saw them then. Up close. Eyes that weren't human. Eyes like yours.' He said all this as though he were delivering the most banal news, reading out the weather report.

Cosmo stopped talking, as if he'd suddenly run out of fuel. His head fell heavily on to his chest, and a light droning sound came from deep in his nose. On the sofa he looked pathetic, wizened, a cowboy who'd been trampled by his own horse. August felt hot. Injustice released itself in him, churning his stomach, melting the marrow in his bones. He gazed unfocused around the room taking in its shapes and colours. On the mantelpiece the dead hollyhocks were still in the big crystal vase. They were tea brown and tissue-like but he wouldn't remove them, not now.

Cosmo snored a little louder.

* * *

Cosmo had been unable to stumble the short distance home. He'd slept the night on the sofa, fully clothed. August had watched him for some time, trying to bring himself to pull off his boots. But by then his head was as light as an atom and his powers of reason were shredded.

He'd also fallen asleep, a shallow, dreamless sleep, from which he'd woken feeling weightless, without any balance restored. Cosmo was still snoring next door. They'd sipped strong, black coffee at the table in the living room. August had opened one of the bay widows, letting in the sharp spring air, and Cosmo had become animated again, seeming to have forgotten what he'd talked about the night before. His hands spun, enthusing about his new market stall. He'd plans to replace Mahmud's Oasis with imported cloth, bits of brass and wood. He'd found some great stock in the Middle East. *Continue the theme*, he'd laughed. He was confident he'd make good money. There was some scam involved, August wasn't surprised. But Cosmo didn't go into the details. He'd dropped heavy hints; he needed help to begin with, an extra person to mind the stock, the cash box. He'd pay a small wage.

August had woken still unclear and doubtful of Cosmo's story. He'd have to be patient with Cosmo, he knew, winkle more information out with a pin. Cosmo's concentration was slippery, and completely self-referential. August needed more information before he confronted his mother, even if it was only Cosmo's version of events. He wanted to know what she was like then, what Cosmo remembered of her moods; had she ever talked about her life with Luke, her feelings for him? A day on a stall would be an opportunity to slip more questions casually in and so he'd agreed to help Cosmo.

Later, in the deli, August felt loosened from the world. Outside the temperature had risen and a young, naive sunshine had thrown itself across cars, the pavement, into the deli's front door. He'd loitered a lot in the café, behind the coffee machine, slowly, quietly distilling his thoughts, serving customers from inside his daydreams.

A delicate lichen clung to the slopes of his groin, as though a second skin was forming there, a herbaceous peel.

It made him feel sleek.

The notion that Edward might be real, a father to find, brought tremendous relief. He'd always been guilty about his lack of affinity to Luke, his lack of response to the photograph, the stories. If Edward were true, he could lose this, let this fall. There might be a man out there he looked like, who'd tried to find him once, who might still want to see him. He could have other family too, brothers and sisters, a stepmother. Other grandparents. Another *name*.

Who was he? August who?

He was slicing pastrami when Leola wandered in.

He sensed her presence first, the sweep of her, as though she'd caught a web of sunshine on her way in, pulling it in with her. He looked backwards over his shoulder as he sliced, amazed that she also brought with her an uplift in his spirits, a small surge of delight. He spied on her knowing he was partially hidden by the battlements of sweets on the display fridge. Her wiry hair was slightly longer and held back and away from her more freckled face. Under her apron she wore a faded T-shirt. Old, battered jeans were stuffed into gumboots. He stopped slicing. The pastrami was for a customer waiting by the till. He wrapped it in fine tissue paper. As he served the customer his whole body pulled towards Leola; he wanted to watch her walk, browse, see what she chose. Wanted to guess her tastes, witness her impulses. He handed over the change, smiling vacantly.

Incredibly, he wasn't afraid of her: not now he was someone else.

'Can I order a cake?'

Leola was standing in front of him. Her tone was polite, trying to catch his attention.

'Oh . . . of course.' He was amazed at his calmness. He realized they hadn't spoken since the cheese flew. *You've missed so much*, he wanted to say. *So much has happened since you've been away*.

She smiled, self-consciously. 'I've been looking after my great-aunt.' She smiled again. 'She likes cake.'

August smiled back, teeth like loaves. He didn't tell her that he knew, that Cosmo had already told him she'd gone away. Couldn't say he was glad to see her again. He nodded. 'Which one would you like?'

'You don't have it at the moment, but I've seen it in here before.'

'What does it look like?'

'Like an Easter bonnet. It has lots of fruit on top.'

'I know the one, white chocolate.'

'*Yeesss*. An oval cake, creamy white.'

'Pistachio nuts inside.'

'Ooooohh!'

'And peach mousse.'

'Yes.' She laughed.

'And passion fruit.'

'Really?'

August nodded. His eyes were stuck to hers. But his face felt cool.

'Can I order one? My great-aunt's well enough now to have a treat. She's a hundred on Sunday, she loves cake, the richer the better. She loves cake and eggnog.'

August pictured a hundred-year-old version of Leola, feasting on an Easter bonnet.

Her cheeks were pink.

Again, he noticed Leola was tall. Tall and big-breasted. Strong jawbones. Her nose was long and straight, curved at the top, a man's nose. Her smile was firm in her face. They stood for a moment, saying nothing. Then she gave him a look, as if to prompt him for the order.

'Oh . . . oh yes,' he scrabbled under the till for a pen and pad. He found them in the tangle of string and tape and old order books, then straightened up.

Leola was grinning at his hair. 'That cheese,' she blushed.

'The Mimolette?'

'Yes. It was delicious.' She shook her head, remembering. 'It was funny, wasn't it.'

August's lips parted. He smiled, wide as a banana.

She laughed.

As he wrote the name of the cake on the small pad he saw the cheese, spinning away from him.

'It was like a meteorite,' Leola grinned.

August gazed at her, eye to eye. A first, a miracle.

'Or a small planet,' he added.

They both stopped, saying nothing. Pink bloomed in both their cheeks.

'Perhaps we're planet-crossed lovers,' August joked.

He smiled and wanted to shoot himself both at once. Leola turned redder and her ears flashed. She smiled and left quickly.

When she was gone August glared at what was left of a newish Mimolette in the cabinet. The cheese had been cut open and its insides were an open mouth, laughing at him. He picked up the cheese and walked through to the café. Henry was in the alcove, making coffee. A man at a table was eating a croque-monsieur. August hurried past them both.

'Excuse me,' he said curtly as he passed. He opened the window and threw the cheese out of it.

* * *

After lunch a delivery man with a large bouquet of flowers walked into the deli. August was behind the counter, filling the coffee bean drawers with fresh supplies. Henry was standing behind the till, bored, cutting up pieces of Parmesan into chunks. Her eyes lit up as the man made his way towards her.

'Rose Finlay?' he asked.

Henry almost nodded her head.

'No,' she sulked. 'I'll just get her.' She disappeared into the café, reappearing with Rose by the hand.

'Here she is.'

Rose gasped when she saw the bouquet.

'Will you sign for them?' the man asked.

Rose nodded, signing quickly.

He handed the bouquet over and it filled her arms. When he left Rose and Henry stood in the middle of the shop, staring at the flowers, heavy, creamy, satin roses, red berries, strings of black-green leaves.

August could see Henry's envy, and that Rose was overcome. There was a small white envelope thrust inside the bouquet. He leaned his elbows on the high cooler and peered across it.

'They're beautiful,' he said to Rose.

Rose was stunned.

He sensed this should be a private moment and wondered if it was possible this was the first time she'd ever received flowers from a man.

'Who're they from?' Henry asked.

'I . . . don't know.' Rose's face was cast downwards.

'Open the card,' she urged.

Rose unsnagged the small white card from the leaves, pulling open the flaps at the back. She slipped out the card and opened it.

'Oh,' she murmured under her breath, reading the message to herself. 'They're from Salvadore.'

'Who's Salvadore?' Henry asked, unable to hide her tone of disbelief.

'A friend,' Rose replied.

Henry looked quizzically at August.

'The man who took you to tea?' he asked.

Rose nodded.

'Who's Salvadore?' Henry repeated.

'Someone I met on a cruise,' she replied, carefully. 'Over Christmas.'

'Is he your boyfriend?'

Rose looked mortified.

August winced at Henry.

'No. Just a friend.'

'He had a Spanish accent,' August remarked.

'Portuguese,' Rose corrected. 'He's Brazilian.' Rose's eyes were a little moist; she was relaxing more about the flowers, enjoying the intrigue. 'He's an ichthyologist.'

'What's that?' asked Henry, almost laughing.

'A fish expert,' August answered.

Henry laughed.

Rose was impressed. 'He grew up by the sea. He was named after Salvador, the city he comes from. He could swim before he could walk.'

August was lost in the romance of this; to be named after a city, to grow up by the sea.

'He seemed very nice.' August remembered the man's unruly hair, the smell of limes. 'Can he samba?'

'He's very good,' Rose smiled knowingly.

'He lives in London?'

'At the moment, yes. He's working on a project. But he travels a lot, like me.'

Henry hadn't been listening. Her eyes were far off, worried; her mouth was turned down.

'Yves hates dancing,' she said, abruptly.

Isabel's flat was standard W11. White walls and wooden floorboards. Abstract art and Indian furniture. Night-lights floating in a stone bowl.

It was only 9 o'clock and the main room was half full of people standing, talking. All attractive. Somehow August could tell they were clever too, smart, fashionable. People who always knew a lot about everything: the Balkans, the ballet, bullfighting. He guessed they were journalists, or filmy people. The last party he'd been to was a year ago. It was a similar type of affair, same type of people. It had culminated in his having an argument with a woman who'd called Birmingham 'parochial'.

He stood at the room's entrance clutching his bottle of wine. In a corner he could see Jim, talking to another man. They both wore dark suits and had thin hair and looked like two cool young priests gossiping. Gabriel was sitting on a sofa nearby. A small group sat round him trying to follow his hands as he recounted a long and involved story.

August made his way over to the makeshift bar to deposit his bottle. Searching for a corkscrew, he felt a hand on his back.

'August.'

He turned around.

'Oh, h-hello,' he smiled too widely, almost puncturing his lips with his teeth.

It was Isabel, trying hard not to laugh at him. 'I'm so glad you could come,' she gushed, looking over his shoulder. 'Gub-gub talks about you so much.'

August squinted, not understanding. 'Gub-gub?'

'Guuubbbb-guuubbbb,' she drawled, as though chiding a Chihuahua. She nodded her head over to where Gabriel was sitting, immersed in a great plume of smoke. 'Gubby. Gongo,' she said, making puppy eyes at him.

'Anna!' she shrieked.

August looked round. Coming towards them was the woman with blood-orange lips. She still had them on.

'August, have you met Anna?'

August turned to look at her and smiled. 'Yes.'

There was an embarrassing split second of silence, then Anna flashed him a prim micro-smile and began scanning the room.

He stood up straighter, his big shoulders blocking Anna's view, his hair a screen of brush fire. She was annoyed and continued trying to peer past him.

Isabel, sensing her impatience, linked arms with her and made as if to move off.

'I may not be pretty,' August said quickly, his eyes pinned to Anna's lips. 'But at least I never chose this colour. It's very . . .' he breathed in. 'Sharp.'

Isabel's smile freeze-dried to her face.

Anna shook her head, incredulous.

August could see this hadn't impressed them; they couldn't care less. Reluctantly, he stepped aside and they slipped past him, with grim lips.

They were tough, August mused.

Tough as old hens.

Much later, he found a bathroom upstairs and locked himself in.

Bathrooms were holes in the world, he thought. *Places of refuge.* They had everything: cold, tiled walls for pressing one's hot head against. Running water. A toilet to throw up in. They were rescue stations.

August flipped down the toilet lid and sat on it, running his hands through his hair. He'd been at the party for two hours but it felt like twenty and he'd drunk the lot: white wine, mint julep, beer, some warm Cava.

Now he felt awful. Woozy.

He studied his hands. On his left palm there was a dim scar about an inch long, at the base of his thumb, stopping just before the artery in his wrist. He'd fallen from a pear tree when he was twelve, not long before he'd left Stonegate. It happened on a nearby farm. The other boys had decided to raid the orchard; they'd climbed the tree with the juiciest looking pears and he'd joined in. He'd fallen when the farmer was spotted coming home, catching his hand on a sharp, broken branch on his way down. He'd picked splinters out of his hand for weeks afterwards, always suspecting some had stayed in.

'They'll work their way out,' his mother had reassured him. 'Through your blood, then through your skin.'

Is that what's happening? he wondered. Were there splinters still trapped in his bloodstream?

August thought about Olivia. He pictured her opening a letter full of questions from him, tearing it up. Saw her ripping it to pieces. He reached across to the roll of toilet paper next to him and pulled a strip off, laying it along one knee. He pulled a pen from his jacket and chewed the end of it. He thought hard for a moment, then wrote in strong well-defined letters: *Dear Olivia.*

He stopped writing and squinted at it, how it appeared. He held the perforated paper up to the light, examining the bold words on the thin grain. Watched them hover in midair. He began to tug at the paper, testing its strength, pulling until at last the perforations gave and the squares of paper came apart in his hands. He got up, lifted the lid of the seat and tossed the pieces in.

After pulling the chain he left the bathroom and went downstairs. Music had been turned up, some Earth Wind and Fire. People were dancing. August hovered near a wall and watched the dance floor, a woman shaking her hips, a man with a trilby going down in the splits. Couples flirting. The music gave him an immediate thrill and he tapped his toes, making sure to stay close to the wall. He found it impossible to let go in public. He was too big, took up too much room. When he danced he forgot himself and that was a problem: he was afraid he might hurt someone with his elbows.

He watched the bodies moving and swaying and drifted into relaxing dreams of Edward. It'd be strange meeting his father, a version of himself, seeing his own face years on, transfigured by age. Would his size be diminished, would he stoop? Would he still have hair? What was he to expect for himself in the future? In what other ways would his face grow and change? Were his legs still in good shape? How did he walk now he was old, how had he ever walked? Were there any ailments he should know about, something which might explain his present condition?

He breathed in deeply and sleepily, thinking he should go. The bodies were still swaying on the dance floor, squid weaving in inky water.

One dancer in particular caught his eye and he peered closer.

Gabriel was dancing.

His back was very straight and his shirtsleeves were rolled to his elbows, as if ready for action. His face held an uncertain expression, his eyes watching other people, their rhythm, wondering what they could hear. For a moment he appeared uncomfortably conscious of the difference, that he was moving to what he could *feel*. He was moving jerkily as the other people around him swayed. His feet, August noticed, were doing a stiff and neat shuffle from side to side, a bit like a sailor doing the hornpipe.

* * *

There was a phone box outside his flat, on the other side of the road by the train depot. August had never used it but had often heard it ring, had once or twice even seen people passing stop to answer it. He'd often fabricated elaborate and romantic adventures around it, the people who used it as their private number, or a secret means to meet. As he walked home down Lena Gardens, still a little woozy, the phone box stood still at the end of the road – an anonymous place, a hole in the world. He found himself stumbling quickly towards it, rooting in his pockets for change.

Once inside he picked up the handset and pressed it to

his ear. He closed his eyes and bit the chrome cord, then opened his eyes. He pushed 50p into the slot and briskly punched in the numbers for his mother's cottage. Heat flared in his ears as he did. He didn't stop to think that it was two in the morning.

'Hello?' he heard his mother's hard voice. 'Hello, who is this? Hello? Is this some kind of joke? Hello.'

August didn't respond.

'Hello?'

A sadness swelled in him; the booze, his past all mixing. It rose and then fell in his chest. He saw his mother and Cosmo in the room with red walls. The sound like panic. He pinched the top of his nose, holding back more. He breathed in deeply, waiting.

The phone clicked off.

August put the phone back on the hook.

He pulled his coat up and around him, as though pulling himself together, then turned and crossed the road and walked up the stairs to his flat.

At quarter past eight the next morning August stood moodily outside Mahmud's Oasis. The market was deserted, a long alley of individual cells, each cell sealed with a corrugated metal wall, each emblazoned with fat graffiti letters. One of the fishmongers had opened, and a butcher further down. Apart from them there was little life. And it was cold. Around him pigeons cooed and flapped their wings. A row of them sat hunched and puffed on a nearby rooftop, peering lazily down at him. A tube train to Hammersmith rumbled by overhead. A zigzag of lights strung the length of the narrow thoroughfare was switched off and hung limply. Steam billowed from a nearby chimney. At this time of the day the market had a remote and tragic feeling.

August found he really did miss Mahmud. His not being there was like a magic trick. Although he knew where he'd gone, his little green stall was weirdly inanimate. Traces of Mahmud hovered around it, but he was irrevocably gone. August shivered into his jacket. Opposite he noticed a handpainted inscription on a stall: *Franco's Glass and China Wear*. Above Franco's was a lavender sign with the words *Dinky Scents – Fancy Gifts*. Both were faintly carnivalesque, faintly vaudeville side-show. High above the sign hung large, unwieldy clouds, hanging cliffs of charcoal, pink and grey. Their edges were ragged with a fierce gold, promising a fine day to come.

August kicked himself for not asking Cosmo what time he'd be there. He'd been to the market hundreds of times, but never this early, he'd never really needed to know or thought about when it opened – or closed. He'd been lost that morning, eager to see him again for more information. He'd imagined a day setting up shop, chatting over the course of a day's work. Waiting for Cosmo was insufferable. The pigeons cooed and puffed and nodded, agreeing.

At nine thirty Cosmo turned up with two Styrofoam cups of coffee.

'Sorry, man. Hope you haven't been here long!' He stumbled towards him, handing him a cup. 'Should've mentioned this market doesn't get going till ten-ish.' He was wearing rainbow-coloured trousers and a long red feather in his cowboy hat.

August was irritated just by the sight of him. He grunted, 'No, not too long.'

'I'll bring the van down with all the stuff. Here, why don't you open up?' He tossed August some keys.

August unlocked the stall, rolling up the corrugated blind. Inside all sign of Mahmud's world had been dismantled; the frying vats, the fridges, the kitchen equipment. All gone north. In its place, a trestle table was folded against the wall, also two chairs. Some empty shelves remained, built into the back of the space. As August unfolded the table the owners of Franco's Glass and China Wear arrived and nodded hellos. The women with the warrior goldfish turbans arrived too. They had the stall next door to Franco. They recognized August and were startled to see him, but nodded and smiled also.

Cosmo reappeared driving a white van. From the back of it he pulled four bulging raffia bags and a cash box.

'Wait till you see this stuff,' he enthused, lifting the bags on to the table. From them he unwrapped vases and ashtrays made from stone and alabaster, quilted cushion covers, bolts of wildly coloured material, little tea sets, copper coffee pots.

'From Cairo,' Cosmo boasted.

August was impressed at the quality of the stock, he'd been expecting cheap junk. He helped Cosmo unwrap and lay things out on a bolt of cloth. He was beginning to feel more relaxed and confident about the day's prospects when Cosmo gave him a price list, handed him the cash box and said:

'I'll be back in half an hour.'

By lunch time, Cosmo still hadn't turned up. August had sold two vases and a bolt of cloth and had once had to ask the women opposite to keep an eye on the stall while he'd gone for a piss in The Bushranger on Uxbridge Road. He found himself fighting a mixture of anger and self-reprimand, also a small glimmer of worry for Cosmo, in case he'd got caught under a bus. The women sensed his unease, offering him cigarettes, which he refused.

By the end of the afternoon he was still waiting. He was furious with Cosmo, furious with himself. The lining of his stomach felt as though it was slipping down an enormous hole, causing a whirlpool in his blood. He'd allowed himself to be used, set himself up. How could he've been so stupid as to have agreed to help Cosmo, knowing what he knew of his past? He should call his mother, borrow Jim's car, go up to see her tomorrow.

The cash box was bulging, Cosmo had been right about the stock. He had half a mind to take the money and go, it was almost four o'clock. Many of the other stallholders were packing up. He was anxious, cross.

Stuck.

When a woman in a low-cut T-shirt bent over the trestle table to examine a vase, her cleavage reminded him of the cleavage of a hammer, the part for extracting nails.

In his chest, something slipped.

He saw Jude.

Sunbathing naked in the big field in front of the copse. Her breasts were long and flat and heavy, a greyish blue, her nipples looked stitched on. He remembered other women too: pink flesh, white flesh, nipples, pubic hair, rolls around stomachs, nests of hair, open legs. Black slits. Men too. Purple goosefleshed scrotums, skin like a turkey's gullet. Long, flaccid penises. Short ones. Grizzled hair, loins, taut hips, sinewy buttocks. He remembered his mother, her white bee-sting breasts. She used to caress herself out on the grass, finger her nipples, taunt the men, women. Laugh, half-naked out there in the field. On hot summer days, when the air was full of dandelion floss, when he longed to go outside, he couldn't.

Instead he stayed indoors, hid upstairs on the third floor.

The woman with the low cut T-shirt was staring at his feet.

August looked down.

Pink petals had slipped from his trousers. A mound, like a pile of flamingo feathers, lay at his feet. He laughed at it, waving his toes to make angels in them. The woman frowned at him as if he was crazy and moved off.

13 July

July brought a heat wave with temperatures lingering in the thirties for a fortnight. Over London the ozone was as thin as a nylon stocking, the sunlight falling through it in an invisible rain, an unrelenting force descending on the city, burning skin in minutes, shrivelling flowerbeds, melting plastic, as insidious and invasive as sarin gas. Smog and dust formed balls behind cars and caught in the eyes and mouth. The parks were dun brown. Wasps were found dead in fridges. People had white raccoon patches when they took off their sunglasses.

August was lying on his bed, naked.

Next to him, on the small table, stood a jug of iced water and a glass. The window of his bedroom was wide open and he could hear the sound of children screaming and laughing coming from the primary school playground nearby. Every now and then he heard the off-key but catchy tune of an ice-cream van as it circled the neighbourhood. He could hear cars speeding past, Sulgrave Road being a rat run through to Hammersmith Grove.

He turned over, his back to these sounds, trying to focus on the jug of water.

His body, his face in particular, was so bad he'd taken a few days off work.

He'd spent the time lying on his bed, drifting in and out of dreams. Mostly he dreamed of dancing, these dreams comforted him the most.

August closed his eyes.

He dreamed he was on the streets of Cuba, in jeans and flip-flops. It was night, a neighbourhood party and he was salsa dancing with a young woman. She had honey brown skin and blonde hair and a short pink dress, but he couldn't see her face, just her long legs and her sinewy buttocks under her dress. She also wore flip-flops. She danced with her hips very close to his, moving in perfect time with his own rhythm. They danced thigh to thigh, loin to loin. Mutely pressed together.

The dream caused his penis to swell and stiffen. He reached down for himself, behind the tip, and gasped a little. He wanted to be swallowed, like the rhythm swallowed him when he danced. He wanted to be danced and fucked. He imagined the woman's mouth closed over him and ran his fingers along the length of his erection.

He ran the dream again as he masturbated – him and the woman dancing in slow motion. He stroked himself and dreamed and it caused an ache in the part of him between skin and bone. He groaned and his penis grew in his grasp. He began to stroke faster. He and the woman pressed close, moulded, his hands on her buttocks, the thin dress. He came very quickly in his hand, a little barb of ecstasy. Like a scorpion sting, it sent fire into his bloodstream, only briefly. His body keened. His skin was electric. And then he was mildly sleepy. He looked at his hand. His sperm was pearly and creamy, an emollient.

Afterwards he lay curled in an afterglow. Somewhere far off, the woman still danced by herself, still tempting him back to the dream. But he was too spent to enter it again. Dreams did that sometimes. Like time, dreams debilitated him. Made him forget, washed him, rolled him in a solution of saline. And a lack of resolve. *Dreams dull the pain*, he thought. *They make me forget.*

Over the last few weeks he'd drafted several letters to his mother, this time on writing paper.

Dear Olivia,
I have always felt . . . . . .

Dear Olivia,
A few months back . . .

Dear Olivia,
I've had some news which you might . . .

Dear . . .

Every one had been torn up. The job was hopeless, one no one else could help him with, one he didn't know how to go about addressing now the initial shock had worn off and he'd absorbed Cosmo's story. How did one go about tracking down one's lost father? He had so little to go on, not even the basic facts about Edward: who he was, where he'd come from, his connection to his mother, what he did for a living.

How had they met? Was it before or after she met Luke, was he an acquaintance or an old friend? Or a stranger, even?

More than anything he wanted to know about their love affair. What had it been? Had it been clandestine? If so, concealed from whom and for how long? From Luke? Not necessarily. He only guessed the worst – a thoughtless affair. No feeling. His mother had cheated on Luke, used Cosmo, other men, why not Edward too?

The door bell rang, interrupting these thoughts. It was midday, Friday, about the time the mailman came with a late delivery. August rose and put on his dressing gown. He padded down the hall, opening the first door and the second. He stood in the shadows, pulling the door back a tiny crack, not wanting whoever it was to see his face.

His mother was standing on the step, in her arms a bundle of flowers.

'I came down last night. Spur of the moment. I've just been to the deli. They told me you weren't well. What's wrong?'

August opened the door but turned before she entered, walking back through the hall into the living room. His mother followed.

'I'll just put these in that vase, shall I?' she said, looking over to the one on the mantelpiece.

August watched as Olivia went to the fireplace and stood for a moment in front of the vase of dead hollyhocks, her mouth pulled down, her eyes on the dried flowers. The petals were woeful, like several dried-up faces of very old women, frail and bled of life; the leaves were curled and brittle, the water having evaporated completely. Gingerly, as though handling something precious, she picked up the vase with her free hand and took it into the kitchen.

In the bathroom, August studied his new face in the mirror.

Lightly, he ran his fingers across his cheeks, then up and into the bridge of his nose, along his eyebrows, along his eye sockets. He could feel a truth dimly, somewhere, one that was an impossible idea.

This is the answer.

He touched his nose, his lips.

My face feels good, my body does. I feel wonderful.

He dropped his hands to his side.

Ask your mother.

Questions were frightening. Like fire, they were ravaging and likely to bring the timbers down around his ears.

Ask your mother.

Questions were like water, they could drown him.

He opened the bathroom door.

The vase was now full of white lilies. Elegant flowers, feline and stark. In the kitchen, Olivia stood in front of them, pushing at a stem.

'Olivia.'

'What, dear?' she murmured, her back to him, still stabbing at the water in the vase. She continued stabbing and plucking at the arrangement for a few moments, as if he wasn't there.

Then she turned round.

'Om*iiiiii*godd!' Her eyes filled up with water.

August straightened himself up.

'What's *happened* to you?' Her voice was a lash, both sharp and soft, almost inaudible.

Slowly, August turned his face one way then the other so she could get a better view.

She said nothing, her breath caught up in her, her face bewildered.

August smiled, lopsidedly, still standing to attention.

Olivia walked up to him and gently took hold of his head by the chin. Her eyes slipped over his face.

His skin was tissue-like, his complexion dun brown. Cracks spread from the corners of his eyes into his hairline, down his cheeks. They were deep, the channels of a droughted delta, running away from his eyes in a manner which suggested his eyes had been leaking acid. Cracks ran along his forehead too. His lips were white with dead skin. The whites of his eyes were red.

'What happened?' she asked again, as if she was asking someone else in the room.

August thought about Cosmo. He pictured the grounds of Stonegate Hall. Again he was a child, holding on to the handle of the door to the room with the red walls. He remembered Jude. He saw his mother, naked on the grass, saw her breasts, small and pert.

His inheritance.

Ask your mother.

'It's some kind of trick,' he said.

Olivia nodded deeply, as if in agreement.

'Of nature.'

She still had hold of his face, surveying it. August felt like a statue, cold, inanimate. He peered down into her small shielded face, into her furrows and faded hair, her eyes which were clear and brown and soft only occasionally.

He saw a woman who'd lost her best years to nothing and had the sense of this in her every action.

August breathed in deeply. Then breathed out.

'Who was Edward?'

Olivia dropped her hands. Her eyebrows knitted, as if she hadn't heard right.

'What?'

'Edward.'

She blinked, shocked.

August kept his eyes on hers, not allowing her to break contact.

Olivia's breathing quickened noticeably and she glared at her son. She said nothing for what felt like a minute, sizing him up.

'How *dare* you,' she cut back, her voice rough with emotion. 'How *dare you*!' Her teeth were bared. 'Just what have you heard? Who have you been talking to? That fucking Jude? Fat, jealous, sad old bitch? *Jee*sus Christ, August.'

August watched as his mother began to pace up and down.

'August, what do you want? What have they said? Whatever it is, it's a lie. How dare you bring all this up.'

She stopped.

August rocked back a little on his heels. His mother's face had swollen and she was shaking her head at him. He was panicked, but pushed on. 'Wh-why did Luke's parents kick you out?' he asked, quietly.

His mother's head pulled back, affronted. 'Oh, I see . . .' Her eyes were darting from side to side. 'I see . . .'

She breathed in deeply, buying time. Somehow, she'd frozen the surface of her face, making it into a taut lie of skin, stretching it over her cheekbones. Then set her lips in it. Her eyes were the only thing she couldn't control.

They were shifty.

'I *left* your grandparents when Luke died,' she snapped. 'I left because I couldn't stay, couldn't live in the same place where we'd lived together. To sleep in the same bed, smell Luke everywhere. See Luke's father – who looked just like him. Every day. No, we didn't like each other, me and Luke's parents. But I *left*. I loved Luke . . .' Her voice smouldered and trailed off.

August was muddled and destabilized. What had he opened up? Here was a truth, or so it felt, and it had the strength of a wind, throwing him backwards. He was picking at something he knew nothing about, another age, another life. He wanted to shake his mother, shake the truth out of her, throw her against the fridge.

'I've s-seen Cosmo again, recently,' he said quickly, his voice breaking. 'He came into the deli a f-few months back.'

Olivia didn't flinch or show any surprise, as if she'd gathered herself up and was ready for anything. 'And he's been telling you stories.'

'No.'

'Then what, the little thieving bastard?'

'Just once,' August began. 'He mentioned . . .'

Olivia nodded.

'And you've believed *Cosmo*,' she hissed. 'He wants to get back at me. I dumped him. Hurt his feelings. So what? Giving you ideas. He's a liar. A drunk. And you believe him and not your *own mother*?'

August wanted to cry. He hated her.

'*L-look* at me,' he said, nervously. 'It seems . . . No,' August stopped himself. 'It's *obvious*. I . . .'

His mother raised her chin, her jaw set. Her eyes were inspecting him, her face still in check, holding it all back. It was so apparent when she stood so close. The truth was alive, just under her skin. He could see it, struggling.

Then it all fell out.

'*Look at me*,' he shouted. He slapped his cheeks. 'Look at what's happened to me. I'm drying up. I'm sick. Look at the face underneath all this dead skin, Olivia. Do you think I'm stupid? Do you think I've never guessed or wondered? Your son. I don't look remotely like you. Or Luke. Small, blond handsome Luke. Am I supposed to believe I'm *his* son too?' He was bellowing. 'Look at me!' he cried, his eyes in hers. 'What do you see?'

Olivia snapped her gaze off her son and stalked out of the kitchen.

August followed her, bereft, holding his face, pushing back tears. He wanted to sleep. It'd felt so right to say what he'd just said. But his sense of entitlement crumbled in the face of losing her for good. She was all he had.

'I'm . . . s-sorry, Olivia,' August started to gabble. 'I don't know what I was saying. It all seemed so possible. Edward, a big man. With the same eyes. That's what Cosmo said. My eyes . . . He said this man turned up once. And it's never made sense, never fitted . . .'

Olivia was walking quickly about his sitting room with her hands over her ears, looking for her handbag.

'I'm leaving,' she said when she found it.

August wanted to scream. *Speak! Speak to me!*

'Goodbye,' Olivia said and left.

August didn't even think about the tube ride; he sat on the train in a daze. He'd been right, right all along. Questions were a bad thing. He should've known they'd end up ruining everything, or worse. A flat denial. Thinking about it now made him flinch, made his eyes sting with shame at her weakness, that in his greatest time of need she'd shut the door on him, denied him his life because she hadn't wanted to expose the dreadfulness of her own. He was wobbly with the humiliation of it, wretched at the sheer magnitude of her rejection. He should've kept his mouth closed, should've gone out to Harrow again, got more information, gone back to see the Chalmins weeks ago, not now.

I loved Luke . . . somehow this had been unexpected. Surely she'd loved his father, whoever that was. What had happened all those years ago? He let his eyes rest on his knees as he bumped along the Metropolitan line, the afternoon heat clinging to him, light yet heavy on his nerves. It seemed the heat these days was uncontrollable, always on full. A young black teenager opposite him was smiling at him, amused. August let him gloat. Before leaving his home he'd wrapped his face in a long piece of cheesecloth and even though he didn't need them, crammed some Raybans over his reddened eyes. He knew he looked like something escaped from an Egyptian tomb, a mummy off to the seaside. He didn't care. He bumped along feeling heartsick, awful.

As a child, summer had been his least favourite season. It brought with it the expectation of being happier, signified a relentless obligation to be enjoying life, having fun, soaking up the longer hours. Summer made his stomach turn inside out, flashed up stark and flippant against his silent inner life. Summer made fun of his quietness, his unshakeable melancholy.

At Stonegate, in the summer, the grass in the field between the house and the copse grew knee high. The rose bushes in the garden grew wild, stretching out their long thorny arms like coils of barbed wire. Furniture was carried around them, out into the field, leaving the house cavernous and dark. Fires were built at night and the adults sat round them until the early hours. In the morning it was common to find the bodies which had been slumped in the house out on the lawn. Refuse built up around them over the weeks: beer cans, bottles, food, polythene bags, cigarette packets, plastic cups. These things crunched and broke, were ground into the grass or eventually blew sideways, across the field, getting trapped in hedges.

In the afternoons, the adults revived. The sky opened its clouds to reveal a sun which beat down steadily and strong.

In the afternoons clothes came off.

August floated backwards.

He saw his eight-year-old self.

Standing behind the barbed wire roses, mesmerized,

watching the large forms, gargantuan swells of flesh, disrobe, clothes falling from them: large, grey flags. August felt the same stir in his gut as he did then, the same sadness – a creeping flood in him, at the sight. Breasts. Pubic hair, bulbous sacks. Like odd and deformed fruit. Ripe and covered with suede or silk. Bellies and inner thighs. It caused a shock. Worried him. Caused his eyes to broil and his bowels to swim as he stared at the men and women draped over each other.

He watched and as he did, he lost sight of them, fell inwards into himself and stood dreaming on his feet. But the images pushed themselves into his head.

'August,' someone shouted his name, catching sight of him behind the roses. The words snapped him back to the world. He opened his eyes.

'Come over here!'

The little boy wanted to run away but his feet were stuck to the ground. He commanded them to move, but they wouldn't.

He closed his eyes.

'Get over here, shy-boy!'

Then rough hands were on his shoulders. He sensed a body behind him, pushing him forward. The smell, all over him. *Sweat turned to acid.* He was marched around the roses, Cosmo's pubic hair at his neck, his sweat wiping against his ears. He was shoved forward and then pulled backwards, drawn up, having arrived at a designated spot.

When he opened his eyes he saw a puzzle.

Men and women joined together, moving rhythmically, backwards and forwards. They were on their hands and knees, looking for something, making loud noises, groans, shouts. A feeling rose in him, a swell. In his genitals, a tug. For a moment he thought he'd come across a battle. But after this moment, this first intake of sight, an idea formed in him and became implicitly understood. As this idea took hold tears slipped from his eyes and he began to cry loudly, with fright.

Sweat turned to acid.

As he cried he could hear Cosmo's hard, derisive laugh, feel Cosmo's hand clamped on his shoulder. And the dull press of his slack suede penis against his back.

Outside the tidy Chalmin home August felt many things, all mildly: mild irritation, mild indifference, he was mildly crestfallen. Pushed about from behind and distracted. He was ready for anything, he told himself; nothing could really throw him, not again, not today. The house was as he remembered it; its greyness and primness giving off an air of indifference. He breathed out deeply, listlessly, then opened the gate and walked towards the door. He stabbed the door bell and the sharp sound it emitted momentarily burnt a hole in his stupor. More alert, he shook himself, his shoulders, tidied his cheesecloth scarf a little so it was off his face. He shoved his hands into his pockets. There was no movement inside at first, nothing for several moments. Then there were sounds in the hall, a slow shuffling. The door was unlatched, opened.

'Hello?'

The woman standing in the doorway was tiny, voleish, with what appeared to be very large false teeth. Her straight white hair was cut short into a girlish bob. She had small, gimlet eyes and a smudge of fuchsia on her thin lips. She was leaning on a walking stick.

'Yes?' She peered at him, at what appeared to be his bad sunburn, her lips stretching into a polite smile.

August found himself taken by surprise; behind his sunglasses his eyes grew larger. He wanted to smile. 'Uuhh . . . I'm sorry to bother you. But . . . are you Mrs Chalmin?'

The woman was annoyed and then polite again.

'Yes.'

He smiled, suddenly wanting to win her, realizing he needed to, needed to soften her stance. She was leaning heavily on her stick, staring at his chest, unable to see quite up to his face. It was clear she already needed to sit down. This was Luke's mother; this small, fierce once-pretty woman. He inhaled, then blew out a long, low breath.

'My name is August Chalmin.'

The woman shut down instantly and stared at the ground, trying to control her face. She remained like this, fighting back her feelings, saying nothing, for several moments.

'I'm s-sorry,' August tried to placate her. 'This must be a shock. There was no other way for me to find you. I didn't want to ring, have the phone put down. I wasn't even sure you'd be here. I tried once before, but . . .'

She straightened herself up. 'What do you want?' Her eyes were defiant.

There was a silence. August imagined himself vaporizing into thin air, wished he could.

'I've only recently found out . . .' he cleared his throat. '. . . about Edward.'

'I thought you said your name was *Chalmin*,' she spat.

He hadn't prepared himself properly for this, for being hated. He stood his ground.

'I've never known any different, I'm afraid. Until recently.'

'Your mother . . .'

'She's always told me Luke was my father.'

The old woman eyed him, his teeth, his nose, his entire burnt and ravaged face. She laughed, sarcastically.

'I'd guessed . . .' he said. He didn't want another door shut on him, he began to speed up. 'But then, someone from Stonegate Hall told me recently, someone I haven't seen since I was a child. A drunk. And my mother won't talk about Edward. I don't know anything about him.'

Mrs Chalmin was leaning even more heavily on her stick, holding on to the doorframe too. She screwed up her eyes and her fuchsia mouth twisted itself strangely, into a bunched worm.

'Do you know something?' she said, her voice saccharine. 'I'm glad you came.'

The sitting room she led him to at the back of the house was cool and colour-bled. It was clear this was a place for strangers and formal visitors. He was being tacitly barred from the heart of the house, another room where she might have a television or more comfy armchairs, a kitchen with an Aga. This was a room for business, social or otherwise. The curtains and the walls were drab, indefinite shades of yellow and blue. The furniture was thinly covered, four armchairs stuck one in each corner of the room. It smelt of dead air. The room had French windows which opened on to a small garden but it appeared they hadn't been opened in a while. She lived alone, August guessed. He dared not ask about her husband, if he was still alive. He sensed an unspoken command to stay quiet. Perhaps she had help. He wondered who drove the green Volvo, if it was even hers. He knew nothing about this woman, he realized, not even her first name, or if she'd had children other than Luke. For some muted, self-deluded reason he'd always presumed Luke was her only child – that he was the only child of an only child. Now he realized this was unlikely. There were framed pictures on a small wooden table near one of the chairs – two women around his mother's age. And a younger woman, in her twenties. A young, pretty vole.

'One of my daughter's girls,' Mrs Chalmin said, falling heavily into an armchair and arranging a thin pillow behind her back.

'Polly.'

'Oh.' August let this sink in. Polly was a stranger. Not his cousin, an unconnected person.

'Are your daughters younger or older than Luke?'

'Younger.'

Her sharp eyes prodded him. Clearly, she wasn't going to like him.

'Sit down,' she motioned with her stick to a chair directly opposite.

August sat.

She studied him, his miserable face, sucking her teeth in and out for several moments.

August smiled gently. 'An allergy . . .' he tried to explain. But her eyes were glazed.

And then sharp again.

'How is your mother?'

'I don't know. We had a fight.'

'Oh.' She smiled with a hint of satisfaction.

This annoyed him.

'Over Edward?'

August nodded.

She was ancient. Her hair, her skin were paper thin, almost ruched in places. Her whole face was the size of his fist. He marvelled at how unlike they were, at the scale of Olivia's lie. Now it was ludicrous, blatant. There was no way he could be related to her. This small, austere woman could never be his grandmother, she had the wrong skin colour, the wrong eye colour; she was from a different tribe. She was breathing heavily through her nose, her mouth pulled down.

'Your mother killed my son.'

August felt the words like a knife, plunging into him. Panic raced in his blood.

'She killed him.'

She was staring at a spot near her feet. Her lips were set in a look of disgust; she was loath to look at him.

August wanted to run, break through the French windows.

'Edward was a nice man,' she continued, matter-of-factly, her undramatic tone making what she'd said sound reasonable. 'Gentle.'

She nodded, still looking down. 'Shy. He worked for us for over ten years. He was our gardener. My husband loved him, trusted him. He was good at his job, knew his stuff. Which was why it was such a shock.'

August's mouth watered. He wanted to go.

'We never liked Olivia though. Knew she was rotten from the start. Didn't trust her . . . No . . .' her eyes became jagged. 'Used to sunbathe topless on the grass. That was how she got Edward to look at her. Otherwise he wouldn't have done what he did. He was a nice man. She used him and then killed my son.'

August was unable to make any kind of retort, he was electrified, burnt by her words.

'I saw them together once, that was how we found out. When Olivia was pregnant. I saw Edward and Olivia in each other's arms. Never said anything to Luke. I couldn't. I told my husband. We didn't know what to do. It was a farce.'

She looked up.

'Then you were born.'

She clicked her teeth. August looked nervously around the room. On a bureau behind her chair he saw another framed photograph. Luke. Tanned, blond, long hair. Lucky Luke.

In the photo he was laughing.

'You had the same colourless eyes as Edward,' she went on. 'Luke guessed the minute you were born. He knew where those eyes had come from. They had a tremendous fight, he and Olivia. Then . . . he came to us. I told him what I'd seen. That they'd been canoodling in the garden. Behind the elms.'

August wanted to laugh. It all sounded like a bad joke. Ridiculous. This woman was deranged by bitterness.

But Mrs Chalmin had gathered momentum and seemed to be enjoying herself. 'Luke confronted Olivia again and she denied everything. It was Edward who told him the truth in the end. That was when he got on his motorbike.

'Luke crashed. He left in a fury. And then he crashed. My son. He was twenty-five years old. He died because your mother . . .' she reached for her stick and banged it loudly on the floor. 'Because your lousy, worthless slut of a mother . . . *cuckolded* him.'

August had tears in his eyes.

Her eyes were dry.

'Now listen to me, young man.' She leaned forward on her stick. Her face was savage. 'You are no Chalmin. Do you hear? My husband would turn in his grave. I never want you to use my husband's name again. Ever. You are no relative, don't come here ever again. Edward's name was Hay. He came from the labouring classes. You tell your mother you saw me. Tell her I've put you straight.'

August nodded, pained and faint. He wanted to leave quickly, but he was stuck in his seat, in the mystery of her story. He wanted more and also had to leave. He was dizzy, but had to ask. One last question.

'Edward,' he choked. 'Wh-what h-happened to him? Wh-where is he?'

For a moment Mrs Chalmin looked as if she cared, then she turned her face away.

'I don't know.'

August could see Luke behind her, laughing.

'We dismissed him.'

Are you lucky? he was saying.

On Sundays, the pool on the Uxbridge Road opened at seven. August had rung to check. When he arrived at ten past, dressed in a raincoat and trousers, gloves, his cheesecloth scarf wrapped round his face and a Kangol fishing hat pulled down low on his head, the man behind the glass near the turnstile had his head in the *News of the World*.

'One swim, please,' August croaked.

The man lowered his paper. When he saw what August was wearing he shot him a look which implied he was being patient. Before he could say anything August pulled a five pound note from his wallet, the note slippery in his gloves, and pushed it through the mouse hole in the glass. The man inhaled and exhaled deeply as he opened the cash register. When he pushed the change and a ticket back through the mouse hole August let the scarf drop and smiled briefly, opening a fresh split in his top lip. His bottom lip had cracks like knife cuts in it.

'Thanks,' August mumbled.

As he squeezed through the turnstile, the man watched him as if watching a ghost float past.

*

In the men's changing room August headed straight for one of the toilet cubicles. Once inside he began to unbutton his shirt, his eyes resting on the cistern. He slipped off his shirt without looking down, then his shoes and trousers, peeled off his gloves. He put his clothes in his rucksack. Under his trousers he had on an old pair of Hawaiian shorts. From the bag he took a large towel and wrapped it around himself, covering most of his torso from his armpits down. Before opening the booth he peeked over the top and saw that the changing rooms were still empty. He hoped no one else would arrive for at least another hour. Even so, he was cautious as he opened the door and walked to the row of lockers. He slung his rucksack into one, locking it afterwards, then walked out towards the pool area. On the way, there was a little shallow pool, ankle deep, meant to disinfect feet. He walked carefully through it and then out.

His steps left a ripple.

And a thin mist, just above the water line.

The empty pool yawned across its indoor quarters, docile and warm. It was a strange pool, a bluey violet, a colour August found familiar. It didn't smell of chlorine, but another chemical: a mild, eggy odour hung in the air.

As he walked along the edge, August began to feel a tightness in his stomach, his heartbeat faltered. He knew if he tried diving headfirst his face wouldn't take the impact, the skin would tear. So he decided to take things slowly. He walked up to the ladder in the shallow end and sat down between its rails, his feet balancing on the top rung. He sat and gazed out across the big blue-violet square. Then it came to him. Bluebells. The pool was the same colour.

He turned and stood upright on the top rung, his back to the pool, stepping down carefully, one rung, then two. The water rose up to meet him, lapping around his calves and then his thighs. It felt delicate and gentle, slippery-cool, as though he were descending into a large mouth. A strange sound pierced the silence as he descended, something like a hiss. Then another, a sound like gas escaping from a fissure. His feet touched the pool floor and he began to walk towards the centre of the shallow end. As he walked, his arms folded up like wings at his side above the water, his body making a small wake behind him.

August closed his eyes as he walked, thinking of nothing at first, then something. Again, he was standing at the window on the third floor. Trees. A big man. Then his head began to flood. Ideas tumbled. The hissing became louder.

In the balcony café near the shallow end, Leola sat looking out on to the pool. She swam most Sundays around this time, when the pool was empty. This morning she could see she wasn't alone. A tall man was wading across the shallow end of the pool. He had his back to her but there was something unusual about him, as though her eyesight around him had blurred. She stared harder at him and then realized it wasn't her eyes.

It was steam.

There was a cloud of steam around the big man, and where his body met the water there were bubbles, as if his body were a big hot stone wading through the water. The man stopped. He began to lower his torso into the water, slowly immersing himself up to his neck.

Curtains of steam rose from the surface of the water,

just above where his shoulders were submerged. Vapours curled off him, evaporating into nowhere, peeling upwards as though lifting off layers of skin.

Leola's eyes lit up with wonder.

* * *

An old hen should cook for at least three hours. The bird should be covered with cold water at first and the flame should then be turned on high. When the water is about to boil, it should be skimmed. The flame should be reduced, salt added, pepper, a bouquet of laurel leaf and sprig of thyme and parsley, one large onion, one large carrot, one leek and two large stalks of tarragon. It shouldn't cook beyond being tender. Before the end, half a pound of mushrooms should be added and let boil in the bouillon for about ten minutes. Afterwards, the hen should be removed from the stock. A cup of double cream and a cup of butter should be tipped, not stirred, into the remaining liquid. This rich sauce should then be poured over it.

The hen should be eaten with croquette potatoes.

August stared at the brown, dumpy bird on his kitchen counter top.

After his swim he'd walked home, on the way stopping at a local grocer he knew opened on a Sunday. When he got home, he'd taken the bird from its bag and laid it on the chopping board, all naked and unexpectedly robust. Since visiting Mrs Chalmin two days ago he'd gone blank. He had no thoughts – about his mother, about Cosmo or Edward. The effect was like trying to start a car with an empty tank. His mind wouldn't give him its version, its thoughts or ideas on his body's most severe reaction yet.

It had collapsed on the job, given up on trying to pick through the mixed evidence. In its place was a kind of fear, like vertigo, as though someone had opened him up and filled him with sky and he was about to free-fall, into himself.

Your mother killed my son. The words had hit him like a loose and uncapped electric cable, their power throwing him, sending him sprawling backwards with shame and remorse. He'd stumbled away from her neat bungalow. Returned to his flat and gone straight to bed. Lain awake for hours in a state of confusion, a gnawing guilt: Mrs Chalmin's tiny face appearing in front of him, her twisted fuchsia lips, her stick banging on the floor, echoing in his skull. Her mental state had scared him. How foolish he'd been, how far away from the truth, from the actuality of another person's inner life; from a bereaved woman's unending grief. He'd been so hopelessly detached from the story of his life. How easy it'd been to float wide and free of what he'd had no contact with, only speculated upon, from the neutrality of innocence. Mrs Chalmin's hatred had been there, all along, waiting for him. Meeting her was like being grazed and then infected by something putrid.

He was amazed to hear that Edward and his mother had met while she was with Luke. She'd loved Luke, she'd said as much. They'd been together for two years before she got pregnant. When and how had Edward intervened: what force had thrown them together? He imagined them behind the long slim trunks of the elms and wondered what passion had moved them, brought them closer.

August filled a deep iron cooking pot with cold water, picked up the bird and put it in. Its skin was goosebumped and hairy in places, the large hump of breast listing to one side; the carcass was macabre, grisly, reminding him of a decomposing roadkill. He covered the pot quickly and turned the flame on.

Now the anxiety of her accusation had waned, fallen to a lower, murkier tier in his thoughts; now it was an idea he was fighting to keep down. His pride had bristled and common sense had stepped in. The old woman had seen events through the distorting veil of tragedy. Granted, Olivia was no saint. But now he sensed the injustice of Mrs Chalmin's words. Was this how Olivia also thought: that she'd killed Luke? Her affair with Edward had wreaked havoc. His birth had caused a death. He tried to piece these ideas together but they didn't quite fit. Mrs Chalmin must have been even more formidable thirty years ago, what had she said to his mother then?

He remembered the copse, the bluebells in it, their fading at the end of every spring. He thought of all the knowledge he'd gleaned over the last few months: Cosmo's story, his mother's, Mrs Chalmin's, the more he tried to examine it all, gather it into some cohesive picture, the more it began to merge and grow worryingly indistinct.

August picked up an onion and a knife and began to peel off its tough copper skin.

* * *

August went back to work the next day. The eggy pool had soldered his body, made it smoother, and the cracks in his face had sealed a little. Outside the sky was cloudless, the sunlight falling brightly, but softly on to the pavement, the Green, its trees. 'Oscillate Wildly' by The Smiths was on the radio, waltzing through the deli, the music exquisitely sad, yet also uplifting.

August stood behind the display fridge, making himself a Virgin Mary.

'Owww!' he half-shouted to himself.

The lemon he was squeezing backfired, the juice squirting him in the eye. He pressed the heel of his palm into the squirted eye and turned the wedge of lemon around, so its smile faced the glass. He squeezed again and this time the lemon drops landed in the mixture.

Since early June, since the days had lengthened, becoming lighter for longer, he'd had to drink much more fluid than usual. With the onset of the hot weather, the cracks in his skin appeared first on his chest. Dim, initially, like the fine silvery lines left behind on women after pregnancy. But as the warm weather continued, the cracks had grown deeper, the splits longer. The palms of his hands became as dry as biscuit, the soles of his feet had cracked and were as tough as cured beef. And so, instinctively, he drank: juice in the morning, water, lemon squash, fruit teas. He had a craving for anything laced with fresh herbs, like parsley, or coriander. Tomato juice, for some reason, was the best for keeping the cracks in his face from appearing, especially around the mouth. Mostly he drank water throughout the day, often as much as six litres. Both Henry and Rose had noticed his new thirst, so he'd joined the gym under the Novotel in Hammersmith, hoping they'd think he was drinking to replace lost fluids.

He drank and drank, but noticed the liquid went nowhere. He never needed to piss it out. Lemon squash seeped into his body as it would have into a dry bed of soil. Tomato juice sank into him. The seeping was always soothing in his blood, as though a cool internal spring was leaking in him.

An eclipse had been forecast.

In recent weeks the country had thought of little else. There'd been talk shows on the television and the radio, articles in all the papers, a media splurge, a drum roll which he knew would continue to build until the middle of August. The eclipse had become a fashionable topic of conversation, an event to have in one's diary. Parties were planned, raves, seaside love-ins. Spiritualists had been predicting the end of the world. New-Agers were planning pilgrimages. Jim and Gabriel had been trying to persuade him to rent a cottage with them in Cornwall. Outwardly, he'd not wanted to know or read anything about the eclipse, evaded the whole subject as much as possible whenever it came up. Inwardly, he was waiting for it. Nervously impatient for it. There was a slow and reluctant give he could sense deep inside him, in his organs, responding to a pull which came from way out on the horizon, from a point well beyond the edge of his vision.

It was Rose's birthday, so August wasn't surprised when Salvadore appeared.

'Hello, August,' Salvadore said, his big eyes and big smile fixed directly on him.

'Buenos dias,' August replied.

August had noticed Salvadore always had a look of amusement in his eyes, as if he didn't quite believe the ways of the English. Over the last few months August had grown used to it and come to like Salvadore's directness. His complexion never ceased to fascinate him. His face blazed shades of colour he never saw on English faces: ochre, sorrel, honey and rust. The whites of his eyes were brilliant. His hair was always oiled and smelt of fresh and unexpected scents: rum, vanilla, black pepper. His moustache was always coiffed. His summer shirts were always vibrant, not loud as they might have appeared on someone with English skin. Today's shirt was a floral print, deep sea blue and white.

Salvadore bowed and on straightening breathed in the early morning smells of the deli, warm baguettes, toasted almonds, Kenyan coffee.

'I have a hunger!' he said loudly, rubbing his stomach.

August beamed.

'What can I get you?'

Salvadore looked at the ceiling, pulling at one end of his moustache as if it might ring a bell somewhere in his head. After a few moments he looked directly again at August.

'One apple puff.'

August nodded and pincered one with his tongs from the pastry basket.

'And a cup of camomile tea.'

August went next door to make the tea at the machine. As he rifled in the boxes for the right tea bag, he wondered if Salvadore had seduced Rose yet. He still found it hard to see Rose as sexual. He wasn't sure if it was her age or something else. Whenever he tried to imagine this part of her, he slipped into neutral. He couldn't see anything at all. He could imagine Salvadore just fine, though, in silk pyjamas and a smoking jacket, pouring Rose a little cocktail, serving her oysters on a bed of ice.

'Where are you going to watch the eclipse?' Salvadore shouted from the deli.

The machine made a hissing sound when it spurted out hot water and August only heard muffled words. When the tea was made he brought the cup back and put it down next to the puff on the counter.

'Sorry?'

'The eclipse,' Salvadore repeated. 'You know, the eclipse of the sun. The moon will pass over it. A total blackout, you must have heard of it. It will be the high point of the summer, of the year.'

August paled.

'I haven't any plans,' he said vaguely, pushing the plate and cup across the counter.

'But you must,' Salvadore retorted. 'It will be a miracle. Once in a lifetime we will get this sight.'

'A spectacle,' August added.

Salvadore nodded. 'Quite.'

Salvadore regarded him intently, as though sharing some private knowledge.

Though the pool had helped, August's face was still delicate, vanquished. Bled dry. He could feel Salvadore's eyes on his skin and was embarrassed.

'I fell asleep in the sun,' he lied.

Salvadore frowned in pity. 'You must be careful with the sun. It is very strong. It can give and take life.'

August nodded, his eyes evasive. 'Is Rose expecting you this morning?'

Salvadore's eyes lit up.

'I am early, half an hour. I will wait and drink my tea. Don't disturb her.'

He turned and took his tea and puff outside.

When he'd gone August stood behind the counter feeling his heart in him, beating with a strange uneven rhythm. Every third beat was timorous, almost non-existent.

When Henry returned from her morning break she was sullen. She was often sullen now, and rude. A month ago she'd cut her hair off into a short bob, and dyed it blonde. It'd made her look even younger than usual, boyish. He guessed Yves had changed her ideas. He'd widened her world, broadened her consciousness. But now Henry was more distant. She'd never brought up the subject of Edward or their kiss, it'd obviously been buried and forgotten.

She was carrying a tray of fresh croissants from the oven. Bending to put them in the window, she looked up and through it.

'Oh, it's Cosmo with that woman.'

August looked round quickly.

'What woman?'

Henry shot him a look of impatience.

'The one you're crazy about.'

August reddened.

'Who?'

Henry released an exasperated laugh, letting the croissants fall in a bundle into the pastry basket.

She straightened up and turned round.

'The woman from Pollen, across the road. Cosmo's girlfriend. At first I thought you were just staring at the tree. But after a while, I realized you were staring *past* it, at the flower shop – at that woman. The one that comes in sometimes.'

'Leola?'

'Leola?' Henry mimicked in a reedy voice.

August stood unable to defend himself, his hands limp by his side. She'd kept coming in after he'd made the ludicrous remark about being planet-crossed lovers.

'I d-don't know what you mean. She comes in occasionally to buy lunch. She ordered a cake once, for her old aunt.'

'I've seen what you do when she comes in.'

'What?'

'You hide.'

August's ears went hot.

'I don't know what you both see in her. She's so . . . big and,' Henry made a face, 'Horsy.'

'No, she isn't,' August said quickly, almost laughing at Henry's jealousy. 'She's tall. Willowy.'

Henry sulked.

'Hummmpph. Anyway,' Henry cut him short. 'Cosmo's got in there first. Look.'

Henry and August peered out the window and up the road at the flower shop. Outside it, on the pavement, Cosmo and Leola were talking. Cosmo's hands were spinning as he talked, round and round, as if trying to make the world around him stop. Behind them stood shelves of plants. Yellows, pinks, small green trees. Leola was holding a small watering can and smiled up into the shade of his hat as he reeled her in. He'd swapped his suede sheepskin jacket for a summer blazer which he wore everywhere – purple velvet. His cowboy hat was at an angle. He chewed on a stalk of grass as he talked and leaned a little towards her on one skinny leg.

'He's quite a character, that Cosmo,' Henry mused, her voice edgy, as though she was trying out edginess. 'I wouldn't be surprised if she *is* going out with him. He has something women like.'

August pursed his lips together. 'What?'

Henry looked at him then crinkled her nose. 'Everyone has something, Gus.'

She left the window, taking the tray back to the kitchen.

August sighed when she'd gone. Outside he could see both Salvadore and Cosmo, one close up, the other further off.

The men were similar ages, both from sunny climates, Latin countries. But very different. The older Salvadore was a tiger in its prime, Cosmo more of a flea-bitten domestic cat. *But they both have something*, August thought. He could see it clearly, anyone could, a physical ease. It was in everything they did: the way they carried themselves, the way they walked, sat, spoke, ate. The way they smiled openly. The way they could so easily give. Cosmo, even with his arthritic legs, still had it. Confidence.

He saw Cosmo and Leola laugh.

Her watering can had tipped as they were talking, watering his shoes. August watched them walk to the end of the pavement where the shop and the flowers ended, deep in conversation. He watched with a sense of impending loss. Cosmo had taken his time with Leola, months. She'd gone away, come back, now he was back too. *He has something*. He watched as they waved each other off. It was obvious they'd agreed to meet later. Cosmo walked on, turning left up along the side of Brook Green, his walk more of an obvious stumble.

So Cosmo had been right about Edward. About his mother being kicked out by Luke's parents.

Lying, thieving bastard.

The truth, it turned out, had been brought to him by a cheat and a liar.

August felt a glow in his chest, of betrayal, as though the hurt he was carrying was a soft wax moving from one part of him to another.

He blinked. His eyes were warm.

August watched Cosmo disappear as though he was walking into a wall of light.

Cosmo was now a fixture in the area, in the deli, in the café at the back, in the market. Café Rouge, a little further along, had become his office. The barber had become his barber. The newsagent his newsagent. Cosmo had never explained or apologized properly for deserting August at the stall. He'd simply turned up half an hour before the market closed, mumbling something about being caught up in other business. It was hard to be angry, especially after Cosmo had paid him. These days Cosmo saw him as a conspirator, a part of a past he loved, and August never knew quite how to react. He half-heartedly went along with it while his feelings about him remained intrinsically locked. Even now he knew Cosmo had simply related the facts, he'd no charity for him, no new respect, no sudden liking or willingness to be his friend. Something in him still wanted to hurt Cosmo, wanted to remain hostile. And Cosmo was seeing Leola, an unbearable weight. But it would be out of place for him to be difficult or rude, it would cause problems serving him in the deli. So he put up with Cosmo – had to.

'That was very nice.'

Salvadore was standing in front of him with his empty

plate and cup, in his eyes there was a look of concern. It'd been more than half an hour since he'd walked in, close to an hour, and Rose still hadn't showed up.

'I wonder if she has forgotten it is her birthday,' he joked.

August was instantly sympathetic. 'I'm sure she hasn't. Shall I go up and knock?'

Salvadore smiled, uncertainly. 'Perhaps. Maybe it would be rude of me to interrupt her. It is improper to hurry a lady when she's dressing. Maybe it's me who has the time wrong. We were going to have breakfast together, at a place I know near the river. Maybe I am too early by far.'

'I'll go and check,' August replied, stopping Salvadore in his trail of excuses.

Salvadore smiled, appreciatively.

In the café he found Henry filing her nails in the alcove.

'I'm going upstairs for a minute,' he said, eyeing her new red nails.

When August reached Rose's door, he was surprised to find it open and her little pug, Hilary, sitting in the doorway watching a beetle waddle past its paws. He'd always thought there was something morbid about Hilary, something of the psychopath. The dog's face was a courtesan's beauty spot: black and velvety and completely flat. Its features were only blurry indentations, hidden under fur. It meant the dog had no face, no way to show its emotional responses.

'Rose?' August said out loud.

In all the time he'd worked for Rose, all their cheese tastings and stocktakings, all their shared hours, he'd never been up to her flat.

'Rose?' he said again, this time knocking at the wood panelling of the open door.

The pug looked up at him and the fur on its face moved, expecting to be petted.

'Where's your mistress?' August asked, petting it behind one ear. The little dog got up, as if it'd changed its mind, and trotted off down the hallway. At the end it stopped and looked back at August. Then it trotted on.

August stepped inside.

The first thing he noticed was a curious smell, two strong aromas, both strong and unmistakable: lavender and bacon.

On the left was a small kitchen. August poked his head inside, briefly taking in the Gustav Klimt calendar, and a faux gold cherub pedestal on the counter, a bowl on its shoulders full of green apples.

'Rose?'

He walked past the living room and couldn't help stopping for a glance inside. Rivers of raw silk orange curtains were thrown open and inner lace ones shivered in a breeze. He stared at the row of dusty elephants on the dresser, the African masks on the walls, one with a tusk in its nose; the tall lamp with its washed-out blue fringes. There were other trophies from around the world, a large latticed wooden chest, a curved sabre strung above it. Baskets and ivory inlaid plates above a book shelf. Strange plants with trunks like lazy spirals of smoke bent from old terracotta pots, casting shadows on to the curtains.

'Rose?'

He walked on. On the right there was a bathroom. He looked inside. This time he started back a little. On a clothes rack suspended over an enormous pink bathtub was a jellyfish of legs. Stockings mainly. Also a large whaleboned corset with suspender attachments, two brassieres with cups big enough to fit his head. Large silk camiknickers. He backed off, feeling irreverent, wrong and unwise to have come in without permission.

Then he heard a little sob, and then another, coming from the bedroom at the end of the hall.

He froze with alarm. Rose was crying; *oh God*, he should never have come in.

'Gus?'

'Yes. I'm s-s-sorry I came in. Shall I go?'

The sobs let up a little.

'Oh no, come in, Gus,' Rose's voice beckoned.

August stood outside the bedroom door, fretting. Wishing he'd left a note. He breathed in deeply, opened the bedroom door and walked in.

Rose was sitting on a large white double bed. Her face was puffy from crying, her eyes bloodshot. Used-up tissues lay like dead seagulls around her and Hilary was lying, also looking dead, beside her on the candlewick. But it was what she was wearing that made August gasp. Again he sensed he should leave. There was something unsettling about what Rose had on, something vaguely horrifying and hard to look at. August tried to avert his eyes, but instead found himself compelled to stare at it.

A lemon negligee trimmed with fluff.

The material was some kind of thin netting, lots of it, so Rose's body was indistinguishable under it, a large grey form. The feathers were what was so disturbing. Rose's shoulders were covered with wisps, the innocent and intimate down of lots of little chicks.

'R-rose, what's wrong?'

She shook her head at him, unable to talk.

'Can I do anything, get you anything?'

She shook her head again.

'Salvadore is downstairs, shall I tell him to come up?'

Her hands flew to her face. 'Oh, no, no. Absolutely not.' She patted the puffiest parts of her cheeks, just under her eyes. 'No, not like this. No. I'm afraid I can't see him.'

August took in Rose for a long moment. There was a lost look in her eyes, a distant sadness. It made August wonder if someone she loved had recently died.

'I'm so sorry, Gus,' she smiled at him kindly. 'But I woke up this morning feeling not quite myself.'

August didn't know what to say.

He opened his mouth and nothing came out. But the sight of a tearful Rose, possibly naked under a lemon negligee trimmed with chick feathers was too much.

'I'll tell Salvadore,' he said quietly, backing out the door. 'I'm sure he'll understand.'

Rose nodded to herself, relieved. 'I'll call him later. Can you make an excuse? Tell him I have a migraine.'

'Sure,' said August. 'I'll tell him.'

The bluebells never died. Like a stain fading into cloth, every summer the indigo ink stain of the flowers simply faded into the haze of the surrounding Yorkshire landscape. It happened imperceptibly, at no certain time. One moment the bluebells were there, the next, as though in a blink of an eye, they weren't – leaving August to wonder if they'd ever been there at all.

Once gone, the copse was less majestic, its purple carpet no longer spread. But he'd still go down there, to look at the long, slim, unadorned plants bedded into the black soil. The trees in the copse would watch him watching, quietly discerning. Old gossips, he always imagined. They rustled their leaves high above, swapping their impressions of him, discussing his weight, his shoe size.

Over the following week August found himself thinking of those trees again. He missed their rooted certainty, the sight of them from the window of the third floor of the big house. Missed their huddle, their air of long-standing comradeship, and their gentle, unassuming air of wisdom. He was so uncertain about Edward. How would he ever find him? His mother had shut him off, Mrs Chalmin had banished him from her kingdom. Neither of them cared.

How could he ever find a man who, like the bluebells, had faded into the haze of a landscape he was only beginning to see the shape of?

August pondered his predicament late into the summer nights. At times it was all he could do to stop himself from flinging his body off the bed, or hitting his head against the wall. He didn't know what to do with himself. He got out of bed sometimes, and stalked about the flat. Or he'd stand on a chair by the bay window and peer out at the train depot across the road. Sometimes he sat alone in the dark. Sometimes he lay on the sofa.

Edward still stood miles away from him, a small and distant range of mountains. The Chalmins had lived in Ditchling. Was it possible Edward was still there, was he still a gardener, a labourer who'd lost his life also, toiling for the well off? He had maps. He would find Ditchling on one of them. *Edward's name was Hay.* He could go there, ask around, speak to people. He could ask in the local post office, or library, a local historian might be able to tell him more about his father, if there had been any other family. This time he'd be careful. Plot and plan. So far he'd been greeted at every turn with derision or rejection. He'd think about his next move: no impulsive trips, no running at things. He'd go to Ditchling in his own time.

* * *

August woke sharply from a barren sleep. His room was full of water. A cool, aquamarine air had roamed in from the open window by his bed, lapping at his body. Soon it would be hot again, in a couple of hours. Hot and disabling. Hot and inescapable. It was too early to go into work, too late to go back to sleep. There was a tape he had in the deli, some Sufi music. There were baguettes he could par-bake while he swept the floor. He could dance and fill up sugar bowls, salt and pepper shakers. Dance and unpack fruit. Make sandwiches. Already feeling the music in him, he got out of bed.

When he arrived at the deli he immediately knew someone else was already there. He could see through to the café and noticed the curtains had been pulled open. The smell of baguettes baking was already wafting up from the kitchen. He walked through the deli, into the café, and looked around. In the kitchen alcove he saw gritty coffee puddles around the coffee machine.

A sense of caution stopped him from calling out and he quietly descended the stairs to the storeroom. He stopped, abruptly, when he caught sight of Henry sitting at the table in the kitchen, her back to him. She sat with her shoulders hunched, her head in her hands. August remained quiet. He could retreat and knew he should. He should leave her and go back upstairs, come back in loudly, banging doors.

But he was fascinated.

Henry lifted her head from her hands. For a few moments she contemplated the large silver fridge in the corner. August stepped a little closer, for a better view. Henry rose from the table and walked across to the fridge, pulling at its heavy handles. In it he knew there were bowls of salads, terrines of pâtés, pies and quiches. Cakes too. Henry took a wall of fudge cake from the fridge, the chocolate black as tar. She carried it to the table, putting it down.

August edged closer.

Henry walked to the sink. On the windowsill above it there was a bottle of Fairy Liquid. She picked this up. She took the bottle over to where the cake was on the table and began to squeeze the contents on to the cake, letting ropes of the dark green liquid fall on it like acid, looping it all over the cake, as though re-icing it. The green on the black was ugly, and Henry began to mash the liquid into the cake as she poured, mashing the tar black and the green acid together.

August watched.

Henry mashed and mashed until the cake was ruined.

When she'd finished it was slumped and crumbled to one side, dignified yet defeated, a dead man; a tramp lying in its own vomit.

'I'm sick of you,' she said to the cake.

August tiptoed backwards into the storeroom, up the stairs to the café. He stood in the middle of the deli, feeling disturbed. He wished he hadn't seen what he just had. Not Henry. Not his little mouse. Not someone so buoyant – her body was once the shape of effervescence. It made him sad to think Henry was unhappy.

He looked outside.

The morning sun had just cracked and its albumen had fallen from the sky, glazing the ground with a thin, silky light. It was lambent, numinous, and he was able to look at it without batting an eye. He didn't care. He went to the door, opened it and shut it again, loudly. He walked heavily across the deli, and bumped into the olive table.

'Oww,' he shouted.

*

When Henry came up, August was listening to the weather report on the radio. The heat wave wasn't going to let up. In fact the temperature was going to increase before it dropped. No rain was predicted for the foreseeable future. He smiled at her when she passed him, his lips sore as they pulled.

Henry ignored him.

'Je vais faire le awning,' she said matter-of-factly.

August said nothing as she walked out. Her French was more or less fluent these days, though she spoke it less and when she did it was without the enthusiasm she'd had months back. Why was she angry, he wondered. And with whom? Why didn't she leave Yves if she was sick of him? What was the attraction, the reason for her to stay? It eluded him why people stuck to other people who were wrong: what was the glue?

He watched as she pulled a chair from one of the tables flanking the door, positioning it directly under the catch. She stood on it and, as she reached up, the light drew a line around her thin body. She was wearing tight denim shorts and a small T-shirt, one which looked as though it'd been made for a child. Although he'd never had a close look at her bare legs, the ones he'd always imagined, had seen under tights and trousers, were different. Shapely. The legs he could see now were shapeless, twig-like and bottle tanned. As she pulled the awning with both arms above her head, her T-shirt rode up and where there had once been a wide, soft stomach, gentle curves, he could see ribs he could count. He heard the awning click into place and smiled, a rubbery smile at her through the window. Henry jumped down and pushed the chair back to where it'd been.

'I'll be downstairs,' she informed him, walking back inside the deli. 'Having a cigarette.'

'Fine,' August replied, cheerfully.

* * *

The plane tree was wearing a boa of green leaves. Its Afro was brighter, a pea green frizz, its arms were still thrown up, reaching above the traffic. Above the heat. As the day grew, heat gathered and, instead of rising, hung low in the air, trapped and desperate, a weight on itself, an unending anticlimax.

For most of the day August didn't go out. He stayed inside, around the fridges, where the temperature was a little cooler. As he tended the till after lunch he saw Cedric and Flora sitting at a table on the pavement, sharing a slice of banoffi pie. August watched them with his usual mixture of pride and envy. He sighed, breathing in his shyness, filtering it through his lungs, feeling it nettle in the pores of his ribs. Cedric and Flora. Olivia and Edward. He squinted, trying to picture his parents outside at the table too. Old, together, in love. What had happened to Olivia and Edward?

A man with Arnet sunglasses pushed back over his crew cut approached the counter, holding a pot of rocket pesto and a bag of farfalle.

'I'd like some of that big orange cheese,' he said, pointing at the Mimolette.

August nodded.

A new one had come soon after he'd thrown the last one out the window. It had sold quickly. This one had been cut into and was almost finished too. He leaned into the cabinet and picked it up and carried it to where the wire was attached to the counter. He unwrapped it, placing an open square of waxed paper under it, and steadied the wire.

'How much?'

'Just a wedge.'

August neatly shaved a piece off and it fell on to the paper. He took the piece in the paper over to the counter, cupping it in his hands.

'Like this?'

The man grimaced.

'Is there something wrong?'

The man shook his head, as though trying to retract his reaction. August stared at the cheese, but couldn't see what was the matter.

Then he could feel it, a searing fire across the backs of his hands. He put the cheese down and brought his hands out from under the wax paper.

The backs of his hands were bleeding. Wet red lines ran across them, like welts from tentacles.

'Errr,' the man was plainly revolted. 'It's okay, I'll just have these.'

When the man was gone August inspected his hands. The splits were fine. The blood had stemmed quickly and there was a clear fluid weeping from them. Under the skin he felt a dullish, indefinable pleasure. He'd stopped wondering about his body months ago, it'd stopped surprising him. It reacted to his sadness, erupted when he was anxious. That much he knew.

In August he would be thirty-four. His birthday was late in the month, two weeks after the eclipse, and the prospect made him nervous. If only he could leave the planet for a fortnight. Disappear into the cosmos. Up there he could find a star and make a wish, that the strange things which had been happening to his body would stop – but the peace they brought would continue.

In the kitchen alcove Rose dabbed one of August's hands with a cotton ball.

'Are you still using the cream?' she tutted.

His hands still looked sore, lightly lasered.

'No.'

'Why not?'

'I don't know, I forget it sometimes.'

'That's no good,' she chided. 'This should make the bleeding stop.'

'What is it?'

'Salt water.'

'Owwww!' August flinched, pulling his hand away a little.

Rose pulled it back. She continued to dab, but he could see she was thinking of something else.

'I'm sorry about the other morning,' Rose said, not raising her eyes from her dabbing.

'That's okay.'

'I wasn't well.'

'Salvadore was fine about it. He understood.'

'Yes,' she started to dab at the other hand. 'I can't believe my luck. He's so adoring. But I've been on my own for so long. Being with him feels odd.'

Yes, August wanted to say, *there is something odd about you and Salvadore.*

He watched her dabbing his hand, her look of concern. His hand, his face, his chest, it was all the same. Drying up.

Rose was dabbing, quiet again.

It was ridiculous, he thought. To continue like this. Making excuses. He wanted Rose to see what was happening. Maybe they could talk about it. She was well travelled, maybe she'd come across his disease. Maybe she knew what it was. She used alternative medicines. *This was something alternative.*

Courage, he thought. *Courage.*

'It's not eczema.'

Rose looked up, alert. 'Oh?'

'It's . . .' He tried to search for a name. Something, anything.

Rose looked worried.

'In winter . . .' his face perked up. 'It *was* frost. Remember? Remember how you thought that was how it looked? You noticed once.'

Rose's eyes widened as far as they could. She kept politely quiet. She nodded.

August decided to keep going.

'W-winter was the worst. Snow fell from my head . . . from my hair, big flakes. In spring . . . I grew buds . . .' He faltered, seeing Rose's increasingly incredulous face. It was all so absurd, he realized, it didn't matter what he said. But it felt so good to be saying it, letting it all out.

'I grew leaves too. From here,' August pointed to his ear. 'From everywhere, really. Now I'm drying up. It's the light, I think, or the sun, or both.'

Rose nodded, uncertain.

'It makes me feel good.' August nodded slowly, as if

he were giving evidence in court. 'I feel better than I ever have.'

Rose frowned. She was still holding his hand. She studied it as though trying to store what she'd just heard for later reflection.

August smiled at her and shrugged.

Rose's face had pulled itself inwards. She continued to dab.

Henry appeared from downstairs. 'What happened?'

August looked sheepish.

'Gus has an allergy,' Rose said.

Henry poked out her tongue and made a face.

'Maybe it's something in the gym, huh?' she mused.

August continued to look at his hand and didn't reply.

'What's this, a field hospital?' Cedric was in the café, stroking his beard.

Henry began to clear up cups and plates from the tables, piling them in the sink.

'There,' Rose sighed, dabbing her final dab.

Cedric leaned in for a closer examination. 'Looks like a birching,' he declared.

Rose looked quizzical.

'I'm fine,' August snapped, fanning his hands away from him.

Flora was standing next to Cedric in a big pale yellow dress which gently fluttered round her like a cloud of butterflies. Flora stared at August's hands and then his face and gave him an unimpressed look.

'Have you come to pay for your banoffi pie?' August replied.

'Okay.'

Flora opened her large handbag and rooted around in

it for her wallet. While she looked, Cedric and August became locked in a staring contest. Rose picked up a dishtowel to help Henry with the cups. The kitchen alcove was suddenly informal, a kitchen in a house.

'Here,' Flora handed over the money.

August broke his staring, disappearing to the till in the deli then bringing back the change. He saw Cedric had taken to staring at the curtains, new ones, with a pattern of suns and half-moons on them.

'There is going to be an eclipse of the sun,' Cedric announced.

August stopped in his tracks.

'We know,' said Henry. 'The whole world knows.'

'Well, the whole world *would* know,' Cedric retorted, imitating Henry's voice.

'What exactly is an eclipse?' asked Rose.

'It happens up to five times a year, in different countries around the world,' Flora said. 'Up to five times a year the moon blocks out the sun.'

'It's very good for the kidneys,' Cedric continued. 'A good eclipse. All that gravity and what-not being stopped for a short time. A relief on the waterworks, I'd say. I plan to be taking a good soak in the dark.'

All four of them turned to look at him with impatience.

'You're a fool,' Flora said flatly.

Cedric smiled, complimented.

'You mark my words,' he continued. 'It'll clear up those hands of yours for a start, August.'

Rose looked mistrustful.

August tucked his hands into his armpits.

He didn't want to hear another word. He wanted his old body back, his world how it had once been. He wished he'd never heard of Edward, whenever he thought of him he felt miserable.

Flora was also staring at him, strangely. Again he searched his memory for her face, a connection. Whenever she was around he felt a sense of knowing, like guilt. *She knows*, he thought. *She understands, somehow.* Her butterflies dress fluttered a little more, but there was no breeze. She smiled at him, her eyes stern, fleecing him.

'During an eclipse you can look at the sun,' she said. She squinted one eye at him, as if to demonstrate.

And then he wanted to go.

'Excuse me,' he said and went downstairs.

In the office August sat down in a chair. His eyes were hot, tears welling behind them. Patience, a liquid bubble in him, was ready to burst. He swayed a little, trying to purge himself of all his thoughts. *You can look at the sun.*

No he couldn't.

No he couldn't.

He'd already been overexposed.

There were violets in the sky the next evening, violets mixed with silvers and greys in the kind of layering usually found in rock. On summer nights it felt cramped and wrong to stay indoors so August decided to go for a walk.

He turned left out of his flat, up Lena Gardens, and left again on to Shepherd's Bush Road. On the corner there was a furniture shop which sold bad antiques, the barber's, then a shop which sold enormous terracotta pots. He stopped to stare at them, all stacked like giant tea cups. Next door was Café Rouge. On a whim, August entered, thinking he might have a beer and read one of the papers hanging up.

He went to the bar and while he was waiting to be served he spotted a table in a corner, near the window, which looked perfect. In another corner, also near the window, he saw a couple talking.

The man was wearing a cowboy hat. A white scarf was tied in a bow at Cosmo's neck. His face was polished, more lively than usual, awakened by alcohol. He was staring at the woman he was with, his eyes full of mischief. Her hair was dark, shoulder length, a dark auburn. It blended with the tones of her dress. Her legs were bare and very pale.

When she uncrossed them there was something about them August recognized.

'Gus!'

August looked left and right for an escape exit. There were only toilets and a door which led to the kitchen on either side of him, neither of which he could hide in for the rest of the evening. His shoes turned to lead. He closed his eyes, trying to hide inside himself.

'Gus, come over!'

He opened his eyes a small crack and saw Cosmo was wiping his mouth with a napkin, his eyes fixed on his face, animated and happy to see him. August smiled, stiffly. Leola turned to see who Cosmo was waving at, and waved too. August felt deflated. His legs carried him without being told to, one step, then two, unsteadily towards their table. When he reached it, he hovered, imagining himself a giant fruit bat. His elbows were suddenly longer, more bony, as though harbouring cold, thin umbrellas of skin.

'Gus, this is Leola,' Cosmo stood up as he introduced her.

'We've met,' she said, smiling up at August.

August felt a flush of happiness just from being near her. She was beautiful and looking *right at him*.

'H-how's your great aunt?' he asked.

'Oh, very well. Much better. A hundred and proud of it.'

'Still drinking eggnog?'

'Yes,' she laughed, visibly surprised he'd remembered. 'She claims it's her secret to long life.'

'Eggnog?' echoed Cosmo, worried he was missing something.

August's lips relaxed a little while Cosmo was still

saying 'Eggnog?' somewhere behind them, somewhere in another place.

'Oh, it's nothing,' Leola dismissed Cosmo, focusing on August's face, examining his features. The dryness had receded a little and now he simply appeared to be tender-skinned.

August shuffled his feet. Her gaze was soothing. It felt cool and calm to be in its wake. It spread in him, pouring like fresh blood through his veins. Very gently, he looked her in the eye and smiled.

'They say longevity is hereditary,' he continued, not knowing what he was saying, the information coming from nowhere.

She nodded. 'I know.'

'Would you like to live to a hundred?'

'If I had enough cake!'

'Cake is full of vitamins.'

'What about trifle?'

August smiled, showing his teeth.

'Packed with iron.'

'And chocolate mousse?'

'Full of fibre.' August blushed and his eyes danced about the room with a sudden surge of pride.

Leola stopped talking. She rubbed her forehead, still looking at August, letting her hand run down to the side of her neck. A thin crack had opened on his face, under one cheek. It looked like the split skin of a tomato, when boiled.

'Are you okay?' Cosmo asked her. Leola's eyes were glazed, then perplexed as she reached for her wine glass.

'Yes, fine,' she replied, not looking at either of them. 'Perhaps I've a headache coming on.'

August felt awkward, as though he should go.

'I should leave you two . . .'

'No!' Leola said quickly, reviving. 'Don't go. Stay.' She glanced confidently at Cosmo, overriding him. 'Please join us.'

She pressed her hand against her chest, pressing herself down.

'I mean . . .' she gulped, 'you don't have to. Obviously. But please do stay, if you'd like.'

August flashed his teeth.

'Are you sure?'

Cosmo looked appalled.

'Yes, of course.'

August pulled out a chair and sat.

Leola took a sip of wine, pleased.

Cosmo smiled, thinly.

August smiled at Leola.

Leola smiled back.

'I think I saw you at the pool,' she said.

'Oh?'

'Last Sunday. I go there early most Sundays.'

August felt his forehead split with surprise. He wouldn't be able to stay too long.

'It was so refreshing. So cool,' he mumbled.

Leola's eyes widened and she nodded briefly as if to tell him she'd seen how cool.

Cosmo, annoyed he was being left out again, poured August a glass of wine and picked up his own glass.

'Cheers.' He smiled at them both, expectantly.

'Cheers,' they clinked glasses.

Cosmo shifted territorially in his chair and cleared his throat.

'We go back a while, me and Gus,' he said.

Leola looked surprised.

'Really?'

'Uh-huh.'

Leola turned to August and raised her eyebrows.

'His mother was an old girlfriend of mine.'

August smiled faintly. His face was beginning to tingle. Cosmo's was oily with wine. 'We used to live in a commune together,' Cosmo continued. 'Years back. Up in Yorkshire. Gus was just a kid. Weren't you?'

Leola looked inquiringly at August.

August nodded.

'Small world,' Leola said politely. 'You didn't know August worked at the deli?'

Cosmo shook his head. 'Didn't recognize him at first.'

August wanted to go, his face and the conversation were making him uncomfortable.

'Not really. I mean I did, and didn't.'

August squirmed and smiled and his face split some more.

'But I think I knew really. His eyes. I recognized his eyes.'

August looked at Leola apologetically. He wanted to close his eyes. Vanish her, vanish them both. He wanted to punch Cosmo, knock him backwards off his chair.

Cosmo smiled at August, and laughed to himself. 'They weren't the milkman's eyes. Nooooo.' Cosmo laughed again, pleased with his impending joke. His eyes were slim, a crocodile's. The corners of his mouth were creased with dimples.

'They were the gardener's. Ha! Weren't they?'

August smiled at him, patiently.

Leola was horrified.

Cosmo leaned forward and screwed up his face.

'Don't think I don't know, Gus, what you want. Offering to help me with my stall, being polite. You just want to poke your nose into things. Find things out. Think I haven't guessed? Think I don't know what you think of me? You had the same manner as a child. The same look in your eyes. Like I'm not good enough. Ha! And with a mother like Olivia.

'Edward. A working man. He wasn't good enough *either*. She wanted none of him. His big dirty hands . . .'

Cosmo began to laugh.

August rose to his feet. His tongue was coated in sand. He put the wine glass to his lips and swallowed its contents in one.

He glared at Cosmo.

Cosmo seemed amused, indifferent as to whether what he'd said had lowered himself in front of Leola.

August smelt his acrid sweat. It made him sick.

Cosmo snorted.

'Goodbye, August,' he waved, as though commanding a performing flea to do a somersault.

'Goodbye,' August said, his voice a broken bell.

Leola gaped at them for a moment, shaking her head. Then she collected her things and followed August out the door.

Holding his face, August walked quickly up Shepherd's Bush Road. He could feel his skin was now loose on his cheeks and the dim pressure of fluid gathered in them, in great discs. He wanted to get away, far away. Not just from the restaurant. From the road, the plane tree, the deli, the whole place where he lived. He wanted to go back to his flat, pack up and disappear. He hurried, glad the sun had set and dusk had descended into the cover of night.

He held his face and walked on.

'August!' he heard a woman's voice behind him.

'August, slow down.'

It was Leola, he realized. He picked up his pace.

'I'm fine,' he said loudly, not turning round. 'Please don't worry. I just need to get home. I've forgotten something.'

'August, please . . . slow down. I . . .'

August hurried on. He heard louder footsteps and felt a hand on his elbow.

'Please stop.'

He stopped abruptly and stood in the middle of the pavement, looking away from her, into the road.

Leola stood next to him, following his gaze.

'That was awful,' she began. 'Awful of Cosmo. He's a child. He just wanted to hurt you. He was annoyed you interrupted us. August . . . please . . .'

August made his hands very straight, like two shutters, and placed them over his face. He breathed in deeply, steadying himself. He wanted to be alone, but also felt better for her presence, liked the tone of her voice. He wanted to say all kinds of things, but couldn't find the words. He sighed and saliva rattled in his breath. He smiled sadly behind his hands.

'I'm sorry,' he said into his hands. 'He gets to me. He always has. But . . . I'm okay. I burnt my face, though, in the sun.'

A few moments passed. Neither of them said a word. Then August punched out a deep breath. He took his hands from his face and turned towards her.

Leola drew her head back a little. She shook her head and exhaled and kept shaking her head as she stared at him.

His house was only a few feet away.

'I just live there,' he pointed and began to walk slowly towards the flat.

Unsure of herself, Leola nodded. And then followed.

As they climbed the steps to his front door she took hold of his arm.

August lay stretched out on the sofa.

While he'd been out heat had collected inside his flat, packed itself tightly into corners, the seams of the sofa, under the carpet. He'd opened the bay window when they entered. But more heat flowed in. On the sofa he lay very still. Above him, the sepia stain of Africa was distant, wavering in his vision. Outside the night lay soft and heavy, a body slumped against the glass of the window. He wanted to go to sleep.

Leola appeared in the doorway with a damp flannel.

'I'm o-okay,' he protested, shakily. 'Really. Pl-please don't worry. You should go. I've ruined your evening.'

'Don't be ridiculous,' Leola tutted. 'I was dying of boredom. You saved me.'

'Oh. I thought . . .'

She smiled at him, half-knowingly. 'What?'

'That you've been seeing Cosmo.'

She threw her head back and laughed heartily. When she stopped she looked at him, her cheeks pink. 'No.'

'Oh.' August smiled at her, big and happy. 'I was just . . . I . . .'

'He's old enough to be my father.'

'But he's handsome. And has a way. I thought . . .'

Leola dismissed this line of inquiry with a shake of the head and a look of disapproval. She walked over to him but appeared uneasy, not knowing where or how close to sit.

'Here,' she said, proffering the flannel from an arm's distance. 'Put this on your face.'

August sat up a little and took the flannel from her.

'I must look a fright,' he apologized. Gingerly, he patted his cheeks with it. 'Aaaaahh-owww.'

'It looks a lot worse than sunburn,' Leola said, wincing also. 'It looks more like an . . . outbreak of some sort.'

August lay back again and draped the flannel over his face, squirming at the coldness of it. Leola perched on the end of the sofa, near his feet.

'You should go and see a doctor.'

He nodded. He saw the doctor, his walnut eyes. And the backs of Leola's legs. They caused an ache, like nausea, in his gut.

'I have.'

'And what did the doctor say?'

'Stress.' The word came out muffled.

Leola smiled.

'How long's it been like this?'

August sat up again. The flannel slipped from his head and he took it away with one hand. His face was heart red, intimately tender. Two large water blisters on his cheeks made him appear comically rag doll-like. In places the epidermis had torn. His hair was rumpled to one side like a fence hit by a strong wind. His eyes were luminescent.

'Since December,' he said, squinting, trying to think of a time, a date. 'Since before Christmas. Since Cosmo moved in,' he jerked his thumb backwards. 'A few doors down.'

Leola was astonished.

'No.'

He nodded.

'Since a cheese arrived, the orange one you like, the Mimolette. We never used to have it before December. I dunno. Maybe it is an allergy. But . . .' he breathed out and smiled reassuringly.

'I feel great.'

Leola frowned.

'It's lovely,' he said, tracing the line of his jawbone with his index fingers. 'Like a force . . . It seems to . . .' he looked thoughtfully, at his knees, '*Flow*.'

He glanced up at her. He knew what to expect but he didn't care.

'With the seasons.'

Leola's brow furrowed.

'Cosmo . . .' he started. 'He was around me a lot as a child. I was an only child, but one of many in the commune. We lived in a big old house in Yorkshire. My father died before we moved there. Or so my mother always told me . . .'

He lightly pressed the cold flannel across his forehead. He closed his eyes. *He was tired.* He opened them again and smiled.

'But now I know about Edward.'

'The gardener?'

August sighed.

'Yes.'

'Cosmo knew him?'

'I don't know. Perhaps. He's jealous of Edward somehow. I don't know. My mother refuses to talk about him. Cosmo told me some stuff. I don't really know what to believe. I've been trying to find out. There was trouble, someone died . . .'

'And your body . . .' Leola interrupted. 'You think it's connected?'

August looked perplexed.

'To what?'

'To Edward.'

August shook his head. 'No. I had all these symptoms months ago. Long before I found out about Edward. If it's connected to anyone it's Cosmo. I've always loathed him. I was mixed up. I thought for a while *he* was my father.'

'Cosmo?'

August nodded.

Leola seemed amazed. 'I find that hard to see.'

'Well . . .'

She looked serious for a moment, thinking, her fingers to her lips.

'I saw your arm once, in winter. It was covered in something . . . I thought at the time how odd it was, it looked like frost. And in the pool. All that steam. You talk about a force. Or a flow. I don't know what I'm trying to say. I don't know you, even. It feels good, you said.'

August nodded.

'Like a connection?'

August nodded.

'With,' she looked around her and forced her hands up through the air like tulip heads. 'This. Everything around you. The air . . .' Her hands bloomed open.

August nodded.

'Well, maybe it's a *gift*.'

August stared. 'What d'you mean?'

'An instinct. Edward must have it. You know.'

'No.'

'Like father, like son.'

August went into a daze. He shook his head slowly. It was ridiculous. He smiled, wanly, needing to be alone. He wanted to feel the dim, sublime ache, the comfort preceding sleep: the pull into the slit in the world.

'No,' he said distantly. 'I don't think you're right.' He smiled at her politely, as if at a child, or someone who'd said something they didn't really know about. 'I've killed every plant I've ever had.'

* * *

August woke the next morning with the sensation of being lain upon. As though another person, or a large heavy form had been lying on him, pressing him down. The form lifted itself off and disappeared the moment he became conscious. He was still on the sofa, fully clothed. Leola was gone. He looked around and saw that a silky white light shone out beyond the window. Cars were passing. He was emotionless, unable to get up. He lay there for several moments before his thoughts came skating back to him, tracing thin figures of eight on his mind.

He smiled, faintly.

Like father, like son. The idea caused a quake in the inner halls of his body, an ecstatic fear. He looked outside, at the pure silk of the sun dropping imperceptibly from the sky.

He thought of his mother, and the fear became more tangible, more potent. His breath quickened. An awareness came to him from nowhere, from outside the window; a sharp and pitying sadness filled him up, made him sigh deeply and want to shut his eyes. He was unbearably sad for no reason, sad for his mother.

The heat wave was good for business, causing an unending demand for salads and sandwiches, fruit and cold fizzy drinks. Thirst was a phenomenon. The whole city was thirsty, or so it seemed. Customers would appear at the till, clutching their throats, parched, craving relief. People couldn't get enough to drink and the deli couldn't sell enough liquid. August filled the fridges with ice cold smoothies and fruit juices; also bottles of cider from Brittany, elderflower water and freshly pressed English apple juice. Wines too: an organic Chardonnay bursting with a melonish grape, a gooseberry flavoured Sauvignon Blanc, a shy and strange vino rosso which tasted of cherries. People bought these by the armload and business boomed.

In an effort to keep the deli cool, Rose had installed a standard fan, its back to one of the windows, and it stood formal and valiant, blowing ordered waves of air across the room.

August's face was less swollen, the blisters had dried and been rubbed off overnight, leaving only the faintest trace of dead skin.

At three-ish, when he and Henry were in the café still

clearing plates, Rose appeared, framed in the doorway, lively and radiant. She'd missed lunch, again having gone out with Salvadore. She was wearing a floor length, colourful shift with trumpet sleeves, on her feet a pair of floral terry towelling sandals. Both seemed incongruous with her short silver hair and her thick square glasses, but she appeared proud of her new wardrobe, liberated in it.

August's face broke into a smile.

'Hello.'

Rose smiled back, graciously. 'How was lunch?'

'Okay. Busy, as usual.'

Rose was momentarily disconcerted by his face, then cocked her head.

'Where's Henry?'

August gestured towards the alcove. 'Washing up.'

Rose looked in that direction. 'Oh, there you are. Have you found the order book?'

Henry's back was to her, facing the sink. 'No,' Henry replied in a small voice, as though trying to make the smallest reply to make Rose go away. She remained facing the wall.

Rose tutted. 'Where could it be?'

August saw Henry raise her shoulders in a large shrug, then put a plate on the washing-up rack to dry.

'That's still soapy,' Rose admonished.

Silently, Henry took the plate back.

Rose stared at her back. 'Henry?'

Henry stopped washing up and stood still in front of the sink, staring at the wall.

Rose walked closer. Realizing Henry wasn't going to turn round, she went closer still.

'Henry?'

Henry turned round. Her face was streaked with tears. She looked past Rose.

'What's *wrong*, dear?' Rose asked, quickly.

Henry shook her head.

'Is it Yves?'

Henry smiled with only one side of her mouth.

August felt inept, out of place; this was women's business.

Rose gave Henry a beady look over her glasses and held the expression.

Henry sniffed. She looked down at her hands. Sniffed again. 'He hit me.'

Rose shook her head slowly, her eyes narrowing. She peered over her glasses.

'Over the back of the head,' Henry continued, carefully. 'Knocked me down.'

August felt a blunt, cold anger in him.

'Mmmmmmmm,' Rose mused.

'I think I've had enough.'

This time Henry's face crumpled and fresh tears began to pour down her cheeks, which plumped up. Rose watched and let her cry for a few moments. Henry leaned back on the sink staring blindly, the tears falling quickly, like water from a tap.

'I wish . . . I'd never met him,' Henry dragged the words through snot and tears. 'I don't like him.'

'No,' Rose agreed. She shot August a look of disapproval and mouthed the word 'rat'.

Henry shook her head and blew her nose into a piece of her shirt.

'I'm sorry . . . I've been unhappy, not myself recently. I'm sorry, August . . .'

August shook his head.

'We're very incompatible, I think.'

Rose nodded.

'I find . . .' She seemed confused. She looked up, into a space above her head. 'Do you find this? . . . it sounds silly. But, sex. It's a strong thing, isn't it?' She sucked her breath in, deeply, bubbling spit in her mouth. 'What Yves wants, it's too much, too strong for me . . .'

'Oh, my dear,' Rose muttered.

August was astounded. Henry's words tolled shamefully in him and he closed his eyes.

Henry took a small step towards Rose and the two women hugged, Rose rocking Henry in her arms.

'Stay here tonight,' Rose soothed, patting and stroking her on the back. 'There, there, dear. Don't cry. It's okay. It's okay. Stay with me as long as you like. It's easy, really. Things don't have to be hard. It isn't a difficult thing to do. To stop doing something that's bad for you . . . there, there,' she patted.

Henry broke the hug and tried to smile at Rose, her mouth pulled down and pursed together, holding back more tears.

Rose smiled, reassuringly.

'Don't worry about anything, dear. I have an extra room.'

* * *

Jim walked into the deli just as August was preparing to leave. It was good to see him, as usual. His hair had thinned a little more, and even the heat wave hadn't managed to prise him from his dark second-hand suit. He was wearing sunglasses, small black spots over his eyes: a blind priest.

August smiled as he came and leaned against the display fridge.

'I was just passing,' Jim smiled, sweetly.

August was aware of a feeling of having his troubles relieved. The sight of Jim sent a wave of comfort through him. Jim was just the person he wanted to talk to. Jim, who was so different, always on an even keel. A man of the world, a father. Someone to whom everything came easily.

'I'll be one minute,' August replied. 'Shall we go for a drink?'

Jim nodded.

August slipped off his apron and went downstairs to collect his jacket.

Henry was in the kitchen, slicing a peach into pieces, arranging the pieces into flower petals on a plate. She looked up with vacant, unhappy eyes. He glanced at the flower, wanting to tell her he understood.

'Are you going to move in upstairs?'

She nodded.

'Do you need any help?'

She shook her head.

'Will you let me know if you do?'

She nodded again and smiled, unhappily.

He smiled back, showing his teeth. 'See you tomorrow, then.'

Henry nodded.

Jim and August sat at an old, weather-stripped picnic table

outside The Green Man. The heat was even closer to the ground and there was a cramped, trapped feeling in the air, as if the ozone's nylon stocking had lowered, pushing down the atmosphere. Around them Londoners were lightly cooked. They glowed prawn pink and perspired. Most had given up on trying to look stylish. Bra straps sagged, hair was pasted to faces. Passers-by were soiled, bothered.

August felt terrific.

'How's Alex?' he asked Jim.

Jim grinned. 'Still training for Glyndebourne.'

August took a large swig of his lager and put it down. 'He must . . . he must have *something* from you.'

Jim was perplexed.

'Must have some of your talents,' August pushed.

Jim thought about it, the corners of his mouth turned down. Then he brightened.

'He's quiet, like me, yeah. And he likes peas.'

August laughed. 'Nothing else?'

Jim shook his head.

'No . . .' August shifted a little and felt strangely watched, strangely duplicitous, '*gifts*?'

Jim laughed at the idea. 'No! What, like my gift for divining water, or healing the sick?'

August blushed. 'Okay, okay . . . I . . . just . . .'

'What?'

'It's nothing. Someone I know had this crazy idea.'

'What idea?'

August sighed and shook his head. 'Nothing.'

'No, what?'

August's face became earnest. He leaned closer to Jim, clutching the table with his fingertips. 'If you . . . if you and Louise had split up, after Kathy was born.'

Jim nodded.

'If Louise moved to Ireland, just say, or, I don't know, Spain. And took Kathy. And she made it clear she never wanted to see you again. And you couldn't see Kathy either.'

Jim's face became serious.

'H-how would you feel?'

Jim shook his head, disbelievingly. 'God, what a terrible thing. August, what's wrong with you? What an idea.'

August blushed and was embarrassed by himself, his gloominess. He wished he'd said nothing. Trying to compare his life to everybody else.

'I'd be heartbroken,' Jim said. 'Heartbroken.'

August looked away and up, catching sight of the sign above the pub. He'd never really noticed it before. In it there was a profusion of greenery, some shrubs, lilies, a garden of some sort. He studied it more closely. In the midst of the greenery two eyes looked out. Then August saw the lilies were in fact a beard, two wide palm leaves were cheeks. Grass was in fact hair, daisies threaded through it in a wreath. In the sign he saw a man, covered in plants. A green man. He looked away quickly, out into the passing traffic. He wanted to run. He smiled distractedly at Jim and picked up his pint and began to breathe slowly, evenly.

August opened his eyes. Immediately he was aware of being covered, softly pressed down. The sensation was similar to the other time: except now, something had been left behind.

It was all over him.

He stared straight ahead, at the ceiling, praying whatever had come in the night, whatever it was, wouldn't be too hard to look at. He breathed in, feeling a lushness flow through his veins. Against one ear he could feel the lightest touch, the kiss of kid-suede lips. Over his legs, around his genitals, his arms, his legs, his back, his face, a second layer had formed. Smooth, silky. Little mouths.

Steeling himself, he rolled back the bedclothes. He swallowed and then slowly looked down.

Lilies.

His body was a bed of stark sunbursts. Hundreds of lilies whose deep throats were speckled with maroon and danced with tiny saffron dragon's heads. Lilies like a suit, like opulent armour. Heads and heads, each in full bloom. Pink trumpets. Salmon stars. Each more marvellous and exquisite than the last. August looked and laughed at the surprise of them. He propped himself up on his elbows.

The flowers moved as if under them his body was fluid, as if they were a flotilla of water lilies. They jostled. He stretched out his hand and ran it over their soft open mouths. The feeling was intramuscular, as though he was being caressed *inside.*

He made his fingers into tweezers and reached out towards where he guessed his navel was. Carefully, he found the base of a perfect pink open flower. Cautiously, he plucked it off.

'Ahhhh!'

A tiny stab of love.

He picked another.

And then another.

He sat up in bed. His upper body was a dense, soft pink trellis of flowers. He stroked his chest slowly, with both hands.

Then he began to pluck each flower off.

When all the flowers were gone, August stood in front of the long mirror in his bedroom. Each had left a tiny pinkish mark, a dim ring of dots, making him look as though he'd had a tussle with an octopus.

When the door bell rang he snatched his robe from the door and pulled on his pyjama bottoms.

He opened the first door, then the second.

'All right, Gus . . . Wow!'

Cosmo was standing on the steps.

'What happened to your face?'

August looked past Cosmo, left and right up the street. Then he saw the three tea chests at the bottom of the steps.

'What are those?' he asked, coldly.

Cosmo laughed a little, as if he'd just noticed them too.

'These? Oh, ah . . . I was wondering if I could leave some stuff with you . . . for the stall. My landlady is giving me a hard time, says she doesn't want any more boxes. And you live so close.'

His eyes were both worried and friendly. 'It won't be for very long.'

'No,' August said flatly.

Cosmo looked taken aback. 'Oh, Gus . . . please,' he whined. 'Oh, man. Why not?'

'You want me to *help* you after the other night?'

Cosmo looked lost. His eyebrows knitted.

'The gardener's son,' August threw the words down at him.

Cosmo suddenly remembered. His expression changed to a unconvincing look of repentance.

'Oh . . .'

'Spineless and cheap, in front of Leola. Trying to make me look small.'

'Gus . . . I . . .'

'You're a liar. And a crook, I want nothing to do with your lousy stall. All stolen goods, I'm sure.'

Cosmo's eyes bulged.

'Hey, Gus, whooaa. What are you talking about? What's wrong? This stuff is all legit. Promise. Really.'

'I don't care.'

Cosmo frowned, not knowing what else to say.

'Funny how you always bring up my past when there's a woman around. You could have told me about him months ago. Who he was, where he'd come from. You were just trying to put me down. Like you did when I was a child. You wanted to know more than me, make me an object of ridicule. Well, you can't hurt me any more. I already knew all about Edward.'

August was shaking. He'd never spoken with so much heat.

Cosmo appeared dumbfounded.

'You just want to hurt me and my mother,' he continued. 'I must look so gullible, a big stupid mug. Because she never loved you, you macho prick.' If there had been a large rock nearby, August would have picked it up and hurled it at Cosmo.

Cosmo shook his head. He stepped back one stair and opened his mouth to speak.

'I . . .' He stopped; he maintained an upward gaze, a look of disorientation in his face.

'I was . . .'

August squinted him down.

'I was hurt by your mother. She used me . . . like a rag to wipe her shoes. She was cleverer than me. That's what it was. I couldn't reach her, make her laugh. I suppose you don't know what that's like.' There was a sad, desperate look in his eyes. He shook his head again, an old man.

August marvelled. Cosmo could still turn him soft.

Cosmo fixed him with tired eyes and his mouth became crumpled with injustice.

'You're right.'

August kept squinting, lip curled.

'About the women, about trying to put you down. I . . .'

August heard a rushing in his ears. Heat rose up from his feet, through his body.

'You're young. You're *his* son. You have it all in front of you. *I'm a mug*. Not you, Gus. You're clever. You'll never end up like me.'

'How's that then?' August asked sarcastically.

'Alone.'

August's rage stopped abruptly. He scowled at Cosmo. He'd never thought of Cosmo as lonely. It was unthinkable.

'Sorry,' Cosmo muttered. 'I . . .' He scanned August's face, openly examining the small rings left by the lilies. His mouth became hollow and narrow, as if to force out what he wanted to say next.

'I guess I'm jealous,' his face fell around his mouth. He nodded, as if to back these words up.

August was stunned. Behind Cosmo the street and the boxes were a blur.

Cosmo smiled in reconciliation.

August wanted to turn around, slam the door in Cosmo's face. Cosmo began to climb back down the rest of the stairs, dejected.

'Okay,' said August.

Something about the way Cosmo moved, feet cramped inwards, something about his lack of coordination, his caved-inness, suddenly became clear.

'Bring them in.'

After Cosmo had gone August looked at his watch and found it was already mid-morning. The tea chests were stacked in a corner of the hall, not too in the way. He'd agreed to keep them for a week at the longest. His next shift at the deli started at two. Enough time for another dip in the pool.

August walked down Uxbridge Road humming a salsa. He was better than he'd been in weeks, sharper, clearer in the head. *Confident* was a word which occurred to him. But this wasn't quite right. He was more alive, more lithe. He found himself fighting the urge to dance a little to the tune he was humming. *Groovy.*

That was it, he felt groovy.

The morning was sunny but the heat wave was cooling off, making him less self-conscious about his layers of clothing, his Kangol fishing hat pulled down over his eyes. He didn't need sunglasses, a continued thrill. The sun was on his face, his eyes were bald and naked in the light. He glanced around him, taking in the busy road. A man cycled past in sandals and white socks, a large black woman crossing was wearing a red lycra jump suit. London was a place for eccentrics, he reassured himself.

He continued down the street, humming and bouncing a little as he walked. As he passed a newsagent a Wall's chest cooler near the doorway caught his eye. On an impulse he stopped and went in. When he came out he stood on the pavement holding an orange ice lolly.

As he licked he recognized a woman not too far away,

coming towards him. There was a hardware store a few shops down with gardening tools hanging outside and rabbit hutches displayed on the pavement in front. Leola was walking right towards him, but her eyes were dreamy, her head lifted up as though contemplating a cloud of midges four feet above her and to the right.

'Owwww,' she cried out, as she walked straight into a rabbit hutch. Clutching her toe, she stretched her other hand out to lean against the side of the shop and a rake fell from a hook on to her head.

'Oww,' she cried out again, walking into more tools. A spade fell off a hook, and a hoe, clattering loudly to the ground.

August grinned.

'Oh, God,' she wailed.

A shop assistant came out, smiling at her politely, and began to pick up the tools.

'I'm so sorry,' Leola cringed. 'I'm so clumsy. I was dreaming. I never look where I'm going. I . . .'

August's feet moved him towards her without being ordered.

'Hello.'

Leola looked up.

August was standing in front of her in his fishing hat and overcoat and long trousers. His face was terrible, covered in strange marks like squid suckers, but his eyes were looking at her timidly, with hope.

'Hello,' she blushed. 'I just knocked all this over.'

August smiled. 'I saw.'

'Oh, dear,' she laughed.

The shop assistant, having picked everything up, disappeared back into the shop.

They stood for a few moments on the pavement, saying nothing. August stared at her, unable to think or talk. His face was peeling, strangely spotted, his teeth hung like tiles. He breathed audibly in and out, his chest rising and falling, but his eyes collected colour the longer he gazed at her. The corners of his mouth began to rise.

'I think you look very graceful,' he said.

Leola turned raspberry. She huffed, as if choking on a dry ball of air in her throat.

'W-would you like to go for a cup of coffee?'

Leola smiled and nodded.

August and Leola sat under a Martini umbrella at a small café on Brackenbury Road. When a waiter came to take their order his eyes widened at the sight of August's face and he kept his distance. August knew he must look a mess or worse, *contagious*; as though he had some kind of plague. Leola was looking at him expectantly, waiting for him to say something.

'I might not look it,' he drew a circle in the air around his face. 'But I feel a lot better.'

Leola smiled, kindly.

'What you said. The other night. After we left the restaurant . . . I've been thinking about it ever since. Maybe you're right. Maybe I'm coming into something. Maybe something has begun, something which will die down or become less . . .' he smiled, 'noticeable.'

The waiter brought a basket of bread and butter and two white filter coffees.

'Anything else?'

August looked at Leola inquiringly.

'Do you do breakfast?' she asked.

'Breakfast?'

'Brunch?'

The waiter nodded.

'I'm starving,' she flashed August a hungry smile. 'Bacon and eggs?'

The waiter wrote this down.

August was staring at the freckles on her nose.

The waiter stood waiting, glaring at him as though he was stupid.

'Uh, times two please,' August added.

The waiter scribbled again and backed away.

'Enough about me, anyway,' August waved his hands at himself. 'What about you? Leola sounds Italian or something.'

'I'm English,' she smiled, amused. 'Leola is the name of a town.'

August almost shot out of his seat. His eyes widened.

'Oh.'

'It's a small town in Arkansas, where my parents met.'

'Oh.'

'They were hippies and went travelling afterwards, in an old Chevrolet, across the States. Very romantic.'

These facts orbited around August's head. He thought of Luke and his mother, they'd done a similar thing.

'What does your father do?' August asked. He reached forward for a piece of bread and began to butter it.

Leola watched him.

'He's a salesman, Yellow Pages. Been doing it for the last twenty years.'

August nodded, stuffing bread in his mouth, his cheeks bulging as he chewed.

'My mother, she likes plants. She grows her own vegetables, has a herb garden. I take after her.'

August nodded again. Her mother was a gardener, her name was a place. She was intuitive, beautiful. Clumsy, dreamy.

'I haven't travelled much,' she continued. 'I grew up around here, in West London. Around Ladbroke Grove. I went to the local comprehensive. We've always been poor. No money to travel, really.'

August gulped.

'No, me neither.' He nodded his head emphatically, in agreement. 'I've never left the country.'

'Where would you like to go, if you could?'

August stared past her shoulder, then smiled. 'Antarctica.'

Leola's face erupted with delight. 'Me too!'

They both blushed and went quiet.

'The emperor penguins,' Leola continued.

'And the seals.'

'Great floes of ice.'

August felt his eyes wobbling in their sockets.

The bacon and eggs arrived, their sharp salty smell halting the conversation. When the waiter had gone, August regarded the two watery egg eyes on the plate, the rashers of bacon. He grinned and stabbed at the yolks with his knife.

They began to eat heartily, not saying much. Their attack was mutual. As they ate with slurpy noises their eye contact was furtive and self-knowing, comically apologetic. Again August saw the Mimolette spinning away from them, on its axis. He saw Leola's great-aunt, drinking eggnog. Leola had egg yolk glistening on her lips. A tiny speck of yellow sat in her hair. He was full, elated at being with her.

They continued to eat, as if they'd done so together many times.

When he was finished August stared down at his empty plate and smiled, showing his big teeth. He picked up the last piece of bread and began to clean his knife and fork with it. Leola watched him and smiled. August put his clean knife and fork down on his plate, popped the bread in his mouth and sighed heavily. He grinned at her as he chewed, then closed his eyes and basked. The sun on his skin was a light but steady flow of happiness.

* * *

In the deli Rose and Henry were still serving a queue of customers. August nodded his hellos and slipped quickly past them and down the stairs where he shed his fishing hat and overcoat and tied on a clean apron. Before returning upstairs he went quickly to the bathroom to check his face.

The rings of dots had vanished. His face was completely clear, unmarked and unlined by cracks or splits for the first time since the heat wave began. He looked like himself. If anything, his skin was better – it glowed a little. He left the bathroom and climbed the stairs with a sense of relief. In the deli he joined Rose and Henry behind the display fridge.

Henry didn't see him when he came into the deli. Neither did August. Rose had her back turned, at the slicer.

Surreptitiously, he joined the back of the queue, his blue baseball cap pulled down over his eyes.

When it came to his turn he simply stood and smiled, as if it would be enough to make Henry change her mind.

Henry's eyes welled up.

'Yves!'

'Oui.'

'Qu'est-ce que tu fais ici?'

Yves shrugged, the collar of his shirt nuzzling up against his stubble which was virtually black. His nose was sharp, his nostrils slanted and scooped deep enough to hold prawn salad.

'Dites-moi,' he drawled, 'où reste-tu maintenant?'

Henry shook her head.

A woman in the queue with a melting beehive tutted and waved her baguette.

'Pas maintenant, chéri,' Henry pleaded.

Yves was restless, dissatisfied.

'*Excuse* me,' the woman said.

Henry looked around quickly for Rose. She was slicing ham, talking to a regular customer on the other side of the glass counter. August was grinding coffee, his back to the deli too.

'Can I pay?' the woman asked, impatiently. Her beehive was listing to one side, her lipstick was running.

'Yes, of course,' Henry replied.

'Excuse *me*, lady,' Yves snapped at her. Her eyes rolled and she stepped back a little.

'*I* am in front,' he turned to stare her off.

'Henry, what's going on?' Rose appeared with the ham in her hands. She glanced at Yves and then back at Henry.

'Is this . . . ?'

Henry nodded.

Rose put the ham down on the counter.

Yves stared at her with contempt.

August turned around and saw Yves. And Rose, and Henry looking nervous, the long queue. He held back, deciding it was politic to let Rose handle Yves, to intervene only if needed.

Rose smiled politely. 'I think you should go,' she said in a firm voice.

Yves glared at Rose with a hard, supercilious face.

'This isn't . . . votre affair,' he struggled. 'Your business.'

'Yes it is. Henry works for *me*. And you are in *my* shop.'

'Oh, *fuck* you, you . . .' He stopped. 'Je veux parler avec Henry.'

August's ears rang. He knew there was a rolling pin somewhere behind him, stowed behind the grinder.

Rose's face flipped to crimson.

The woman with the beehive flattened herself against the shelf which held the chutneys. There was a silence as the other customers settled in to watch.

'If you don't go immediately, I'll call the police.' Rose grew inches in her moccasins.

'I'll speak to him for a minute,' Henry said, frightened. 'We can talk outside.'

'No you won't.' Rose pushed her away from the counter.

'Where are you staying,' Yves asked her one more time.

'None of your business,' Rose replied.

'I've had enough of you, you stupid . . . old *lesbian*,' Yves threatened, pointing his finger.

Henry visibly quailed.

August started looking for the pin.

The bouffant woman closed her eyes.

The other customers clutched their bags of fresh basil, their pots of artichokes.

'Get out,' Rose whispered.

Yves smiled.

'Get out!' she roared. Her face was livid.

'Lesbian,' Yves sneered.

Rose lifted the counter lid up and for a moment they stood with nothing between them. A mild look of surprise flickered across Yves's face.

August was frozen.

Rose laughed. Then punched Yves in the face.

'See how it feels,' she shouted. She hit him again, sending him reeling backwards. 'You bully, you coward, you bloody bully, come on,' she punched him again. *Thwack*, this time there was a crunch.

'You fucking crazy bitch,' Yves muttered, cradling his face.

It was a Monday afternoon. It was summer. Sunlight was smiling into the shop. Seven or eight customers were staring at him, shocked. And there was a small, strong woman in a kaftan who had battered his face, standing with her fists bared, ready to polish him off.

Yves glared at her, at the situation, with disbelief.

'Now get out,' Rose repeated.

Yves slipped past her, and walked out of the shop.

In his kitchen that evening August was intent on making a flummery of raspberries. Over the years he'd perfected his own recipe: two glasses of raspberry jelly melted with one and a half cups of water and the juice of half a lemon. One glass of milk. Fresh raspberries, mashed. Pour the mixture into a mould and refrigerate. Serve with single cream. Drink with it a fine claret.

August was mashing raspberries when the door bell rang. He leapt. Perhaps it was Cosmo, wanting his boxes back. He hoped it was, he could sit down with him again, push him down in fact, on to the sofa, approach him from a different angle. He left the raspberries and hurried down the hall, opening both doors with a sense of conviction: he would pump Cosmo, ask him all the right questions.

Two policemen stood on his doorstep. Both had thin lips and thin eyes and walkie-talkies stuffed under the epaulettes of their navy jumpers.

'Mr Chalmin?' one of them asked.

Guilt swelled instantly in August. It poured out his eyes, making his sight blur.

'Y-y-es,' he blinked.

'I'm Detective Barker and this is PC Michaels. May we come in?'

August nodded. He turned stiffly and led them down the corridor; on the way his eyes landed on the boxes and his stomach plunged. There was a short, perceptible silence as the policemen followed him in.

'Are these yours?' Detective Barker stopped in front of the boxes, as if he'd expected them to be there. He budged one a little with his toe. August felt stupidity rumble up behind him. *Stupid, stupid, stupid. Gullible and dumb.*

'No. No, they're not.'

The two policeman looked at each other, as if they knew they were in for a story.

'Can we have a look inside them?' asked Detective Barker.

August nodded, vigorously.

He went to the kitchen and brought back a sharp knife which he used to slit open the tape along the joins of the flaps. He stood back. Detective Barker looked into the first box. August could see it was full of very colourful cloth and wooden boxes and objects made from brass, just like the objects he'd sold on the stall months ago. He remembered how he'd been impressed by the quality of the merchandise – it *must* be stolen, he decided. *Bloody liar, bloody thieving lying bastard.*

'I see,' said Detective Barker.

PC Michaels stared into the box too. 'Looks like the same stuff,' he said.

'Yes, it does,' agreed Detective Barker.

'I-it's. Not m-mine,' August stammered, trying to look each of them in the eye. 'It belongs to a friend, well, not really a friend. It belongs to someone I know who has a stall in the market. I'm keeping them for him.'

The two policemen stared at him, patiently.

August was angry, mainly with himself. He was a beginner, a ridiculous bumbling beginner in the art of using others; what had he been thinking? He'd say nothing, he silently vowed to keep in whatever he could. He'd find Cosmo later, for now say as little as possible.

Detective Barker reached into the box and took out a fat bolt of colourful cloth. He sniffed it deeply and made a knowing face. He began to unwrap the bolt, letting the cloth fall to the floor. August watched, with growing disbelief.

'Yup,' said Detective Barker.

The cloth lay like a drunken python on the floor. In his hands the detective held a small flat package wrapped in plastic, about the size of a thin book. He sniffed it again.

August stared at the package. His breath had thinned and he felt faint.

'What is it?'

Detective Barker grunted. For the first time since he'd come in his manner became flinty.

'Black Lebanese.'

August stared at the package as though it was a piece of Noah's Ark. He wanted to sit down. He grimaced at it, at Cosmo, amazed Cosmo could be up to anything so serious or organized. His face turned a deep pink, his forehead was damp.

'Probably a lot more of it in there,' said PC Michaels.

August glared into the box.

Detective Barker looked around. 'Can we sit down?'

August showed them into the living room where the two policemen sat down on the sofa. PC Williams took out his notebook and began to scribble. August pulled a chair from the table by the bay window and positioned it, interview style, in front of them.

'Mr Chalmin,' Detective Barker began.

This was no time to put him right, August thought, explain his name was Hay. August nodded.

'How long have you had these boxes?'

'Uh . . . a few days.'

The policemen looked at each other.

PC Michaels made a note.

August felt his bowels loosen. He tried to smile, hoping that a bright face might stop this from happening, but his lips were heavy.

'We won't beat around the bush, Mr Chalmin. We've been trying to catch Cosmo Rodriguez for some time. Do you know where he's gone?'

August stared at the policeman as if he'd just uttered a sentence in a different language.

'Gone?'

Detective Barker sighed, long and deliberate.

'Yes, gone. We thought you might know where. He's always in and out of the country, always in and out, in and out.'

August flinched, his throat constricted.

'Gone?' he repeated.

Detective Barker looked thoroughly fed up.

'Cosmo Rodriguez skipped the country yesterday,' he said. 'We were wondering if you might know where he went.'

'N-no. I don't.'

Detective Barker's chest swelled as he sighed inwardly, deeply.

'I'm afraid we're going to have to take you in.'

August didn't know exactly what he meant.

'In?'

'For questioning.'

'To the station,' said PC Michaels.

August was shocked and calm. He imagined the station: filing cabinets, plywood walls, concrete cells, a room with a desk and chair, a tape recorder running. He stemmed the urge to vomit.

'Yes, of course,' he said and stood up. 'I'll just get my jacket.'

He went into his bedroom and stood for a minute, thinking. He knew he was innocent of anything to do with Cosmo and his dealings. The truth would come out. He knew he had to keep a cool head, be serious, and he'd be fine. He knew this, but was still shaken. Deeply betrayed. Cosmo, a drug dealer, the idea was silly . . . And then obvious. Why would time change things? Cosmo had dealt drugs twenty years ago, why not now? It was an easy trade, one he knew. August sighed – Cosmo and his mother, they were buoys. Bobbing in his life. Light, unsinkable. Attached to him. Surface anchors.

He went into the kitchen. He took the bowl of wine coloured mush and put it in the fridge.

He went back into the living room and signalled he was ready.

'Okay then, let's go,' said Detective Barker.

* * *

The phone rang.

'Hello?' August said sleepily into the receiver. He'd been dreaming about a whale.

'Hi there.' It was Jim.

'What time is it?' August groaned.

'Early.'

August squinted at the alarm clock by the side of his bed. It was 7.30 a.m.

'Why are you ringing me so early, what's wrong?'

'Nothing.'

'Then why are you calling, where've you been?'

'We're off to see the eclipse.'

'Oh, God.'

'Wanna come?'

'No.'

'Are you sure? We're leaving in a couple of hours. We're going to stay at a friend of Isabel's in Cornwall so we can be there for it tomorrow. Get a day off. We'll pick you up.'

'No. I can't. I've had too much time off work recently. Besides, I don't want to see the eclipse.'

'Why not?'

'I don't know.'

'You're not still . . . . sick?'

'Yeah, I think I am.'

'Come to the beach. It'll do you good.'

'I've had too much sun already.'

'Okay, Gus.' Jim sounded sad.

'Really, I'm fine.'

'I'll think of you.'

'Thanks.'

'Bye.'

August put the receiver back down.

The eclipse. The word made him sink into a dark green pool.

He thought of the dream he'd been having before Jim

called. In it an enormous whale was tethered to the bottom of a dark green bay in a tiny, volcanic island. The whale was moored like a buoy, unable to move. There was a long, slim jetty which stretched from the shore into the middle of the bay. An otter trotted down the jetty and stopped at the end, where a rope was tied to the end of it. The otter had begun to clamber along the rope.

Finally, the weather cooled. Early on the morning of the eclipse it rained for the first time in weeks, settling the dust and pollen, leaving behind a pebble-smooth, minty feel to the air, a relaxed and mild depression.

Before the deli opened, August took a pastry and a cup of coffee out to one of the tables on the pavement. It was good to be outdoors, with his shirtsleeves rolled up. There were hardly any cracks left on his forearms. His face and body were welded, smoother where the cracks once were. He could feel a breeze run up under his shirt, wrap cool milky arms around his face. As he bit into his pastry he closed his eyes.

At last, he thought, *things could be turning*.

At the police station there'd been a regulation questioning and fingerprinting. He'd been as helpful as possible. Cosmo was small fry, they'd said, a small-time smuggler, hashish and cannabis. They'd said he was lucky he hadn't had his legs broken yet by the competition. This was the reason they'd been slow to catch him, he wasn't a priority. Small-time smugglers were more likely to be scared off by the bigger fish than by the police. After a couple of hours they let August go on bail. The boxes had been impounded. So was his passport. That had been the hardest thing to suffer. Though he'd never used it, now he couldn't. It was an imprisonment of sorts – of his inner life.

After his release, August had been numb, disorientated. He couldn't work out what threw him most, that Cosmo had blatantly used him, or that he was gone. His disappearance made him feel at a loss.

At five to eleven, August checked his watch. The eclipse was due in fifteen minutes.

'Henry,' he called and went out on to the pavement, where she was waiting with some customers.

There were lots of people on the street, most wearing UV filter sunglasses, some wearing regular sunglasses, others shielding their eyes with newspapers. Someone had a mirror, another had a piece of paper with a pinhole in it. Strangers were talking to one another, shop owners had come outside. They were all gazing up to the sky, as though waiting for a flying saucer.

'Henry, I'm going to take a break, go downstairs. Can you watch the shop?'

Henry furrowed her brow.

'No, I'm staying out here.'

Frustrated, August went back inside. On the counter a bowl of French beans and prosciutto needed covering. Hurriedly, he began look for clingfilm; he would wrap it and then sneak away. No one would steal anything while Henry was outside.

'Hello, hello!'

August looked up.

Cedric and Flora were standing in the middle of the shop.

Cedric smiled, arms open, as though hosting the eclipse himself. A hibiscus was pinned behind one ear, his shirt was a washed-out salmon colour, with salmons leaping on it. Flora had on UV filter sunglasses. She stood looking at him, her face placid. August felt disconcerted by her hidden eyes, as if she was doing things with them behind the squares, winking or trying to send him a message.

'Are you coming to watch the show?' Cedric asked.

'No.'

'Why not?'

'I don't feel like it, in fact I'm just about to go on my break.'

Flora moved closer.

'It will do your kidneys the world of good,' Cedric said, encouragingly.

'My kidneys are fine.'

'Fine, fine fine,' Cedric muttered, mockingly bored.

'I'd like some cheese,' Flora interrupted, edging closer. She motioned to the cabinet. August wanted to bolt.

'Can it wait?'

She shook her head. Her eyes were squares. Her tight curls had grown outwards and clasped her head like a helmet made of sponge. She pointed to the Mimolette. August's heart sank. *That bloody cheese.* It'd be hard to slice, the wire had snapped recently.

'Okay,' he said quickly, reaching into the display fridge and taking the Mimolette out. It was a whole sphere, a ball of lava. He put it on the counter and looked up at Flora.

'How much do you want?'

'I don't care.'

'What?'

She smiled and August stared back, annoyed.

Then the world went darker.

'We-heeey!' Cedric exclaimed, dashing outside.

August and Flora stood alone in the deli. The cheese sat on the counter between them. August rested his hands on it. His insides swam. Flora's mouth twitched sideways. Her nostrils flared a little. Then she took off her glasses.

Her eyes glittered.

She smiled.

'C-c-can I borrow those,' August asked nervously.

Flora shook her head.

'Nooo,' she replied in her long flat east European tone. 'You won't need them.'

August stood on the pavement and looked up at the sky.

A big black disc was moving slowly across the sun, eating it. The disc moved like a dream, silently, steadily, imposing itself on the light. Around it the clouds were purple, grey, mauve. The sky was overcast. The moon-dream was sad and cool as it slid across the face of the sun.

August quivered.

He saw a small boy, maybe five or six, standing on the third floor in the big house, looking out the window. It was autumn and a swarm of copper leaves floated around the heads of the trees in the copse. To the child the copse was always eerie in late autumn, a small graveyard, the black skeletal trees poking up, wet with the ashes of decomposing leaves.

The child looked down.

He saw a man sitting on the steps of the house. His hair was long and wet. Dandelion heads of steam bloomed in front of him. He was rubbing his hands and staring out at nothing, waiting. The boy stared down and wondered if he had come to take his mother away, in a jeep. She had only just returned. Months ago, she'd disappeared into a slit in the world. But she was back. The little boy stared at the man for an hour maybe, willing him to go, praying and feeling sick.

Eventually the man stood up. There was talking on the steps and he disappeared inside the house. Some time passed, not much. There were more voices on the doorstep, this time he recognized his mother's terse tones. The front door slammed shut. Then there was silence. Then the man began to walk down the long drive.

August stood on the pavement outside the deli, looking at a big black spot which was the sun.

His shoulders sagged.

In the sun he saw the man walk away from the house. He was enormous. His walk was slow and heavy, his hands were hugged around his body as if he were keeping something safe inside his jacket. His gaze was fixed on the ground. When the man reached the part of the drive which swung past the copse he stopped. He pulled what looked like a long paper-wrapped bundle from his jacket and left the drive, heading for the small group of trees.

He disappeared into them.

The little boy fixed his eyes on the spot where the man had gone, stared until the copper trees merged and blurred in his vision.

14 October

In bed, August turned his head.

More of his hair had fallen out and lay scattered on the white pillow. It had fallen from his head as if it had no roots – his hair had fainted off. Inches long, it lay brittle and scattered. In the last month his hair had turned a deep copper as it fell, a rich and exalted shade of death. Catching sight of it on the pillow was startling – strange to see a part of himself so close up, to see what others saw. He picked at a few strands, making a small sheaf, bringing the hair to within inches of his face. As he stared at it, he felt empty. Autumn had heralded a new feeling of detachment from his body.

Losing his hair meant nothing.

It wasn't that he didn't care; not caring would have been a reaction, a feeling of some sort. He was finally confounded. The changes had been happening for so long he'd used up all his responses. These days he was distanced. To deal with them he'd moved over into another body and now he lived as if he were two people, his old self and a new one which ate and breathed and slept and watched the older self wither.

* * *

When August arrived at the deli he was a little later than usual and surprised to see the bread hadn't been put out in the window and the blind on the door was still pulled down. When he unlocked the door the deli was deserted, but Henry was sitting at a table in the café.

'Hi,' he said from the door.

Henry turned her face his way. Gravely, she put a finger to her lips as he advanced, then pointed to the kitchen alcove. August was instantly intrigued, cautious; when he came closer he saw Rose was standing by the sink, stirring a cup of tea. Her face was bloated, her eyes turned gluey. She said nothing as she stared into the tea. August looked at her and then at Henry, who looked grimly back at him.

'What's happened?'

Henry remained clamped shut. She had a mug of coffee in her hands, clasping it dutifully, as if it weren't her place to speak.

Rose stirred her tea.

'What's wrong?' asked August, this time more than concerned.

Rose looked up. Her skin was transparent, faintly jaundiced. Fine mulberry veins were vivid and busy on her cheeks. He'd always found it hard to age Rose. Now she had no make-up on he could see she must be in her sixties.

'It's Hilary,' Rose said, her tone serious.

August searched. Hilary, Hilary, an aunt, a friend? He looked uncomprehendingly at Rose.

'Hilary?'

'Disappeared.'

Henry shut her eyes in shame.

Then he remembered. 'Oh, *no*,' August murmured. 'When?'

Rose pursed her lips together and peered deeper into her cup of tea.

'I left the door *and* the gate open,' Henry said, bleakly. 'When I was moving out last night.'

'Oh, dear.' August saw what had happened. Rose's front door opened on to a small open space and then a flight of stairs which led to a tiny courtyard just outside the deli's back door. There was a gate in the yard which opened on to the street.

'He must have slipped out, run away.'

'*She*,' Rose snapped.

Henry gritted her teeth and frowned. 'I'm sorry, I thought Hilary was a he.'

'She's a she. She used to be a she,' said Rose, edgily. 'I had her neutered.'

'How . . . how long's she been gone?' August interrupted.

'We're not exactly sure,' Rose sniffed. 'Probably since last night. Maybe this morning. My front door was open this morning, it may have been open all night.' She glanced at Henry, her anger all the more effective for being subdued.

'I'm so sorry . . .' Henry bleated. 'I thought I'd pulled the gate closed. I didn't realize it was on a latch.' She put her mug on the table and her face began to brew up pink and get plump.

'He . . . She's probably here somewhere,' August tried to placate them. 'In the deli. She's probably come in through the back door, she must be downstairs in the storeroom, asleep somewhere. You know. She slipped in while you weren't looking, this morning.'

'We've looked,' said Henry.

Rose nodded.

'We can look *again*. I'll look. We can phone the RSPCA, the police. We'll find her. Don't worry.'

Rose sniffed again and Henry looked away, out the back windows.'Come *on*,' August encouraged. 'She can't be far. I bet she's here somewhere.'

But neither woman was listening to him.

While Rose and Henry slowly began to bring the salads and the olives up from the fridges, August checked the cold rooms and the storeroom, behind the big boxes of tins, the wine rack, the sacks of dried pulses. He checked in the office and in the bathroom, behind the fridges in the kitchen, the stove, the sink. But no Hilary. When he went back upstairs Rose was on the phone to the RSPCA.

'There's nothing they can do,' Rose sighed, hanging up. She stood for a moment, staring vacantly at the handset. And then her face began to fall apart. Her cheeks moved further away from each other and broke off, her eyes looked about to slide off her face. Her mouth trembled, her lips quivered. Rose's face was a miniature earthquake.

'Oh Hilary . . . she's gone!' Rose crumbled into tears.

August stepped closer to her, putting his arms round her shoulders. Her small head bounced on his chest as she sobbed, small and hot and smelling weirdly of *crème brûlée*.

'Don't worry,' he said, patting her back. 'I'll find her. I'll go out on the street. I'll find her. You'll see. Don't worry,' he patted.

Shepherd's Bush Road was wet and dirty. Above him, the sky was a washed-out and watery blue-grey. Restless winds rustled the leaves of trees, combing the skies and causing the spine to jerk with a sense of one's unspoken crimes. Around him August noticed people were somnambulant, walking cowed and preoccupied. October was always the most melancholy month, he decided, bringing with it a feeling of defeat. His body had slowed with it, slid into a humbling mode, a silent daily wilt. The eclipse had only served to make him more cautious, more wary of his secret assignment. Could he be sure of what he'd seen? Had it been Edward in the sun, the big man, walking towards the copse? Flora had disappeared while he'd been staring upwards and he hadn't seen her since. There were questions he'd wanted to ask her. Ideas had formed.

A gift . . .

In the last few weeks Leola's words had wrapped themselves around his consciousness with long and thread-like tentacles. It'd sounded crazy at first, *a gift*. From his father. Cosmo, the cheese, these had been his only theories early on. And then he'd given up, simply let the strange things happen to his body, let himself be overtaken. Now, casting his mind back to the previous winter, he'd remembered the changes had started *before* the Mimolette came, before Cosmo turned up. The frost had arrived by itself. Now Leola's idea seemed extraordinarily simple. Maybe his father was looking for him. Maybe his body had somehow, subliminally picked this up.

The truth was, he was frightened of meeting Edward. Frightened of who he might be, of another rejection, the final one. Was that what was waiting for him at the end of all this? Was he about to have the rug pulled out from under his feet? Would the world again rock with laughter at his naivety? His mother, Mrs Chalmin, Cosmo. No one wanted him to meet Edward; in their own ways they all wanted Edward dead, or vanished – not present. Edward had caused a tragedy, yet he was supposed to be a quiet, gentle man. Shy. Would Edward have become bitter? Or changed unrecognizably from the young man he was. Would he be sealed up like Olivia; would failure have rubbed the young man out?

August headed west, towards Hammersmith, whistling and calling the little dog's name, feeling a little sad to think of such a small creature out on its own, especially one bred to be kept indoors. He found it hard to believe Hilary would be at all interested to leave the comfort of Rose's home and he shuddered, recalling the jellyfish of pantyhose and stockings he'd seen the day he'd found Rose crying on her bed. Her lemon, fluffy gown. Since then her relationship with Salvadore had become more stable. In the summer Rose had blossomed.

August continued on up the road, past Hammersmith library and the Palais, past the fire station and the tube. When he reached King Street he stopped. There was a throng of people on the pavements, vegetable stalls set up. Traffic. There was no way he'd find Hilary on such a busy high street. He remembered the dog had a little disc attached to its collar with her name and Rose's number on it. If Hilary was found, it was likely the dog would be returned. If Hilary had been a baby Labrador, or a spaniel, perhaps it'd be different. If found, people might keep something cute. But Hilary was creepy and morose; she was diffident and looked expensive. Whoever found Hilary would return her, hoping for a reward. August turned around and headed back to the deli.

As he neared the deli he passed a café. It had grease-smudged windows and a board with holes in the window. Plastic letters were stuck in the holes which spelt out meals and their prices.

August looked in.

Cedric was sitting at one of the red Formica tables in the window.

Surprised, August stopped and went inside.

'Hello,' he said, standing above Cedric expectantly.

Cedric was sitting in front of an empty mug. He looked far away, as old and chipped and peeled away as the table his elbows rested on. He studiously cupped his hands to his temples, shielding his eyes from August.

August frowned. Rose and Henry knew he was out looking for Hilary. He could spare some time.

'Can I sit down?'

Cedric still didn't reply. He continued to fix his eyes in the mirage in front of him. August slipped into the seat opposite and rested his hands on the table top. He'd never seen Cedric so unhappy.

'Cedric?'

'Yes, August,' he replied heavily.

'You don't look well.'

'I'm fine.'

Cedric's oystery eyes were leaking a little.

'Good. I'm fine too.'

'Good.'

'Fine.'

Cedric's lips wavered a little, trying to suppress a smile.

August giggled.

Cedric laughed a little. His eyes began to focus, the corners crinkle.

'So, you're fine,' August repeated.

Cedric laughed a little more.

August smiled and shook his head.

Cedric nodded, nobly. 'I'm fine.'

'Good, I'm glad.' August looked over towards the counter, hoping for a waitress.

'Actually, I'm not.'

August nodded slowly, ready to listen.

Cedric bunched up his cheeks and lips making his long beard wriggle, a live catfish.

'Men's problems.'

August was puzzled. Cedric's usual mirth was like a fine layer of oil, slipping off his face. Cedric looked as though he'd been crying, or was going to. He was staring at the table.

'My pecker doesn't work,' he said, addressing the table.

August's eyebrows shot up.

Cedric nodded to himself. His face underneath was tired, the tide drawn out.

'Impotent.'

August didn't want to hear any more, and was fascinated.

'Oh . . . dear.'

'It hasn't worked for years,' Cedric continued. 'In fact it's never worked that well, even when I was your age. It happens to some men, you know. The urge is hardly there at all. Low sex drive, they call it. Like electricity. My surge is faulty. Always has been. Now the lines are down completely.'

August was amazed. *Let me drill a hole in your bole . . .* He half-smiled remembering this.

'I know what you're thinking,' Cedric said. 'But my eyes are bigger than my stomach,' he laughed, softly. 'The spirit is willing but the flesh is weak, and all that. I'm all bark and no bite. All salad and no salami.'

August was unable to say what he should, to tell Cedric he sort of knew what he meant.

'And now I'm in love for the first time in my life,' Cedric muttered. 'And I . . .' He stopped and shook his head. 'My body's not up to it. It's a joke.'

August nodded.

Cedric squinted at him, mistrustfully.

August's hair had holes in it where bits had fallen. Long bits hung randomly, as though birds had been plucking at his head, for bedding.

'Sometimes I forget how I look,' August reddened. 'For a split second. Some mornings I forget what I look like completely. I pretend that I'm someone else. Someone handsome or cool. The kind of man women like. It only lasts a second, though.'

He looked sadly, but matter-of-factly at Cedric to stop any pity.

Cedric chuckled. 'You're crazy. You look . . . splen-diferous. Bold. You have *du chien*, as the French say. Something else. Something different. Haven't you noticed women looking at you?'

August blinked.

Cedric laughed.

'You're very striking. Flora thinks so too.'

August's ears went hot. The old man was being kind. He smiled politely and changed the subject.

'We've lost Rose's dog, Hilary,' he said. 'You haven't seen her, have you?'

When August returned to the deli mid-morning there was still no sign of Hilary. Rose and Henry were hardly speaking. A piece of paper was taped to the plane tree outside with Hilary's face photocopied on it and the word *Reward* under it. Rose had given a bundle of the posters to Salvadore and had sent him to tape them up all over Shepherd's Bush.

By four in the afternoon a coldness had set in which hadn't been there in the morning. October also brought with it a new feeling in the deli, new orders for a new season. The deli was packed with home-crafted savouries: Cornish pasties like great bulging stomachs, encased in robust pastry, dainty lentil croquettes, light and crumbly but also thickset and stubby – a giant's fingers; mushroom burgers and soya bean curd cut into blocks, a large jar of grim but seductively abrasive pickled onions, autumn's acid bombs; a rude and dense venison pie sold with a green pepper poivrade and redcurrant jelly; silky grey herring fillets in a shallow sand bar of vinegar. Plum bread. Damson jam. Seville orange marmalade. The Vacherin was back in production and August had decided to order more English cheeses. A big, brave barrel of Colston Basset Stilton governed the display fridge, its pate a creamy yellow shot through with ink, its rind the colour of a dried, pale earth.

Rose was upstairs, attending to a sudden, blinding migraine, leaving August in charge and Henry relieved she was gone. Rose had taken her in, looked after her while she'd moved out of the bedsit she'd shared with Yves. Rose hadn't charged her rent, had been patient and kind while she found somewhere else. In return, Henry had lost, possibly killed, her dog.

August looked at her, fondly.

The blonde hair had gone. She'd dyed it over black again and was growing it into a longer, shaggy style. She was no longer bossy, he'd noticed, or trying to be edgy, or speaking French. But she'd lost some of her sunny disposition. While she still had a disarming openness and directness, there were periods, hours sometimes, when she seemed preoccupied with her thoughts, periods he recognized and knew where she was. Henry had become more self-examining, more introspective. His fantasies had stopped too, he realized. He couldn't remember when, but they had.

Henry was cutting up a freshly made pizza with a wheel. It was crisscrossed with anchovies and smelt fishy and oily and cheesy and had moist, cooked black olives on the top. All of a sudden August was hungry.

'You know what?' said Henry.

'What?'

'I miss Cosmo.'

'Humphf,' August replied, grumpily.

He'd forgotten about Cosmo in recent weeks. It was almost two months since he'd disappeared. The police hadn't been back, August's passport was still confiscated. He'd half expected a postcard, a phone call, a message via his old landlady slipped under the door. But nothing. Not a word.

'He stank,' August said, firmly.

'He was funny, though. I liked him.'

August imagined Cosmo stumbling past the deli, saw his cowboy hat, his upward stare, his jumble. He pursed his lips.

'I didn't.'

'So, was he seeing *Leola*?' Henry used a silly voice.

'No.'

'*You* should.'

'What?'

'You should, Gus. I've seen her looking at you.'

'When?'

'Whenever you walk past the flower shop.'

'Oh, rubbish.'

'She likes you,' Henry laughed. 'She does. And you haven't noticed.'

'Don't be ridi-ridiculous.'

'I'm not being ridiculous. You're shy, and she's so . . .'

'What?'

'*Vague* . . . or something. You know, she thinks too much . . . Either way, I've been watching you both for months. You like each other.'

August was suddenly giddy and overcome with a child-like joy. His cheeks flushed. Since they'd had brunch he and Leola hadn't met up, just passed each other occasionally on the street, nodded and said hello. He still felt faintly sick whenever he saw her. Still went red. But it was easier, at least, just a bit. His ears got hot just thinking about her.

'We . . . we had coffee, once.'

Henry turned, her face plainly surprised.

'When?'

'In the summer.'

'And?'

August shrugged. 'I . . .'

Henry shook her head, incredulous. 'Did it go well?'

August thought about it. 'Yes.'

'And?'

August wanted to escape. He winced. 'I . . .'

'You haven't asked her out again?'

'No.'

'Why not?'

'I don't know. I thought about buying flowers once. As an excuse. Then, you know, then ask her to go out. But I wouldn't know what to buy. I'm no good with flowers. I'd be embarrassed.'

'Then buy a plant.'

August watched Henry cut a small piece of pizza for herself, glad she was stealing food again.

'A cheese plant,' she said, chewing.

'A what?'

'A cheese plant.'

August squinted, disbelievingly.

'No, really,' she said. 'There *is* such a thing.'

August imagined a palm tree sprouting from a Mimolette.

'They're very common house plants, easy to look after.'

'Really?'

'Easy as pie. As pizza,' she laughed.

'Oh.'

'I can't believe you've never heard of them.'

'No, I never have.'

'Well, you should get one. I'm sure they sell them across the road.'

A cheese plant. August thought the idea sounded ridiculous. *Cheese plant*, he ran the words through his head. *Cheese plant, cheese plant.* He was standing near the window and looked out at the plane tree. On the tree he could see Hilary's sad little face again, taped to the trunk. At the base of the tree one or two leaves had fallen, dried and yellowed. The first to fall this season.

Half an hour later August was arranging almond croissants into a kind of yurt on a large platter when there was a tapping on the deli's window. He looked up to see the poster of Hilary's face stuck to the glass. Someone was holding it there, but their face was obscured. From the neck down he could see the person was wearing battered jeans and brown suede desert boots.

Hilary's face wobbled on the glass and the person made a little doggy paw with one hand.

'Gabriel!' August laughed.

The joke was a welcome relief, he'd been hovering around the window all morning. Since the dog had disappeared the deli had become a funeral parlour. Henry had spent over an hour unpacking a box of organic teas, without talking, and Rose hadn't been seen since the previous day.

Gabriel came in, sheepishly holding the poster. 'This dog robbed a bank?' he signed.

'Mean?' August grinned and signed back.

Gabriel signed that there were *Reward* posters on every tree up and down the road.

'Owner's dog,' August signed. 'Missing.'

Gabriel gasped.

'How are you?'

Gabriel flashed him the thumbs up.

'Isabel?' August signed.

Gabriel made the sign for breaking, then the sign for over.

August nodded and showed concern.

'Communication problems,' Gabriel signed and laughed and danced his knuckles along the marble counter top.

'You okay?'

Gabriel nodded.

August watched Gabriel's hands and thought of his mother. Silence was her medium too, her chosen cover.

Henry appeared behind the display fridge, wiping her hands on her apron, her mood still penitent; she ignored them and started to wipe in between the cheeses with a J-cloth.

Both men gazed at her for a moment.

August looked back at Gabriel. Gabriel's face was glowing a little, with interest. He looked back at Henry again, pushing her lengthening hair behind her ears as she leaned forward into the fridge.

'Henry,' August beckoned.

Henry looked up.

'I want you to meet a great friend of mine.'

Henry's face was serene, her body movements lethargic. 'Okay,' she said, obediently.

She floated over and stood next to August with one arm held behind her back, her mouth pulled back at one side.

'This is Gabriel.'

'Hi,' Henry said quietly, as though she were ten and

meeting a friend of her parents. She lowered her head and looked up at Gabriel through her lashes.

August stared at Gabriel in amazement.

His face looked as if it'd been slapped. It'd turned red and soft, a bit moist.

Gabriel smiled and his lips rolled up.

'Gabriel and I went to school together,' August said quickly. 'We grew up together in Yorkshire.'

Henry nodded.

Gabriel was staring at the counter, embarrassed, as though thinking something through, his face wrinkled up in concentration.

August was concerned. Usually Gabriel had no problem meeting hearing people. He used a mixture of signs and words he could say to every and anybody. If they couldn't understand him, it never bothered him, as long as they got the gist.

Henry winked at Gabriel.

Gabriel's cheeks flushed.

They stood for a moment on either side of the counter, silent.

'Nice to meet you,' Henry said, looking into his eyes.

Gabriel nodded.

Intuitively, Henry seemed to guess he was deaf. She beamed and then pointed to the poster of Hilary behind the counter and made a lynching gesture, as if hanging herself.

Gabriel put his hand over his mouth to stifle a laugh.

Henry pointed to her chest. 'I lost the dog,' she said, defining her words.

Gabriel's eyes widened.

Henry bit her lip and nodded and then looked sad.

Gabriel followed her movements with a keen awareness, his eyes narrowing as he did. Still, he didn't sign anything.

Henry smiled.

'Must go,' she said, motioning her head back towards the fridge.

Gabriel nodded.

She grinned and left.

Gabriel tried to smile back but August noticed his lips wouldn't go up.

* * *

In the catacomb under the deli a sound rang out unheard.

Thin, piercing yaps.

The pug could only keep it up for a few minutes at a time before collapsing and chewing on the small book, a passport, which had fallen from the box in the cupboard. In the cupboard it was dark and stuffy and hot.

After Gabriel's visit August still hung around near the window, occasionally looking out and up the road. He'd been outside once and paced up and down in front of the shop, seen Leola standing outside Pollen with a customer. *I've seen her looking at you.* Henry was making it up.

Cheese plant . . . He thought about Henry's suggestion. Gabriel and Henry's mutual attraction had made him even more painfully aware of his passivity. It'd taken him almost a year to build up the courage even to think about approaching Leola. In that time Henry and Gabriel had had entire relationships and were open to new ones. It was as if he missed things, always, which other people got. He was too slow or too trapped or in the next room when things happened. He was always somewhere else. *Where?* he wondered. *Where have I been all my life?*

Henry was still mooching around the shop. After stocking the shelves with tea, she'd pulled off all the mustards and the vinegars from other shelves and had been dusting and rearranging them in alphabetical order.

'Henry,' August said, tapping her on the shoulder. She turned, but he could see she was lost in thought.

'I'm going out for a minute.'

August emptied his head, of his mother or Edward of old Mrs Chalmin. Of Hilary and Rose, of Cedric. As he left the deli, he touched the plane tree for good luck. He kept his apron on and walked slowly along the pavement. He stopped at the lights. The green man flashed without his having to push the button. He crossed. The pavement was crowded with plants as usual: red cyclamen, pink kalanchoe, indigo hyacinths. Nests of white narcissus bulbs. He entered the shop and found Leola bending over a bucket of gerberas. Each head was big and yellow, the flowers a bucket full of suns. He walked straight up to her bent-over form.

'Hello.' His voice sounded echoey in the plant-choked shop.

'Aarrghhh,' Leola gasped, straightening up.

'I'm s-sorry, I didn't mean to interrupt.'

'You're not, don't worry. It's nice to see you.'

August examined her close up: her freckles, the small bump at the top of her nose, her eye colour, hazel. Her naked lips. The lines around her mouth were long and slim, like the muscles women have on their inner thighs, high up.

'I'd like to buy a plant.'

He smiled at her, proud of himself. He blinked, then looked around the shop. It was a jungle, great arcs of leaves and flowers, palms and giant weeping figs; a vine of some sort, bony and dancing with lantern-like leaves, clambered up one wall. Behind him he could hear the trickle of a fountain. *Another oasis*, he thought.

Leola nodded. She was a little crumpled under his body

which was leaning forward. She slid under and away from him and straightened out her skirt.

'Did you have any particular plant in mind?' Her voice was light and compact.

'Yes.'

'Oh, what?'

'A cheese plant.'

Leola smiled, amused.

'I've been told it's easy to look after.' August reddened.

'That's right. We have one or two.'

She reached into the stadium of benches behind her and selected a plant. It was small, a spangle of dark green leaves with holes in them.

'It looks healthy,' August marvelled.

'Water and love,' Leola replied. 'That's all it needs.'

She walked over to a high wooden bench which had rolls of paper and string and scissors and bits of flower stems on it. She cleared away a space and set the plant down.

Her back was to him and August saw the stretches of opal white between the hem of her skirt and her gumboots. Chalk blue subterranean rivers. He was tired all of a sudden, tired and relaxed. A warmth spilt from his lungs, spreading into his chest, downwards, a sweep of reassurance. The muscles between his shoulder blades released themselves, his shoulders fell. He stepped a little closer as she began to wrap the plant in a sheet of marbled paper, so close he could see the pearly skin in her parting, her peach-velvet outline through her T-shirt, the curve of her neck and shoulders. He could smell the bodily warmth which came from her centre and also, on her arms and hands, a cold, wet freshness from all the water and plants around her. He sensed a presence behind him, calm and strong.

It pushed him.

He stepped a little closer.

'There you go,' she said, sticking a piece of tape around the plant's pot.

They were inches apart and she knew it but was untroubled by his closeness. It meant she didn't mind, he realized. *She didn't mind!* Didn't mind he was close enough to touch her. He could breathe on her and send a tiny ripple of air into her ear, graze her neck with a chain of atoms which had come from dark and porous chambers inside him. Make lung to cochlea contact. His organs, his innards, could be linked to hers. He could kiss her right then, even, touch her if he wished. He felt a dull pleasure, a swell of erotic anticipation. He stood still, saying nothing as she cut and snipped.

A customer came in and Leola picked up the plant. 'Remember, water and love,' Leola said, pressing it into his hands. For a moment they both stood clasping the pot, fingers interlaced. Leola smiled and August smiled back, exposing his great teeth.

The customer stood waiting in silence, her eyes cast into the small, artificial pond full of goldfish.

* * *

Henry was attaching a new cheese wire to the counter when August returned with the small, wrapped plant held aloft.

'So, you bought the cheese plant, huh?'

August didn't hear or see her. He walked past Henry with the plant held up to his nose. He strode into the café and then back; then walked round the deli's floor in small, tight circles.

'Are you okay?' Henry asked.

August nodded. 'I'm fine.'

'So you spoke to Leola?'

August smiled. 'Yeah.'

'Gus, what're you waiting for?'

August stopped.

'This plant.'

'What?'

'This plant is what I've been waiting for.'

Henry looked dumb, and then impatient.

'You sure you're okay?'

'Yes.'

Henry pulled at the wire she'd just fastened to see if it held tight.

'I suppose you think you're in love.'

'What?'

'Love.'

'Yup,' August continued to stare at the plant. 'Water and love.'

'You're impossible!' Henry said, exasperated. 'Look, there's washing-up to do next door. I've done it three mornings in a row. It's your turn.'

In the kitchen alcove August rested the plant on top of the barrier which shielded the units from the customers. He ran warm water into the sink and squirted Fairy Liquid into it. As it filled he let his hands soak in the warm water. He was hollow, void of any coherent line of thought. The moments he'd been so close to Leola had slipped into a hole in the world; they'd vanished for good, but left him with a buzz of happiness.

With his hands in the water he hummed a wordless

tune. When the level had risen enough he switched off the taps and put the plates and cups into the water. He hummed as he scrubbed the plates and stacked them on the wooden rack, then the cups and cutlery. When everything was finished he pulled the plug, keeping his hands in the sink, letting the water suck through his fingers, liking the way Fairy Liquid made water slippery.

When he heard the gasping from the throat of the pipe as the last water was sucked, he looked down at his hands. They'd shrivelled and pruned with all the soaking, but something else was wrong with them. He looked more closely.

His fingernails.

Where the nails had been there were only opaque squares of pink, the flesh around them dimly indented. He spread his fingers into stars and held them closer to his face.

His fingernails had come off.

Or rather, slid off, like stamps unglued from an envelope after soaking. His fingers were nailless. Completely uncapped. Bald. He wriggled them – and oddly wormy. August peered down the plughole. His nails must have been sucked into the swill, he realized. He crumpled his hands to his chest.

'Oh,' he said to himself.

* * *

Rose wandered down to the deli in the afternoon. There'd still been no sign of Hilary and she looked pale and drawn.

'It's been two days,' she said in a tired voice. 'I know she's lost for good. If she was somewhere close, she would've come back, she would've found her way back, she's a clever little thing. I know she's been stolen, or worse. She's been run over.'

Henry cowered by the slicer.

'Don't give up,' August urged. 'My mother's dog once disappeared for a week and came back.'

Rose perked up. 'Really?'

August nodded. 'She was a wire-haired dachshund. Disappeared while they were out on a walk. They searched everywhere for her, all over the moors, then gave up as it got dark. A week later she turned up thin and hungry, with a raw nose. She'd been trapped down a badger's hole.'

Rose screwed up her face.

'There are no *badger holes* on Brook Green,' she warbled. 'No rabbit warrens. This is west London. Hilary hasn't gone out chasing voles!'

August was distracted. The sight of Hilary chasing Mrs Chalmin flashed in his head, making him smile when he shouldn't have.

'I'm sorry,' August back-pedalled.

'That dog was so special, so clever and intelligent,' Rose said, heavily. 'My child.'

Henry and August cringed.

August thought of Hilary's featureless face. The dog had always appeared nonplussed, indifferent to Rose, to anyone and everything; it had no personality, no charm, no appeal whatsoever. It was difficult to understand how such a creature could inspire any emotion, let alone love. The dog was horrible.

As if reading his thoughts, Rose began to cry.

* * *

At home, August unwrapped the cheese plant and placed it on a saucer on his kitchen windowsill. The stalk of the plant was strong and new, the leaves sprawled like the legs of a newborn foal. The plant appeared to have spirit, he thought, a playful way of holding itself. He turned on the tap and filled a glass with water, then tipped the water into the soil around its base. He sighed as he poured, sensing a tide in him rise.

He felt cool as he poured.

Later, August found himself loitering in his kitchen, searching for eggs. There'd been no conscious decision, no real plan of attack. He began poking, abstractly, in the fridge, in his cupboards, on his shelves. He didn't know why he felt like making a cake; he just did. More accurately, it was as though the cake was trying to make him, calling him: wanting to be made. He sensed a pull from the various ingredients in his kitchen; he imagined bags of angelica and chopped dates lying on their sides, neglected or hiding, languishing in racks or wire bowls. Wanting to be transformed into something beautiful. He imagined the cake that was trapped in the air around him, waiting to be sculpted. A château. A glorious, three-tiered emporium of sponge. Jewel studded and strutted with chocolate fingers, hanging with cream. Bobbling with gooseberries. Strung with fairy lights and beads: silver balls, glacé cherries. A cake which would erupt from the tin, a palace forced up through the earth's skin; a mountain of a cake. He would make one of these.

He found three large, brown eggs at the back of the fridge. Flour in a jar on a shelf. There was some butter in a dish, just enough. Soft enough. He took down his favourite mixing bowl from a stack on a high shelf by the wall. He flipped a cupboard open and looked in; a tall bag of caster sugar was standing surreptitiously at the back. Some baking powder too.

In the bowl he grabbed the butter with both hands, separating it into pieces with his fingers, enjoying the slap of it in the hollows of his palms, the squishing up of the yellow mud between his fingers. With a fork he creamed the pieces of butter together with the sugar and a pinch of salt. There was some acacia honey in a pot on the counter. He poured some in and mixed. The honey would make the sponge moist and sticky and heavy. He poured a little more in. And mixed, thinking of Leola, and how much she liked cake. He imagined her skating down Shepherd's Bush Road in a long, diaphanous gown, holding a fiery baton aloft, the cake he was about to make on her head. He smiled to himself and added a pinch of baking powder, then sifted the flour in. He cracked the eggs and mixed them in separately and carefully, stirring with the concentration of a child. The lurid, viscous yellow was like sun's blood, somehow magical, slippery-weird, growing the more he stirred. It would bind the mixture, give it weight and smoothness. He stirred and thought about Leola's skin. Her neck curve, the backs of her knees.

August poured in some red rum and mixed. Threw in a fistful of chopped black dates. He stirred until the mixture was heavy, sluggish. Finally, ready. He gazed into the bowl then lowered his head and breathed in deeply; the substance he'd made was perfect: lumpen, oozing and sweet-smelling.

While waiting for the cake to rise he wandered into the

sitting room. For the first time he felt conscious of the dead lilies his mother had brought him, months ago. He saw her storming about his flat, her hands over her ears. Now he was less upset at her outburst. He added together the stories he'd collected: Cosmo's jealousy, his mother's denial. Mrs Chalmin's bitterness. They all balanced out. They were all pieces of the same story, just different tellers telling it their own way. He went over to the mantelpiece and picked up the large crystal vase. He walked back to the kitchen and set it down on the counter, pulling at the dead stalks. The flowers were wizened, their mouths frozen in a wordless gasp. One by one, he picked them out then threw them into the bin. Then he rinsed the vase out.

He went back to the living room and stood at the entrance, peering in. The last of the day's sunlight was filtering through the top of the bay window, throwing gold on to everything. The sofa was gold, the wooden coffee table was dusted in gold mildew. The carpet, normally a rusk brown, glowered in the sunlight, bone white, a desert. His home had a tint he'd never seen before, the colour of sunshine. He moved closer into the room and perched himself on the arm of the sofa.

He thought of Edward.

He saw him emerging from the copse, a big man, mist rising from the grass, trying to rub him out. He saw his slow and elegant walk as he headed towards the drive, big-boned, a light step, his back straight, a brace in him somewhere, holding him upright. A ballerina in gumboots. Wiping soil from his hands. The memory came but lingered only a moment in front of his eyes, receding into a bizarre backward time lapse, the man growing smaller, fainter, finally disappearing, as he was sucked back into time.

August shifted, uncomfortably, when the memory was gone. Edward had tried to make contact once. Now it was his turn. He should go to Ditchling as soon as possible. Tomorrow was Saturday. He'd call Jim, tell him he'd baked a cake. Ask to borrow his old car in return for it. His children would love it. Ditchling was a couple of hours away at the most. He'd drive with the windows down to let fresh air in, stop if or whenever he became panicked. He'd listen to the radio. Sing to himself. He'd drive slowly.

* * *

Overnight torrential rains fell accompanied by driving winds, causing floods in many places in the south of England. Trees and electricity lines were down, roads were closed, rivers had swollen and in places burst their banks. The town of Lewes, only a few miles from Ditchling, was the worst hit. Flood waters had entered the town, driving people from their homes. When he woke up, August glanced immediately at his bedroom window, but couldn't see out. The window was too smeared.

He hopped out of bed and switched on Ceefax on the television.

The A20 and the M25 were the only motorways which hadn't been closed. The weather report forecast a window of good weather for the early part of the day. Then more rain. He'd picked up Jim's car the evening before. Louise had loved the cake, the kids' eyes had bulged. On a road map he'd never used, he found he could pick his way east through to Tunbridge Wells and then over through smaller roads to Ditchling. He looked outside, the sky was morose, inconsolable. The weather, he decided, was the last thing to put him off. If anything, the sky, its downpour of grief, gave him the sense that the journey was all the more urgent.

The A20 was fine. The M25 was only slightly flooded in places. Small bellies of water had collected where the road dipped. The rain had mostly stopped over this stretch of road. But the wind was still strong and he saw higher vehicles swaying in front of him and kept well clear. When he reached Tunbridge Wells he found it almost deserted, silent. He stopped for lunch at a café but could only get a sandwich, the waitress explaining the electricity had been cut off.

On the way to Uckfield he saw the fields were bloated with water, transforming the scenery, turning England into China. The land appeared wider, more panoramic. He drove on past the River Uck, looking down into the broad band of flowing steel, a sense of wonder and humility settling on him. Nature was out of balance. It made him feel subdued, guilty.

He turned on the radio for company. On it, Cilla Black was singing 'Alfie'.

* * *

Ditchling was a red village, almost entirely made from bricks and tiles made from Sussex clay. Pantiles hung on most of the buildings making them look frilly and Quakerish. The walls of the buildings were rugged, August noticed, made from flint pushed into mortar, giving them a milky, crystalline glint. He parked in the village hall car park and made his way to the centre of the village – one main street which intersected with another. On a hillock behind he could see a church, just back from the road. There were three pubs, some shops, two estate agents.

And a post office.

Behind the glass there was a young man, younger than himself. He smiled at August when he entered. August approached, glad to have found Ditchling was so tiny. He'd begin here, he decided. A few simple questions, maybe pick up a lead.

'I'm looking for someone who used to live here,' he explained. 'He may still live here. But I'm not sure.'

The young man was immediately interested.

'Oh?'

'His name is Edward Hay.' August said the words too loudly, nervously. He'd never said them before.

The young man scratched his chin. 'You'll have to forgive me, I've only just moved here myself, been doing this job six months.'

'Oh, I see.'

'But there is a Mr Hay here. He lives in the village. On this road in fact. About a hundred yards up. Just after the shops. Been here for years. Spindles the house is called.'

August wanted to sit down. Terror clawed his stomach.

'But I'm afraid he's not an Edward. His name is Stanley Hay. Nice gentleman he is. Lives alone. Has done for years.'

August expelled breath heavily, unable to conceal his dismay.

The man was eager to reassure him.

'He might know anyway.'

August smiled and left.

Spindles was shaped like a boot. It was small and red and crooked, as though it'd been built on and added to over the years. A crowd of dead sunflowers stood in front of it, mute and shuffling slightly. Their once enormous seed pads were black and shrunken, cast downwards. They looked fragile but friendly, somehow kindred. The rest of the garden was unkept, full of other high, dead plants which needed cutting back. In an empty window box a row of brightly coloured plastic windmills spun excitedly.

This is more like it, August thought, opening the gate.

Next to the door there was a long rope. He pulled it and heard a jangle inside the house. He smiled, imagining the man inside rising from a meal of Marmite soldiers.

'Hello!' a voice said behind him.

August jumped and turned around quickly.

On the path a big old man was propping up a bicycle against his hips.

'Oh, h-hello,' August replied.

The man's eyes were small and plump and black, sunk deep in his face. 'Can I help?'

August nodded.

'Are you . . . Stanley Hay?'

'I am,' he said, wheeling his bike closer. He had keys in his hands and August moved aside as he put one in his front door and turned it. Before he opened the door he stopped, his mouth friendly, his eyes slightly disconcerted, looking into August's. He shook his head and smiled. 'Come in, come in,' he beckoned.

The kitchen was small, painted cerulean blue, and very full – a magpie's kitchen. Every shelf was clogged with jugs, jars, vases, bowls, boxes, books. Much of the wall space was plugged with pictures and paintings.

'Sit down.' The old man motioned to the small wooden table next to a window. On the sill there were several jam jars full of dead flowers. Also several upturned dead flies, their legs cramped, as if they'd died laughing. A crossword was half done in a folded corner of the *Independent*. Next to it stood a small bust of Lenin.

Stanley began peeling off his layers of clothing and rubbing his hands together.

'Tea?'

Sitting, August nodded.

He stared at the friendly old man's back as he went about making the tea. Stanley, he warned himself, like Mrs Chalmin, might turn out to be no blood relation. He must be guarded, he checked himself. He must stop liking this man so much so quickly.

'I c-came to find someone,' August started.

'Oh?' Stanley replied, with interest.

August nodded.

'A relative.'

'Who used to live here?'

'I'm not sure. Or around here. He used to live in Ditchling.'

'A Ditchling man, ah . . . good. Good stock.'

The kettle clicked off and Stanley poured boiling water into a teapot and pulled a cosy over it.

'I've lived in this house a very long time, forty-odd years. Before me there was a family. The Turners. An old house this is, long history. What was your relative's name?'

'Edward Hay.'

'O*oooooooooooh*.'

Stanley's outburst was like a train sliding to a halt. He stopped what he was doing, sliding to sad.

He stood in the centre of the kitchen, holding the pot of tea. It had a hand-knitted cosy on it, striped and multicoloured. His feet were oddly turned out, a seal's flippers. His eyes receded further into his large face as he watched a film flicker past them. His mouth opened and August saw the flash of his big teeth, and began to sway inside, feeling a swell of relief. A tear slid from one eye.

'He was my brother. I'm afraid Edward died last year.'

More tears began to slip from August's eyes, slip like liquid light, like laughter. Tears slipped like the seasons passing, like petals from a flower, like leaves from a tree. Tears slipped, silently, easily. They made his lips very wet.

He sniffed water.

Stanley frowned. He stroked the teapot as though it were a small dog.

'My name is August. August Hay.'

'Oh,' Stanley's eyes fattened up even more. 'Oh . . . my. Oh dear. Oh. Dear.'

August nodded. His eyes were opaque with grief. He smiled.

'I'm o-okay,' he reassured Stanley.

Stanley came to the table and put the teapot down and wrapped his big arms around August and held him for a long time.

* * *

The tea was strong and delicate, a feminine drink. It calmed him as it flowed down his centre, spreading in his network of vessels, stemming his feelings of grief. The two men sat on either side of the small wooden table. Stanley was still sad but smiled.

'He didn't talk about you much when he was alive,' he started. He stopped and then puffed loudly.

He began again.

'Edward always got on with the Chalmins. They'd been good to him, and Luke . . . he was a friend. Luke respected him.' Stanley shook his head.

'Ed was such a quiet man. Kept to himself. I was always amazed he'd got caught up in the whole thing.' He studied August's feet, still not having understood.

'But he fell in love. That was it.'

August nodded.

'Lost his head, I think. Neither of them thought things would turn out like it did. But after Luke died she wouldn't have him. Ed understood. Then she disappeared. The parents were bereft, as they would be. Asked Ed to leave. It was a scandal round these parts. A terrible scandal. The parents moved soon afterwards.'

August could only nod and let the information float into his empty head. The events were so intimately connected to him, but they felt like nothing; the information died in him.

'What . . . what happened to Edward?'

Stanley sighed.

'He had a council flat, just west of the village. He went to ground. Took Luke's death bitterly. Blamed himself. It was a tragedy, especially Luke being so young. Tragic, what happened. Ed sat and stared out the window mostly, for a year or so. He'd killed a man, or so he used to say. He'd killed Luke. Lost the woman he loved. And his son.'

Tears appeared and sat in the old man's eyes. He poked them with his finger, then wiped them away and sipped his tea.

'Slowly he got out more. After a while. Went back to work. He was good at what he did, you know. He had a way. Could make anything grow. People knew him. He had a good reputation. Slowly he went out again.'

He stopped and looked keenly at August.

'He went once, you know? Up to Yorkshire. He tried to see you. But she wouldn't let him.'

August nodded, frowning.

'That was the end I think. He was forty-three. He stopped living a long time before he died. Died with nothing, I'm afraid. Never married, no other children. Nothing. That's what he said, kept saying it before he died last winter. He'd left you nothing.'

August was suddenly alert.

'He died last *winter*?'

Stanley nodded.

August narrowed his eyes, shaking his head slowly. 'When, exactly?'

'Just before Christmas.'

'But when, exactly when?

'Ummm,' Stanley scratched his chin. 'A fortnight before Christmas.'

'What date?'

Stanley looked at him, strangely. 'December the eleventh.'

August couldn't sleep. Images of his father's life took hold of him, pulled him down, laying him in a shallow stream.

He couldn't stop seeing his father staring out the window of his council flat, feeling his father's guilt, his loneliness. His shyness. He knew this life too well. *Alone*. Cosmo's words curled themselves around his vision, the opposite of a prediction. A sudiction. Edward had died alone in his flat on the eleventh of December, of a strange and undiagnosable disease, a series of system failures. He'd died, or so Stanley had said, leaving nothing; died at the same time as August's first outbreak of frost.

He'd lain awake all night, eyes open, seeing his father, imagining his life. Stanley had given him some photographs and he'd lined them up on the small table beside his bed, staring at Edward, a big, bearded man with pale eyes. It was the face he'd been seeing everywhere, in his dreams, in the sign. It was the face of a man who had spent a lot of his time outdoors. It was hardy, weathered. His features were similar to August's. But whereas his always seemed crammed, overcrowded on his face, Edward's features were worn down, stretched apart. Time had softened Edward's face. In one photo, he'd recognized something in his mouth, a smile he was trying to control. In others Edward was smiling, flashing his great big teeth. His father had been attractive, there was no doubt about that. Edward had had a quiet magnetism.

He'd stared at the photos all night. His father – in a

stiff collared shirt and tie. His father – holding the harness of a Clydesdale at the South of England Show in 1989. His father – standing next to a hay wagon at harvest time. Behind him the Sussex hills were blood-orange. He'd stared at him all night. The images were vibrant, alive, capturing life, the camera having snatched bits of his father's existence inside it. It was surreal, freakish, to see these scraps as all that was left – live bits of the dead. He'd stared at them and cried, silently, with tears at first and then when none were left, without; mourned his father most of the night.

In the early morning he'd wanted to get out of his flat.

Downstairs, in the deli's office, he sat with a mug of coffee. Even though he'd found out so much, found his father dead, found his uncle, he'd only discovered facts and fragments of history about a stranger, a man called Edward. He had photos and dates, different accounts, but nothing which had changed his life. The story was somehow still remote.

The office was almost redundant, full of empty boxes and paper. Rose made phone calls from there occasionally and apart from the accounts once a month, there wasn't much office work to be done. It was dark in the early morning, dark as a den. The light was brown and satiny and there were bits in it, swirling and settling around him. He was sipping coffee, imagining his parents 'canoodling' behind the elms, when he heard a small noise, a shuffling, and then a muffled squeak.

August looked round.

The noise stopped.

He sat still.

There was silence. Under the shelves along the side of

the wall there were cupboards with sliding doors. August stared at them. The shuffling started again, this time accompanied by a noise.

'Woo, woo,' came the noise from the cupboard.

August cocked his head.

The noise stopped.

'Hilary?'

'Woo, woo,' the sobs continued. This time he imagined the woos were a little more panicked. August put down his mug and began sliding back the doors to the cupboards. If it was Hilary she'd have been in there for three days and would be in a bad shape. As he continued to slide and unslide the doors he became aware of a scuffling inside the last cupboard. When he slid back the door the stench of urine hit him in the face.

Hilary was sitting in a nest of shredded papers, an upturned shoe box next to her. Her velvet face hung in pleats, her eyes were full of reproach. In her mouth she gripped a small, slim, chewed-up book.

'Hilary!'

The dog collapsed, still gripping the book.

August leaned into the cupboard and picked her up with the book still in her mouth, resting her on his lap.

'There, there,' he murmured, reassuringly, rubbing up and down along her back to bring back circulation. 'There, there,' he continued, patting. He felt a strong surge of relief, an urge to squeeze the dog in his arms, crush its stubby, velvet body. Squash Hilary to death.

The dog lay motionless and limp, her eyes expressionless, as though nothing would bring her back from the abyss. August continued to pat her body and ease the book from her mouth. Turning it over, he saw it was a passport. The dog wriggled her squat body as he flicked through the first pages. He stopped at one page. He stared hard at what he saw, not being able to understand it.

It didn't seem possible.

There was a picture of a man in the passport, with a small goatee. August flicked back a few pages, to the front. The name in the passport was Ross Finlay, born 1934. August tried to think hard, think carefully. Rose never talked much about her family; she'd never mentioned a brother, let alone one who was a twin, near-identical. He studied the accompanying details, height, eye colour. The same as Rose's. Did Rose have a brother who was five foot six? Did he have the same lively grey eyes, the same complexion? The dog wriggled again on his lap. And then an idea floated up like a bubble from his feet, through his blood. Something Rose had said.

'*She used to be a she.*'

He looked at the dog. Her body was shapeless, squat.

He remembered Rose in her lemon negligee, the way he'd been drawn to the shape of her body underneath, how he'd been fascinated and repulsed at the shapelessness of it. How he'd backed off.

'*Neutered.*'

He heard Rose say this again, in a clipped voice.

He patted the dog.

He'd seen it that day under the negligee, the body of something else. He'd seen it and let it through the filter in his head. Rose was old. He'd already neutered her. He'd not wanted to see what he had, had submerged the sight. But now he saw her again, on the bed. A body too wide, too thick to be a woman's.

August pressed his lips to the top of Hilary's head. Rose

had once been a man. Rose had been Ross. He looked down at the little dog. In a second it all made sense. He saw what he'd never noticed. Hilary was a flag, a marker, deliberate or not. An ally. *She used to be a she*. Rose had gone from being a man to a woman, in a way cancelling herself out. She had become something different, a third sex – two sexes poured into one.

August stared at the photo again. It wasn't another person, a twin or a brother. It was Rose. The same eyes, the same lips. Rose had been a small, effeminate man. He wondered when he'd made the change. Rose was mid-to-late sixties. She'd owned the deli for at least three years and he'd been there half this time. The deli. Had it been a dream life Ross had escaped to? He wondered if there'd been surgery. He thought of Salvadore, their relationship was a happy one. He guessed there had.

Hilary began to woo again.

August remembered the shoe box in the cupboard. Hilary had obviously knocked it open, had chewed and peed and ripped most of its contents to pieces. There may have been other personal documents in it. But he wouldn't look. He'd keep her secret, let her think he hadn't seen the box; tell Rose he'd found Hilary in the office, that she'd managed, somehow, to get out of the cupboard by herself.

He put the passport back in the box and left the strange shredded nest as it was.

Upstairs in the deli he set a small saucer of milk down for Hilary. The little dog began to gulp. He gave her another bowl. As she gulped this too, there was a rap at the door. It was far too early for Henry, or customers. At the door he pulled aside the blind. A young blonde woman was standing outside, she had neat black eyes. Wondering what she wanted, he unlocked the door and opened it.

'Yes?' he inquired.

The young woman glared at him with disdain. The neat eyes narrowed.

Then he remembered.

He hadn't seen her since the winter before. She'd once delivered the cheeses. Rose must have placed an order without him knowing, a flush rose up from his chest and blossomed in his face.

'Cheese?' she asked sarcastically, then openly showed a look of repulsion at his clumpy head.

'Oh,' August's lips crumpled. The walls of his windpipe stuck together. 'I d-didn't know . . .'

The woman glared at him, stopping him from speaking. 'Well, there's twenty kilos in the van.' She turned back towards where it was parked.

August followed.

As he walked behind her he felt a weariness wash over him. Perhaps nothing had changed, would ever change; perhaps he was doomed to remain in the same invisible prison, forever. When they reached the van she opened the back door. There were large boxes in it.

'It's that one,' she pointed.

August nodded and went to heave it out. The woman stood and watched without looking at him. August filled his arms with the box, lifting it from the van. The woman closed the door and he let the box down heavily on the pavement.

'Can you sign for it?' she said, thrusting a clipboard under his nose.

'Sure.'

The woman stared at his hair as he scrawled his initials.

August was suddenly angry.

'Here,' he said, placing it in her hand.

'Thank you.' Her smile was facetious, insincere.

She was afraid of him, he realized. With or without his orange hair, he was something she wasn't sure of.

She looked away again.

'*Boo*,' he said loudly.

The woman was startled.

'Yaaahhhhh,' August shouted, flapping his hands by his ears.

She stepped back quickly, her eyes open, pinned to his.

August smiled at her, exposing his teeth.

The woman stepped back further.

August gave her the best werewolf impression he had, his eyes slim, icy, hungry. He growled.

The woman dived back in her van and sped off.

When he returned with the box of cheese Hilary was slumped behind the counter, bored. He picked her up gently and tucked her under his arm.

He let himself out the deli's back door and climbed the stairs to Rose's flat. On the way he had to remind himself about the passport. Rose had been Ross but now she was Rose. The new information was both bizarre and unimportant. He didn't care what Rose used to be, he needed her as she was.

He rang the bell and waited.

Rose opened the door.

'Hilary!' she squealed. Her eyes swelled and she clasped her hands to her face.

August handed over the little dog.

'My baby, my precious, my love,' Rose was overcome, swamping the dog with kisses.

Hilary listlessly licked Rose's face.

'I found her in the office,' August explained. 'She'd been locked in a cupboard.'

'Oh, my baby, my baby.' Rose was delirious.

August glanced at her silky housecoat, her cerise turban.

'I'll see you later,' he smiled.

'Oh of course, Gus thank you so much. Thank you.' She was still caught up in her reunion.

The dog began to make wooing noises again.

Rose was horrified.

'Oh, my love, my love, you're not well.'

August left quietly as Rose took Hilary inside.

In the storeroom August unpacked the cheeses, stacking them in the fridge. As he did, he thought about Leola. In the flower shop he hadn't asked her out, as he'd meant to, hadn't arranged to see her again. In the excitement of being so close to her, he'd just left with the plant. He was worried; he'd gone to Ditchling instead. He'd become unravelled. Distracted. If he didn't follow things up, his life would revert to how it was.

He selected a few cheeses for the fridge upstairs. There was a new Mimolette and he slipped it under his arm and carried it along with a few other cheeses, up the stairs. When he entered the café Henry was sitting at a table with a cappuccino.

'I won't be long,' she said, eyeing his full arms.

'No, don't rush.'

She raised her eyebrows gratefully. Then stared at his head as he passed.

'August . . .' She was about to say something, then stopped.

'What?'

'No, nothing.'

'What?' he persisted.

'It's just . . .'

'What?'

'Your hair,' she sighed.

August stopped and smiled happily. 'I know,' he said. 'It's awful.'

'It's worse than awful, it's like a disease.'

'Scrofula,' he joked.

'No, really, Gus, it's a disaster. I can't stand it any more.'

'Oh?'

'Let me give you a haircut. My treat.'

August thought about it. He rarely had it cut, he hated having it done, it embarrassed him. Clumps had been falling out and he knew he couldn't avoid it for much longer.

'I'll think about it,' he said, casually.

He placed the goat's cheeses and the large Brie in the display fridge. For a moment he held the Mimolette in his hands. It was heavy and warm, a baby's head. This one was cantaloupe coloured on the outside but still had the same pockmarked rind.

'How's the cheese plant?'

August looked up.

Leola was standing in the deli, smiling. The cheese became warm in his hands, alive.

'It's fine,' he said walking towards the till. On his way he put the cheese in the fridge.

Leola rested her hands on the counter top. She was wearing a head scarf, red and white checks; it made her look wholesome. Outdoorsy, yet elegant. Again, he could smell the freshness of the plants she was always around.

Right then he didn't feel embarrassed about his looks, his hair like a palm grove after a hurricane.

'I watered it this morning,' he said. 'It's on the window-sill, in the sun.'

Leola laughed.

'What is it?'

'A cheese plant shouldn't be in the direct sunlight.'

August's face fell. 'Oh no!'

She was amused.

'I kill plants,' he groaned. 'I killed a cactus once. Oh God!'

'Move it out of the sun,' she smiled.

He wanted to run home and do it right then.

'Anyway, I didn't come because of the plant.' She moved her hands closer to him.

August looked at them, they were white and slim. He inhaled and smiled and picked up one, then the other, holding her hands in his.

She seemed surprised but pleased and drew a deep breath. They smiled self-consciously at each other. Leola pushed on with what she'd come in to say. 'I wanted to know if you'd like to go out for dinner, tomorrow night.'

August's ears burnt. He closed his eyes, his mouth was full of fudge. Then he squinted, seeing her through the shadows of his lashes.

'I'd love to.'

Leola seemed relieved.

They beamed and held hands.

'Huhmmmm,' Henry cleared her voice loudly as she came into the deli.

They kept beaming.

Henry inspected them curiously, as though they'd just fallen from the sky.

'What time?' August asked.

'Eight-ish?'

He nodded.

'The tapas bar next to Pollen is good. Good wine. I know the people there. How about there, at eight?'

'Fine.'

Reluctantly, they let go of each other's hands.

Henry was hovering behind the cabinet, sulking.

Leola left.

August turned to Henry. He smiled but she didn't smile back. Her mouth was pulled to one side and her eyes were hot, her eyebrows knitted.

'I suppose you're in love,' she said.

August laughed at her childish tone.

'I don't know.'

Henry huffed.

'Look at your hair,' she snapped. 'She must be blind.'

August giggled.

'Don't giggle,' Henry commanded.

He began to laugh at Henry.

'Don't laugh at me,' she laughed. 'I mean it.' Henry huffed again and her arms went limp.

August smiled. 'What's wrong?'

Henry pouted and shook her head slowly and screwed up her nose.

'No one loves me.'

August went over to her and wrapped her in his arms.

'I love you,' he said.

Henry made a weird sound, like a groan.

'And Gabriel fancies you.'

Henry grumbled. Then grumbled some more.

He held her for a few moments, then Henry looked up at him with a grin.

'Does he?'

August nodded. He stroked her hair.

'And we found Hilary.'

'Really?' She quickly divided herself from his arms.

He nodded vigorously.

'In a cupboard in the office.'

'Thank fuck.'

August laughed.

'She's upstairs with Rose.'

Henry inhaled deeply. She looked him in the chest and brushed some fallen hair from his shirt.

'I'm happy for you,' she said.

August was disconcerted. Love affairs were public affairs, he was learning quickly.

'Do you think Gabriel really fancies me?' she asked.

'Yes.'

She smiled.

'Really?'

'U-huh.'

A customer came in, the first of the morning rush. Henry went to the counter. August stood behind the display fridge for a moment. It was early morning, but the day felt as if it'd just ended. His eyes flicked to the Mimolette in the fridge and it looked back at him and winked.

Instinctively, he looked out the window and saw his mother was standing on the pavement.

Olivia couldn't look at him. Her eyes were lowered into her lap. She sat on a chair by the table in the alcove of his sitting room, one hand clutching the edge, the other wrapped across her stomach.

August felt sorry for her; for once, he knew more than she did. But this knowledge sat in him, in pieces, each part in its separate corner. If he told her what he knew, it might alter what she'd come to say. There was one story left and he wanted to hear it plainly.

Olivia's eyes flicked across her knees, searching for how to begin.

As he watched, August caught a feeling, ever so lightly. He was a child again, a child of five wanting to know something way beyond his years. Her past was full of failure, her own personal experience of coming upon failure in herself. It was uniquely hers, her life's disaster and a quill of understanding passed through him. She hadn't hidden the truth from him. She'd *shielded* him from it. Her trauma wasn't for a child to know about. Between a parent and a child the subject of intimate love, of passion, was unspeakable.

Olivia looked up. Her face was grave. Her eyes were

heavy, small piles of rocks collected in them.

'Edward was a surprise,' she said with no emotion. 'He came on me quietly . . . like . . . a storm. I'd never expected anything like it. Known anything like it. I was happy with Luke. We were happy. Young. We thought we were in love. We *were*.'

August squirmed.

She opened her mouth, as if to say something else, then closed it and pushed on. She still wasn't looking at him.

'The first time I saw Edward, he was in the garden at The Elms. It was a shock. The attraction was instant and unsettling, a strong, worrying feeling, like fear.' She broke off and looked at her son for understanding. She breathed long and sharp, then continued.

'I watched him without his seeing me at first. He was in the flowerbeds, tending the rhododendrons, a great mass, a bush like a monster in the garden, I hated them. But I was caught up watching him. I saw the gentle way he moved. I could see through his clothes. I saw his body. Long limbs, the heavy bones underneath. How slow he was. He moved amongst the garden, amongst the great heavy plants, disturbing nothing. Walked with the pace of the garden. When he turned and smiled I was . . . drawn.'

She cleared her throat. She stared past him, as though reciting these events, as if she had to. If she wavered from what she'd practised, she might lose control. August wondered if it was the first time she'd ever said any of this to anyone.

'It was like being descended upon,' she continued. 'By a mist. By a bond you can faintly see. I knew so much about Edward the minute I saw him. It made Luke seem . . . like a choice. Something without grace. Luke was so tangible, so outlined. When I met Edward I felt a different kind of life. Exposed to a mystery. To something which had slipped out from somewhere secret, from a dream.'

She was embarrassed.

August nodded.

'It happened almost without words. Very quickly. Being near him was very easy. Like being in a space cleared by an atom bomb. It had no time. No sound. I forgot myself. Luke became a figure on the horizon. When I became pregnant, he was so excited. I couldn't explain Edward. I said nothing. I've never said anything about him. Been dumb for years. I thought once you were born I'd leave Luke. But before then I didn't know . . . whose child I was having.'

August saw the catastrophe coming. His birth. Luke's death.

'It all ended when Luke died. The mist dissipated. The world became surreal. There was so much noise. Mrs Chalmin shouting. She wailed for days. Death is stronger than love, you know, August. I've learned that in my life. It flattened me. I ran away. To Jude's house, to Stonegate Hall with you. I stayed there and was burnt by guilt all those years. Cosmo, other men. Jude's boyfriend. They were invisible.'

She gently rubbed a finger under one eye, tracing the socket in her skull. Slowly, she shook her head at herself, tired.

She went on.

'You and Edward are so alike. So, so, so very much the same. You walk the same way, have the same expression in your eyes. The same mannerisms. I've always brought you flowers, whatever was in season. It was all I could think of. I was trying to bring you something on your father's behalf, a gift. He had a gift.'

August's eyes swelled. The flowers she brought were like dust. Everywhere. He saw them every day, always had them in sight. Now he knew why she was always so impatient with him. He'd hated her impatience so much.

He winced.

'Edward came to see me years after you were born,' she continued. 'By then Luke's death had worn through me. I felt very old by then. Another person. I'd only just stopped being overwhelmed by what had happened. I couldn't be with Edward. We'd been severely punished for being together, I knew it was wrong. I told him I wanted him to leave me . . . and you. I wanted him to vanish. I lied to you the other day.' She stopped.

She had a sick look on her face. Then she looked at him directly.

'It's become normal. The lie I made became solid. It formed levelled ground over Luke's death. I even gave you Luke's family name. I wanted to forget what I'd done. For a long time afterwards I wished I'd never met Edward.'

She stopped talking, her throat was dry. She stroked herself under her papery neck and looked out the window on to the street. It had all come out. Uncoiled itself from her like a snake uncoiling after a long gestation in a cupboard. She was calmer, satisfied.

August knew he should tell her. She probably didn't know. He wanted to hug her, take her in his arms and protect her, always from now on, but knew this wouldn't happen.

'Edward died last year,' he said, quietly.

His mother moved her face towards him. She seemed

uncertain, as if he'd spoken from the top of a hill, way in the distance.

'What?'

'I m-met his brother, Stanley, recently. He told me Edward died, last December.'

Olivia stayed very still for a moment, as though listening to something very quiet. Then her face broke, her mouth collapsed like the lip of an unset clay jug. It poured forth sorrow.

She keened forward.

Quietly, she began to sob.

In the night there was an electrical storm. August woke to a thunderclap so loud it sounded as though God had put his hands into his bedroom and hit them together, commanding his attention. He woke up and was sharply aware. His curtains were only partially drawn and when he heard a rip in the sky he looked out to see phosphorescent veins illuminated against the blackness, a delicate fan of reef coral. He shivered and continued to look out his window while there were more thunderclaps and spears thrown at the ground. Strangely, the sky's violence made him feel calm.

In the morning he could feel something stuck in the corner of one eye, something itchy and bothersome. He rubbed gently at the corner, feeling for dried sleep, or something lodged. As he rubbed, he felt a give along the top rim of his eye, a light ripping sensation.

He pulled his finger away from his eye and examined it.

'Oh, Jesus.'

His top eyelash was stuck to it, perfectly whole. It looked quite glamorous, August thought for a moment, like a fake one used by a showgirl. A tiny hula skirt. He knew his eyelashes were orange, but had never known they were so long and fluttery.

He stared at the orange fringe on his finger. He thought about the Mimolette, the same colour. About Cosmo. How wrong he'd been all his life. Jealous of Cosmo, hateful. Crushed by Cosmo's indifference. His stench. The commune. What he'd seen there, on the grass. Not knowing anything about his life, his father, the terms of his birth. Thinking Cosmo might be his father. Knowing it wasn't Luke, knowing this deeply. He'd been trapped for so long with his child's ideas and conclusions. The fringe on his finger . . . Leola had been right. His body, the changes. They'd led him to what he now knew. His father, in death, had released spores of himself. They'd carried on the wind. He'd inhaled them. Or perhaps they'd travelled some other way – in his dreams.

He got out of bed and went to the bathroom. In the mirror his one eyelash fluttered like a bird with one wing. He touched it and the eyelash moved. He touched it with a little more pressure and the eyelash came off on his finger. He stared at himself. He was eyelash-less. His pale eyes appeared smaller, more vulnerable, as though his eyes could easily fall out of his head – they balanced in their sockets. And his hair was atrocious. The bald bits could no longer be hidden by longer strands. He thought of his date later that night, his first in years. He considered cancelling it, then realized he couldn't risk it. Leola might get the wrong idea. And he wanted to see her more than ever now, there was no more shyness left in him. As he stared at himself he realized the self-hatred which usually rose up when he saw himself in the mirror wasn't there.

It had moulted. *He looked like his father.* For the first time in his life he saw his face and didn't wish it was different.

He smiled.

He was eyelash-less and balding.

* * *

Salvadore and Rose were standing in the deli like a couple who'd just had their baby baptized. They had on smart clothes and polished shoes. Rose was wearing a broad-brimmed hat and was holding Hilary in her arms like a newborn infant. They'd just returned from the vet.

'Phantom pregnancy,' Rose said grandly.

Salvadore peered at Hilary as if he knew how this felt.

August gave them a look of incomprehension. 'What's that?'

'She thought she was pregnant,' Rose explained, kissing her pelt. 'Poor thing, you thought you were pregnant, didn't you?'

Hilary stared vacantly out the window.

'That's why she hid in the cupboard, she was nesting, she wanted to find somewhere to hole up and give birth.'

'But I thought she was neutered,' August replied. 'How could she think she was pregnant?'

'It happens,' said Rose authoritatively. 'It's psychological. She doesn't know she's been fixed.'

August shrugged.

He had new respect for Rose. He felt foolish. Rose had been through a tremendous struggle, probably for most of her previous life. Probably still.

'Anyway,' she said. 'We're taking her upstairs. She needs to recuperate, build up her strength.'

'She's a very brave girl,' Salvadore nodded. He winked at August. 'You are brave too.'

'Me?'

'Yes.'

'Why?'

'To go around with such terrible hair. You need a haircut.'

August patted his hair. 'I know.'

Rose eyed him, strangely.

* * *

In The Green Man Jim was laughing and Gabriel was pink when August joined them on his lunch break.

'What's so funny?'

Gabriel turned pinker and shook his head.

August glanced at Jim for an explanation.

'Who's Henry?' Jim asked.

August smiled at Gabriel.

Gabriel studied his trouser legs, blushing deeply.

'She works with me. In the deli. Gabriel met her the other day. Didn't you?'

Gabriel didn't reply.

'Gabriel?'

Gabriel twitched his nose, still looking at his trousers.

'I don't believe it!' August exclaimed. 'You're shy!'

Gabriel lip-read this, and reddened more. He shrugged helplessly and leaned forward and picked up his pint.

* * *

Late that afternoon August sat on a chair in the café with a tablecloth tied around his shoulders.

The deli was closed, the day was over. He'd agreed to let Henry at his hair, even though the idea made him nervous. His hair wasn't just hair. It claimed more of him than he'd ever wanted it to, occupying the space taken up by a limb. A haircut was never a simple thing for him, it was more of an amputation.

Henry appeared from the storeroom with her scissors.

It'd been a long time since he'd been physically close to her, not since their kiss, and he felt awkward. He'd promised Gabriel to ask Henry out for a drink and get him along too. He wondered if he should bring the subject up, then decided it was best to play Cupid in silence.

Henry stood behind him, her soft belly very close.

'August,' Henry said in an impatient tone.

'What?'

Henry began to run her fingers through his hair. 'Look.' She shoved her fist in front of his eyes. Then opened it.

A copper cloud of hair hovered in it.

'I don't think I can cut it. It's *all* falling out.'

August grimaced. 'Can you try?'

Henry continued to rake his hair and pull at strands.

August remained quiet.

Henry combed slowly backwards and forwards, then began to level hair along her closed fingers, snipping at it.

August remembered her reaction to his body in the spring. He wished he could explain he wasn't diseased. Explain it was some kind of gift. A life for a life. Now he could see this, *a graze*, a brush with his father. In his sleep.

He stared at his knees and listened to the snipping.

'Wh-what about you and Yves?' he said after a while.

There was a louder snip.

'What about us?'

Henry continued to rake and snip.

August's ears became hot. Half a minute went by which felt like three.

'I hate him,' Henry said.

August nodded.

'Keep your head still!'

August obeyed.

'He's seeing someone else, someone who looks just like me. He was perverted.'

August frowned.

'He cramped me.'

As Henry snipped August saw Henry bent forward over a table. Biting her lips in pain. He shook his head trying to shake the image.

'Oh, August!' Henry exclaimed.

'I'll keep still, I promise.'

'This is impossible!' she gasped. 'Look!' She began to rake her hands quickly through his hair and it began to come away like fibreglass.

'Look, see, it won't work.' She raked and raked, and more hair spun into her hands.

August saw the ball of orange, like a baby.

'No, no, stop!' he said, quickly, jerking forward and away, holding his head as if to shield himself from a crash.

'Stop,' he said again, half-crouching over his knees. He didn't move, his heart was beating fast. He closed his eyes. He was frightened.

'Don't touch me,' he cringed.

Henry dropped the hair to the floor and wiped hair from her skirt.

A cry exploded from August's chest.

Henry shook her head in amazement.

August rocked and hugged his knees. His hair lay around him like storm debris.

He groaned.

'August,' Henry moved round and knelt by him. 'Sweetheart,' she rubbed his back. 'What's wrong, what's wrong?' she soothed. 'Tell me . . .'

August shook his head. There was a cramp in his gut, something round and hard and solid was forcing its way up his insides.

He could only shake his head.

Henry stared. She knelt next to him on the café floor, rubbing his back as he rocked.

In his chest the hardness began to grow warm. As it did, a thin sea swirled in him. He saw himself floating inside a ruff of water on a sea, a creamy curl wrapped round him.

The sea began to spin.

His body racked and he hiccuped.

'I guess I'm worried,' he whispered. Henry was kneeling next to him.

'It's okay.'

He stared at his hair on the floor.

'It's your body, isn't it?'

He nodded.

'It's never frightened me – till now.' He picked up some of his hair and examined it.

'I . . .' Then he stopped.

He looked at Henry. Her face was startled. He was startled too.

'I don't want to lose my hair.'

She nodded.

He sighed, defeated.

Slowly he began to pull what was left from his head and Henry helped. They pulled and scraped for some time, until there was nothing left. Henry picked at his eyebrows and they came off too. When they were finished his head looked very smooth. Round and pink and naked.

The world was on edge after the previous night's storm. The sky was low and grey, the air fat with the possibility of more rain. The clouds rumbled and stroked themselves high up in the heavens.

August tried to ignore it all.

At eight o'clock he sat perched on a stool at the bar in the tapas restaurant. He'd ordered a beer and sat with his back to the door, thinking Leola couldn't miss him. His head felt extraordinary – cool and bare. For the first time in his life he felt completely nude, almost indecent. He was aware of people looking at him. The barman almost couldn't. The place had emerald green walls and small wooden tables for two, people were eating. It was a homely, friendly place, he thought. As he waited he flicked through the menu. He was wearing his lucky shirt, a pale pink dinner shirt, embroidered with white stitching.

At eight forty-five the muscles in August's face had slackened. He could barely contain his disappointment. He'd been stood up. The barman had made it worse by saying nothing, and this had somehow been a condolence. He paid for his two beers and slipped off his stool. He didn't care what the possibilities were: wrong day, time, bar, an accident, a mishap. She hadn't come. He felt stupid. The other couples had seen him, the whole restaurant had seen him waiting. He knew they thought he'd been stood up because he was bald.

He left the restaurant and walked out on to the road. When he came to the crossing he pressed the button at the lights and waited. He could see nothing in front of him, the night and the road had become one, a blackness. He blinked, and when the green man flashed he stepped out into the road, his eyes blurred.

'Owwww,' a woman cried out.

'I beg your pardon,' August said earnestly to whoever he'd bashed.

'August?'

It was Leola.

August hovered above her, smooth as an elm. 'Oh, h-hello.'

The pips from the crossing were going. Cars revved their engines.

'Out the way,' shouted someone from a new VW Beetle.

August pulled Leola on to the island.

'It *is* you,' she said, slightly stunned. 'Oh . . . I feel like a fool. I've been walking past the restaurant for the last half an hour. I didn't recognize you.'

'All my hair fell out. It doesn't matter,' August said, trying to make light of it. 'I probably look like some-one else.'

Her hair caught a little in the upsweep of wind caused by the cars passing. She shook her head.

'No. Actually, you're unmistakable.'

They stood watching the traffic clattering past. Noise

and lights. The two streams sucked any other words from them. Again, it felt natural to be so close. So right he slipped his arms around her waist and filled his arms with her. She sighed and leaned back into him. They stood like this, supported and sagging into one another, as the cars hummed and rolled past. Lights and noise. They stood saying nothing, their bodies absorbing one another, charging and slackening. Her blood and his blood were as warm, her breath and his breath rose and fell. The pulse in his temple was hers.

The pips went again and they walked back to where Leola had been standing.

'What about the restaurant?' she asked.

August glanced back across the road. He shuddered into his jacket. More rain threatened. The sky was darker, more muscular, pushing its weight about. He didn't want to go back.

He felt brave.

'I'm a good cook.' He smiled at her, showing his big teeth.

Leola blushed.

'Can I cook you dinner?' August tried to make his face honourable. 'I have a good recipe,' he grinned. 'For Mimolette.'

Leola scanned his features, smiling at what she saw.

August pushed on.

'A salad. With chicken and mushrooms.'

She grinned from ear to ear. 'That sounds perfect.'

August looked down at her and felt a blurred mixture of excitement and fear. The idea of being with her made him nervous. And lit him up. It started a warmth in his gut, a slow meltdown of his strength.

They were standing outside the deli. August looked up. Above them the plane tree was a black mamba up in the darkness, writhing to the rustle of its own leaves.

'Let's go then,' she said.

Leola slipped her arm under his as they walked a little further and turned left towards his flat. The rain broke as they reached his doorstep.

* * *

Leola ran her eyes over August's naked body. Over the smoothness of his hidden places, valleys and cleavages, depressions and curves. The dimples at the base of his spine were like decoys in the skin of a deep sea fish, a skate perhaps. Her eyes wandered over the wings of his groin. His skin was translucent and perfectly bald.

'It all came off,' August apologized, when she saw there was no hair around his genitals.

No hair at all.

None in the caves of his arms either. It made him something rare, a sleek and gentle creature, a beluga whale of a man. A dolphin boy. August's nakedness was like the inside of bone, or the outside of an organ.

'You're beautiful like this,' she said, kissing his chest. Their bodies were entwined, a twisted rope of legs and torsos.

He hid his face in her neck.

'You were right,' he whispered.

'About what?'

'What's been happening to me.'

His hands reached down behind her, his fingers traced the backs of her knees.

'My father died. Last December.'

Her skin there was soft, as though he wasn't touching her at all, as though he was caressing an invisible, unknowable warmth.

'That's when I first noticed the frost.'

He began to draw on the rest of her body with his fingers, and the tip of his tongue, write words all over her until she writhed – and then relaxed. His tongue was the shape of the centre of an orchid. It came from somewhere as intimate, the same dusky fluted throat. His lips left a trail of iridescent dust on her hips, her abdomen. His eyelids were the palest iris mauve. She kissed them. He kissed her back, fully, slowly. In each of their mouths was the end of a rainbow.

In the autumn light the plane tree was regal. As they finally died, the leaves turned pink and then caramel. When they caught the light, they were a coppery head of hair.

The wind blew and the hair shook gently.

After lunch August was in the deli, beaming, radiating warmth. Leola had stayed the night and the imprint of her body, the bits which fitted into him as she slept, was still all over him. Earlier they'd walked to work together, all of three minutes, holding hands. Neither of them had talked, both shy, speechless after the night's encounter. But they'd agreed to meet later.

Flora appeared in the shop, behind a customer in the queue. August hadn't seen her and when her big body and big face appeared at the counter it occurred to him that he never saw her appear or disappear. She came and went in a blink. She stood in front of him clutching two bread rolls. He couldn't help smiling inwardly at the way she looked: her face, shaped like a germ, flat but irregular around the edges, her mauve complexion, her straight lips, implying a readiness for battle.

She put the two white bread rolls still stuck together on the counter.

'Kissing crust,' she monotoned, pinching the breads.

'What?'

Flora pointed to the Siamese twinned breads, the join in them. 'Where the lips of the breads meet.' She smiled childishly, and winked at him. 'It is the softest crust. These breads are good to eat.'

August blushed. 'How are you?' he grinned, trying to seem easy with his new head and face.

She frowned. 'You look like an egg.'

'I know, I know,' August shuffled his feet. Flora was hard to distract with small talk. But he wasn't in the mood for any more of her tricks and wanted to avoid the subject of the eclipse.

'Soon you will hatch.'

August laughed politely.

'How's Cedric?'

Flora shrugged. 'Not bad.'

August thought he saw her cheeks flush. 'He was a bit down the last time I saw him.'

'He told me.'

August was surprised. This implied she didn't find the subject of impotence difficult. He remembered Cedric had said Flora thought he was attractive.

'You look lovely today.'

She pinkened even more.

'It's love,' she shrugged again, happily. 'He's a fool who makes me laugh.'

August nodded.

'And that's just his poetry.'

They both smiled and tittered.

Flora stared at his shoulder. 'You feel whole when you find your other half.'

She made her eyes small, her mouth upturned. 'But love found in later life is different.'

August wanted to know why and didn't.

'Sex is different.'

Where had he met her before?

Flora's neck stretched out a bit like a turtle and her big face came nearer. She peered at him.

Had she lived in the commune? Was she a friend of Jude's?

'It's no longer for creation.'

August nodded, absorbing this.

'Sex becomes creative – in the imaginative sense,' she continued, then paused. 'You know what I mean?'

August cast his eyes downwards.

She shifted her weight from one leg to the other, not caring if he wasn't listening.

'Anyway, how much are they?'

August had forgotten about the breads. They *were* kissing.

'Sixty pence.'

She reached into her bag and tweezed in her purse for money. When she found some coins, she held them up in the air, as though at ransom.

August smiled, patiently.

Her eyes were fiery. 'How is your father?' she said, slowly.

August's face muscles fell, dropping his mouth.

'Dead,' he replied, letting the heavy word drop.

Flora's soft eyes became solid.

'And buried?'

August crinkled his face, trying to understand her tactlessness.

'Cremated, actually.'

She nodded.

'Nothing left of him?'

'No, nothing.'

'Nothing buried?'

'No.'

'No visits you have to make.'

'No.'

'Okay,' she said briskly.

August ignored this. 'That's sixty pence please.'

She sniffed at the kissing breads on the counter, then put the coins back in her purse.

'I've changed my mind. You have them.' She huffed. Then she turned and left.

Rose came down from her flat late morning, poised and gracious. She stopped in her tracks when she saw August in the café, kneeling on the floor. A woman with two small children was sitting at a table next to him and August was letting them feel his head. Rose looked on as the children laughed and tried to pick it up as if it were a balloon they could keep. When August saw her, he was also overcome with surprise and mouthed the word 'Sorry'.

Rose shook her head and began to gather plates and cups from the other tables.

'That's enough,' the woman said eventually.

August was relieved. The little girl let go and began to bite her fingers as she stared at him, pleased with herself. The little boy was touching his own head and staring at August with interest. Their mother sighed with amusement as she began to gather up their things.

'Kids,' she tutted.

August smiled at them. His ears were burning. When

he stood up he felt light and a little nervous. He waved to them as they left and then retreated into the kitchen alcove. He'd never been so physically close to children.

'I'm glad you shaved it,' Rose commented. She was changing the tablecloths. 'I didn't know what to say. All that stuff about snow and leaves . . . It's been a bad year for you, hasn't it? I know a good nutritionist you really should try, August. It's something in here, in the deli. Milk or cheese or the bread. It could be yeast.'

'Maybe,' he said, flatly.

'Or fruit.'

Still she chose not to see anything unusual about him but August reined in his disappointment. He knew she'd come as close as she wanted to.

He watched her as she fussed around the tables.

Sensing his gaze, she looked up quickly. Behind the tidy square frames her eyes blinked, disconcerted. He saw they were small and grey, the dots in them a little jittery.

'How's Hilary?' he asked.

'Eating like a pony. We're taking her on holiday with us.'

'Holiday?'

Rose smiled demurely. 'Sardinia for a fortnight. Not until next month, I was going to tell you nearer the time. Salvadore is going to study pilchards.'

'Sardines.' August said the word loudly, testing to see how it sounded.

Rose smiled. 'Yes.'

He pictured Rose, Hilary and Salvadore on a fishing boat in the middle of the Mediterranean Sea. Rose was in a flowery beach coat with a wide floppy hat. Hilary was staring over the edge, looking for pilchards. Salvadore was mending a net.

'I was wondering if you could manage the shop for those two weeks, on extra pay.'

'No problem.'

'Will you be all right with Henry?'

'Of course.'

'How is she?'

'Fine. She doesn't talk much about Yves.'

'Good. He was a thug. She has terrible taste in men. Whatever happened to that slimy older man who used to come in here?'

August tried to think.

'He looked like some kind of cowboy.'

'Oh.'

'He had a strange name.'

'Cosmo. He disappeared.'

'I didn't like him either. He was a lady's man. Never trust that sort.'

August smiled.

Rose was patting down a new table-cloth, smoothing down seams.

'He was an old boyfriend of my mother's, actually,' he replied.

Rose stopped and looked up with raised eyebrows. Her cheeks coloured. 'Oh . . . you never mentioned it.'

August made a point of turning around to wipe down the coffee machine. He coughed, clearing his throat. 'Some things you don't want to talk about, you know.'

Rose straightened up and glanced around the room, taking it in. She smiled a pert, glazed smile in August's direction, excused herself and went downstairs.

August had saved the kissing breads.

After Flora had pinched them the crust was broken and they were unsellable. When the lunch-time rush died, he took them downstairs to the office with some honey roast ham and black mustard on the side. He was glad to be on his own, so he could get his mother's story out again, examine it under a glass, slowly, carefully. It was as interesting as a bug.

Though she'd been full of remorse, there was something which had been bothering him about the way she'd told her story. As she went on, her voice had taken on a plodding tone. There was a look in her eyes which showed the events she'd talked about, after thirty-three years, had eventually been diluted. She'd managed to get away from them. Make them dull.

He wondered how this might feel. Diluted. All he knew was immediacy. His current life, its sharpness. In forty years would he remember the vividness of his feelings now? Would he remember his disappointments? Or would they get layered over also . . . *levelled ground* . . . would each decade form a layer of protection over the one that went before? Would age change not just his face but his memory? He hoped not. He never wanted to lose his sharpness, never wanted to end up like his mother. Lose any more of his life.

He pulled apart the kissing breads and began to slice one roll open with a small, serrated knife.

Something began to fall from the bread. A strong, surprising colour. It fell like flakes of snow, like slivers of suede.

Indigo.

He sliced deeper. Indigo petals were buried at the centre.

Petals fell on to his lap.

On to his feet.

He flung the roll on to the desk, staring at it, shocked – as if in it he'd just found a mouse. He snatched up the second roll and pulled it apart. Indigo petals bloomed upwards from it in a fountain. They landed in the Rolodex, in the wastepaper basket, on the floor. On his bald head.

He brushed them off.

He picked one petal up, balancing it on the end of his finger.

Buried.

He saw Edward.

Walking from the copse at the end of the field.

Wiping soil from his hands.

Flora again. But he wasn't going to go to Stonegate. Not for her, or for anyone.

* * *

August waited three days for Cedric to come back into the deli. He wanted to find Flora, tell her to leave him alone. Or else give over her information, tell him, point-blank, anything she might know about his father. He was annoyed.

He lay in wait.

Cedric didn't come in, neither did Flora. By Friday morning he was bearish and so distracted he poured pineapple juice instead of milk into his mid-morning coffee.

It tasted of vile witch's brew.

The idea of going back to Stonegate Hall was intangibly frightening. A quicksand slowly filled his stomach the more he thought about returning. He hadn't slept since he'd found the petals in the bread rolls. Hadn't needed to. He'd been existing in a suspended state of living, of feeling. He saw himself hanging over his day-to-day routines, an enormous bird in a flow. The flow he hung in was dread. He didn't want to go back to the old house.

Ever.

Time didn't heal, he realized. It only dulled and smothered. Time was whipped air, lots of it. Opaque as gelatine. Soporific. Time was a smoke screen. It lay softly over fear, over dread. And now the idea of going back to Stonegate Hall reared very solid. And time fled from it, like rolling clouds from the tip of a mountain. Exposing and recalling his old feelings. A gut-churning wretchedness.

This wretchedness floundered in him all Friday morning.

Buried.

At lunch time he rang Virgin trains. He booked himself on the six forty-five to Skipton. He knew a pub there with a few rooms upstairs. He rang them too. Then he ran across the road to the flower shop to tell Leola he was going away for a day or two.

A soft, needle rain fell steadily as August walked along the grassy verge of the road. He'd asked the taxi to drop him off half a mile back, not wanting to be seen by anyone getting out of a car near the house, also wanting the walk. He pushed his fists deep into his denim jacket pockets, already regretting the snap decision to come all this way without the right clothes or shoes. Without a plan. He had no idea what he would find, or what he was looking for. It'd all been so urgent in London, so apt. Feeling the rain soaking through his clothes, seeing the sturdy countryside around him, familiar, uncaring – he felt absurd.

He walked with his eyes on the ground, a large, thin, bald figure, unmissable, car or no car. Blue-pale, elegant, passing silently in the rain. When he neared the gate to the paddock at the bottom of the property, he stopped and looked left and right. The road was empty. He vaulted over the gate and began to walk up the narrow path to the paddock, his ankles sinking inches into thick, buttery mud. He had to concentrate on his steps. Each foot sucked as it came out of its hole, then squelched as it was put down, into another, his trainers turning heavy, like clogs. This part of Yorkshire had been rain-soaked and flooded for weeks. The earth had become something else: tremendous, shifting, full of minerals forced up from some reservoir underground. All around him he could feel a fullness, as if the world had a swollen lip. Many of the trees still held their leaves, faintly yellowed. Long green grasses brushed him on either side of the path. He continued to walk. The rain broke and began to pour softly, hurling millions of small winged insects to the ground.

At the end of the path he came to the paddock. A fat brown horse stood in the rain at the far end. It turned and stared impassively at him, steam jets blowing from its nostrils. He held the strands of barbed wire open enough to slip through and skirted the field. At the other side was another gate. He looked over it.

The field was a choppy sea of green. To the left was the copse, to the right, far off and up on raised land, was Stonegate Hall.

The house seemed to sweat in his vision – from the surprise of being seen. It pulsed at him as though it were alive and could uproot itself from its foundations. Walk towards him. The pub's landlord had told him it was now owned by a millionaire and his Swedish wife. A poisonous yellow frog of a sports car crouched outside the entrance. Otherwise it was the same. Ivy still clung to half its face like some hideous birthmark. The same grey, porous stone. It was a disturbingly emotionless house, even now. His gaze fixed on the top row of rectangular windows – not even eyes, but shut lids. He felt a sudden rise in him, a fearlessness, and opened the gate.

*

August tramped across a short corner of the field in plain view of the house, plainly trespassing but uncaring about being seen. *So simple*, he thought. He owned this place implicitly, this field, more than the present owners ever could. It owned him. He'd have enough to say to them if caught.

The copse stood in its familiar huddle, the trees with their backs turned to him. Each tree was different, none he knew the name of. Some were firs, others more squat and bushy. Their leaves rustled a greeting as he approached, the sound like a great crowd gossiping, friendly and intimidating, as curious and unsure of him as he was of them. He picked up his pace, aware now he'd made the right decision.

The eye of the copse was quiet. The floor was tongue shaped and thick with leaves. Once inside, August sensed he was being stared at, that he was being intrusive. The wind blew and shook the leaves and he knew the trees were discussing him. But there was a barrier between him and them, a language he would never crack. He looked from trunk to trunk, wondering if his father might have carved one with his initials or a date, something to guide him to the right spot. There might be a marker, he reasoned, if his father had buried something here. He began to wander from one tree to another, gliding his eyes over their slim trunks. Some were lightly green with moss, others were rugged with ivy. It soon proved unwise. As he walked, touching each tree, looking down at their feet, he realized his father would never have buried something at the foot of a tree. He wouldn't have damaged their roots.

He abandoned this idea and wandered back to the centre of the group of trees. The rain had stopped. A bird croaked. Another made a dib-dib sound. Further off, a car quietly roared past. An aeroplane rumbled in the clouds. Nothing. No sign. He dropped to his haunches and sat down on the mattress of leaves. He examined his big hands, spread them on his knees. Knuckles like the paws of a great hound, his father's hands. Clues he'd seen every day of his life. He thought of Edward lying ill in his council flat.

Nothing.

He couldn't shake the feeling of being sneaked up on from behind. His past, the people who'd made him, his body. It was all so much easier to think about, all in some kind of order now.

Lined up.

Behind him.

He was tired. He took his hands from his knees and spread them out behind him, tempted to recline completely flat. As he did, one hand came up against something hard, a large stone or a rock. He moved his hand away to avoid it, still contemplating curling up and going to sleep. The trees shook their leaves hard, the noise like thousands of seed pods cracking against a hollow tube. He sat up. He peered upwards. The trees rattled. He stared back at the spot where he'd bumped against the rock. He couldn't see where it'd been, it was buried again, under leaves. The trees heaved their branches, the sound was like panic in the air. Louder, wilder. August began to dig up leaves, clearing them quickly with his hands.

The stone was bald.

Crystalline white. Only its tip showed above the earth, the rest of it was sunk deeper in. It had come from a river bed, August realized, it'd been taken from the small stream which ran past the copse nearby. He began to dig around it, the trees dying down. The earth was cold and packed up tight into his fingernails. He dug until the full size of the stone became exposed.

It was squat and bulky, smeared with olive green slime, a small hill buried to its knoll, easy enough to push over. Using his body weight, he heaved it with both hands. The stone rocked and landed heavily on its side. In the newly exposed basin a worm oozed back into the soil, flat beetles wriggled.

August stared at the uncovered patch of earth.

It pulsed.

Like the house, it sweated with the surprise of being seen. His father was the last person to touch this earth, August realized. Be this close. He spread his hands and planted them squarely on the ground, touching the last of his father, where he'd touched. Mingling his flesh with his father's dim traces. He breathed in distant chains of atoms of his father's breath. He picked up handfuls of earth and wiped it across his face. He shoved earth into his pockets, rubbed it all over the back of his neck.

He began to dig some more, scooping up great clods of black soil; it was harder and more compact the deeper he struck. He scooped and was drunk. His ears rang. His stomach knotted. What was down there? A body, a box? Adrenaline flooded into his hands, making his arms weak and fiery all at once. Then his fingers scraped against something hard. He scraped some more. Something long and thin was buried a little deeper, a neck or a pole. He scraped some more, his breath quickening. A stick of some sort was impacted into the cold, black earth. He scraped along it until he came to one end which was square and flat. He cleared earth away from this too, scraping carefully, as an archaeologist would, until he at last made out what it was.

The spade was decrepit.

Its long wooden handle was waterlogged and eaten by worms. The square head was cancerous with rust. It lay in the mud like a relic of some terrible event – a victim of Vesuvius, or an Ethiopian famine. Starkly naked. Emaciated and forgotten. August reached out and stroked it gently along the length of its narrow belly. He imagined himself buried deep, asleep under the copse; how peaceful it must have been under the earth. Asleep and untroubled. Supported and secure. He took hold of the handle and pulled. The spade came out of its tomb with a suck. It was light in his hands and he sloughed off the excess mud.

He rose from his knees and looked up. The trees were quiet, leaning inwards, as if to have a good look at what he'd found. He smiled and they nodded with approval. His father had singled them out, chosen them as guardians for his only valuable possession. *Nothing*. Had Edward forgotten the spade, or had he been embarrassed at such a humble gift? August looked around him, at the leafy green-yellow cloud he was in. Light danced around the tips of the leaves, mottled and pretty. There was something about the trees, their solemnity, their great brown trunks, so solid, their quiet, confident permanence, that made him somehow know Edward.

He knew there was a train back to London in just over an hour. He could catch it if he hurried. Carrying the spade, he made his way back to the open field and the paddock.

He walked quickly, in a vacuum, no thoughts came to him: nothing. Just a feeling of being watched.

The feeling lasted until he reached the road.

* * *

The next morning August woke up in his flat in Shepherd's Bush.

A topaz light had leaked from the slit in the curtains, invading the room. He rolled over to face the far wall. On the dresser in the corner he saw the cheese plant, its leaves supple and shiny. He'd had it a couple of weeks now and it was doing well, he noticed, the first plant that had ever lived as a result of his care. Leola would be impressed.

His head itched.

He scratched and felt his scalp was rough as sandpaper. He rubbed his hand all over the surface of his skull and stared at the ceiling, wondering anxiously if it was what he hoped.

He went to the bathroom.

In the mirror his head glowed copper. What was on his head was on his chin also.

Stubble.

He wanted to clap. Relief bloomed up from his belly, spreading into his chest.

August sat down heavily on the edge of the bathtub. He stared at his slim, white thighs, his craggy knees. He twitched a toe. He reached across the toilet bowl for a strip of paper and blew his nose. He threw the moist, dumplinged tissue in the bowl. He sat for a little longer on the edge of the tub, glad he was alone. He wanted to understand why he was so relieved, but didn't. It was just a feeling, a wash. He wanted to cry but didn't. He hiccuped.

In the kitchen he flipped on the kettle.

Outside, he noticed the light was growing cautiously and a pale mist was lifting. He filled a glass with water and went back into the bedroom. He walked to the dresser and poured the water into the plant's pot, watching as the earth around the base soaked the liquid, turning it blacker, softer.

Acknowledgements

Thanks to Emma Daly for housing and often feeding me in the early days, for never writing me off. Also to my teachers Linda Anderson and Bill Herbert at Lancaster University for their wisdom and encouragement. I also owe a debt of gratitude to Joanna Pocock, Saleel Nurbhai, Alison Hilton, Julia Bell, Amanda Glyn, Hydrox Turner, Tessanna Hoare and Richard Salmon – each of whom contributed in some way to the writing of this book. Thanks also to Nigel and John at Sutherland's deli on Shepherd's Bush Road and to Alice B. Toklas for her recipe on how to cook an old hen. Thanks to Ben Ball for making this a better book and to Simon Trewin, my agent.

Thanks to my mother, Yvette Roffey, for a lifetime of unconditional love and support. Also thanks to Ian Marchant, for laughter every day and sharing the adventures of writing.

THE WHITE WOMAN ON THE GREEN BICYCLE

Monique Roffey

SHORTLISTED FOR THE ORANGE PRIZE FOR FICTION 2010

When George and Sabine Harwood arrive in Trinidad from England George is immediately seduced by the beguiling island. But Sabine feels isolated, heat-fatigued, and ill at ease. Her only solace is her growing fixation with Eric Williams, the charismatic leader of Trinidad's new national party, to whom she pours out all her hopes and fears for the future in letters that she never brings herself to send.

As the years progress, George and Sabine's marriage endures for better and for worse. When George discovers Sabine's cache of letters, he realises just how many secrets she's kept from him – and he from her – over the decades. And he is seized by an urgent, desperate need to prove his love for her, with tragic consequences . . .

ISBN 978-1-84739-522-1
PRICE £7.99